Praise for the Love and Honor Series

"Hallee writes with such authentic detail that I felt the sweat drip off my brow, heard the buzz of the African jungle, and ran for dear life with Cynthia and Rick. A rich story of courage and seeing the world with new eyes. Riveting, this book will get under your skin and into your heart. Absolutely fantastic."
Susan May Warren, USA Today bestselling author, on *Honor Bound*

"Hallee Bridgeman weaves a military suspense with romance for a fast-paced adventure. Word of Honor kept me turning pages all night long."
DiAnn Mills, author of *Concrete Evidence*, on *Word of Honor*

"What a fabulous story with perfectly crafted characters who grab your heart from the opening page. I loved everything about it—from the witty dialogue to the breath-stopping suspense to the tender romance. Once I started, I couldn't put it down. I highly recommend this book and can't wait for the next one."
Lynette Eason, award-winning, bestselling author
of the *Extreme Measures* series, on *Honor Bound*

"This book has something for everyone—action, adventure, romance, and true-to-life sadness and grief. Hallee crafts a complex story infused with spiritual truth, wrapped around intriguing lead characters with complicated personalities and backgrounds. Phil and Melissa will have you rooting for them the whole way through."
Janice Cantore, retired police officer and author
of *Breach of Honor*, on *Honor's Refuge*

LOVE MAKES WAY

HALLEE BRIDGEMAN

USA TODAY BESTSELLING AUTHOR

LOVE & HONOR

Published By

Olivia Kimbrell Press™

Dedication

This book is dedicated to Brandon and Joy, our real-life
Army nurse and Special Forces soldier love story.
I would have made my main character a spunky brunette
if I didn't already have a cover when I started writing.

Thank you for your friendship,
even in the darkest of times.
And thank you for your love that inspired a story.

Prequel novella
Love in Any Language

Novels by Revell
Honor Bound
Word of Honor
Honor's Refuge

More Love & Honor
Love Makes Way
The Seven Year Glitch
Chasing Pearl

Learn more online:

www.halleebridgeman.com/series/love-and-honor-series/

"For I know the plans I have for you,"
declares the Lord,
"plans to prosper you and not to harm you,
plans to give you hope and a future."

Jeremiah 29:11 (NIV)

Glossary of Military Terms & Acronyms

People

18 series: a US Army soldier who is Special Forces qualified or, in the case of 18X, a candidate for the same.

DOD: US Department of Defense/The War Department

DV: Distinguished Visitor. A VIP.

HVT: a high-value target, usually an individual

LT: Either a first or second Lieutenant.

NCO: a Non-Commissioned Officer. In the US Army, an enlisted soldier ranked corporal or higher.

ODA: Operational Detachment Alpha (typically refers to an SFODA)

POTUS: The President of the United States

SFODA: Special Forces Operational Detachment Alpha (an A-Team)

VIP: Very Important Person. A DV.

VPOTUS: The Vice President of the United States

Nautical Terms

Bow: the front of a vessel

Port: the left side of a vessel

Starboard: the right side of a vessel

Stern: the rear of a vessel

Clothing and Gear

CAC: Common Access Card/Military ID Card

ACUs: the standard US Army Combat Uniform, formerly BDUs or the Battle Dress Uniform. ACUs have been through numerous redesigns, with the Operational Camouflage Pattern (OCP) camouflage pattern replacing the ineffective Universal Camouflage Pattern (UCP) in 2015.

Five eleven tactical: Registered trademark (rightly 5.11 Tactical®) of a civilian brand of clothing designed for tactical use, often khaki in color

NODs: nighttime optical devices. The generic acronym encompasses the GPNVG-18 (Ground Panoramic Night Vision Goggle), also called quads by the tier 1 units who use them, the AN/PVS-14 monocular device, the AN/PVS-15 binocular device, and the BNVD (Binocular Night Vision Device). Some Special Operations Forces may also employ thermal/image-intensifier fused devices like the AN/PSQ-20 for increased detection capabilities.

Places

AO: area of operations

CASH: Combat Support Hospital (CSH)

CHU: Containerized housing unit (a small, climate-controlled shipping container)

CONUS: The Continental United States, aka the lower 48

DFAC: Dining Facility

Fort Breckinridge, KY: a fictional US Army base hypothetically located in Central Kentucky, loosely based on a combination of Forts Campbell, Bragg, and Benning.

HQ: headquarters

Karpovia: a fictitious former Soviet Eastern Bloc non-NATO affiliated nation hypothetically located in Eastern Europe.

Katangela: a fictitious African nation hypothetically near the Congo

SCIF: sensitive compartmented information facility (a secure location where classified information can be reviewed)

Terms, Jargon, Slang, Acronyms:

exfil: exfiltrate (withdraw)

Bird: Among paratroopers, a bird is any aircraft, such as a fixed-wing or rotary-wing aircraft. A rotary wing aircraft (helicopter) is also rarely referred to as a chopper.

Brown shirt: nickname (often derogatory) used by Special Forces to describe personnel in other government agencies (OGA) who often wear khaki tactical civilian clothing when in the field. The "brown shirts" were also the paramilitary forces used by the German Chancellor to eliminate his enemies in the 1930s.

Fast rope: Fast rope rappelling is a military technique for rapid deployment from a helicopter into an area where landing isn't possible, using a thick, gloved rope that personnel slide down with their hands and feet to control their descent and speed.

HALO: High Altitude/Low Opening. An airborne operation in which paratroopers exit the aircraft at very high altitudes (15,000–35,000 feet) and activate their parachutes at a much lower altitude (2,000–4,000 feet), usually near their objective or target.

IED: Improvised Explosive Device, a homemade bomb.

infil: infiltrate (move in)

JP-8: JP-8 is a kerosene-based, multi-purpose fuel used by the U.S. military and NATO, similar to commercial Jet A-1 but with added corrosion inhibitors, anti-icing agents, and anti-static additives.

klick: one kilometer, or a distance of 3280.84 feet.

medevac: a medical evacuation of wounded personnel to treatment areas such as a CASH, MASH, or hospital.

mike: one minute or 60 seconds of time.

MRE: meal ready to eat, the primary field rations of the US military

NATO Phonetic Alphabet: NATO nations agreed upon designations and pronunciations for letters and numbers (e.g., A is *Alpha*, B is *Bravo*, 1 is *wun*, 3 is *tree*) to allow all NATO nations to communicate more effectively across language barriers.

OD/OD green: OD green, which stands for "olive drab/green," is a dull, greenish-brown color that was historically used for US military uniforms and equipment, particularly during World War II, Korean conflict, and the Vietnam War.

OGA: other government agencies, used in place of the actual designations such as DIA, CIA, NSA, FBI, DHS, and more, which occasionally conduct joint operations with US Department of Defense personnel.

PCS: In the U.S. Army, a PCS (Permanent Change of Station) is a transfer of a service member to a new permanent duty location, typically involving a move to a new base or installation.

PT: Physical training, usually organized morning exercises consisting of calisthenics and a two-mile run.

Ricky-tick: quickly and efficiently

Roger: understood and acknowledged

Roger, Wilco: understood, acknowledged, and will comply

ROTC: The Reserve Officers' Training Corps is a college-based program for students to earn a degree while also training to become an officer in the US military.

SIPRNET: secret internet protocol router network (a network the Department of Defense uses to transfer classified information), aka "the high side."

SITREP: situational report

TDY: Temporary duty travel (TDY), also known as temporary additional duty (TAD), is a designation reflecting a US Armed Forces Service member's travel or other assignment at a location other than his or her permanent duty station.

Wilco: Will comply

CHAPTER

ONE

Undisclosed Location in Northern Africa

August

Gerald "Jerry Maguire" McBride could smell cinnamon. Which didn't make sense because—strapped to the hanger seats in the MH-47 Chinook flying over the dunes of the Sahara Desert—he should smell JP-8 exhaust, hydraulic fluid, gunpowder, sweaty men in 115 degrees close-quarters with no air conditioning. He closed his eyes, wondering about the smell and trying to place it, and suddenly found himself in his parents' living room, with the Christmas tree in the corner where a chess table usually sat. Wind beat snow against the windows in the way only a South Dakota storm could.

He heard his mother's voice, and it drew him to the kitchen. There, at the sink, her gingerbread apron covering her too-thin body and the silly snowman handkerchief covering her bald head.

"Mom?" he whispered.

She turned, hazel eyes lighting up. "Jerry! We didn't expect you home!"

He shook his head. "But I didn't make it home in time."

She held her arms out. "Oh, it's okay, son. I understood."

He opened his mouth to tell her how much he missed her, how much he wished he'd made it home before she died, but a slap on his shoulder whisked away the cinnamon, bringing the sharp bite of JP-8 exhaust back into his olfactory processes.

Captain Rick "Daddy" Norton stood in front of him, hanging onto the strap above his head. "Wakey wakey, eggs and bakey," he said. "Six minutes!"

Everyone in the helicopter then yelled, "Six minutes!"

Jerry nodded and unbuckled, joining his team in the center aisle of the helicopter. They would fast-rope out of the bird from each side of the rear ramp.

As he flexed his knees to the motion of the bird, he tried to reclaim the dream, the look on his mother's face, the joy he felt at being in her presence again, but it eluded him. He shook his head to clear it and focused on the mission.

Jerry stood at the rear of the starboard stick behind Lieutenant Phil "Ozzy" Osbourne, a 180 Alpha who had trained as a Delta and served as the team's medic and Jerry's backup spotter. Sergeant Calvin "Hobbes" Brock, one of the team's 18 Bravos or weapons specialists, loomed in front of Osbourne, his helmet nearly touching the top deck of the Chinook. Second from the front of their stick stood Master Sergeant Wade "Commando" Chandler, the team's newly frocked first sergeant and a former 18 Charlie combat engineer now 18 Zulu. Lieutenant Jorge "Piña Colada" Peña, a recent 18 Alpha or team commander, led their stick. For the time being, Peña—who had trained as a Foxtrot or intelligence specialist—served as the team's second in command and occasional detachment commander.

"One minute!" Norton yelled while holding up his index finger.

"One minute!" Everyone in each stick yelled back.

On the port side stick, Captain Rick "Daddy" Norton, the team commander, would grab the fast rope first upon arrival at the landing zone, or LZ. Behind him and nearly attached to Norton's hip stood Staff Sergeant Travis "Trout" Fisher, the team's 18 Echo, their signal NCO. Behind him stood Staff Sergeant Eric "Gilligan" Gill, an 18 Charlie, followed by Sergeant Daniel "Pot Pie" Swanson, an 18 Bravo, carrying a whole lot of ammunition and the team's only M249 machine gun. Behind Swanson and beside Jerry at the end of the other stick stood Sergeant Bill "Drumstick" Sanders with an MOS of 18 Foxtrot. Sanders had an uncanny ability to read people. He could have conned hundreds performing as a carnival psychic.

The crew chief shouted something none of them could hear as the nose of the 160th SOAR MH-47 rose to a nearly 40-degree angle and the stern dipped toward the earth. He then simultaneously activated the rear ramp and manned the port side mini-gun. The Army had equipped the MH-

47 Chinook with twin miniguns, one near the ramp and one forward in the aircraft, as well as a 20mm cannon in the nose. All of them now actively scanned for any kind of enemy presence on their LZ.

"Thirty seconds!" Norton yelled while holding up his finger and thumb in a pinching gesture.

"Thirty seconds!" Everyone in each stick yelled back.

The ramp fully lowered, filling the compartment with heat, JP-8 exhaust, noise, and a whole lot of rotor wash. Peña and Norton kicked the coiled and very heavy fast ropes down the ramp until they hung free like poles in a fire station, only made of OD green nylon instead of brass. The ten men would slide down these ropes exactly the same way firemen of old would slide down a brass pole. The aircraft beneath their feet never budged despite the change to the center of gravity. Special Operations Aviation Regiment (Airborne) pilots were the best of the best in the US Army, if not the world.

Norton made his hand signal and hypothetically yelled, "Go!" though no one could hear it. Then he and Peña departed at nearly the same time. One long second later, the second man in each stick followed, and so on, until Jerry grabbed the rope and slid down to the desert floor. The first eight men out of the bird had already formed a circular perimeter around the LZ and had their weapons up and ready for use.

The Chinook departed rapidly and without ceremony. Each man in the team held up two fingers as they cleared their lanes of fire, assuring that they could not detect any enemy combatant activity. Over their team's comms, Norton used NATO-designated number call signs and phonetic pronunciation to announce, "Objective is *wun* klick to my *tree* o'clock. Bounding overwatch. Move out."

A chorus of clicks acknowledged his orders, and they moved out tactically toward the objective. Five men would set overwatch while the other five men moved out forward past them toward the objective. Then they would hold in place, weapons ready, covering the movement of the five men behind them, who then overtook them as they bounded forward.

Twenty minutes later, the tang of burned cordite burned Jerry's nose as he pressed his back against the sun-scorched mud wall. The heat from the sun bounced off the dirt to burn his neck and the underside of his jaw. Sweat soaked his jacket and headband. A heartbeat later, a bullet chipped the edge of the wall above his head, showering him with grit.

Jerry ducked and moved—surprisingly fast considering his bulky gear and the long rifle he carried—and crouched behind the front tire of a rusting Land Rover Defender, a relic left over from when Algeria had provided them to Sahrawi Polisario Front insurgents during the Western Sahara conflict. He kept the engine block between himself and the shooter.

Carefully, he shifted the strap of his M110A1 Compact Semi-Automatic Sniper System, or CSASS, which he had affectionately named "Cassie," and examined the area around him. He needed to make that umbrella thorn tree ten yards to his left.

"Bravo Four? Status? Over." Captain Norton's voice crackled through comms, calm but with a nearly undetectable edge.

Jerry keyed his mic, voice low. "Six, this is Bravo Four. Pinned by the wall behind the Land Rover. One hostile, three-zero meters north. Need covering fire to make the tree to my 10 o'clock. Over."

"Roger," Norton replied. "Pot Pie. Show Jerry Maguire the money. Lay down cover fire on my mark—short bursts until directed to cease. North. Bravo Four, move on burst, break." After a two-second pause, Norton transmitted, "Mark."

A breath later, Swanson's M249 Squad Automatic Weapon, or SAW, rattled off short bursts after short high-volume bursts of deadly fire, stitching the alley with suppressive fire.

Jerry bolted, boots pounding the dry earth. With practiced ease, despite the sixty pounds of gear weighing him down, he grabbed the lowest branch and swung up into the tree. Bark and spiny thorns bit his palms as he scrambled higher, making him regret not taking a second to pull on his gloves. Once high enough, he pulled Cassie around, checking the optics, zeroing in on the target. "Bravo Four. On objective," he confirmed into the microphone.

Commands barked in his ear as the team stormed the thatch-roofed adobe building. He scanned the building by peering down Cassie's left side. Normally, his spotter, Osbourne or Swanson, would handle calling out targets for him. However, Phil had stayed with Peña's group, and

Gill's additional bulk would have proven problematic had he tried to perch alongside Jerry in this tree. Not for the first time, that left Jerry alone in his current perch. He saw a flicker of movement and instantly acquired the target through the powerful optics atop his rifle.

Years ago, Jerry had reconciled the lethal facts and results of his occupation with his Christian faith. Throughout the Bible, scripture makes many references to Godly men who take the lives of their enemies in combat, ranging from Gideon to Joshua to Samson to King David. God created all men with an intended purpose. Sometimes, God's intended purpose meant he created warriors. Like his father and his grandfather before him, Gerald Adam McBride knew beyond any doubt that God had always intended him to lead the life of a warrior. Keeping the men of his team alive was his mission, and he felt assured that one day he could hold himself blameless before the God of the universe.

That certainty did not stop occasional nightmares from visiting him. He would have worried much more about his spiritual and mental health if he never experienced a drop of remorse over the lives he took in battle. But the math worked in his favor. He could remove one evil life from this world and directly safeguard the lives of his team members. And perhaps that act would also save a dozen, or a hundred, or a thousand innocent lives.

Through the powerful scope, he caught an insurgent popping up from behind a rusted Toyota Hilux, deadly AKMS rifle poised to fire on his team. Jerry calmly squeezed the trigger—smooth, precise, like making a slow fist—and the man dropped before he could fire his first shot. "Strike times one," Jerry announced over comms, a bowling analogy meaning he had not left any pins standing.

Norton responded with two clicks, meaning "good work."

Another hostile leaned out a window, but Swanson's burst cut him down before Jerry could fully line up the shot. "I had him, Pie," Jerry broadcast.

"Too slow," Swanson replied.

"*Lentus est teres*," Jerry said, Latin meaning slow is smooth.

As the team claimed the building, a Humvee crested the hill. Irritation crawled up Jerry's neck. DHS had pitched this op as a quick snatch-and-grab. Nab a known Al-Shabaab informant, get in and out. No muss. No fuss. At no time did they suggest a firefight in a nowhere village miles from Djibouti. At least his team had come prepared and knew how to respond.

Norton broadcast, "Bandit. Rooftop. My two o'clock. Over."

Jerry pivoted and scanned the building facing their objective until he detected movement on the rooftop. He captured the movement in his crosshairs, seeing only a red-checked headpiece flapping in the wind. His finger tightened on the target, but he did not fire. Then his scope filled with the sight of a child, perhaps eight or nine years old, a boy, peering over the escarpment with eyes full of fear and curiosity.

"Six. Bravo Four. Bandit is a non-combatant. Not an

aggressor. Maintaining overwatch. Over."

Jerry kept the child trained in his crosshairs. The bad guys had used all kinds of dirty tricks in the past, and he knew if the situation changed, he would do what needed to be done, much as he did not desire that outcome. Duty always trumped personal preference.

The team cleared the building. As they moved through the structure, the men below began to yell, "Clear!" Finally, Norton broadcast, "All clear. But stay frosty."

The boy in his crosshairs dashed away, presumably back inside his own building now that there remained little "excitement" to see across the street. With a sigh of relief, Jerry carefully laid Cassie on her side, mindful of the optics, and visually scanned the entire area, hypervigilant against any unforeseen opposition. He would not put it past these terrorists to use women and children as human shields or walking IEDs.

"Pie, Maguire, Daddy requests the pleasure of your company. Over," Sanders drawled over the radio.

"Roger," Jerry said. He picked Cassie up and tucked her into the pit of his shoulder. One last sweep through the scope—clear—then he shifted, slung Cassie, pulled his gloves on this time, and started climbing down.

Suddenly, shocking pain tore through his left biceps, a searing punch that stole his grip. He heard the echo of the shot only after the bullet tore through his flesh. Had that kid come back and shot him?

He crashed to the ground, dust exploding around him. Blood soaked his sleeve fast—too fast. The bullet must have hit the brachial artery. "Man down. I'm hit!" he barked, clamping his right hand over the wound as bullets shredded the tree trunk above him.

"Identify hostile! Identify hostile!" Norton ordered over their comms, the sound very loud in Jerry's ear. The reports from the semi-automatic fire sounded wrong. They were not the now familiar thundercrack of Kalashnikov 7.62 supersonic rounds. They sounded much more familiar, like 5.56 NATO rounds.

"Probing fire," Swanson broadcast, then his M249 roared, but he had no target, and no enemy appeared. Blood oozed between Jerry's fingers, more with each heartbeat, as Osbourne slid in beside him, ripping open his kit. "Not like you to go running into bullets," Osbourne quipped, a wry grin flashing.

"You know me. Attention seeker," Jerry muttered, but his voice sounded weak, strange to his ears.

"Always that one diva in every crowd," Osbourne shot back, gray-green eyes focused, hands steady. He tore open Jerry's sleeve and observed the wound. "Jerry, you might be in the hurt locker, buddy."

Jerry nodded. "*Calamitas virtutis occasio est.*" Calamity is virtue's opportunity.

The incoming fire ceased. Jerry estimated at least 30 rounds had come in his direction. Then more fire came in, shredding the tree above where Jerry had formerly perched.

Norton's voice came over the comms. "Hobbes. Shut that idiot down. Now!"

Osbourne raised an eyebrow. "Artery's nicked—I need to

clamp it." He paused. "It's gonna hurt."

"Expect so," Jerry said, spots dancing in his vision, nausea churning his gut.

"*Semper* Gumby, Jerry," Osbourne breathed before he got to work. Stay flexible.

Shock dulled the pain—he didn't feel Osbourne's clamp, just a vague, uncomfortable pressure. Orders crackled from Norton, but it all came through his earpiece as if from a hazy distance.

"Are you kidding me? Come here!" Calvin "Hobbes" Brock screamed over the comms. Jerry looked up in time to see Brock rip the M16 rifle right out of the hands of the DHS "observer" who stood in front of the recently arrived Humvee firing into the tree, then grapple the man to the ground.

"Oh, man. That is not going to end well," Osbourne said. Jerry and Osbourne watched Hobbes, wearing armored gloves, calmly punch the downed man in the face with a timed precision that echoed his boxing days as a youth in the Bronx. "Oh, that will definitely leave a mark."

Norton transmitted again, "Doc. Sitrep? Over."

Osbourne replied, "Hit an artery. Gonna need medevac most ricky-tick, Boss. Over."

After a brief moment of silence over the comms during which Jerry felt certain Captain Norton had just verbally expressed his true and sincere feelings on the matter, he transmitted, "Roger. Stay on Bravo Four. I'll call it in. Out."

Jerry said, "You cannot be serious. Did that Five Eleven Tactical fashion model actually fire his weapon? And hit me? I got shot by a brown shirt?"

"Just the usual friendly inter-agency rivalry." Osbourne keyed his microphone. "Daddy? I do believe Hobbes found the shooter. Want me to call him off? Over."

After a brief pause, Norton replied, "I have no idea what you mean, Ozzy. I don't see a thing."

"Roger that, Six," Osbourne grinned. "I will render aid once our highly skilled and properly trained DHS partner finishes accidentally falling out of his vehicle."

"Negative, Doc. Stay on Jerry. They can clean up their own mess," Norton replied. Then he ordered, "Hobbes, check his ID before you scramble his face too much. Over."

Through blurred eyes, he saw Osbourne rip the cap off a hypodermic needle, felt the cool swab to his right arm just before a tiny prick. "Bird's on the way. Stay conscious, and try not to bleed so much. Your dry-cleaning bill is going to be massive."

"Shot by DHS about 8,000 miles from their nearest legitimate jurisdiction," Jerry said. "Imagine that."

Osbourne said, "Stranger things have happened."

"I'm sure," Jerry quipped. "Just not to me and not today."

Uncomfortable burning from the injection site finally reached his heart. The first heartbeat transformed the burning sensation into a warmth that spread through his entire body, flooding his veins, easing the fight in his chest. "Maybe tell me a joke to keep me entertained while I wait."

Osbourne chuckled. "What do you call a sniper who gets himself sniped?"

Jerry grinned. "A liability?"

Osbourne mocked disappointment. "Aw. You heard this one already."

Jerry closed his eyes, a silent prayer that he would open them again flickering in the back of his mind.

Landstuhl Regional Medical Center,

Landstuhl Army Base, Germany

As she scrubbed out at the big metal sink, First Lieutenant Olivia "Olive" Duncan bopped her head to the beat of the music coming from her earbuds. She'd just assisted on a chest wound. Shrapnel from an IED lodged into the thoracic cavity of a barely twenty-year-old private while fighting in an undisclosed location. They'd had to work fast, combating the loss of blood in the field and the time it took to get him to Germany.

She smiled, thinking of the private lying in recovery. He would have some scars to show off and a story or two to tell if he were permitted and felt so inclined.

For two years, she'd worked as a surgical nurse in Landstuhl, catching patients from Europe and Asia's hotspots. She couldn't have imagined this life back in her Auburn University ROTC days. Living in Germany gave her easy access to so much of Europe, and she spent every single day off traveling to the next place on her bucket list, including the Brandenburg Gate and Neuschwanstein Castle. She would miss living here when her time ended.

She dried her hands with coarse paper towels, glancing

at the clock—1400 hours, aka 2:00 PM Central European Time. She had two hours left on her shift. Through the glass window, she could see the surgical board and scanned it while tossing the used towels into the trash. She could spare five minutes for a vending machine sandwich.

She tugged off her surgical cap and unwound her long braid, letting the red plait fall down her back. She rolled her shoulders to loosen the tight muscles and rolled her head on her neck, already imagining the salty bite of processed turkey on that vending machine sandwich. She wouldn't even read the list of ingredients this time.

Hand on the door, she paused as Captain Nathan Adams called from behind her, "Good work in there, Lieutenant."

She popped her earbuds out, and he repeated himself. "Thanks," she said, half-turning. "You too."

He nodded at the clock. "Took a little longer than expected. We missed lunch. Want to grab something with me?"

Captain Adams, ROTC at the University of Oregon, Olympic silver medalist in track, medical school graduate from Johns Hopkins, tall and dark-haired—he had set the nursing ranks buzzing since his arrival. His attention straightened her shoulders, a faint flush warming her face, but she shook her head. She had a very iron-clad no-fraternization rule. Even for charming, tall, dark, and handsome docs. Oh, but was that temptation she had to push aside?

"No, thanks," she said with a smile. "Have my heart set on a special meal right now."

Her stomach rumbled, loud enough to mock her, and she prayed he hadn't heard. Before she could slip out, the trauma bay's alert buzzer blared, announcing an incoming critical. She snatched up her stethoscope from the sink shelf and jogged after Adams, his long stride forcing her to half-run.

CHAPTER

TWO

Ramstein Air Base, Germany

As Osbourne rolled him off the bird at Landstuhl, Jerry had some rare moments of introspection. He knew his wound could kill him. The look in Osbourne's eyes every time he checked his vitals belied the outward confidence the medic projected.

Even through the drugs, he could feel the dull ache in his arm with every heartbeat, with every movement of the helicopter. A chemical bitterness coated his mouth, like aspirin dissolved on the back of his throat, chasing the fog in his veins.

"Hey, Ozzy," Jerry said, his tongue thick with morphine, "You think that DHS guy's gonna make it?"

Osbourne nodded and unsympathetically answered. "Might need a new face."

"I'm kinda fond of my left arm, Oz. Think I can take it home? Attached and all?"

Osbourne stared down at him, and something in Jerry's eyes made his false grin fade. "It's bad, Jerry. Not gonna lie. But we're here, and we made good time. Odds are better than not."

Jerry wondered what he would do if he lost his left arm. No matter what scenario he imagined, his career as a sniper would come to a proverbial screeching halt. His team days would be over. That was a given.

What would he do? Where would he go? Even if he passed a medical board and they let him stay in, they would want him to do something else, and the team was his home. It was the only life he knew, the only life that mattered.

Maybe he could drive a forklift or take up supply or ordinance. Or he could pack parachutes. He was already Airborne qualified, and if he reclassified as a parachute rigger, he could wear that cool-looking red baseball cap.

Probably not. Hard to pack parachutes with one arm. He would have to go. But where? He couldn't go home, not forever anyway.

For whatever reason, he suddenly missed his mother. Throughout all the moves and permanent changes of station he experienced in his childhood, all his friends and neighbors and chaplains had changed, his schools had changed, and even the weather and landscapes had changed. The only constant in his entire childhood had been his mother and his sister, Mabel. His father, a legend among Green Berets, had either been in the field, on TDY, or serving in undisclosed locations for nearly his entire life. He barely knew the man until the day he retired.

Mom and Mabel, though. He had known them. Mom had loved him. Would he end up completely alone? Without even a wife, or a child, or an *arm*?

Doors banged open, and they rolled him into trauma. Osbourne never left his side.

In the trauma room, Olive yanked sterile trays from the carts with efficiency, anticipating the doctor's needs while Adams scrubbed at the corner sink. She slotted her CAC into the computer's card reader, logging in as the curtain parted. A bearded medic wearing dirty ACUs, whom she did not recognize, shoved the gurney through. The smell of desert and sweat filled the sterile room. With a clipped voice, he said. "Staff Sergeant McBride, Gerald A., twenty-seven years old. GSW, left biceps, brachial artery nick. Clamped in the field. Tourniquet in flight. Morphine times two. Last dose 40 mikes ago. Type O-Negative. One unit type specific onboard."

Adams said, "We got him from here." He looked the medic up and down. "Go get cleaned up, Lieutenant. Grab some food. We'll find you when there's news. Promise"

Without a word, the medic ducked out, letting them work in their familiar arena without getting in their way.

Blood stained the field dressing, but McBride was awake, jaw clenched, full chestnut beard screaming Special Forces even before she could see that he wore no patches, no identifying anything on his uniform other than a patch proclaiming his blood type. Olive stepped forward with Adams to slide him onto the bed. She slipped off a glove and brushed her bare hand over his dust-streaked forehead, giving him skin-to-skin contact. His hazel eyes, half-lidded under the heavy morphine doses, locked on hers—hard, searching. "Welcome to Landstuhl," she said softly. "You're in good hands."

Adams sliced off the dressing, eyes narrowing. "Clamped for hours. It's mush. We'll have to graft. Tourniquet's held, but we need the OR stat to save the arm. Fluids, cefazolin IV, prep for vascular repair."

As Olive turned to the computer, McBride's right hand snagged her wrist. He had a strong grip, despite the circumstances. The fingers of his hand felt burning hot. She froze, bending closer. His gaze dropped to her cross necklace that had slipped free from her scrubs, then lifted, intense. "Do you pray?"

She smiled, twisting her wrist until their hands clasped briefly. "Continually."

He nodded, grip firm despite the drug haze clouding his eyes. "Please do that. And maybe pray for the guy that shot me."

Wow. She had never heard such a request. Pray for your enemies? She patted his hand until he let go of her wrist. "I will. I'll pray for you, soldier. Promise. And I'll see you in recovery," she said. "You've got this, soldier."

She typed Adams' orders as an orderly wheeled him

out. Logging off by snatching her CAC from the reader, she headed to the scrub room, a prayer flickering for Staff Sergeant McBride, Gerald A.—Special Forces, O-negative, 27 years old, with hard eyes she suddenly wanted to know more about.

Despite his earnest request, she could not bring herself to pray for the man who shot him.

Jerry floated in a haze, the recovery room's white walls blurring like a rifle scope lens caked with dust. His left arm throbbed under a fresh dressing, the biceps stitched tight. He fought the fog, then suddenly felt a burst of adrenaline as he recognized the fight-or-flight feeling welling up within him. He remembered the story his dad told him of clipping him in the jaw when he came out of anesthesia after his wisdom teeth surgery.

Taking deep, slow breaths, he silently recited the soldier's Psalm—Psalm 91—ensuring he mentally formed every word as his muscles gradually released their tension and his heart rhythm slowed.

Muffled voices hummed beyond the curtain, a distant cart rattling like loose change in his ears. The smell of this room annoyed him. It smelled like iodine mixed with Pine-Sol mixed with alcohol and a hint of ammonia. His white blanket and linens smelled overwhelmingly of bleach. Nausea swirled in his stomach. He realized he was having a bad reaction to the anesthesia.

He drifted off again, or maybe not. Couldn't be sure.

Everything smelled the same, and he still felt like he might lose yesterday's lunch.

Anesthesia fogged his brain, softening the sharp edges into a fuzzy dream—coffee steaming, a porch beneath a vast sky, a smile he couldn't place. The monitor's beep drilled into his skull, and he squinted, his eyes fighting to focus. His mom's voice echoed in his memory, but he could not make out the words.

Had he dozed off again?

That nurse stepped into view—copper red hair with highlights of gold spilling over her shoulder in a braid, green eyes bright like summer pines, freckles dusting her cheeks like a star map. He had briefly wondered if he had dreamed her before, but apparently not.

"*Quam pulchra es!*" Jerry exclaimed the Latin phrase for "How beautiful you are," though his voice sounded thready and slurred.

"Hey there, soldier," her southern drawl purred, soft as a hymn, "back with us, I see."

Jerry grinned, lopsided and slow, the drugs prying his tongue loose. "You look like an angel." His voice slurred, sweet and flirty, miles away from his usual dry clip. He tried to sit up, but the room tilted hard, and he flopped back, chuckling. His arm felt like it weighed as much as a car. "You smell... really nice. Like strawberries."

She laughed, quick and warm, like she'd dodged worse than his mushy charm. "Anesthesia's talkin', soldier. Men come out of it throwing punches or proposals. You're the sweet kind—lucky me." Her touch grazed his wrist, cool as she checked his pulse, the IV, steady as stone.

When he opened his eyes again, she had her back to him and was apparently leaving. Must have dozed off.

"Hey, don't leave on my account," he said, but his voice sounded weak and contorted in his own ears.

"Hey, welcome back again," she said, her voice low.

"What's your name?" he managed.

"Nurse Duncan."

"Dunkin. Like Dunkin Donuts."

She chuckled. "Close enough."

"Coffee," he mumbled, blinking slow, her face doubling then steadying.

She drew nearer. "You can't have coffee just yet. Water for now."

"Oh, I'd love some water."

She held a straw to his dry lips. He tried to gulp it down. The cool water soothed his throat. The icy liquid trickling into his belly gave him something to focus on besides the antiseptic smell of the room.

"Thanks," he said with a grateful gasp.

"I'll be back soon and give you some more. Try not to move too much. You got shot, you know. And just had some pretty major surgery."

"Coffee, though."

She shook her head. "I told you, soldier. You can't have coffee."

He shook his head. "No. No. Listen. Like to buy you a coffee. Two. Whole pot. Get to know you." His head lolled, words spilling with a goofy sincerity he'd never claim unmedicated, half-cognizant and half-lost in her green eyes.

The nurse's smile softened, crinkling those eyes as if she found him more amusing than pitiful. "I do love my coffee. It's a tempting offer, I'll admit. Best one I've had all day."

"You smell good," he slurred.

She patted his hand, stepping back, and he drifted, her braid a red blur in his fading sight. His mind slid back to that warm porch, the coffee cup steaming, only now green eyes danced with mirth, and a dusting of freckles joined the scene.

Until the smell of cinnamon lured him inside, and his heart ached again with the memory.

CHAPTER

★

THREE

Olive slipped her uniform cap onto her head before getting out of the car, then grabbed her travel mug of coffee and a backpack containing her scrubs. The early morning held a quiet stillness, as if taking a moment in preparation for the day. Once she crossed the parking lot, she looked up at the sky, savoring the view of the bright blue and purple sunrise. She closed her eyes and breathed in the morning, smelling the crisp bite of dew-kissed grass and distant pine, saying a silent prayer for her day.

"Most people look at the sunrise with their eyes open."

Startled, she turned and spotted Staff Sergeant Gerald McBride, the gunshot wound to the left biceps from yesterday. He sat on a bench, wearing an Army PT uniform. His left arm, bundled in layers of bandages, rested in a sling.

"Sometimes things are better when your eyes are closed," she said. "Smells, tastes, you know. Vision tends to dominate your other senses." She crossed over to the bench and gestured at the seat next to him. "May I?"

"Oh, by all means."

She set her backpack on the ground and sat next to him, turning sideways to face him. The metal bench was cool, a faint chill seeping through her uniform pants from the morning dew.

When she took a sip of coffee, he said, "I'd still like to buy you that coffee."

With a smile, she said, "Ah, so you remember that, do you?"

He cleared his throat. "Well, you left an impression."

Flirtatious soldiers were part of her day. She didn't even get embarrassed anymore. "Are you headed home?"

He nodded. "Just waiting on my medic. He's finalizing some paperwork."

"Where's home?"

"Fort Bragg for now. Center of the universe in case you didn't know."

Memories of the two years she spent in North Carolina flew through her mind. "Oh, I know. I was stationed there right after school."

"Not my favorite place," he said. "But I have a good team, so that makes it palatable."

"Why not a good place?"

He shrugged. "A lot of training happened there. Like, a lot. Hard schools, harder instructors." He paused. "Better chow than at Benning, though. I'll give them that." His words slurred, and his eyelids drooped.

She gestured at his arm. "How are you feeling?"

"Kind of like I got shot in the arm."

"Really? Get shot often?"

He stared at her silently for one heartbeat, then two, clearly deciding what he was allowed to say. "Maybe."

"That so?" She giggled. "Why get shot so much?"

"Thought it would be a good way to meet hot chicks." He scrubbed his beard. "Turns out I was right. Still, I wouldn't recommend it."

She chuckled. "So, I'm a hot chick, am I?"

"Hotter than a jalapeno pepper in a sauna," he said with absolutely no irony.

"Well, Staff Sergeant, I am also a commissioned officer."

All dry humor, now, he replied, "Oh, ma'am, yes ma'am, I am aware. But I would never hold that against you, ma'am."

The doors to their right swished open, and a man in clean ACUs marched out. As he walked, he effortlessly donned his green beret and straightened it. She recognized him as part of the crew who brought Sergeant McBride in. She stood and scanned his uniform rank and name before she said, "Good morning, Lieutenant Osbourne." She found it curious that a medic held an officer's rank and wondered about the story behind that.

He glanced at her nametag. "Good morning to you, too, Lieutenant Duncan." He stopped in front of Jerry. "Ready to roll, Jerry Maguire?"

"Maguire?" she asked. "I thought it was McBride?"

He grinned, a twinkle in his eye, "You had me at hello, ma'am."

Relentless flirt!

Lieutenant Osbourne asked, "Oh, did I come at a bad time?"

"Not at all. He's just enjoying the excellent narcotics provided to him post-op," she explained.

Lieutenant Osbourne scoffed. "Should have flown here with him. He was all over me. I am not just a piece of meat, lover-boy."

Jerry said, "You know what I think? I think my spotter should have been up in that tree with me. That's right. Right there by my side, tucked in right next to me all lovey and snuggly, right where you belong, Oz."

Olive rarely saw an interchange like this between a Staff Sergeant and a First Lieutenant. Clearly, Special Forces had its own culture of respect that did not necessarily always conform to the norms and standards of the regular Army.

"Well, I would have been. But then that clown might have shot both of us."

"Fair." Jerry conceded. "What's all that?"

Osbourne looked elaborately surprised as he held up the thick presentation folders and small decorative boxes he carried. "This? Oh, you don't want any part of this."

"Is that a medal?" Jerry's voice sounded suspicious.

"No," Osbourne said firmly.

"Oh, thank you Lord, thank you Jesus!" Jerry declared.

"It's actually two medals," Osbourne announced with malicious delight.

"Oh, then no," Jerry said. "And also no."

"Come on, now, hero. Somehow, the President of these

United States—well, we're in Germany, but you know what I mean—our Commander-in-Chief decided you merit a Purple Heart."

Jerry shook his head. "Not again."

"Oh, it gets better," Osbourne said with barely contained glee. "You, my friend, have been honored with the Homeland Security Distinguished Service Medal from our wonderful friends and fellow patriots at the Department of Homeland Security."

Jerry gave him a look of unabashed astonishment. "You, sir, are a liar and a scoundrel."

Osbourne couldn't contain his laughter now. "You can't make this up, Jerry. Look. Look here. This is the highest DHS honor for exceptional meritorious service or achievement in a duty of great responsibility, and it can be given to any member of the Armed Forces—across all branches—for actions supporting homeland security missions," Osbourne had to stop and chuckle, "such as joint operations, or disaster response. Or, you know, when some DHS knucklehead shoots you."

Olive could not believe what she had just heard. Friendly fire? How could that even happen anymore? Should she have heard that?

Jerry sat back further on the bench. "Ozzy? I hate you. I really do. You know that, don't you?"

Osbourne slid the medals into his kit bag. "Well, I love you, brother. And I am so thankful to our heavenly father that you still have that arm. Now, let's make tracks. Whatta ya say?"

"Yeah." Jerry slowly rose to his feet.

Olive could tell the movement hurt despite the painkillers. "Take it easy, Sergeant. Give that arm time to heal."

He studied her for a moment before he said, "Keep those eyes closed, ma'am. Never know what life might show you when they're closed."

Port-Au-Prince, Haiti

Marie Desalin pressed her back against the wall of the adobe building, praying that her black dress and black head scarf would hide her in the light of the new moon. The Kenyan soldiers strolled by, and she held her breath, keeping perfectly still. They looked neither left nor right.

As soon as she felt safe enough to dart, she ran across the street and tapped the secret signal on the door. It opened to a dark room. Once inside, the door shut behind her, and a flame lit a low lamp, highlighting her brother Jean's face. The air inside carried the faint, acrid bite of kerosene from the lamp, laced with the earthy damp of rain-soaked adobe.

"News?"

She shook her head. "Nothing good. Kenya is bringing in more troops. I saw Americans there, too. Not in uniform, though, so probably CIA." They spoke in Haitian Creole, voices low so as not to carry out of the thin walls. "They're going to come for you, Jean. They think you're the problem."

Jean's wife Daphnée slapped the table with her hand.

"The only people who think he's the problem are the ones we're trying to overthrow."

"Yeah, the ones with the guns." Henri Desalin, Jean's oldest son, spat on the ground. "We cannot fight all of them with what we have."

Julien Desalin, the youngest son, laughed. "We can one at a time."

Marie looked from one nephew to the other and finally settled back on her brother. Her breath hitched. "I can't lose you, too."

Her mind went back to her tenth birthday. She went with her family to church, but the American soldiers burst in, screaming in English. Her mother had grabbed her and held her against her while they searched the men. Out of the service, they took seventeen men, including their oldest brother, Marcus. They'd never seen him again.

Jean put a hand on her shoulder. "We will prevail. I'm working out the plan now. In the morning, I'll make contact with the Chinese spy. I'll find out what they want from us and hash out what I want from them."

Marie waved her hands in the air. "Why bring more foreigners in? Huh? Other countries have stepped in and tried to solve Haiti's problems for decades. Can't we, as Haitians, just be the ones in charge of our own destiny?"

Jean laughed low and opened up his leather-bound notebook. She knew how intricately he planned, and how he organized the lists and diagrams in the pages of his precious journal. "I can assure you, sister, that I will be the only one in charge in this situation. Anything I offer will be only what I'm willing to give and nothing more. The people of Haiti deserve true power and true independence. I will not negotiate that away like this current fool."

He pulled her into his arms. "Go with Daphnée to the estate. Prepare the meal. The boys and I will meet him there."

She looked up at him. "You all risk capture if you go to the estate."

He shook his head. "No danger. I will be giving a speech in Cap-Haïtien. We found a double to serve as a decoy."

Daphnée grabbed her shoulders. "We must persevere, sister. Even when we're scared."

Marie took a deep breath and slowly let it out. The lingering salt of unshed tears coated her tongue,

"You're right. I know you're right."

She went to the door and put her hand on the handle. "*Liberté ou la Mort*," she whispered, quoting the early nineteenth-century slogan from the Haitian Revolution. "Liberty or death."

"*Liberté ou la Mort*," he replied. "Be well, sister."

CHAPTER

★

FOUR

Clarksville Memorial Hospital

Clarksville, TN near Fort Campbell, KY

November

Three Years Later

The operating room hummed with controlled chaos, the sterile air sharp with antiseptic. Olive stood at the ready, her gloved hands steady despite the adrenaline pulsing through her. Overhead, the surgical lights blazed, illuminating Tommy Davis, a young man in his mid-20s who'd happened to be visiting his grandparents when assailants burst in, intending to rob two elderly people, not expecting the presence of someone young and spry who could fight back. The ER nurse who had brought him up to surgery said he'd wrestled the gun away from one guy only to be shot by the other.

Back in Landstuhl, she routinely dealt with this type of trauma. Not so much in Clarksburg, Tennessee, just outside the gates of Fort Campbell. Usually, appendectomies and bodies crushed by vehicle collisions filled her Saturday nights.

His vitals flickered on the monitor, heart rate erratic, BP crashing. "Scalpel," Doctor Marian Schneider barked, voice taut. Olive slapped the instrument into her palm, her movements precise, automatic. The patient's chest was already prepped, drapes framing the entry wound—a jagged mess just below the left clavicle. Blood seeped despite the suction, pooling in the field.

"BP's dropping—80 over 50," the anesthesiologist called. "Tachycardic at 130."

"Push another unit of type specific," Dr. Schneider ordered, slicing through subcutaneous tissue. "We've got a bleeder. Suction, now."

Olive leaned in, maneuvering the suction tip, clearing the field as the surgeon clamped a spurting vessel. Her eyes flicked to the monitor. His oxygen sats dipped. "He's desatting," the anesthesiologist said, voice calm but urgent. "Increasing O2."

"Retractor," Dr. Schneider said. Olive handed it over, anticipating the skilled surgeon's next move. The bullet had torn through the pectoralis major, nicking the subclavian artery. "We're in deep—possible lung involvement." Dr. Schneider looked up at her student, who hovered just behind Olive. "Come closer. I want you to see how I do it." Dr. Schneider refocused on the patient as Olive shifted, giving the medical student room to get closer. "Get me the

4-0 Prolene."

Olive passed the suture, then prepped the chest tube kit. Blood loss was critical, and the young hero hung by a thread. "Another unit's up," she announced, hanging the bag, watching crimson flow through the IV line.

"Pulse is thready," the anesthesiologist warned. "We're losing him."

"Stay with me," Dr. Schneider muttered, tying off the artery. "Chest tube, now."

The medical student hesitated only slightly before inserting the tube all the way, blood and air hissing through the line as the lung reinflated. The monitor blipped—sats climbing, but the BP still teetered. Olive's heart pounded, but her hands didn't falter, passing instruments, adjusting the light, keeping the field clear. "Come on, God," she whispered under her breath, eyes on the patient's ashen face, "we really could use a miracle."

Dr. Schneider worked furiously as she repaired the artery, but the clock was cruel. Every second a risk, every suture a prayer.

Memorial Chapel

Fort Campbell, Kentucky

The faint hum of Sunday morning chatter floated through the chapel as Olive came through the doors and slipped off her coat. The November chill had seeped through her faded teal scrubs, and it felt good to step into the warm and out of the wind.

She made it with five minutes to spare. She honestly didn't think she would. However, young hero Tommy Davis pulled through in the end, and she would have gladly missed chapel to ensure he received the best post-surgical care she could provide.

Her heart ached for his poor grandparents, for the trauma of their Saturday evening and the stress of waiting for the news of whether Tommy lived or died. He had a long road in front of him, but the glimpse of the family she'd seen in the little surgical waiting room assured her he'd complete the journey.

As she accepted a bulletin from one of the children at the door, she smiled and felt some of the tension of the night dissipate from her neck and shoulders.

She had served at Fort Campbell as her final duty station before leaving the Army six months ago. She'd always intended to return home to Alabama, but had completely fallen in love with the area and decided to stay.

She'd applied to Mobile hospitals to please her parents, but Clarksville Memorial, just over the Kentucky line in Tennessee, had made an offer she couldn't refuse—better pay, her friends nearby, a drive home short enough for long weekends, and no state income tax.

She might still end up in Alabama one day, but she wouldn't mind staying here, either.

Instead of seeking a local civilian church off post, she'd kept the Army chapel as her church community. Several friends—also former Army—still attended the chapel instead of a local church, so despite the transient nature of the military, she had a solid community here.

As Olive headed for her usual seat, she glanced at the praise team on the platform, getting ready to start. She waved to her friend Mina, on the drums, as she set her Bible on the chair.

"Hey, stranger," said Kerri, a wiry blonde who stood a good five inches taller than Olive. She held Jenkins, Mina's youngest son. "Long night?"

Olive grinned an exaggerated grin and leaned close to the toddler. He had straight black hair like his Korean mom, a round face, and the prettiest eyes she'd ever seen in a baby. "It *was* a long night," she said in a playful, singsong tone that made Jenkins' face light up. "Full moon on a Saturday night. Always a good time."

Jenkins laughed, emitting joy in his special 10-month-old way, and Olive gave him her finger to grip while she looked at Kerri and spoke in a normal tone. "How are you?"

"Good. Trying to get everything ready to host both sets of parents for Thanksgiving." She looked over Olive's head and lifted her chin. A second later, Mina's husband, Chief Warrant Officer Archie Knowles, arrived, wearing his dress uniform.

"Thanks," he said warmly, scooping a chattering Jenkins from her.

"Any time. Jenkins is our favorite."

He walked to the front, and Mina slipped out from behind the drum set to meet him at the edge of the platform. Olive felt a familiar tinge of envy at the easy way her friend greeted her husband, at the hand on his shoulder, and the happy look on her face.

She turned her attention back to Kerri. "Both sets, eh? You swore you'd encourage one of them to pick a different holiday."

Kerri grimaced. "Everyone insisted. And here we are in the middle of such a divisive political season. Dear Olive, what have I done?"

Olive laughed. "You can do it. Four days." She thought of Kerri's daughters. "The girls will love all the attention."

Kerri's gaze swept over her, lingering on the braid now frizzed and unruly after fourteen grueling hours, then trailing down her scrubs to the toes of her Crocs. "You just getting off?"

"Was supposed to get off at seven, but didn't walk out of the OR until nine thirty. I figured if I went home first, I'd crash and not make it here."

"Glad you made it."

Olive turned to find her seat and barreled into the solid chest of a man. "I'm so sorry," she said as she stepped back and looked up. He put his hands on her shoulders to steady her.

"No worries." His voice washed over her, low and deep. His hazel eyes felt familiar, like she should recognize him.

His eyes widened in recognition. "Lieutenant—" he paused as if searching for her name. "Davis? No. What is it? Donut?"

Donut made her giggle. She tilted her head. If he'd been in uniform with a handy nametag on it, it would have helped, but he wore a pair of black jeans and a cabled blue sweater, neither of which did anything to help place him in her memory. "Lieutenant would be either Bragg or Landstuhl," she said. "I made Captain right after I got here."

He immediately removed his hands. "Sorry, ma'am, Captain, ma'am. Yes, Landstuhl." He took a small step backward. "Imagine you met a lot of people coming and going there." She searched his face, trying to place him. "I did promise to buy you a coffee."

Mentally, she overlaid a beard onto his smooth cheeks and remembered. "Sergeant McBride," she said with a smile. "Left biceps. Ran into an unfriendly friendly bullet, if I recall. Unofficially, of course."

"Unofficially," he confirmed. "Wow. How do you remember that?"

"Well, you left an impression," she said, echoing his words from their last meeting.

A sudden blush rose in his cheeks, and he cleared his throat. "Well, uh, so you're stationed here now, Captain?"

With a little shake of her head, she said, "Past tense. I've been out for a few months."

Everything about him suddenly relaxed. He opened his mouth just as the band started playing. "I see. In that case, I'd love to see about that coffee."

Something about him made her want to have coffee with him. Or tea. Or anything that might let them have some time alone just talking. "That would be great," she said, then hesitated and did something she had never done before. "Meet me at the food court after service?" She paused. "Maybe lunch?"

The smile on his face lit up his eyes. "That's a date, ma'am." Anything else he might have said got interrupted by the worship leader beginning the service.

Olive slipped into her seat and tried not to sneak a glance behind her to see where he sat down, or with whom. Instead, she intentionally faced forward and tried to pay attention to the song.

CHAPTER

FIVE

AAFES Main PX

Fort Campbell, Kentucky

Ten years in the Army taught Jerry McBride one truth. Stateside Post Exchanges, or Base Exchanges—the military equivalent of department stores—looked like carbon copies: the same products, the same fluorescent hum, the same smells. Even the architecture may as well have followed a single master blueprint. Food courts, too.

He could almost always count on steak sandwiches, burrito bowls, or Louisiana fried chicken, irony not lost on him here in Kentucky. The competing aromas of grease and spice hit him as he stepped inside, scanning the Sunday crowd for that coppery red hair. He didn't spot her—Lieutenant turned Captain turned civilian now— among the crowded tables. He hadn't had a chance to catch her name before worship started. Something with a D, he remembered. He shifted around a sticky high-top, scanning the room.

He hadn't lingered in Landstuhl. He'd gone straight back to Fort Bragg, North Carolina from Germany and finished his recovery in his barracks room, complete with regular visits from Osbourne and lots of physical therapy at Womack.

Running into the nurse at chapel hadn't surprised him too much. This was a small army, and people usually crossed paths more than once. What did surprise him was the instant delight that spread through him at seeing her.

"Hey there, soldier," she said at his elbow, soft southern lilt cutting through his thoughts.

He turned, a grin tugging his lips. "Snuck up on me. I was thinking about Germany."

"I loved being stationed there," she said, her smile making her eyes crinkle under faint shadows. "The work was hard, though." She wore faded teal scrubs and a gray sweater.

"Expect so," he said, shoving his hands into his pockets. "Major trauma center for—" He paused, dodging the prospect of uttering something possibly classified in this environment. "Well, you know."

"Indeed." She slipped her hands into her sweater pockets. "I'd like to think there's less trauma here, but this morning, spent the better part of six hours with a 19-year-old and a gunshot wound to the chest, so today's not the best day to talk about that."

He studied her face, the shadows that came and went out of her eyes when she talked about her patient. "Image that takes a toll on you."

She shook her head, "I'm tougher than I look."

"Don't know about that. You look pretty tough," he said. "Did he make it?"

"So far."

"So far is good," he said, then tilted his head. "Please tell me your name. I tried to remember it at chapel, but I don't remember much about my time there. There's like a fog where details should be." Other than green eyes and the smell of strawberries, he thought.

Her smile lit those eyes, bright as summer pines. She held out a hand. "Olivia Duncan. Olive. Nice to meet you."

"Gerald McBride. Jerry. Pleasure's mine." He shook her hand, thinking how small it felt, and tested her name. "Olivia Duncan." It rolled off his tongue, savoring the flavor of it in his mouth. "Very Irish."

"Indeed," she lilted, mimicking a brogue. "My gran'd approve uv ye." She chuckled, voice softening, returning to normal. "Always been Olive, though."

"Even better, means peace." A porch flashed in his mind—sunset, steaming coffee, a safe haven, maybe a family—his perfect idea of peace. Tranquility. Funny, he remembered having the same mental image coming out of his surgery.

"My parents did that on purpose," she explained as they stepped to the coffee counter. Her words, though well-articulated, stood in the not-too-distant shadow of a deep southern drawl. "Older brother's Frederick, little sister's Irene. Both names also mean peace. My dad's parents' families hated them getting married. Our names were intended to battle a long history."

They ordered coffee and turkey sandwiches. He paid for it before she had a chance to dig out her wallet. "I said I'd buy you a coffee," he explained before she could protest.

They found a table away from the after-church crowd. They sat, and he asked. "Mind if I say grace?"

Her countenance brightened, and she smiled in a way that made his heart skip. "That would be great," she said.

He bowed his head and offered a sincere, short prayer of thanks to God for the food and for the company.

"Where's your family now?" he asked, peeling the lid off his cup. The rich coffee aroma rose with the released steam.

"Mobile, Alabama." She blew on her coffee, steam curling up. "Well, just north. Daddy's a preacher. Mama's retiring from the school system this year."

"So, you're a preacher's kid," he observed.

"Yup. PK," she confirmed.

He sized her up and said, "I enjoyed today's sermon." he kept his tone casual. "I like the idea that God has a plan for all of us, even if we can't see it or don't understand it. I know, in my life at least, I've seen God using me to fulfill His plans."

Olive sipped her coffee then said, "I've never seen you at Liberty Chapel before, and I've been there going on three years."

Jerry nodded. "When I'm not in the field, I attend chapel over by the hangar near Fifth Group. It's being renovated right now."

Instead of responding, she just smiled. "When did you get here to Campbell?"

"We moved our guidon about two years back," he explained. "We're supposed to be taking on a new JSOC mission, but right now we're hurrying up and waiting. They can't decide if we are going to cohort here with Fifth Group, or have our own station on another base, like Breckinridge."

Jerry could not tell if Olive looked hopeful or doubtful when she said, "So you're coming up on three years, here. No PCS orders yet?"

Jerry shook his head. "Not so far. This is the longest I've ever been assigned to the same place since Robin Sage."

The United States Army Special Warfare Center at Fort Bragg was a necessary home base for every Army special operator. Green Berets euphemistically called it the "hub of the wheel." Training to become a Green Beret could take anywhere from a year and a half to three years, from the Special Operations Preparation Course, to the Special Forces Assessment and Selection course, to the comprehensive Special Forces Qualification Course, and culminating in the Robin Sage exercise in the nearby North Carolina forests.

Additionally, Jerry had attended the US Army Sniper School at Fort Benning in Georgia for his Level 1 training in the middle of that, only because the Special Forces Sniper Course or SFSC at Bragg had overallocated available slots. He had returned to the "hub of the wheel" at Fort Bragg to attend his Level 2 sniper training at SFSC, a seven-week program focused on advanced marksmanship, fieldcraft, surveillance, and precision fire in support of special operations.

"So, what's your mission here, if you can say?" she asked.

He nodded around a bite of turkey sandwich, "Well, apparently, today's mission was to buy you a cup of coffee."

She smiled, clearly understanding he could not discuss his mission. "Well, then," Olive took a slow savoring sip of her brew, then pantomimed a toast, "Mission accomplished."

"How did you end up in the Army?" He leaned back, sandwich in hand. "Big jump from PK to LT."

Her cheeks pinked. "Well, way back then, there was a boy."

He raised an eyebrow when she didn't elaborate. "I assume that didn't pan out."

"Sadly, no. College wasn't for him—too much temptation, not enough backbone." A shadow flickered in her eyes, gone as quickly as it came. He wondered about the story there. She shrugged. "Even so, I followed him to an ROTC scholarship to Auburn. I loved it. Best decision I ever made, despite the boy. I made good friends, saw the world, and practiced combat nursing. Who gets to do that?"

"What made you decide to get out?"

She gave a small shrug. "I have no idea. It felt like God wanted me to, but honestly, I don't know why. I loved my job, and I'm good at it. I'd gotten the promotions. But the longer I ignored God's voice to get out, the more I knew I was supposed to do something else."

He stared at her for several moments, then said, "Interesting. That lines up with the sermon today about how we need to trust that God has a plan."

She raised an eyebrow. "Go on."

He tried to put into words what he inherently knew. "When we look at a big picture objective, the concept can be overwhelming. Here are bad actors, and we need to apply force in a certain way. But there's a lot of players and a lot of moving parts—air, land, sea, ops." He took a sip of coffee to give himself a moment to mentally assemble his conclusion. "In the end, when it all works together according to plan, we have a successful mission. But it didn't happen by accident. There was always a plan."

She pursed her lips. "Are you reckoning my life to a combat mission?"

He gave a slow smile. "I wouldn't go that far. But I believe God has a plan. Sometimes the setup for that plan happens back here." He held his hands apart and waved his left hand up and down. "But we can see where it mattered here." He lifted his right hand up and down, then picked up his coffee. "I can't tell you how many times I've looked back and said, 'Ahh, that makes sense now.'"

She took a bite of her sandwich and chewed slowly, clearly considering his words. Finally, she swallowed and met his eyes again. "In that case, I look forward to the day I can say, 'Ahh. Now I get it.'"

He chuckled. "Trust the plan, Olive."

"What about you?" she challenged. "Why Green Beret?"

He sat back. "Army brat. Third-generation Special Forces. I don't think I had much choice in the matter. Grew up everywhere. My dad retired in South Dakota, which is where my mom was originally from. Ever been?"

"South Dakota? Never."

"He has this place on the prairie that sits dead center between Mount Rushmore and Laura Ingalls Wilder's home. More than a hundred miles from either. Midland. Literally in the middle of nowhere."

She balled up a napkin and set the last bite of her sandwich aside. "So, you went Special Forces to fulfill expectations? Or do you actually enjoy it?"

Hard question. Could anyone enjoy what he did? "Not either exactly." He chewed slowly, mulling a reply that didn't sound dismissive. "I mean, dad's proud of me, sure, but that isn't why I did it. My childhood just made me aware that this career was an option as my future career. But if I had never joined, I wouldn't have been *persona non grata*. As for the work itself..."

He took time to carefully think through his next words before speaking. "I'm good at it. I think God designed me for it. But enjoy? There are aspects I enjoy—my team, strategy, and hitting the bullseye from 2,400 meters. I like those things. And, as much as it sucks sometimes, I enjoy the training. I kind of embrace the suck."

He paused for a few breaths, considering his words yet again. "But the real-world application? I think I'd be worried about myself if I said I 'enjoyed' that. It's a terrible duty, but a very necessary duty." He paused again. "I enjoy living in a free country, and I know what keeps it that way. *Non sibi sed patriae* and all that."

"I get that. Not for self, but for country." She studied

him, her eyes holding his for a long beat, then nodded. "I appreciate the honesty."

"Olive, I'll always be honest," he said, washing the remainder of his sandwich down with the last of his coffee. "I have no reason to lie to anybody,"

Once more, Olive toasted him with her cup. "I'll keep that in mind before I ask something risky."

Beijing, China

Liang Wei stood in the busy tea shop and closed his eyes, relishing the sound of Mandarin Chinese filling the air from a dozen different conversations and the rich, earthy aroma of oolong steeped in hot clay pots that enveloped him.

His last assignment in the Dominican Republic required him to master Spanish. Before that, he operated a covert organization in Miami, Florida, where he had to play a simpering fool while also learning to speak French and English.

He could not wait for his time in the west to end. He just wanted a nice, local assignment to complete his last five years of service to the People's Republic of China's Ministry of State Security, or MSS.

He took the paper cup of tea from the attendant with a bow and carried it outside. The cool November breeze felt refreshing in comparison to the humid air of the Dominican Republic. He all but closed his eyes and breathed it in, instead choosing to casually take a deep breath. He would be alone soon.

He spied his contact on a bench by an old war statue. He casually walked over and sat next to him.

"You've done well."

Liang nodded. He knew he'd done well. "And?"

His contact remained silent. Liang watched a flock of pigeons descend on the statue and wondered at the freedom of a bird, but the hard life of scraping for every bite.

Finally, the contact said, "We are sending you to Haiti."

Liang threw his head back and laughed. "Haiti? Are you mocking me?" The question was met with stony silence. Finally, Liang asked, "Why?"

"It's a short assignment. We are providing weapons for rebels in exchange for unfettered access."

With a gasp, Liang clarified. "Unfettered?"

He nodded. "That's the deal." He lit a cigarette, and the wind blew the smoke away. "Your French is impeccable. Your English is good. Your Spanish is passable. Go make the deal. Give them what they want. Make nice. Let him think we're on his side. Then you can have a team of twenty trained men to set it up."

The idea of such access to the monolith in the West. His heart beat a little faster. He hated the tropics. He hated the languages, the people, and the food. Oh, but he hated the United States of America more. What he could do with so much access and a puppet under his command!

"I will be in touch," he said, standing. He tossed his untouched tea into the trash bin next to the bench.

SIX

Clarksville, Tennessee

November

Olive eased the front door shut and dropped her keys in a dish on the little entry table.

She walked through her living room, the late afternoon light spilling through the big window onto the worn hardwood. Her beige couch held a riot of mismatched pillows—pink, yellow, orange. A crocheted blanket from her sister draped over the back, its bright stripes a splash against the brick hearth's quiet gray.

As she kicked off her shoes, she pulled the band off the end of her braid and finally freed her hair from its confines. Her scalp sighed as the auburn strands spilled free, and she rubbed the ache loose, fingers gently massaging her scalp.

She needed a shower and bed, but as tired as she felt,

her mind raced ninety-to-nothing, reliving the three-hour lunch with Sergeant First Class Gerald A. "Jerry" McBride, thirty years old, O-negative, decorated Special Forces sniper. She went into the kitchen, the white tile cold against her socked feet. After she turned on the kettle, she grabbed an herbal tea bag from the box on the counter and plopped it into the waiting mug.

A mischievous grin pulled on her cheeks when she thought about the way he'd retreated when she first said the word, "Captain". Clearly, lunch would not have happened today if she had required Jerry to render her a parade ground salute from time to time. Jerry continued to serve as a Non-Commissioned Officer. Mixing ranks like that would break so many rules, hers and Uncle Sam's.

That didn't matter now, did it? Her mind flickered back to the way amusement filled his eyes while he told her an anecdotal story, his hand strong when he shook hers, his grin that made her heart thump like a cannon inside her chest. She hadn't felt anything like this in a long time.

Post surgery, he'd oozed with a careless kind of anesthesia-induced charm. Today, he radiated a sober strength and steady character. He'd stirred something inside her she didn't really recognize yet.

She poured steaming water over the teabag. The chamomile's soothing floral mist rose, already relaxing her before even taking a sip.

With a sigh, she carried the mug to her couch. She settled in, pulled her legs up under her, and stared blankly into the cold hearth of her fireplace, letting her mind relax.

The vibration of her phone startled her out of an almost doze. She glanced down and read her sister Irene's message to their family chat.

> Irene: Thanksgiving! Excited to do Tennessee instead of Mobile.

Thanksgiving already? How had the last week gone so quickly?

She wrote back:

> Olive: So excited. Can't wait to see everyone and show you my new place.

It took seconds for her mom to reply.

> Mom: Freddy's flight arrives in Nashville Wednesday morning. We'll pick him up on the way to your new place. Dad confirmed we'll be in the motorhome.

She glanced around her home. Her sister could sleep in the spare room. Her brother could take the couch in here. She had plenty of room for the motor home next to the house and an outlet right there for her father to plug into. She could not wait to open her home to the people she loved most in the world.

> Olive: Sounds good.

She hesitated, her fingers hovering over the keys. Even though she knew her mom well, she went ahead and asked:

Olive: Did you already buy food?

She chuckled at her mom's reply.

Mom: Turkey's already in the fridge, getting ready for dad to brine it. We'll bring it with us. I'll send you a shopping list for the fresh items we'll need once we get there.

She took a sip of her tea and leaned further back against the couch cushion, yawning a jaw-cracking yawn that made her eyes tear up a little. Her phone buzzed again, and she glanced at it, expecting to find her mom's shopping list. Instead, to her delight, she saw a new text from Jerry. Her heart rate increased slightly as she opened it.

Jerry: Enjoyed coffee. Hope we can do something again soon.

The grin she couldn't erase after leaving the food court matured into a toothy smile. Her fingers hovered over the screen, then she typed back.

Olive: Do you have plans for Thanksgiving?

While Irene unpacked her suitcase, Olive sat on the corner of the bed with her legs pulled under, chatting with her sister and catching up.

"So, tell me about this guy you invited tomorrow?" Irene asked.

Heat flooded Olive's face. "Argh!"

"Argh? Why Argh?"

"It was so spontaneous." Olive covered her face with her hands. "We just finished chatting about Thanksgiving, and then he texted me, and I was sleepy, and I just invited him without thinking about it."

Irene playfully shoved Olive's shoulder. "It's a good thing! I approve." She slipped a dress onto a hanger and put it in the closet. "It's been a long time since Bryan. Have you even gone out with anyone since then?"

She'd met Bryan at her father's church when they were five. They didn't attend the same schools, they had church, and their families spent a lot of time together growing up. He asked her out during their senior year of high school. As soon as they started dating, people around them talked about marriage. He encouraged her to apply for an ROTC scholarship with him, and they both received one. Once they got to Auburn University, something inside of him changed. He started partying, drinking, and the more he drank, the meaner he got. She broke up with him very quickly. He dropped out midway through their sophomore year. She had never seen him again.

"No. Well, a lunch or a coffee here and there, and then nothing. I mean, obviously, being surrounded by so many military men. I do get asked out. A lot, really. There was just never any desire to date anyone. I didn't want any fraternization to affect me or my career." She smiled. "There was this one doctor in Germany, though. I will admit I was tempted."

Irene closed her empty suitcase and plopped on the

bed. "I would be interested to hear about the man who almost made you break your own rules," she said with a giggle.

Olive toyed with the end of her braid and told anecdotal stories about Germany.

An hour later, she left her sister getting ready for bed and moved quietly through the living room so as not to disturb her jet-lagged brother, Freddy.

Working nights for the last two months threw her off her sleep schedule. In her kitchen, she'd organized the dishes for tomorrow. She had grouped dry ingredients with their serving containers. On index cards inside each serving dish, she had listed required refrigeration and wet ingredients on one side and recipes on the other. She flipped the oven on and started on the pies.

Normally, when she cooked, she had music pumping through the speakers above the cupboards. In deference to her sleeping family, she slipped earbuds in and turned up the music. While she measured and poured, she danced and moved.

Just as she put a pumpkin pie into the oven, her back door opened and her mom came into the kitchen. Olive pulled the earbuds out. Her mom glanced at the organized ingredients on the counter.

"Oh, I was coming in to do the pumpkin pie myself. You beat me to it."

Olive turned the kettle on and gestured at the collection of sugars and nuts next to a glass pie plate. "We still have to do the pecan." She opened the fridge and pulled out the plastic-wrapped crust she'd made. "I made a double piecrust when I made the crust for the pumpkin."

Her mom slipped on an apron. "Perfect. If you roll it out, I'll mix the batter."

They worked in silence and very quickly had the pecan pie in the oven as well. Olive poured them each a cup of herbal tea, and they sat at the little table.

"As much as I loved my time in the Army, I sure wish all my holidays could have been spent with you guys. I'm really happy you're all here."

Her mom rubbed her back. "You have a beautiful home. I'm glad you're so happy here." She blew on the surface of her tea. "I mean, obviously, I'd be happier if 'here' was in Alabama."

Olive shook her head and chuckled. "Did Freddy ever have a second date with that one girl?"

Her mom shook her head. "No. They still work together, though. My understanding is there was no chemistry."

"That's too bad. He seemed to have high hopes."

As if sensing their conversation, Freddy appeared in the kitchen doorway. His tousled red hair gave him a mischievous look. "Delicious smells woke me."

Cinnamon and nutmeg swirled thick in the air, laced with the caramelizing sweetness of browning sugar from the oven.

"You've been asleep for hours," Olive said, glancing at the clock and performing a quick calculation to determine her brother's normal local time in the UK. "We were trying not to wake you."

"I'll be fine. It's just jet lag. It's mid-morning in London." He joined them at the kitchen table. "I don't mind getting woken up. I don't get to see y'all very often."

The timer for the pumpkin pie dinged. Olive checked it, pulled it out, and set it on a wire rack.

"Dad's putting the turkey on the smoker at seven. What time did you tell your friend to come over?"

Nervous energy darted through Olive's stomach at the ready agreement Jerry gave to her invitation. Why had she done that? "Uh, noon. He has duty at five, so we had to do early."

"Noon is plenty of time." She waved in her direction. "You go on to bed. Get a couple hours sleep. I'll handle the pecan pie."

"Yes, ma'am." Olive tousled Freddy's hair. "Help yourself to coffee and food."

"Thanks, sis."

When Jerry rode his Indian Super Chief Limited motorcycle—painted teal blue and bright yellow gold to match his Special Forces patch and tab—into Olive's driveway, an older man with graying red hair came from around the side of the house. Jerry cut the engine and doffed his helmet.

A haze of applewood smoke and sage clung to the air, making Jerry's mouth water.

"That's a beaut," the man said in an Irish lilt. He wore an apron with a comical turkey face on the front. He wiped his hands on the towel hanging from his waist and extended his hand to Jerry. "Tobias Duncan."

"Jerry McBride," he said. "Thank you. My father had it customized for me after I graduated from Ranger school." He ran his palm over the edge of the windshield. "He built this himself."

"That is a lovely machine," Tobias declared. "And such good weather today. Wonderful day for a ride."

"Yeah, seemed too sunny to waste it on my pickup truck."

Olive opened the front door. Jerry dismounted from the bike and took an autumn flower bouquet out of the saddlebag, offering it to her as she approached. As she drew closer, Jerry's heart leaped like a paratrooper practicing parachute landing falls. He spent the last four days just waiting for the moment he could see her again. In thirty years, he'd never felt like this before.

She wore a rust-colored loose top over leggings covered in comical turkeys. For the first time, she had her hair loose instead of in a braid. It cascaded down her back, well below her shoulder blades.

He looked down at his own jeans and black T-shirt, glad he'd chosen to wear casual clothes instead of dressing up.

Her welcoming smile lit up her eyes as she accepted the fall bouquet he offered. "Welcome," she said. "Happy Thanksgiving."

"Thank you for having me."

A red-haired man who looked close to Jerry's age joined them outside. Olive gestured toward him. "My big brother, Frederick. Freddy, this is Jerry McBride."

Jerry shook his hand. "Nice to meet you, Freddy."

"Likewise," Freddy replied in a southern drawl that echoed Olive's cadence.

"Nice donor-cycle," Olive quipped.

"Thanks. It was a gift from my dad," Jerry responded. He smiled a toothy smile. "You want to ride it, don't you?"

Freddy laughed, "Oh, he got you, sis!"

Olive joined in the laughter. "Not today. But it is really nice."

"Thanks." Jerry secured his helmet to the seat. Glancing at Freddy, he said, "Olive said you came from London. How was your trip?"

"Long flight. But I was able to get a nonstop between Heathrow and Nashville, so it wasn't terrible."

Jerry nodded. "That trip does me in on this side."

"Yeah. I crashed pretty hard yesterday. At least I'm home for a couple of weeks this time. Last time, it was just four days. My brain didn't know if I was coming or going."

With a sympathetic chuckle, Jerry said, "Been there, done that."

"This the Super Chief?" Freddy asked, walking around the bike.

Jerry nodded. "Yeah. Obviously custom. My dad actually makes these windshields." He indicated the custom acrylic shield. "Makes some crazy amount, like a thousand a year."

"No kidding?" Freddy asked, folding his arms.

"Well, Sturgis is big in South Dakota."

"Right!"

Soon, the entire family joined them. He met her sister, Irene, and her mother, Nancy, while he showed her brother and father the bike. Eventually, they all went back inside.

"Where is your family, Jerry?" Tobias asked.

"Uh, South Dakota, sir."

"That's right. You said that. Is that where your people hail from?"

He nodded. "My mother. My father's family originally came from South Carolina."

Tobias nodded. "Big Scottish settlements in the Carolinas."

"Yes, sir. But my grandfather was career Army, as was my father. So, I've never actually lived in South Carolina. We just used to go there when we were close enough to drive down for holidays." He accepted a glass of iced tea from Olive and sat next to her on the couch. "What about you? Where are you from?"

"I was born in Belfast, but my parents moved to Alabama in 1975. My mother's Catholic, and my father was Protestant. It made for a rather dangerous situation at the time."

"The Troubles," Freddy said in a perfect Irish accent. His father gave him a scolding look.

Olive interjected, "How's the turkey, Daddy?"

"Your mom's about to get it out."

Olive stood. "I'll get the platter for her." Irene followed her out of the room, leaving him with Freddy and Tobias.

"Olive tells me you're a preacher. Did your mom stay Catholic?" Jerry asked.

Tobias gave a small shrug. "She wanted us raised Protestant. I don't think she ever converted per se, but she was very active in our church lives. And she loves the Lord."

Freddy held up the remote. "You guys care if I turn the game on? Auburn's playing"

Jerry shook his head. "Of course not."

"War Eagle!" Olive shouted from the kitchen.

Jerry enjoyed watching Olive move and talk within her core family. At first, she seemed a little nervous, a little tense. By the time the delicious meal of smoked turkey and all the trimmings had disappeared, followed by pies and coffee, she had relaxed, and her laughter sounded lighter, her conversation more ready.

They cleared the table and played dominoes for hours. Jerry had never enjoyed a Thanksgiving so much. They laughed and teased each other, tripping over one another as they shared anecdotes and stories, and constantly affirmed each other. By the time the afternoon ended, Jerry felt as though they had folded him into the fabric of their family.

Olive walked him to his bike, giving them the chance to share a moment alone for the first time that day.

"I can't tell you how much I enjoyed this," he said, slipping his leather coat on. He gave in to the impulse and reached out to tuck a strand of her hair behind her ear. "But I have to go to work now."

She crossed her arms over her chest and looked up at him. "I'll admit that I asked you on an impulse and immediately wished I hadn't."

He let go of her hair and rested his hand on her shoulder. With a raised eyebrow, he asked, "Oh?"

Red covered her cheeks. "I wanted to see you, but I didn't want to sign you up for the whole Duncan family experience."

"I had a wonderful time. You have an amazing family. I'm honored that you gave in to your impulse and shared today with me."

A slow smile spread across her face. "Honored? I like that." She looked down, then back up. "I'm happy, too."

He brushed a finger down her cheek, then swung his leg over and straddled the bike. "Enjoy your folks." He pulled the helmet down over his face. His voice muffled, he said, "See you Sunday."

After handing her father the turkey platter, she sank into the kitchen chair and yawned. He stood on the step stool and set it in the cupboard above the refrigerator.

"And, that's the lot," he said, draping the dishcloth over the edge of the sink.

She looked around the clean kitchen and thought of all of the leftovers in her refrigerator. The room smelled like dish soap and lingering smoke from the smoker outside the kitchen door. "Another one in the books," she replied with a slow smile.

He joined her, clasping his hands together and resting them on the table. "I'm glad you invited Jerry. He seems like a man of solid character."

That uncomfortable cringe she felt for the last few days at inviting him had disappeared. Instead, she thought of the look in his eyes as he ran his finger down her cheek, the spicy smell of his aftershave in the air, and the way his hazel eyes looked dark brown with the black shirt. Her own fingers hovered over her cheek, remembering his touch. "He does."

He looked at his hands, then at her again. "What would that look like for you?"

With a raised eyebrow, she asked, "What would what look like for me?"

After moving his shoulder with a small shrug, he said, "Well, I mean, you're settled here, right?"

Was she? Settled? She considered the question, not wanting to demur. "You know, God pressed me to get out of the Army. I know we talked about it at the time. It didn't make sense. I could have gone a few more years and even made it to retirement, but there was this pressing need to get out."

He nodded. "I remember."

"At the time I didn't understand why." For some reason, she felt tears burn the back of her throat. What about this conversation caused such an emotional response? "What if it was for such a time as this?"

He didn't answer right away. Finally, he said, "What makes you say that?"

"Well," she said, drawing out the word, "let's say I was still in. I'm at chapel last week, and this really handsome soldier invites me out to coffee."

"You find him handsome, do you?" her father teased.

"Uh, Dad. You saw him, too, right? You have eyes?"

He chuckled. "Go on, then."

"Okay. So he asks me out, except he's a sergeant and I'm a captain. That means the answer is no, without exception."

"Seems early to have this conversation."

"It is early. Doesn't mean I'm not thankful I was able to have lunch with him last week, or to have him in my home today. And, I really hope I get to see him again. Soon." She propped her chin in her hand. "What do you think about that?"

He gave her a small smile. "I think I love you, daughter, and I like this excited energy coming from you right now." He reached out and squeezed her shoulder. "Your experience with Bryan was traumatic. What he did to you could have easily ruined your life, but you didn't let it. You rose above it." He tilted his head to look at her. "I can see that now. But, to be honest, I've worried about you for the last ten years. Not worried about your career choices. Worried that you would never let another man get close enough to you after that heartbreak."

Dark memories tried to assault her. Her father had never brought this up before. Only her parents knew the trauma Bryan put her through and the toll it took on her soul to rise above it. "It's my past. I can't let the past steal my future." She rubbed her jaw, remembering the pain of the dislocation caused by Bryan striking her with a closed fist when she dared suggest he'd had too much to drink at a tailgate party.

"There's strength in that. I respect that," her father said in his Irish lilt. "And I like your handsome Jerry."

"He's a Green Beret."

"Impressive," her father said, nodding.

She sat back in her chair. "He's a sniper."

Just like that, she set that down in front of her father and gave him time to process it. She could almost see her father integrating that fact with the personality of the man he had just shared Thanksgiving dinner with. Finally, he said, "That must take a terrible toll on him."

Those tears she'd felt threaten before filled her eyes. "Daddy, how do I –"

When her breath hitched on the end of her sentence, he reached out and took her hand. "How do you reconcile that?"

A tear slipped down her cheek. "Yeah."

Her father pursed his lips and contemplated the question momentarily. Then he said, "If God made you for a time such as this—and I'm neither confirming that nor denying that to be the case—but if He did, then He certainly will have equipped you for that. You consider the man—is he a *just* man? A *righteous* man? Then consider the missions. Are they *just* missions? Are they *righteous* missions? Then you think to yourself, what if he did not do what he does? What would that look like for the mission?" He squeezed her hand and let go, sitting back. "Not everything is a zero-sum. Work it out. Then, only then, you go back to the man you know."

They sat in silence while she contemplated that. After a full minute, she said, "I really like the man I know." She smiled and brushed that lone tear away. "Like, really like him."

"Like, I really like him, too," he teased. "Trust God's plan."

Jerry's words reverberated in her mind. *Trust the plan, Olive.*

CHAPTER

SEVEN

Arnold Air Force Base, Tennessee

December

Jerry hugged the tiled wall of the kill house, a long-abandoned hospital with plenty of rooms and hidden secrets. Simunition smoke stung his nose as he edged around a corner. He held Cassie tight to his chest. Fisher tapped his shoulder, signaling him to move forward. Through the earpiece, he could hear Master Sergeant Wade "Commando" Chandler giving quiet orders as his team cleared the second floor.

They had run six scenarios since 0700 hours this morning, rotating through roles, playing "dead man out" and "wounded man out," and other gigs while still achieving their objectives. Jerry had yet to take point on the breaches, and, since this run-through butted up against midday chow, he had the pleasure this round.

He looked over at Captain Peña, who motioned with his gloved hand to go through the next doorway. Jerry silently moved to the other side of the door and waited for Fisher to kick it open. Jerry and Timothy "Bourbon" Waller went through first, followed by Peña and Fisher.

"Clear!" Fisher subvocalized, and they moved back into the hallway to clear the next room. The infrared lights on their weapons illuminated the hallway like a bright green carnival ride in their optics. Jerry struggled against the distraction of the shadows and the dusty smell. He always hated training here.

Peña made a motion with his hand, and they all froze as one, waiting. A faint sound of a woman's whimper came from somewhere ahead. Peña gestured, and they took their positions. This time, Jerry would breach first. He nodded, signaling his readiness. This time, Waller kicked the door in.

In the center of the mainly empty room, the hostage knelt on her knees, her hands clasped behind her back. Her shoulders shook. Jerry immediately lined up the kid standing behind her in his sights. Young, very young. Maybe fourteen. Then the world blinded him for less than half a second, while his optics compensated for the fact that the kid had shone a flashlight in their direction.

Jerry hesitated, confusion at finding a child in his crosshairs combined with the blinding light making it difficult for his brain to connect with his fingertip. In that split second of hesitation, the young gunman fired his pistol, and his hostage slumped forward. Jerry fired three times, all three rounds hitting the aggressor in the chest plate inside a space no bigger than a US nickel.

An airhorn sounded. Everyone lowered their weapons and pulled off their NOGs as the lights in the entire building came up.

Peña spoke into the comms, "That's a wrap, Top. Mission fail. Team intact. OPFOR dead. Hostage deceased."

It took several seconds for Chandler to reply. "Roger. What I'm hearing is that some of you will be cleaning weapons tonight. We'll conduct the after-action review in ten minutes. This afternoon, our hostage is very much alive, and our OPFOR has been arrested and will be spilling valuable intel as soon as we finish our side of the conversation."

The "hostage" stood up and brushed off her pants. She held her hand down, and the teenage gunman accepted it and let her help him stand under the weight of his heavy gear. "See you next time," she said with a smile.

Jerry clenched his jaw. He never hesitated. This should have been "one and done." Jerry held up the motto of the US Army sniper school, "One shot, One kill," as his professional watchwords. Now he had to explain his actions to his First Sergeant. He did not look forward to the ribbing he knew would most certainly come his way.

They walked out together, the group silent. Jerry hung his helmet on his vest by its strap and rubbed his eyes as he stepped out into the December morning. Fisher slapped him on the back as he went by. Jerry sighed as his phone vibrated in his pocket. He recognized Osbourne's number.

"Well, well, well. Look at the rich civilian Florida doctor Philip Osbourne, MD, condescending to call little old me. What's up, Doc Oz?"

"Nothing like working at a Miami trauma center during the holidays."

A few years ago, after getting injured on a mission in the jungles of Katangela, Africa, Osbourne had lost his leg, after which he had medically retired from the Army. That's when Waller had joined the unit.

The Army is a small community, and the Special Forces community is an even smaller subculture within the Army. Everyone kind of knew everyone else. Waller and Osbourne had gone through 18 Delta school together, and Waller had actually medevacked Osbourne out of the jungles of Katangela.

Jerry liked and respected Waller, and called him a friend. Waller, an excellent medic, a believer, and a family man, had a generous nature and a childlike sense of humor. Even so, Jerry thought of Osbourne more like a brother.

For a year after Katangela, every time Osbourne spoke to him, Jerry could hear the depression in his voice. It worried him and directed his prayers. That all changed last year after Osbourne began dating Melissa Braxton. Jerry could hear the happiness, the contentment in his voice.

"I imagine it's about as fun as Mogadishu in July."

"About as hot. Not as dry, though. You ever get us that timeshare there?"

Jerry laughed and chatted with Osbourne for a few more minutes until Waller called him back to the group.

"Great to hear from you. Have to go get schooled by Top now. Dead hostage, and all that."

"Ah. There are still some ways in which being in a trauma center in Miami is better than running a shoot house course. Love you, brother. Say hello to the team for me."

Jerry trotted over to the team. Chandler looked him up and down. "Not like you to hesitate, Jerry."

"No, Top. It is not my default setting." Heat filled his cheeks and he cleared his throat. "The kid threw me. Didn't make him a hundred percent as the aggressor before he hit me with the flashlight."

Chandler shrugged. "You've been doing this long enough to know—sometimes kids are the bad actors, or made to be."

Jerry sighed. He thought about the missions over the years, the people he'd seen through his scope. "I am aware, Top. Just threw me this time. Won't happen next time."

Peña added. "In the real world, I know you always have our back, Jerry Maguire. Usually from a klick away in your nest. But when you're on point. the lives of the hostage and the team depend on your rapid assessment and judgement."

Jerry felt a muscle tick in his jaw. "Yes, sir," he said. "Small point of order, though, Colada. In today's scenario, the team members are all alive, and the doer is very much unalive."

"Fair point," Peña conceded. "So D minus, not F."

"Distracted by a certain redhead?" Waller asked with a grin. "Trust me, I've been there."

"Shut up, Bourbon," Jerry explained. He could hear the

teasing in his friend's voice, but he didn't want to leave the impression this morning's momentary lapse represented some kind of ongoing control issue, especially when it mattered.

Major Norton, with hair just as crimson as his freckles, raised a single red eyebrow and ran his fingers over his ginger beard. "Thinking of me, Jerry Macquire? Did I have you at hello?"

"Sir?" Jerry answered. "You complete me."

That immediately diffused the tension. A barked laugh escaped Norton's throat. "Miss me already, Jerry?"

Jerry answered, "Sir, when you get called from on high to go entertain the top brass somewhere near the five-sided puzzle palace on the Potomac, you will be missed."

Norton's face didn't change except for a slight slitting of his eyelids. "Yeah, sooner than we realize."

Peña stepped forward. "Let's get loaded up. We have to make chow, then run at least six more exercises before dark." He pointed at Fisher. "Trout, clear our tech, secure sensitive items, and pull the recordings. I want to debrief back at the treehouse before we run the next scenario."

"Yes, sir," Fisher said, playfully nudging Jerry to the side as he jogged back into the building.

After everyone else disbursed, Chandler pulled him aside. "Anything you need to talk about?"

He shook his head. "No, First Sergeant. I assumed he was the target. He could have been another hostage the bad actors had there as a strawman. Anything's possible. I simply had not made a 'zero doubt' assessment before he blinded me."

"So, just thinking like a Bravo Four, not a door kicker?" Bravo Four was the additional skill identifier enjoyed by US Army qualified snipers. Wade Chandler, the highest-ranking enlisted man on the Team, had no condemnation in his voice.

"That's it, Top. Nothing more to it."

"Got it." Quick, single, nod. "We'll try to keep you from being our door kicker in the real world unless we absolutely can't help it."

Norton interjected. "That's for the best." He met Jerry's eyes. "You're probably the best sniper I've ever seen."

"Your wife would know, sir."

Norton grinned an ironic grin, acknowledging that Jerry recognized his personal bias. In Katangela, Jerry had taken out a terrorist while he held Norton's wife at gunpoint from more than a kilometer away. "That she does."

Turning back to meet Chandler's steady gaze, Jerry said, "I assure you, in a real-world scenario, I don't think I would hesitate. *Vivere militare est.*"

Life is warfare.

Chandler nodded, "Enough said, Jerry. All good."

Clarksville Memorial Hospital, Tennessee

Olive came out of Clarksville Memorial's front door and looked up at the gray December sky. Last week had been warm enough that it didn't feel like December at all. But that changed overnight, and she was glad she'd had her sweater with her.

Her shift had thankfully ended on time, but she had definitely clocked overtime this week. She looked forward to the next three days off.

She glanced at the incoming text displayed on her smart watch. Seeing Jerry's name erased her fatigue and made a smile stretch her cheeks. Even though his unit had gone to central Tennessee to train for two weeks, she got texts from him most mornings and evenings.

Jerry: Buy you a coffee?

She kept walking, looking through her bag for her silent phone. She didn't look up until she needed to cross the parking lot to her car. There, leaning against the door, stood Jerry McBride, a cup of coffee in one hand and a white paper bag in the other. She grinned and trotted toward him.

"Good morning," she said. She found it ridiculous how happy seeing him made her. "For me? You shouldn't have."

He held the cup out to her with a slight bow of his head. "Happy to oblige."

He wore his ACUs, the green and brown camouflage clashing with the red paint of her car. He wore his trousers tucked into the tops of brown suede boots and had his green beret pulled down over his right eye like a brim. Her eyes skimmed over the various badges and patches on his uniform, duly impressed with his accomplishments as a soldier. "You should be happy I got off on time today. Sometimes I get stuck."

"I'm really happy you didn't get stuck."

The mostly hot brew tasted delicious. "I didn't expect you until the middle of the week."

He set the bag on top of the car, then leaned against the door and crossed his arms over his chest. "We got called back. We have to, ah, go somewhere."

"Unofficially."

He nodded. "Unofficially."

She raised an eyebrow. "I'd ask if you could tell."

"Don't ask. Don't tell. Wasn't that a military thing?"

She laughed, "Now I really want to know."

"Best not. Just trust the plan. And there is always a plan." He tilted his head and looked down at her. Her heart rate accelerated slightly as she looked into his eyes. "But I'm free tonight. Can't promise when again. Would you like my company?"

"What if I have plans?" she teased.

"Change them," Jerry answered without a hint of humor.

Their schedules had not meshed since Thanksgiving two weeks ago. She relented, "Jerry, I would love your company."

His eyes shone as his mouth formed a smile. "What time's good for you?"

She took another sip of coffee and looked at her watch. "I need to sleep this shift off, or else I would be no fun. How about any time after five?"

"Let's call it six-thirty. I haven't slept in a couple of days myself." He straightened and picked up the bag. "Hey. Close your eyes."

"Close my eyes?"

"Last time I saw you in Germany, you were watching the sun rise with your eyes closed. Never seen that before." She could not believe he remembered that. He nodded again with a tight-lipped grin. "Olive. Close your eyes."

She raised both eyebrows but complied. Suddenly, the rich buttery smell of pastries filled her nose. Her mouth immediately began to water.

"Croissants, from my favorite bakery. I was going to bribe you if you said no."

She opened her eyes and grinned up at him. "I could still change my mind," she teased.

"That could be fun. Then I could change your mind back again." Jerry chuckled and held the bag out to her. "See you at six-thirty."

On an impulse, she shifted the bag of pastries to her right hand, which also held the coffee cup, and stood on her tiptoes to hug him with her free left arm. He barely hesitated as he returned the embrace. His strong arms felt good as they came around her. She didn't mind the smell of his musky sweat and the faint smell of gunpowder and gun oil. He smelled very much like a man. "Thank you," she said as she stepped back. "Get some rest."

He ran a finger down her cheek. "You too."

She could feel his touch long after he walked away. Feeling lighter, freer than she had just minutes before, she slid into her car and set the bag in the passenger seat. She caught her reflection in the rear-view mirror, trying not to cringe at the disheveled hair pulling out of her braid or the shadows of fatigue under her eyes.

Since when did she care about how she looked after a shift?

Shaking her head, she pulled out of the parking lot. The aroma of the croissants tempted her to dig into the bag before she was properly secured at home and could enjoy them to their fullest. She smiled and bit her lip, thinking about the handsome soldier who'd waited by her car. He'd clearly come straight from the field. The fact that he'd come to see her before going home meant a lot to her.

She remembered what it was like, coming in from the field, and all you could think about was a shower and a meal that didn't involve opening a foil-lined bag and scooping the cold contents out with a long brown plastic spoon.

But he'd come straight to her. It electrified her to think that he might like her as much as she liked him, that he might miss her when he didn't get to see her the way she missed him.

When she pulled into her driveway, she parked the car and dug her phone out of her bag, sending a text before she forgot.

> Olive: Thanks for breakfast. You made my day. Just need a dress code for tonight.

As she walked in the door and set her keys on the table, he replied.

> Jerry: Casual and warm.

Excited, she pulled the band out of her hair and started to undo her braid, humming a bright Christmas carol as she walked toward her bedroom.

Miami, Florida

Jean Desalin kept his infrared blocking sunglasses on as he wove his way through the throngs of tourists in the heart of Miami's Little Haiti Christmas parade. The sun beat down on his head, causing sweat to bead on his forehead. Food vendors hawking their wares had fans pointed at the crowds, sending the scents of grilling meats and spices out to tempt hunger.

He stepped out of the way of a man pushing a toddler in a stroller. He didn't mind the crowds. More crowds meant more anonymity. The sunglasses would help defeat any facial recognition cameras that happened to record his image.

Jean ducked into a cigar shop, and the man behind the counter gestured with his chin toward a beaded curtain. Jean went through the beads into the back room. A large Chinese man in a linen shirt stood next to a closed steel door. Jean approached and spoke quietly. "Good to see you, Hao."

Hao Jun, Chinese MSS agent assigned to the Caribbean, nodded in greeting. He and Hao met in the early days of this deal and had spent several weeks together hashing out details and plans. In that time, Hao and Marie had, surprisingly, become extremely close.

Jean wondered if Hao's masters in Beijing, who directed his mission, also knew of his romantic involvement with the sister of *Papa Libète.* Or, he thought—and not for the first time—perhaps they had ordered it?

"You as well," Hao said in perfect French. "I am happy to facilitate this meeting." He punched a code into the panel near the door, and it swung silently open.

From his perch just inside the doorway, he stood for a moment in the cool room, his eyes running over the cutting-edge technology lining the walls—at the screens and computers displaying market data and a live feed of Congress, as well as various CCTV feeds from different cities.

His sister, Marie Desalin, approached him, arms outstretched. She spoke their native Haitian Creole in her greeting. "*Bonjou, frè.*" She hooked her arm in his and turned to the man sitting in an armchair. "I would like you to meet George Schwartz."

The old white man with the pudgy face and blue suit did not stand, nor did he extend his hand for a handshake. Jean could not have cared less about his lack of manners or decorum. "Mr. Schwartz," he said, "I appreciate you agreeing to meet with me."

"Get to the point quickly."

Anger burned deep in his chest, but he did not react. "I need ten million American dollars."

The old man raised a thin eyebrow. "I know that. What will I get for my investment?"

"I have made preliminary arrangements with China. I already have half the money. In exchange for deeply discounted arms, I will grant them access to my country, deep water ports, surveillance outposts, and a home base for any anti-Western operations."

Schwartz sat silent for several seconds. "Why do you think I care about that?"

Jean laughed and sat in the chair opposite the billionaire. "It is no secret you hope to destroy this administration. And you don't care about the collateral damage in the process."

Jean's mind drifted off to the 2010 earthquake, when armed American "relief" helicopters buzzed overhead but delivered more troops than tents, followed shortly by the ceaseless cycle of UN missions that imported cholera and exported nothing but excuses. "I want to save my people from the endless gang wars and give my nation a strong leader."

Schwartz looked him up and down. "The people call you *Papa Libète.*"

Marie answered. "The people love him. He has rallied an army. We just need weapons."

The billionaire glanced in Marie's direction but did not respond to her. Instead, he stood and said to Jean. "I will give you twenty million. Save your money to feed your men."

Jean lowered his head and said, "You will not regret your decision."

"I trust I will not."

CHAPTER

★

EIGHT

McGregor Park, Clarksville, Tennessee

Jerry zipped his flannel jacket tighter, the high 40s air nipping his ears as he guided Olive through the crowd at Christmas on the Cumberland. McGregor Park's Riverwalk glowed from over a million colorful lights strung along the path, their reflective colors dancing in the Cumberland River's dark ripples. The beauty made him forget his upcoming mission and allowed him to pretend for a moment that life was fun and bright.

"Ever come to this before?" he asked.

Olive glanced up at him, then looked out at the water again. He appreciated that she'd listened to him about casual clothes. She had on a pair of comfortable jeans, a white top, and a thick gray sweater. A matching gray cap covered her ears, featuring a cute white pompom on the top.

"No," she breathed. "It's incredible."

"I like the reflection of the lights on the water," he said. "My dad was stationed in Florida when I was like ten. On Fourth of July, our family watched fireworks from a sandbar. The way the reflection of the lights rippled with the water was really cool."

She glanced up at him, her eyes wide. Something in her face made his mouth dry. A smile tugged at her lips. "Why, Jerry McBride, you're about to become poetic."

He reached over, letting a soft, auburn curl wrap around his fingertip. The smell of strawberries danced in the air between them. "Something about you inspires poetry in me, Olive Duncan."

"Oh?" she asked, breathless. "Are you a modern David? A poetic warrior?"

"I think I could be." Just then, a little boy, maybe nine or ten, ran into him and looked up at him with shock. Jerry shifted and smiled reassuringly and said, "It's okay, buddy."

The kid ran to catch up with his family. Jerry watched him until he rejoined his mother. "Cute kid."

Unfortunately, the moment between him and Olive had passed. He put a hand on the back of her arm and steered her around the group that had mingled and converged around them. "I didn't expect it to be so busy on a weeknight."

"'Tis the season," she said, looping her arm through his. "What a perfect night, too. Just cold enough to honor the season but not arctic."

"Don't guess you get a lot of snow around Mobile."

She chuckled. "Reckon not. But they do up the French Quarter downtown pretty good with lights, and there's carriage rides. Nicer than New Orleans if you ask me. And it becomes festive enough."

The child who had bumped into Jerry walked back by with his family and gave Jerry a little smile and wave. Jerry smiled and waved back.

"You're good with kids," Olive said.

"I love kids. *Maxima debetur puero reverential*, you know?"

"Afraid I don't know. I recognize it's Latin, but please translate."

"Oh," Jerry stopped walking. "Roughly, 'The greatest reverence is due to a child'."

She grinned. It made a dimple appear on her right cheek. "You're a little bit of a show-off, Sergeant First Class Gerald McBride."

He cocked his head and gave her a tight-lipped grin. "Just trying to impress you, Olivia Duncan."

"I think it's working. Just a little bit."

They strolled, pointing out displays that caught their eyes. Several times, they took selfie photos, and once, an older man offered to take a picture of the two of them. Olive readily handed her phone over, and Jerry pulled her close to his side, smiling broadly.

Jerry would get mission details in the morning. He only knew he would board a plane and fly to a place that required cold-weather gear. That could mean any number of places. As much as he didn't enjoy getting his photo taken, he wanted her to have a photo of them together if something happened. Silly, considering they'd spent no more than a few hours breathing the same air. But he could feel something here—something deeper and more than a casual evening with a friend.

A riverboat trudged by. "Beautiful," she whispered.

He stared at her profile. "Definitely."

She glanced over at him, a delighted smile covering her face. "You are such a flirt. You hungry yet?"

"Starved. And you are more beautiful than anyone or anything I've ever seen." He took her hand and they continued through the crowd. "There's a ChristKindl Market here. Did you ever eat at one in Germany?"

"I did. Best brisket I've ever had, and that's saying something. I used to eat at Dave's in Mobile."

They waited in line, chatting about German Christmas, a festival she went to in the Black Forest, and the uniqueness of that region. Laughter and muffled carols swirled around them, a merry cacophony blending with the chatter of the crowd. The savory smell of the smoky char of grilling meat contrasted with the sweet smell of cinnamon-dusted nuts from nearby stalls.

Soon, they carried beef sliders with onions on rye buns and small paper cups filled with a warm, spiced cider to a nearby picnic table.

Jerry waited for her to finish adding pepper to her fries, then held his hand out to her. She asked, "Okay if I say grace this time?"

"Of course."

He bowed his head and listened to her voice float in the

chill air to him. "Father, You're wonderful, and Your timing is perfect. Thank You for tonight, for this food, for this time together, and let this food nourish our bodies as we commit our bodies to Your service." He started to pull his hand away, but she squeezed it tighter and added, "And keep Jerry safe from harm wherever he's headed to."

Jerry cleared his throat, emotion suddenly tightening it. "Thank you," he said, then took a sip of the spicy warm cider.

She squeezed his hand one more time, then released it, picking up a fry. "Thanks for this."

"One day, I'll feed you a meal that doesn't come with packets of condiments," he said.

Her laughter floated around him, pulled him in, lit something inside him he hadn't known was dim. "Tell you what. I'll cook for you when you get back."

He swallowed the flavorful beef and wiped his fingers on a paper napkin. "Having eaten at your house once before, I already know that's something worth coming back to."

Olive sank into the passenger seat of Jerry's truck, the heater's hum chasing off the December chill as the Cumberland River's lights faded behind them. She would only admit to herself that she'd felt a little disappointment that he hadn't shown up on his motorcycle. She would have liked the excuse to wrap her arms around him as they rode.

Her gray cap sat in her lap. She ran her fingers over it, enjoying the fuzzy feel, and briefly toyed with the pompom.

His flannel jacket hugged his broad shoulders, his strong hands steady on the wheel. She would think that after seven years in and around the Army, she would be immune to the strong, handsome, dominant male type.

Apparently not.

"What a fun night," she said, voice soft, breaking the quiet. "Thanks for dragging me out."

Jerry stopped at a light and glanced her way. "I'm happy to bribe you with pastries any time."

As she laughed, she shifted and turned her body toward him and tucked a leg under her. "Challenge accepted."

A beat, then softer, "Glad you liked it, though. It's always good to do something normal. Otherwise, what are we doing?"

Her chest tightened. His mission loomed tomorrow. "Normal's good," she said, fingers brushing his arm.

He nodded, gaze back on the road, but his jaw flexed like he wanted to say more. They rolled through Clarksville's quiet streets, Christmas lights winking from porches and shrubs or glittery trees peeking through windows; lights wrapping streetlamps and telephone poles like candy canes, until he pulled into her driveway. The truck idled until he cut the engine, silence settling thick.

"Guess this is me," she said, unbuckling but not moving. Her heart thudded. A strange tension, an energy, filled the cab.

Jerry paused. "I don't want to leave tomorrow." He turned to her, one hand resting on the wheel. Her heart started thudding. "I've never not embraced a mission." He hesitated, opened his mouth as if he was about to say something, then he shook his head and opened the door. That strange tension dissipated.

She grabbed her cap, sliding out of the cab when he opened her door. The cold nipped her cheeks, but his hand found hers—warm, callused, steady—guiding her up the path.

At her door, she fumbled with her keys, the porch light casting his shadow long. "Jerry, I—" She looked up, words stalling as his eyes locked on hers, intense, searching.

"Olive," he cut in, voice low, "I don't know when I'll see you again."

"I'll be here." She stood on her toes and slipped her arms around his neck. He pulled her close for a hug, squeezing her tight. For a tiny moment, her mind went back to seeing him on a gurney, bleeding from a bullet that hit too close to an artery. "I'll be praying for you."

She started to pull away, but his arms didn't release her fully. She looked up at him, searching his face, heart pounding. He lifted a hand to her cheek. His fingertips felt cool, callused, and purposefully gentle.

"Close your eyes, Olive," he said, his voice so low she could almost feel it.

A small smile came to her lips as her lashes fluttered down. The next moment, his warm lips covered hers.

Nothing in her life had ever felt as right as the feel of Jerry's kiss. It was like everything she'd ever waited for, ever wanted, culminating in one single press of his lips. She pulled him closer, standing on her tiptoes, her fingers running through his hair. His hand gripped the back of her head, his other arm around her waist, steadying her.

His scent—clean soap laced with the fresh outdoors they'd enjoyed—filled her senses. She could taste warm cider, a touch of cinnamon on his lips.

She trailed her fingers down to his cheek, the day's stubble rasping like a secret against her palm, warm and rough and alive under her touch. He eased the kiss to a murmur, lips lingering a breath away before he drew back just enough to lift his chin. There, in the glow of the porch light, his gaze locked on hers—dark, unblinking, a slow hunger uncoiling like smoke. Her breath hitched, mirroring the pull in her chest, her free hand fisting the collar of his jacket as if to steady them both against the tide rising between.

"Promise me you'll stay safe. Promise," she murmured, breathless. She intentionally relaxed her fingers.

"Promise I'll try." He brushed her lips once more, soft, then stepped back. "Goodnight, Olive Duncan."

"Goodnight," she echoed, watching him retreat to his truck.

She slipped inside and locked the door behind her, her lips still tingling. She set her keys in the dish on the table and pulled her jacket off, a silly grin covering her face.

Outside of Thomazeau, Haiti

Liang Wei watched a scrawny chicken dart around a bush, a thick worm clutched in its filthy beak. Its sharp, erratic clucks scratched the air, mingling with the low buzz of flies orbiting a nearby midden heap.

Liang commonly observed squalor and filth here in Haiti. The differences between this despicable island nation and his home province of Fujian seemed infinite. In Fujian, he could at least look forward to cooler winters, and though coastal, the humidity never smothered him. Here, the humid Haitian air pressed against him from all directions, and a trickle of sweat slipped down his back under his linen shirt. The temperature and humidity here never changed, no matter the season, and the near-daily rain squalls only made the air harder to breathe. The water tasted of iron. A variety of insects made themselves at home in all the food. The streets smelled of waste.

Mainly, though, Liang despised the Haitian people and their tolerance for filth. In his mind, he despised them even more than Americans.

Still, the Ministry of State Security had assigned him this mission, and he had a duty to hide his ever-growing contempt while he accomplished his nation's goals.

He looked across the table at Hao Jun. Hao had started all of the wheels turning with this project. Had made the original contact and hashed out a lot of the deals.

Marie Desalin sat next to Hao, her hand on his thigh, his arm over her shoulders. It took everything in Liang not to sneer at the spectacle. Did Hao play a game with Marie to smooth the process, or did he have real feelings for the woman? Liang couldn't tell, but he knew if the answer fell to the latter, things could get messy fast.

Jean Desalin approached, lighting a cigar, his French Creole as rough and low as the man's sweaty dark bulk stood tall. "My friend. Fortune brought you back."

Liang turned, sizing up the rebel leader. Last time they met, Jean had worn green fatigues and a black beret; today, he wore cotton pants, a loose shirt, and a straw hat that shaded his scarred face. He hardly looked the man to topple Haiti's current teetering regime. But Liang knew looks deceived. He hated having to look up to meet the man's eyes.

He had two younger men flanking him, both as tall as the rebel leader. They had hard eyes that looked between him and Hao with suspicion.

"My sons, Henri and Julien."

Liang stood, and they shook hands. Liang never bowed to any of the Haitians. They would have misinterpreted it as a sign of weakness. Also, he had no respect for them. He mentally toyed with how he could disable and kill Jean and his sons if this meeting went poorly.

Jean's wife, Daphnée, rolled out a cart of glasses and a pitcher of ice water. The water looked clean, though Liang knew it likely was not. The wife had long dreadlocks, a twist of gray and black hair. It made her look slightly mad. Liang ignored her and kept his voice flat. "Hao confirmed your funding came through."

"Indeed." Jean poured water, and everyone settled into metal chairs. "A billionaire unhappy with the US election felt the need to tip the scales."

Liang nodded, unblinking. "My leadership agrees to

your terms—five thousand small arms: 3,000 AK-103 rifles, 1,000 Type 56C carbines, 500 QSZ-193 pistols, 200 QSW-06 suppressed pistols, and 300 Type 69 RPGs. We will provide six extra magazines for all rifles and one extra magazine for all pistols, along with 500,000 rounds of ammunition and 1,000 RPG rounds, including anti-armor and high-explosive rounds. Additionally, we will provide 2,000 Type 67 fragmentation grenades.

"For heavy weapons, we agree to supply you with 100 Type 35 60mm mortars and 1,000 mortar rounds, 2,000 Type 69 anti-personnel mines, and a full complement of Semtex explosives and fuses. All in all, more than enough for your rebels to take Port-au-Prince and maintain power in exchange for our cooperative presence here."

Jean kept his expression blank and exhaled a huge puff of smoke. But Liang imagined the man could not ignore the excitement and anticipation that danced up his spine.

Henri added, "We need some sniper rifles."

"You have trained snipers?" Liang knew for a fact they did not, and he probably should not have jabbed the rebel's son, though he did feel a tiny thrill at the minor loss of face the seemingly innocent remark caused.

Jean grinned a joyless grin. "I pay you to provide the guns. Let me worry about the shooters."

Liang nodded, struggling not to let his contempt for this useful idiot shine through in his eyes. "I will see what I can do. Fewer than 3,000 AK-103 rifles should make up the difference."

"Good." Jean puffed his cigar. "Final price?"

"As we agreed, twenty million US dollars. Ten now, ten on delivery." Liang's eyes flicked to a guard shack a hundred yards off, catching the glint of binoculars. "Normal shipping channels are unsuitable. America's tightened everything. Their constant 'aid' to your president's crumbling regime presents a challenge to our arrangement."

Jean quickly exhaled a plume of smoke and fanned it away dismissively, as if also fanning away the current president. The sick smell enveloped Liang's face, making his nostrils flare.

"He's feeble, clinging to power by licking their American boots and gobbling up their scraps like a dog," Jean sneered, pulling a phone from his shirt pocket. "Shipping will not present a problem. You don't even need to come all the way back to Haiti. I have a plan." He typed, somewhat gracefully given his large hands, then handed the phone over.

Liang entered his bank account details, the screen flashing. His own phone buzzed as the screen confirmed the transfer of ten million US Dollars. He handed the phone back nonchalantly, trying not to make physical contact with the giant again. "Efficient. What do you need from me?"

Jean stood, cigar smoke curling. "Nothing once we have secured the weapons. To get them here, I will need some of your trained people to facilitate the delivery. Your team of 'military advisers' who've been here for the last few months would do nicely."

Liang kept his features perfectly schooled. "I will have

to discuss changing the scope of our direct military support with my superiors." He looked directly at Hao. "You know I do not have the authority to give them orders that vary from their current assignment."

Hao nodded his head. "Understood. I have written a report. If you back it, then that will help matters."

"Copy me on the report and I will consider it."

Hao nodded again.

Henri laughed, sounding much like a kettle drum with a sense of humor. "It will be remarkably easy. We will make the transfer at sea in international waters between your ship and a ship we will acquire."

"Acquire?"

Jean nodded just once. "This is why we will need some assistance. Most of my people are on lists. None of your people would raise any alarms."

Liang had begun to lose patience. "You had best give me the details of your plan so that I can brief Beijing."

"Of course. This is why I have asked Hao and Marie to join us. We will discuss it over lunch."

Liang felt his stomach tighten and churn. He would have to eat this horrible food and drink this filthy water to complete this deal. Even now, the faint, chalky grit of local dust coated his teeth, an omen of the spiced, overripe plantains and dubious stew to come.

The thought of it sickened him.

Karpovia, Undisclosed Location

Despite thermal layers and a Level 7 Extreme Cold Weather Parka and overgarments, cold seeped through Jerry's Generation III Extended Cold Weather Clothing System like icy fingers probing for weakness. Snow crunched under his kneepads as he very slowly shifted, steadying a whited-out Cassie against the rough bark of a towering spruce tree. The new moon left the Karpovian mountain night pitch black, save for the faint, scattered glows from Vozhd Yevgeniy Kovalenko's ancient fortress half a klick downhill—a sprawling stone castle perched on a high ridge, its medieval towers and battlements retrofitted with modern antennas and floodlights, hugging the edge of a frozen alpine lake.

Kovalenko's hybrid war through militias, cyberattacks,

strategically executed asymmetric attacks, and arms smuggling had Karpovia teetering on the edge of genocide. Eliminating him from power served the best interests of the whole of Europe and Russia. No escalation, no war—just a removed oligarch.

Jerry's breath puffed white in the ten-degree air, stinging his lungs with each inhale, while his left biceps ached under the relentless grip of the chill. At this altitude in the Karpovian High Tatras, the wind howled through dense forests of spruce and fir, carrying the distant noises of winter-hardened wildlife.

They had spent the last nine days on this op, but the real grind started 26 hours ago when Jerry and his spotter, Waller, had stealthily marched overland through the snow-blanketed terrain, humping all their supplies and cold-weather gear to establish their overwatch position. For this mission, the pair needed to get eyes on the target, confirm intelligence, and maintain surveillance until the kinetic strike.

In Top Secret negotiations, the NATO powers of Europe and Russia all determined they could neither initiate nor participate in kinetic missions against Kovalenko. If any such activity could ever be attributed back to them, international relations with non-affiliated nations would suffer decades of setback. Thus, the US had taken the lead in exchange for favorable trade status agreements and other political concessions.

In other words, the US military personnel on the field should not be here. Yet here they found themselves on a frozen mountainside in Karpovia. No matter how this mission went, assuming everyone did their jobs, the world at large would never know a thing about what happened today.

Since arriving at their current location shortly after 2100 hours local time the previous night, they had spent their time identifying the hostiles in the fortress, tracking their movement, and remaining undetected. Their clothing consisted of the ECWCS, and they had employed the COLD method throughout their mission, which meant they stayed clean, avoided overheating, wore loose and layered clothing, and kept dry.

In sustained cold environments, any movement required more energy and often resulted in sweating. In this environment, sweat could actually freeze and—aside from discomfort—cause illness or injury.

The previous night, the moon rose as a thin sliver, spraying silver and shadows over the landscape like a scene from a macabre nightmare. Tim Waller had quietly sang a song to himself, which Jerry overheard.

"I see the moon, and the moon sees me. The moon sees somebody I'd like to see." Waller's breath froze as soon as it left his lips. "God bless the moon and God bless me. God bless somebody I'd like to see."

Jerry had felt a tiny pang of envy for Tim in that moment. He had an amazing wife of five years waiting for him at home. Jerry could not wait until he had that same peace, that same adoration, that same respect waiting for him at home, too.

"Sure wish there was a tuantaun around we could cut open and crawl inside," Waller muttered.

They had griped good-naturedly about the gusts of wind biting through their gear, the snow soaking their knees and elbows, and how the forest's evergreens provided cover but also dumped fresh powder on them with every gust.

Surveillance devices, including some night vision devices, would almost instantly detect any out-of-bounds heat sources. Consequently, to avoid detection, they had not used the chemical heating packets included in every MRE to warm their food. Instead, they ate frozen beef stew and chicken à la king like candy bars.

They had pitched their single shelter in defilade on the lee side of the ridge among trees and underbrush, then slept in three-hour shifts until the sun rose. The sun did not bring heat, but it did speed up the biting wind. They had swapped out in short shifts, observing the position and sheltering throughout the day. The constant wind turned to gusts at sundown, and the present moonless night enveloped the world in brittle darkness.

Now, after packing all of the gear except what they used currently, they each lay atop white sleeping mats salvaged from their modular sleep systems. This afforded them at least some separation from the snow and the hard, frozen ground.

On this utterly moonless night, the shadows cast shadows, and everything that touched them felt frozen and remorselessly cold. The inside of Jerry's nose felt raw and chapped with every breath. He had to exhale sideways to avoid misting his optics. While the cold closed all around him like a fist squeezing warmth out of his fingers, toes, and face, he experienced the worst fear of every sniper in the cold.

He feared he might start to shiver.

Once shivering started, it became nearly impossible to stop, and hitting your marks while shivering presented insurmountable challenges.

All things considered, Jerry decided he would pay real money for a hot shower, a hot meal, a warm bed, and never to feel this cold for this long ever again.

Beside him, Waller shifted slightly, his breath controlled to avoid fogging his own optics. "Man, this cold is brutal. Feels like we're auditioning for a Siberian vacation."

Jerry tried to keep his teeth from chattering. "T.O.T.?"

Waller checked the time. "Time on target, 72 mikes and counting."

Several frosty breaths later, Jerry wondered, "Does your place still have that hot tub?"

Waller chuckled. "We moved outta that apartment complex about a year ago, man. Think warm thoughts."

Jerry wiggled his toes against his two layers of woolen socks. "What do you think I've been doing since yesterday?"

Waller said, "Other than leaving Cassie out in the cold?" The weapons had to acclimate. Bringing his rifle into and out of the cold conditions nearly assured the optics would frost over, despite the sophisticated systems built into his Swarovski scope to mitigate just that problem. After Jerry grunted, Waller continued, "Just think, Leanne's back home, probably sipping some Christmas flavor of hot tea by the fire. Here I am, eating ice and turning into a popsicle."

Again, Jerry grunted softly, scanning the fortress through his Swarovski ranging reticle scope, its nitrogen-inert-gas purging, keeping the glass crystal clear in the Arctic temperatures. They'd identified 30 out of the 36 souls inside from their intel packet—Kovalenko's platoon of 24 security goons, plus about a dozen domestics scurrying around like shadows in the lit windows. All but six matched the profiles. Those six troubled him. They looked like ex-military personnel, all wearing matching winter camouflage, armed with whited-out Kalashnikovs and sidearms, patrolling the walls or lounging in the heated barracks. "Yeah, well, at least you've got Leanne waiting on you."

About a minute later, Waller whispered, "She's pregnant. Leanne's pregnant."

"Really?" Jerry felt a rush of welcome warmth flood his body.

"Yeah, man. Three months now."

"So," Jerry teased. "Does the father know yet?"

"I'll let that slide this time. You're cold and a little whiny like a four-year-old. Even your nose is runny," Waller teased back.

"You'll be an incredible dad, Tim," Jerry said without an ounce of irony.

A few long minutes passed before Waller said, "We lost

the first two. The first one—we were stationed in Colorado, married less than a year—she made it to 19 weeks. Lost her. Little girl. I was in Alaska doing stuff like this at NWTC. Wasn't even there."

"Seriously?"

"Lost the second one about two years back. We were PCSing to Campbell. I was home on leave then. Really hard on her."

"Tim, that sucks, man. I'm so sorry."

"Happens more than you realize," Waller said. "Harder on Leanne, of course."

"I'll definitely keep y'all in my prayers. Baby Waller, too. Especially."

"This one seems different. We're praying every day, and Leanne has a good feeling about it. We have a really good OB." Waller slapped Jerry on the shoulder appreciatively. "Hopefully, I'll move on up soon. Another mouth to feed and all that."

"Get in line, bro. That Zulu slot is mine all mine."

Waller chuckled quietly, though there was an edge of sympathy in it. "Oh, right. You're promotable. Nail this, and you'll slide right into that 18Z slot when Commando finally hangs it up. Master Sergeant McBride. Now that kind of has a ring to it. Leaves a certain flavor in the mouth. Kind of like burned beans and turpentine."

A radio call interrupted their whispered banter. "Silent Peak, this is Cloud Breaker. Authenticate Alpha-Niner-Six Uniform. Over." The words came through over the thunderous noise of four turboprop engines.

"Focus up," Jerry muttered, though he appreciated the banter—it kept the mind sharp against the numbing cold.

Beside him, Waller pulled out his mission-specific authentication cards, read the code, and responded. "Cloud Breaker, this is Silent Peak. I authenticate Whiskey-Whiskey-Sierra-Two. Over."

After a long twelve seconds, Major Norton responded, "Good copy, Silent Peak. Read you five by five. This is Six. Tango Oscar Tango. ETA 67, I say again, six-seven mikes. Bravo Four. Sitrep. Over."

"Roger," Jerry whispered into his comms, his voice low and steady despite the chill numbing his fingers inside his gloves. Following Norton's lead, he transitioned from mission code names to their more familiar call signs and designations. "Bravo Four set. Read you Lima Charlie. We are half a klick from objective on the south-west corner. Break. No defenses observed on rooftop. Break. Obstacles are ramparts all around, one stairwell north side, one flagpole west side, and one dish west side. Break. HVT confirmed in the main keep—pacing near the eastern tower window. I have a clear line of sight. Over."

"Roger, Bravo Four," Norton crackled back. "Hold position. Deploy Hornets at one-five mikes. Break. Flare and lasso at 5,000 feet. Will send, 'lasso.' Break. Remove all OPFOR while we are inbound. Confirm. Over."

Jerry nodded superfluously. "Roger. Confirm Hornets at one-five mikes. Confirm lasso at 5k. Confirm fire at will to remove bandits. Standing by, over."

Norton sent, "Out," ending the conversation.

Minutes ticked by in frozen silence. Jerry fancifully imagined he could detect the sound of the aircraft flying at more than 33,000 feet and the maximum standoff distance from where they lay in the snow. Not possible. Finally, the comms crackled, "Cloud Breaker to execute in—" Norton shouted the next words, "six minutes!"

Jerry knew that everyone aboard the Antonov An-12, which NATO forces referred to as a Cub, all shouted back in unison, "Six Minutes!" in response. The jump commands would proceed from there to one minute, thirty seconds, and finally to go.

The team would perform a high-altitude-high-opening airborne insertion from a distance of more than 30 kilometers. Then, they would glide along with the prevailing winds the entire distance to the objective.

"*Per Terram, Per Mare, Per Aerem*," Jerry whispered. By Land, By Sea, By Air.

"Roger that," Waller whispered back. "*Mors Ab Alto.*" Death From Above.

Two rapid clicks came over the comms. The entire team had successfully deployed their parachutes. In all, 14 well trained and well-armed men including Major Rick Norton, Captain Jorge Peña, Chief Warrant Officer David Morita, Chief Warrant Officer Zachary Hanson, Master Sergeant Wade Chandler, Staff Sergeant Calvin Brock, Staff Sergeant Eric Gill, Sergeant Min-Jun Johnson, Sergeant Darius Brown, Staff Sergeant Jared Ibrahim, Sergeant Dasa Yazzie, Sergeant First Class Travis Fisher, Sergeant Andrew White, and Corporal Michael Mendoza would soon land one by one on the roof of that fortress.

Vozhd Yevgeniy Kovalenko was about to have a very bad day at the office.

Jerry's heart rate ticked up. Through the scope, three sentries patrolled the outer walls—bundled figures in white-wrapped gear, one smoking a cigarette that lit up like a beacon in his night optics. "Bourbon, three bandits visible. North wall, east gate, and south parapet. Confirm?"

Waller peered through his rangefinder, his M4 carbine with attached M203 grenade launcher within easy reach. "Affirmative. Distance four eight zero meters on the north one. Deflection fifteen degrees downhill, adjusted elevation up point five mil. Wind nominal, but watch the gusts from the north—top snow dusting at three zero meters."

Jerry peered at the field of snow between their position and the target. Occasional gusts of light wind dusted the powdery top snow. He would factor the gusts into his shot solutions.

Indicating the sentry enjoying the cigarette, Waller said, "Might as well have shot up a flare."

"I'm planning on letting him enjoy his smoke break for a few more seconds," Jerry said.

Waller said, "Scanned the structure twice. I identify just the three visible bandits."

"Confirmed," Jerry whispered, then exposed his right index finger by folding back the finger flap on his heavy gloves. "Engaging most distant bandit first. Splash one on your mark."

He lined up the first sentry in his crosshairs, wind

whispering through the pines. The sentry in his crosshairs was an enemy soldier. That enemy soldier would certainly kill any one of them if possible. This was not a question. Leaving him alive would at best raise an alarm and at worst end up with dead teammates. The only means of accomplishing their mission rested squarely below Jerry's right index fingertip.

Waller focused on the wind while Jerry focused on his target. Waller said, "Deflection unchanged. Distance unchanged. Standby for nominal wind."

Jerry kept his breathing as normal as possible while exhaling out of the side of his mouth and lightly stroked Cassie's trigger to keep his fingertip from cramping.

"Mark," Waller prompted.

Jerry exhaled, slow and controlled, and squeezed. The elongated suppressor coughed, a dull thwack louder than a baseball hitting the catcher's glove but much quieter than the sonic boom of an unsuppressed supersonic round, and the precision bullet made its way through the icy air until the sentry dropped, snow swallowing the body. He shifted seamlessly to the next, Waller calling adjustments, and two more suppressed shots followed. He took out the smoking sentry last. Their bodies fell silently into the white blanket of snow. In the silence that followed, no one raised any alarms.

"No movement. Clean shots," Waller whispered.

"Confirmed," Jerry agreed, then keyed his mic. "Turkey," Jerry broadcast, meaning three strikes in a row, then shifted his focus to the main keep. He knew without having to engage in a lengthy tongue wag about it that Waller had reverted to scanning for any new targets.

Precisely fifteen minutes after the incoming team above had deployed their parachutes, Waller deployed the eight Teledyne FLIR Black Hornet nano-UAVs—tiny, hand-sized drones marked with black IR tape. He guided them silently to the eight cardinal points around the fortress, their thermal cams feeding back real-time intel on his tablet. "IR Markers set. Eyes in place. All quiet— scratch that. Movement on the roof."

Jerry swung Cassie around. A fourth sentry emerged on the rooftop, fumbling with a radio. Another thwack, and the man crumpled before he could transmit. "Six. Bravo Four. Strike times four. Be advised, new obstacle on the north side near the staircase. One bandit. Over."

Norton replied, "Roger, Bravo Four, this is Six. Lasso. I say again, Lasso. Out."

Waller retrieved his M203, loaded an M992 infrared illumination cartridge, and fired it skyward. The round arced high, bursting silently into an IR glow beneath a tiny parachute visible only through NODs —marking the rooftop for the incoming team. Then, he activated his laser sight and drew a long circle in the black sky as if leading some kind of crazy PowerPoint presentation. He continued to draw circles with his muzzle for long seconds.

In their night vision, it looked like a solid beam that left the muzzle of Waller's M4 carbine and reached so high the International Space Station could see it. To the team in the air, it fully marked their position, the eight cardinal points marked by the tiny drones, and the location of their intended landing zone.

They heard a series of rapid double clicks come over the comms. Finally, Norton broadcast, "Batcave."

Waller turned off the "bat signal" and set his M4 down within easy reach, then reverted to spotting, peering through his rangefinder.

Above the objective, Jerry watched as the team began their final descent. Each man had a one-square-inch infrared reflective patch on his left boot and right shoulder, making them almost entirely visible to him through his sophisticated optics. They all maneuvered into a practiced stall and moved into a corkscrew formation above the castle. The formation looked like a moving spiral staircase.

Jerry watched through his optics as the rest of his SFODA glided in like ghosts, one by one, with perhaps an eighth to a tenth of a second between quiet landings. Daddy first, then Pina Colada, then Mr. Miyagi, and all the others—Hobbes, Gilligan, Rocky, Truth or Dare, Honest Abe, Dicey, Trout, Snowflake, MMMBop, Commando, and finally Cobra on his very first mission—touched down one by one silently on the rooftop, stacking up without a sound.

They prepared to breach the upper doors until Jerry hit the handle with his laser-aiming device, which illuminated the door handle brighter than the old Vegas strip in their night-vision devices. Norton reached over and slowly operated the handle, quietly opening the unsecured door.

They tightened their stack then surged through the

opening like a black tide, carbines sweeping in precise arcs, NODs glowing faintly in the dark. Long, tense seconds stretched into what felt like agonizing minutes—or even hours—in Jerry's mind, his pulse pounding in his ears as he strained to track their progress.

Radio silence held, broken only by clipped whispers over the comms: "Clear... moving... contact left." Then, suppressed muzzle flashes erupted like staccato lightning in his optics, painting the interior corridors in bursts of green-tinged fire as the team methodically cleared room after room—doors opened silently, corners sliced, threats neutralized with ruthless efficiency.

Suddenly, chaos erupted below. Kovalenko's remaining security force rallied in a desperate counterattack, a dozen swarthy and well-equipped guards scrambling into position in the great hall, their Kalashnikovs barking in defiance. Through the arched windows, Jerry caught glimpses of the frenzy—figures darting behind overturned tables and granite pillars, muzzle blasts blooming in the dim light, bullets ricocheting off stone walls with sharp cracks that echoed faintly across the frozen valley. The air filled with the acrid scent of cordite even from afar, carried on the wind from the lake.

In Jerry's crosshairs, Kovalenko paced inside, broad shoulders and close-cropped gray hair, with a phone pressed tight to his ear. Apparently, someone in a high office in either Europe or Russia had decided to distract their target at the appointed hour. Kovalenko had ducked out of Jerry's visual window at the first sound of his men returning fire. He broadcast, "Six, Bravo Four. HVT out of my picture. Over."

"Roger. OPFOR dug in," Norton hissed. "Taking fire. Can you bring the thunder? Over."

Jerry's grip tightened on Cassie. With Waller in his ear, Jerry picked off exposed targets—thwack after thwack—dropping four before the rest dove behind thick tables and stone pillars.

"Strike times four. Remainder now concealed," Waller broadcast. "Sending grenade."

Jerry nodded. "I'll clear the window." He sniped out a pane of glass with precision, then keyed his mic: "Six, Bravo Four. Fire in the hole—great hall. I say again. Fire in the hole. Over."

Waller fired the M433 high-explosive dual-purpose round through the opening. It detonated amid the group, the blast muffled by stone but lethal, killing most outright, leaving two severely wounded, groaning and firing wild pistol shots. Jerry admired their tenacity, even in defeat—no surrender, just fight to the very end. The infiltrating team advanced, finishing the survivors with controlled bursts.

Jerry and Waller immediately pivoted back to searching for Kovalenko. Finally, he spotted him and reported, "Six. Bravo Four. HVT now in southwest corner. Painting now."

Once again, Jerry activated his laser aiming device and circled the window. When Waller began a slow lasso, Jerry deactivated his laser and placed Kovalenko squarely in his crosshairs.

It felt like only seconds later when Chief Morita broadcast, "Fire in the hole."

Jerry closed his eyes so that the bright flash of C4 explosive from the improvised shaped charge didn't blind him. After he heard the report of the explosion, he opened his eyes and scanned the target area. Brock had folded Kovalenko like a lawn chair and was very effectively applying restraints to the man.

"Bravo Four. Good work. Six has HVT secure," Norton broadcast. "Be advised, exfil inbound. Over."

Jerry slung Cassie, and he and Waller quickly stowed what little gear remained. They could leave no trace of their presence here that would attribute today's activities to US forces. The drones silently returned home. Jerry counted his expended cartridges and handed them to Waller, who also counted and confirmed that he had not left any expended brass on this mountainside.

Inside the fortress, the team had begun a similar cleanup which, no doubt, their State Department colleagues would finalize. After all, no one had more experience cleaning up messes like this than the CIA.

The sound of an approaching cargo helicopter's thrum grew, and Jerry could feel the movement of the air. He brought Cassie back on target and observed the fortress.

The Soviet era HIP landed almost weightlessly and effortlessly on the roof, exhibiting a grace that nothing that large should. The ramp lowered as the aircraft landed, and more than twenty men wearing civilian clothes exited the aircraft. Some carried large cases, and others carried AKMS rifles.

Through his scope, Jerry watched Norton greet one of the men, shake his hand, and wave his team on board the aircraft. Upon seeing this, Jerry slung Cassie and prepared himself for the descent down the mountainside.

Boots sinking into snow, Jerry slid down the ridge, Waller sliding along beside him. Behind them, the fortress displayed a preternatural calm. Light radio chatter and clicks revealed the team had turned Kovalenko over alive and neutralized all resistance.

They moved through the dark woods, the world an eerie green through his NODs, using terrain for cover. As they approached the clearing, the huge helicopter touched down, the crew chief simultaneously dropping the ramp. The rotor wash blasted loose snow into a cyclonic vortex, making approaching the thing from the allegedly safe thirty-degree angle feel like trudging through a blizzard. Jerry vaulted in beside Fisher, then Waller entered, marching backward with his carbine facing outward, pulling rear security.

Seconds later, Peña shouted, "Go!" over the engine noise as he simultaneously pounded the chopper's ceiling with a gloved fist. As they lifted, Jerry caught a glimpse of the fortress lights with his naked eyes, not fully appreciating how different it looked when unobstructed by reticles.

What the CIA planned to do with Kovalenko didn't come under the heading of his "need to know." Well above his pay grade, in fact. They had spared Karpovia from a tyrannical rule and granted the surrounding nations a few extra years of peace. He understood the politics of the region well enough to know they'd done a good thing on this mission.

He peeled back his glove and checked his watch. Back at Campbell, the time was Eleven fifty-nine on December twenty-third. The ramp closed, and the warmth in the cabin surrounded him. Shudders wracked his body as he relinquished the tight control and allowed himself to shiver.

"Who else is ready for a Kentucky Christmas?" Norton grinned ironically. "I hear it's a white Christmas this year. Lots of snow."

"More snow!" Jerry yelled in protest.

Sergeant Darius "Truth or Dare" Brown, an 18D and the team's newest medic, asked, "You cold, Jerry Maquire? I just jumped from about 40,000 feet above sea level and then glided on the arctic wind for half an hour, man."

"Really, Dare?" Jerry's voice quaked with his shudders. "Thirty *whole* minutes?" He gave him a mock impressed look.

Waller added through teeth that chattered with shivers, "Try thirty whole *hours* on that frozen ridge."

Brown grinned, pulling out a thermos of MRE hot cocoa. He poured two steaming cups, handing them to Jerry and Waller. "Warm up, heroes. And thanks for that HEAT round. Knocked the wind out of the bandits for sure."

Jerry sipped, the rich, warm chocolate melting the chill from his bones. His teeth chattered as he sipped. He longed to feel warm again. He'd never tasted anything so wonderful.

Except maybe one thing. His mind kept thinking about strawberry colored hair and lips that tasted just as sweet.

TEN

Clarksville Memorial Hospital, Tennessee

As she helped wheel the bed through the double doors, Olive caught sight of the patient's father pacing in the hallway. He wore a black sweater emblazoned with the image of Darth Vader adorned with a candy-cane striped scarf and the words, "I Find Your Lack of Cheer Disturbing" written in typical Star Wars font. It made her smile. Obviously, his family had come from a Christmas party.

She looked at his son's sleeping face. He'd come into the ED symptomatic of appendicitis. Unfortunately, his appendix ruptured before they could get him into surgery. She knew the two-hour surgery had felt like a lifetime to those parents.

She handed him over to the recovery team, then returned to the operating room to finalize her notes. Using the access card attached to her scrubs shirt, she swiped it into the system and began clicking through the prompts.

"Lieutenant Duncan," Grayson barked from the doorway, his nasal voice cutting through her thoughts like a scalpel. "Chart's a mess—fix it before you clock out. And next time, anticipate my moves. I shouldn't have to ask for the curette twice."

Her neck muscles tightened. "That would be 'Captain,' doctor. It's been a long time since Fort Bragg." She'd had enough of his mouth today. When she saw him listed as the doctor for the surgery, the temptation to claim her mild headache had grown more severe, and head home on that excuse had nearly affected her professional judgement. He'd asked her out in North Carolina five years ago and had taken great offense at her reminder to him that he had a wife. When he started working here in Clarksville, she actually began contemplating finding a different job.

She glanced at him. The years hadn't been kind to him. He was tall, thin, balding, and his skin had a faint yellow cast. She watched as his cheeks turned red. "Nevertheless."

"I'd be happy to review the video of the surgery with you so you can explain to me how having the curette in hand before you even knew you needed it is a violation of any written rule. But I will require my rep to be with me during any such post-mortem. I assume for the sake of transparency, you would not object." She turned her back to him and finished typing, then logged out. It should have surprised her that he still stood there, his eyes narrowed, as if trying to decide what to say. "Was there something else, Doctor?"

"Duncan, you will not like even one single minute of crossing me," he said.

She smiled and pulled her surgical cap off her head. "Doctor Grayson, I'm not trying to cross you. I'm simply standing up to a bully." She walked forward until she had to look up at him. "You see, unlike your, shall we say, unfortunate wife, I'm not afraid of you."

His eyes narrowed, and a muscle ticked in his jaw, but he finally spun on a heel and marched away. Olive considered the stark contradiction that humanity could produce men with the character and moral fiber of Doctor Grayson and, at the same time, men like Jerry McBride.

"Girl, that was something," Audra Green said from behind her.

Olive looked over her shoulder. "Someone has to say something. The Army might have forced a retirement to get rid of him, but I doubt this hospital will do anything. They're short-staffed, and he's cheap."

"I heard Becky made an official complaint."

"Yeah. Expect a lot of those."

"Better watch your back."

Olive scoffed and said, "He can't hurt me." She tossed her cap into the laundry bin next to the door. "In our current culture, having cameras on everything we do is all the transparency I need." She waved her badge at the door sensor, and the door swung open. "I'm headed to lunch."

She went the back way to the cafeteria. At three forty-five on Christmas Eve, few people worked in the clinics and offices, though it had been moderately busy earlier in the day. Her phone dinged, and she saw an incoming message from her mom. Instead of texting back, she just called her.

"Merry Christmas Eve," she said. She grabbed a tray and walked over to the salad bar. "How's Alabama?"

"Busy. Your Aunt Hilda got in this morning."

"I'm so glad."

"What are you working tomorrow?"

"Seven to seven." Olive scooped green peas on top of her lettuce. "I can video call when I get off. We can open presents."

"Sounds perfect. Love you."

"Love you, too," she said, then slid the phone back into her scrubs pocket and finished making her salad. Impulsively, she grabbed a slice of red velvet cake to go with it. Christmas Eve only happened once a year, after all.

She sat down at the table and just took a moment. She closed her eyes and let everything relax. After a silent prayer, she picked up her fork and looked around.

Tasteful decorations adorned the space without excess. Traditional images covered the windows, and giant ornaments hung from the ceilings. A large tree stood in the corner, covered in handmade ornaments made by patients in the children's wing.

The father in the Darth Vader sweater appeared in the dining area, holding his wife's hand. She wore a sweater with a llama and a menorah that had the words, "Happy Lamannukah" on it. It made Olive chuckle.

The worry that had etched their faces hours ago had

gone. Now they just looked tired. Olive suspected this Christmas/Hanukkah season would go down in the books, and the family would reference this near tragedy many times in the years ahead.

As she had done at every meal break for the last couple of weeks, she swiped on her phone and pulled up the photos of Jerry and her at the Christmas light festival. She stared at his smiling face, wishing he sat in front of her right now so she'd know he was okay. The idea that if something bad happened to him and she'd never even know it increased her stress.

She'd spent time reading through every text, every email, remembering every conversation. Every day, she felt her feelings for him growing deeper and deeper.

Had she occupied his thoughts the way he had occupied hers? Did the time apart make him realize they shouldn't be together, or did it make a longing for her grow the same way she longed to see him again?

She swiped back to his face and enlarged the picture, studying his eyes, thinking back to the way his kiss felt, the way his arms had pulled her close. "Please God," she whispered, praying for his safety and security.

After she finished her salad, opened the plastic wrap covering the cake. The first forkful yielded a velvety crumb, its tangy cream cheese frosting blooming sweet and cool on her tongue, erasing the bitterness of working with Grayson.

She washed the bite of cake down with a sip of coffee, the brew perfectly mingling with the flavors of the cake.

With eyes closed, she savored the experience.

After finishing her meal, she still had fifteen minutes left of her break, so she pushed the tray away and leaned back in her chair, stretching her legs out. Her phone dinged and vibrated again.

Assuming it was her sister making some plan or another in the family chat, she almost didn't check it in the midst of her melancholy mood. But, when she glanced at her phone, the name threw her. Jerry? Her heart skipped a beat. She sat up straight and quickly unlocked it.

> Jerry: Be home for Christmas. See you soon.

She blinked, reading it twice. Her lips suddenly tingled, bringing back that kiss, his warm mouth, his strong shoulders. A grin spread on her face, silly and wide, chasing off the earlier shadows.

She typed back, fingers trembling with joy.

> Olive: Can't wait. Merry Christmas, soldier.

She whispered a silent, "Thank you," to God, a short prayer filled with so much more than those two words. *Thank you for keeping him safe. Thank you for bringing him home. Thank you for having me be on his contact list.*

Campbell Army Airfield, Fort Campbell, KY

Soon after the wheels of the C-17 hit the tarmac, they began unloading their cargo. Everyone moved with practiced efficiency. Jerry swung his duffel bag over his shoulder and grabbed the handle of his rifle case that housed his beloved M110A1, and followed Fisher down the plane's rear cargo ramp. The cold Kentucky night air greeted them, and Jerry took a deep breath, thankful for the safe return home.

The arms room NCO met them at the armory. "Merry Christmas, gentlemen," he said, clicking on his laptop. "Any surprises?"

Major Norton set his weapon on the table in the center of the room. "Everything's accounted for. We'll be back next week to clean. Just get them racked and logged in, and you get back to Christmas evening with your family."

"Yes, sir. Thank you, sir."

Ibrahim, an 18F or Operations and Intelligence NCO, dropped his duffel on the ground outside the weapons locker and handed his M4 to the sergeant taking inventory while reciting the last four digits of the weapon's serial number. He gave Norton a glance and offered, "I can stay."

Norton looked at him as he accepted the weapon from the armory sergeant and confirmed the serial number. "You have a new baby and a pregnant wife, Honest Abe. Holidays aside, much as I appreciate the offer to take up the Christmas slack, go on home."

Ibrahim rubbed his black beard and smiled with white

teeth. "Yes, sir."

Before he could turn, their Group Commander, Colonel Longstreet Beauregard Jenkins, callsign LBJ, came through the door. He wore jeans, winter boots, and a tan sweater. Jerry didn't think he'd ever seen the Colonel out of uniform before. He almost hadn't recognized him. "Welcome home, Coppertop," he greeted Norton using his official callsign. "I read the brief you sent en route. Well done, men. The brass are mighty proud of you boys."

Norton received a weapon and verified the serial number as he nodded toward the Colonel. "Yes, sir. No hitches."

"Tough time of year to focus on mission."

"Yes, sir. But liberty never takes a holiday. Neither do bad guys."

Jenkins slapped Norton on the shoulder and turned to face the team. "Expect I won't see a single one of you until January second. We'll debrief then. Except you, Abe. Our state department counterparts will likely call you in for a little palaver here in the next few days to get your assessment, but we can roll the dice."

Norton raised an eyebrow. "I doubt we'll be complaining, sir." After the Colonel left, he said, "We'll gather in the ready room before you all leave."

Jerry stepped up to the counter and handed his weapon through the cage window. As soon as he got a confirmation from Norton, he picked up his duffel bag and made his way to the ready room.

His eyes burned, and he checked the time. Christmas Day, 1732 hours, or 5:32 PM Central Time for civilians. No, not day, evening. Christmas evening. He sank into the leather couch and startled when Peña grabbed him by the shoulders from behind. The clock now read 5:41. "Wakey, wakey," Captain Peña said. "Daddy's home."

Jerry sat forward and rubbed his eyes as Norton came into the room. "Well done. Couldn't be prouder. Colonel Jenkins wouldn't have come out on Christmas Day if we hadn't done a respectable job." He looked around. "Cynthia and I want to invite anyone who needs a seat at the table over for a late Christmas dinner tomorrow. Sixteen hundred. I'll be frying a turkey, and rumor has it my father-in-law will also be there."

Waller whistled under his breath. "Rubbing shoulders with the VP after this somewhat black bag op?"

"Even better, Drumstick intends to join us. I know he'll be glad to see everyone who can make it," Norton announced. Years back, Bill "Drumstick" Sanders had gotten out of the Army and almost immediately stood up a personal security company that also performed private investigation work.

Norton started taking RSVPs. When he looked at him, Jerry shook his head. "Sorry, Daddy. Got a date."

"Don't want to get a selfie with the VP again?" Norton probed.

Jerry had met the Vice President of the United States two years ago when he hosted a medal ceremony followed by a luncheon at Number One Observatory Circle. "My date's better looking," he said.

Norton rubbed his red beard. "I thought you liked redheads. Cheating on me already? Doesn't really speak well for our future prospects."

He thought of Olive's red braid. "Oh, definitely like this female redhead. No offense, sir, you are permanently afflicted with being a redhead of the male persuasion." Everyone laughed as Jerry stood. "Merry Christmas, everyone. And happy whatever, Abe."

Abe grinned at the good-natured jab. "This year, I call Christmas Day, Monday."

"Happy Monday, then."

Every bone ached for a hot shower and a warm bed. He wanted to call Olive, but he honestly didn't know if he had the energy. He felt drained, tapped out. He tried to remember the last time he slept more than three hours at a stretch and couldn't recall.

He crossed the compound to his barracks building and slowly climbed the stairs to his floor. When he got to the door, he mentally patted himself on the shoulder for fishing his keys out of his bag in Karpovia and putting them in his cargo pocket. Experience told him he'd not sleep well—or at all—on the multiple-stop flights home, and jet lag would break him on this side of the Atlantic.

He let his bag hit the tile floor with a thud as the metal door swung shut with a loud clang behind him. If he sat down, he'd sleep, and he'd rather wash away the last several days first, so he stripped his uniform blouse off on the way to the bathroom. While the water heated, he turned the room's thermostat up to 75 degrees, then pulled his boots off for the first time in four days, relief washing through every toe.

He examined his reflection in the mirror. White and gray camouflage paint hid inside his chestnut beard, in the lines of his eyelids, and against the hair at his temple. His eyes stared back at him, bloodshot with deep dark circles under them. The cold had chapped the skin around his nose and his cheeks, leaving them raw and red. But he was alive, whole, home, and starting to feel warm.

Hot water pounded his shoulders, steam fogging the tiles as he scrubbed Karpovia off. The spicy smell of his soap gradually filled the steam in the air, clearing out the fuel smell from his sinuses that came with riding in the cargo hold of a C-17. He thought of Olive and his intent to spend Christmas with her after her shift ended. Not happening tonight.

Wrapped in a towel, he grabbed his phone—1829 local. She'd finish up her shift soon. He typed, his thumbs slow and clumsy.

> Jerry: Just got in. Beat. Crashing hard. Tomorrow okay?

He flopped on the bunk, barracks silence pressing in like a hum, the warm air seeping the last of his strength away. Her reply dinged fast.

> Olive: So glad you're home safe! I'm off tomorrow. Breakfast at my place? 9?

A grin cracked his tired face.

He gave her text message a thumbs-up, then pulled the OD Green Army issue wool blanket up over his shoulders, asleep before he could even plug in his phone.

CHAPTER
ELEVEN

Clarksville, Tennessee

Nerves jittered in her stomach as Olive slid the pan of biscuits into the oven, then wiped the flour off the countertop. She knew how she had left things with Jerry, but she didn't know what that looked like nearly two weeks later. She stirred the corned beef one more time, put the lid on the skillet, and turned the stove off. Before she could pull the fruit salad out of the refrigerator, her doorbell rang.

Heart pounding, mouth suddenly dry, she turned down the Christmas music she'd had pumping through her Bluetooth speakers and made her way through the living room, eyes looking around for anything possibly out of place. When she opened the door, unexpected joy burst through her at the sight of Jerry.

He was clean-shaven, wearing a gray cable sweater and an OD green skull cap that made his hazel eyes look emerald green. The bridge of his nose and his cheeks looked chapped red. He carried two gift bags.

"Merry Christmas," he said with a smile that made her heart flutter.

"Welcome home, soldier," she said.

She stepped into his arms as if God had designed them for her to perfectly fit there. They wrapped around her, strong, sure, and his lips met hers as if they'd kissed a thousand times already. The days since she last saw him slipped away. He smelled of spicy aftershave, a light musk unique to him, and fresh air. She just wanted to breathe him in.

He lifted his head and looked into her eyes. "Worth coming back to."

"You have been missed." She cupped his cheek, liking the smooth feel, then stepped back and gestured toward the room. "Come in."

"Thank you." He held up the bags. "Where should I put—"

A grin stretched across her face at the secret gift she had snagged for him, even though they had skipped any talk of exchanging gifts. She snatched the bags from his hands and plunked them onto the end table beside the package she had wrapped that morning. "I didn't do a tree this year because I knew I was working all week."

"I didn't do a tree, either. Had other things on my plate."

She laughed. "Unofficially."

"Unofficially." He nodded. "You have such a beautiful

home. Thanks for having me again."

"Have a seat. I just have to check the oven." Instead of sitting, he followed her into the kitchen.

"Smells great."

She glanced at him as she grabbed a dish towel off the counter and opened the oven door. Something about the way he casually leaned against the door frame did something funny to her pulse rate. "I love breakfast smells. Especially mixed with coffee." She turned the biscuit pan, then shut the door. "Would you like some? Coffee?"

"Absolutely."

She remembered he drank it black from their post-church lunch and Thanksgiving. The slight tremble in her hand as she poured the coffee surprised her. She forced herself to take a deep breath and let it out slowly. Olive handed him the steaming mug, then turned the burner on beneath the skillet she'd staged with beef tallow. While it heated, she cracked two eggs into a ramekin. "How was your mission?"

If she hadn't looked at him, she wouldn't have seen the shadow that crossed his eyes. But his face remained calm, relaxed. "*Veni Vidi Vici*," he answered unironically, quoting the Latin phrase meaning we came, we saw, we conquered.

"Good." She waved her palm over the skillet, judging the heat, then slid the eggs out of the ramekin. They immediately started hissing and popping, and the air filled with the bacon smell of the beef tallow. Olive sprinkled the eggs with salt and pepper and cracked two more eggs into the ramekin. "I watched the news to see if I could guess where you were, but nothing clued me in."

"Like I said, we did our thing." He took a sip of the coffee. "If you hear about us, something went very wrong. There's a reason they call us the quiet professionals."

"No news is good news, then."

"For our side, anyway. We don't make movies about our work like the Navy does. Usually, movies about Green Berets are dudes suffering from debilitating PTSD who burn down a town or something." He set the mug down and slipped his hands into his pockets. "Wow. That's good coffee. Like really good."

"Thanks." It took her a second to take in his previous words. "Does that false perception ever bother you?" She loaded a plate with corned beef hash, topped the mound with the eggs, then slid the other two eggs into the pan. After seasoning them, she pulled the biscuits out of the oven. She had a bread plate ready for them.

Jerry said, "Sure, sometimes. But we can't talk about what we do—and some movie star or screenwriter in Hollywood has no idea what we actually do, or who we actually are—so, they just recycle the same decades-old fictitious tropes they used when my granddad was in Vietnam."

Olive detected some annoyance in his answer, not with her, but rather with the culture, so she decided to change the subject. Based on every fact she knew about the handsome, strong man standing in her kitchen, sipping her coffee, she could never imagine him fitting into the "crazy vet" mold falsely perpetuated by mainstream media and entertainment outlets.

"Is your grandfather still with us?"

Jerry shook his head. "He passed just after I turned ten. I remember him, though."

"He and your father sound like great men."

Jerry sipped his coffee and slowly said, "*Magni viri in adversis gaudent, sicut fortes milites in bello triumphant.*"

Olive grinned. "Meaning?"

"Oh. It's from De Providentia. Great men rejoice in adversity, just as brave soldiers triumph in war."

After turning the eggs in the pan, Olive picked up the biscuits and retrieved the fruit salad from the refrigerator. She held them out to him. "Could you be a great man and take these to the table?"

"Triumphantly."

Before he came back, she had loaded a second plate with the corned beef and topped it with the eggs. She turned off the heat under the skillet and picked up both plates. "All set," she said.

"Let me take those." He took the plates from her, and she refilled her coffee mug and grabbed his.

She'd set the dining room table with a dark blue tablecloth covered in silver snowflakes. Silver candlesticks held white candles. She'd filled a glass bowl with glittery silver pinecones. A silver butter dish sat next to a silver bowl filled with homemade strawberry jam. She had orange juice in a glass carafe on the sideboard and water in the glasses on the table.

"This looks wonderful," Jerry said as he placed the white

plates on top of silver chargers. "Thank you."

"My pleasure." Her nerves had started to settle once they took their seats. "Would you pray?"

He held his hand out and she folded her fingers into his. His strong, warm fingertips closed over hers as she bowed her head. She could feel the callouses on his palms. "Father, thank You for the promises of this day, the gift of Your Son, safe travels, this great company, and this food. Please bless us and bless this meal and this time we share."

She offered him a biscuit, then split one open with a fork. Steam rose up, and the warm, bready smell filled her nose. "What would your day have been like yesterday if you'd been home?" she asked.

He smiled in a way that tugged at her heart. "My mom loved holidays. She taught elementary school, so her life kind of moved from one holiday to the next. And my sister, Mabel, always makes it easy to celebrate."

"Oh?" She cut into an egg, pleased that the over-medium yolk spilled out perfectly. "How old is Mabel?"

"Two years older than me, but she could be ten. She loves every holiday. On the first of every month, she decorates her bedroom door." He pulled out his phone, tapped it, then swiped through it, and held it out. She saw the red and green wrapped door, tinsel creating a sparkly chevron pattern. Next to it, a dark-haired woman stood. She clearly had Down Syndrome. That explained why Jerry's older sister still lived at home.

Olive grinned and handed the phone back to him. "That's so fun. I love that she uses her door."

"Mom did that with her for her entire life. She said that way everyone can see it." He turned the phone screen back off, pocketed it, and smeared jam on his biscuit. "My mom would have made her traditional eggnog pancakes, and my dad would tolerate it all with a big smile and few words."

"You're talking about your mom in the past tense."

He nodded. "She passed three years ago today."

"I'm so sorry," Olive gasped. She wondered if his heart was truly here with her in Clarksville, or back home in South Dakota with his grieving father and sister. "That must kind of throw a wet blanket on Christmas."

He shrugged. "Not really. We knew it was coming. Just wish I had more time. We left some things unsaid." He cleared his throat. "Mable loves Christmas. You know?"

"Sounds like you miss home."

He washed a biscuit bite down with coffee. "Never actually lived in South Dakota. I was an Army brat, born in one country, graduated high school in another, and grew up mostly between Benning and McDill. But I miss them. Colonel released us last night through next week. I bought plane tickets to go visit this morning. Didn't want to risk Space-A to Ellsworth Air Force Base during the holidays."

She propped her elbow on the table and rested her chin in her hand. As much as she hated to see him leave again, she didn't begrudge his opportunity to see his family. "'Middle of nowhere,' South Dakota?"

"Midland, South Dakota," he confirmed.

"Brr."

"Yep," He laughed. "Rapid City got snow yesterday, as

a matter of fact. Nearest decent airport. About two hours out," He shook his head. "Our family text was filled with Mabel's photos in the snow."

"Do you need a ride to the airport?"

He shook his head. "Oh, no thanks. I'll only be gone three days. Just a quick trip. I'll park in the long-term lot in Nashville."

"I'd love to drop you off and pick you up."

He smiled and his eyes lidded slightly, considering the offer. "I would love that, but I checked the schedule you sent me. You'll be in the middle of your shift when I get back."

They spent the next two hours chatting about families, sharing stories about parents and siblings. Eventually, they moved from the table to the living room and sat on either end of the couch facing each other. His presence filled the room, and he fit in her home perfectly—like a final missing piece clicking into place and solving the entire puzzle.

He set his water glass on a coaster on the coffee table and said, "I have to get to the airport. My flight leaves at three."

She stood and crossed the room to where she'd set the presents. "Well, you can't go until you open your gift."

The nerves had returned. She held out the gift bag to him, trying to keep her hand from trembling. "You first," he said.

With a grin, she said, "If you insist." The first bag contained a travel mug with a drawing of a nurse with crazy red hair and wild eyes. "Be a nurse, they said," it read at the top, "it will be fun, they said." It made her laugh.

"That's perfect." She gestured. "Your turn."

He pulled out the figurine of the soldier kneeling in prayer, the words taken from Psalm 91, the Soldier's Psalm, carved into the base. "He will cover you with his feathers, and under his wings you will find refuge."

He ran his finger over the words, then looked up at her. "I really like this."

"It made me think of you." She fought the desire to lighten the tension that filled the room. "I was hoping you'd like it."

"I do. Very much." He paused, then said, "When something about a mission or something else stresses me out, I recite the Soldier's Psalm."

She gasped. "I love that."

He put it back in the bag and pointed at her. "One more."

When she opened the jewelry box, the necklace with a pendant shaped like a stethoscope forming a heart made her gasp out loud. "Oh, Jerry," she said, tracing the heart. "How beautiful. And how thoughtful." She shook her head. "How did you even have time?"

He shrugged. "I saw it weeks ago and thought of you. I went this morning to pick it up, hoping it would still be there." He winked. "The benefit of Christmas deployment is the ability to take advantage of after-Christmas sales."

She stood with him and easily went into his arms, still holding the box in her hand. "It means a lot to me. Thank you."

He wrapped his arms around her and pressed his lips to hers. She thought she could stay in his arms all day. He cupped her cheek with his hand and slowly gentled the kiss. When he raised his head, it was just to rest his forehead on hers. "I suddenly don't want to leave, again."

She squeezed him and stepped back. "You go see your family. Enjoy them."

"I will." He slipped his hand around her waist and pulled her forward again. "In a minute."

CHAPTER
TWELVE

Midland, South Dakota

Jerry's dad, Leonard "Leo" Adam McBride, set a cup of coffee in front of him. Jerry smiled and said, "Appreciate it."

"Course you do." His dad sat across from him, his hazel eyes taking in everything. His once brown hair, still cut close in the military style, now salted with gray.

"How was your night?"

The weather had delayed his flight. He'd arrived just before midnight. "Fine. Been a long couple of weeks, though. Lots of snow and lots of flying." He rubbed his eyes. "We got in on Christmas Day."

"Didn't realize you were even gone." A wry smile curved his lips. "But when we didn't hear from you Christmas morning, I assumed."

"Yeah." He took a sip of coffee and closed his eyes,

appreciating his father's special roast. "Man, that's good coffee."

"Life's too short to drink bad coffee."

"Well, when all you got is MRE coffee for a few weeks, you'll take most anything else." He raised his cup in a toast to his dad. "Business still good?"

His father sat back in his chair. "I used to get enough orders at Sturgis to see me through the year. Now, with all the social media stuff your cousin keeps doing, I have a three-month waiting list and work twenty-hour days just to fill orders at Sturgis. If you ever decide to get out, I can add an '& Son' after the name, and we could make a killing."

His father built custom windshields for any kind of vehicle that needed one, but motorcycles dominated his trade. The work involved in customizing the windshields and forming them by hand went back to the days of old when blacksmiths crafted swords and shields on anvils from raw metal using hammers and pure human strength.

Jerry raised an eyebrow. "Get out?"

"Yeah." His dad rubbed his smooth jaw. "It's not the same Army I was in. Very different."

True. A lot of things about the military had changed in the last decade, and some things had changed back. "Granddad said the same thing about you. Didn't he say, '*Tempora mutantur, nos et mutamur in illis*'? Times change, and we change with them," Jerry smiled when he said that. It wasn't intended to be an insult or a gotcha. "Everything changes from one generation to the next, does is it not?"

"Renaming ships and tearing down memorials? When they renamed Bragg, that was kind of the final straw for me," his dad said frankly.

"They named it back," Jerry countered.

His dad shook his head. "One shot, one kill. No take backs."

Jerry considered it. He understood why rewriting history and generations of tradition would have this effect on his father and other veterans of his generation, but Jerry had not emotionally invested himself in this particular argument. Like his father, he thought the initial effort and the motivations for it were steeped in inexplicable ignorance. However, on balance, he also thought most politicians were either deeply stupid, irreversibly corrupt, or both, allowing him to frame the issue from that perspective.

Jerry chuckled. "Sounds like you're holding a grudge."

"You got that right. Me and every other vet who ever served there, probably. And that new PT test? What a joke. Why not just sign everybody up for hot yoga? *Si vis pacem, para bellum*. If you want peace, prepare for war."

While he had no intention of arguing with his father on this point, Jerry felt his dad was mistaken. The new annual Army Physical Fitness test may be many things, but it was certainly no joke. He remembered how shredded his thighs had felt after his last test. He would much rather sign up for hot yoga.

"I hadn't planned on getting out any time soon," Jerry said.

His father prompted, "So you looking to go warrant? You're a little long in the tooth for the team these days,

Sergeant First Class."

Jerry shook his head. "I'm promotable. Move up to Zulu. No reason I shouldn't. Our team has had an overstrength slot for a while now, and Wade Chandler is getting close to either getting E-9 or calling it done."

An 18Z is the Senior Sergeant on the team, typically a Master Sergeant of pay grade E-8. Jerry, as a Sergeant First Class, held the pay grade of E-7. "If that doesn't work out for some reason, then I'll go warrant. My plan is to go warrant after I get done with the Zulu slot."

His father said, "Then when you burn that bridge, you'll finally accept a commission? You'll be like a real mustang."

"Sir. Doing everything I can to avoid ending up as a commissioned officer, sir. No offense, Colonel sir."

His father shook his head, and his eyes suddenly stared into the past. "I understand completely. You're a team dog, through and through. The politics alone would make you want to choke some dummy out on a daily basis. Your mother, however, would not have approved."

Jerry felt himself tense up. "Yeah. She made that abundantly clear."

The kitchen door burst open, and Mabel rushed in wearing a pink coat and a pink hat with a pom-pom on top of it. The crisp bite of winter air clung to her coat, laced with the faint, earthy tang of hay and feathers from the henhouse. She carried a basket filled with eggs. Leo immediately stood and took the basket from her, while she removed her coat and hat. "Seventeen eggs! Even though it's cold." She walked over to Jerry and put her arm over his shoulders, crossing her feet at her ankles, standing like a street tough kid on a light post. "My girls are happy girls."

Jerry's grin stretched across his face. "Seventeen! It's eight degrees outside. That's great. How many customers do you have now?"

Mabel shrugged her shoulders in a fluid motion. "Daddy knows." She looked at their father. "Daddy, give him his present now?"

"Not yet. Your day's not done yet." He pointed to a whiteboard with a chart. The columns had the day of the week and intersecting rows labeled with pictures. Jerry understood the tasks of feeding the hens, watering them, collecting eggs, and placing the eggs in cartons.

Mabel reached into the left pocket of her coat and pulled out a wooden bead, then made a mark next to the picture for feeding the chickens. Once she made her mark, she put the bead in a little box under the chart and pulled another bead out of her pocket, repeating the process. Once she emptied her pocket, their dad said, "What's next?"

Mabel tapped the picture of the cartons.

"I know what's next." She capped the marker and took the eggs into the utility room. She looked at Jerry and beckoned him with her hand. "Come on. You can help me. I'll teach you how."

He got up and followed her. In the utility room, he saw her workstation, the pictures on the wall, and the calendar hanging above the workbench. She carefully filled the cartons, matching the sizes of eggs, then closed them. Jerry noted she had twenty-four eggs, not seventeen. She pointed at the calendar. "Twenty-seven."

He assumed she meant the date. "Yes. Twenty-seven."

In her child's handwriting, Mabel wrote the date on the egg cartons. Then she stacked them next to several other cartons and crossed out the date on the calendar. "Now presents!" She took Jerry's hand and led him back into the kitchen. "Now presents," she repeated to their dad.

He smiled and nodded. She rushed out of the room.

Jerry reclaimed his coffee mug. "You're very good with her."

"Your mom was better." Leo shrugged. The grief in his voice from years back had vanished, but the loss still echoed there. "There was a learning curve. I was gone a whole lot when you two were little. After your mom passed, I suddenly had this amazing daughter and truly no idea what to do. But your mom had perfectly written everything down for me in a notebook. I can follow simple directions."

"I miss her too, Dad. God knows, it's hard to even be here without her."

His dad sharply cleared his throat. "I know, son. But life has to go on, right? *Tempus vivendi et tempus moriendi.* There's a time to live and there's a time to die. Much to our grief and dismay, your mother's time to die came too soon. It's hardest on your sister."

Almost before he realized it, Jerry said, "I met someone."

"That right? Met someone like casual, or met someone like you're making plans?"

Was he making plans? In his heart, he felt like he ought to start making plans, but he could hardly be that serious just five weeks in. "Just a few dates. Spent Thanksgiving with her family. Had breakfast at her place yesterday morning before I flew here."

"You didn't spend the night before breakfast—"

"No, Dad. I had just come back from—somewhere."

While his father maintained a Top-Secret Clearance, he still had no need to know, and classified details rested on that two-pronged fork.

"But you like her?"

"What's not to like? She's former Army. Officer. Captain, actually. A nurse."

"That's what she did and does, but how do you feel about her? Do you like her, son?"

He studied his dad for a long breath before saying, "She reminds me a lot of Mom."

"Well, in that case, you should probably start making plans."

Jerry walked over to his dad and put his hand on his shoulder. "I'm sorry, I don't visit enough. I think it's part of the job. I love you and I love Mabel."

His dad grabbed him in a fierce hug and quickly let him go. "We know that, son. I'm proud of you, and I know exactly what your life is like. You don't have to explain. We're just happy to see you when we can."

Mabel called from the front room. "I'm ready! Come

on! I'm ready! Presents!"

Jerry raised an eyebrow. "I didn't bring her anything because, as you know, I mailed her present weeks ago."

His dad slapped him on the shoulder, and they walked to the door. "I know. She loved it, by the way. When you said you were coming. I went ahead and got her something from you. She's gonna love it just as much."

Jerry couldn't help but look behind him as they left the kitchen. But his mom was not at the sink. Nor did she labor at the stove, filling the house with Christmas baking. And she never would again in his lifetime.

Fort Campbell, Kentucky

February

The wind beat against the ready room window as a late February snowstorm howled outside. He should be at the chapel, sitting next to Olive, enjoying a sermon from his favorite chaplain in the rotation of chaplains. Instead, he stared at a Monopoly board, battling Fisher and Brock for Realtor dominance. The room smelled like microwave popcorn and coffee.

"Show me the money, Jerry Maguire," Fisher grinned, shaking the dice cup. His lean frame slouched in the leather chair, socked feet kicked up on an empty ammo crate they used as an end table. "Two hotels on Park Place—five hundred bucks."

Jerry snorted, shoving fake bills across the table. "Robbery.

You're worse than the brass with TDY cuts."

Brock laughed, a New York Yankees baseball cap covering his head. "Says the guy who owns all the railroads. You're just mad Trout's fleecing you first."

"Strategy," Jerry said, dry as the desert in Djibouti. He rolled a six, then moved his top hat past Fisher's remaining hotels. "This is the dumbest game. You're both toast when I can build that hotel on Baltic."

Two inches of ice topped by an inch of snow, followed by another ice storm in a thirty-six-hour timespan, had grounded everything. It was barely safe to walk outside, much less drive. The commanding general had closed Fort Campbell to anything except emergency services. As much as he enjoyed the break in training, he'd love to have the ability to get to Clarksville and spend some time with Olive.

"This game may be stupid, but we're not dumb enough to challenge you to a dart game ever again," Brock explained. "Who throws seven bullseyes in a row? You're not human, man."

Fisher said, "It's like playing golf with Waller."

Jerry had made it back to Fort Campbell in time to take Olive out for New Year's Eve. They'd enjoyed a movie, Chinese food, and a long kiss under a gazebo covered in Christmas lights. Between her shifts and his training, they'd managed a couple more breakfasts, two lunches, and two dinners. He'd also met her at her car after an all-night shift again, coffee in one hand, a bag with buttery croissants in the other.

But they talked every day on the phone, texted each other all day, and had not missed a chapel service together yet. Now, snowed in, he missed her—the strawberry smell of her hair, the smile always present in her eyes, that constellation of freckles across her nose.

"You know something boys?" Jerry mused. "I am getting pretty sick and tired of snow."

Fisher rolled, landing on Jerry's railroad. "Hundred bucks. No free rides. Cough it up, Trout." Fisher smirked, tossing the cash. Before he could retort with a quip, Jerry's phone chirped. He expected to see Olive's name, but instead saw Phil Osbourne's.

"Pause, boys. Gotta take this."

Brock made kissing noises, and Jerry shook his head as he swiped. "Ozzy, what's up, brother?"

"Ozzy!" Fisher yelled, loud enough for Osbourne to overhear.

"What's up, Doc Oz?" Brock yelled.

"Hang on, Ozzy." Jerry put Osbourne on speaker phone so he could talk to the other two. They traded friendly insults for a few minutes, then Jerry moved to the other side of the room. "How've you been? What's up?"

He could hear the smile in Osbourne's voice. "Better than I have ever been."

"Glad to hear it."

"What about you? How is it going with Olive?"

Just the thought of her made his heart beat faster. "Weird, really. Strange. It's like I no longer count time by days, just by moments with her."

"Sounds like true love to me, man."

After a brief pause, Jerry said, "Expect so."

"You made any serious plans yet?"

Despite the fact that Osbourne could not see him, Jerry instinctively shook his head. "Not yet."

"Well, make plans and trust the plan, brother."

"Sounds like a plan," Jerry quipped.

"I'm guessing after hearing from the guys, you're not conveniently snowed in at her house."

"Yeah, unfortunately, she had a shift last night, so she's actually been trapped at the hospital since yesterday. Too much ice to risk her going home."

"The way people there drive in the snow, I wouldn't blame her."

Jerry chuckled, "Not to give too much credit to drivers in Tennessee or Kentucky, but you and I know the worst drivers on earth are in..."

"...are in North Carolina," Osbourne finished along with Jerry.

Osbourne chuckled and said, "Worse than Kuwait. No joke." Jerry watched Fisher lace up his boots and don his coat. He glanced at the clock. Lunch time. "Listen, I called for a reason."

"Aw," Jerry clicked his tongue. "I thought you just missed me, Doc."

With a chuckle, Osbourne said, "Melissa and I have started planning the wedding."

A grin spread across Jerry's face. "We talked about this. I cannot be the maid of honor, dude. Seriously."

"Keep that up, and you won't even get invited." He cleared his throat. "We're going to do it on a cruise ship."

"A cruise ship?" Of all the things he might have predicted, that did not make the list. "Interesting choice."

"Comes with the ability to completely secure the area," Osbourne said. Again, Jerry nodded, even though his friend couldn't see him. Jerry knew Melissa's sister was in witness protection. Clearly, they planned something around the security and containment of the cruise ship so she could attend. Since Phil's dad was a federal judge, he could probably make that happen with few hitches.

"What do you need from us?"

"Just you, brother. I can't ask you to be my best man, but I want you to be a groomsman. My best groomsman, let's say."

Emotion clogged his throat, and he couldn't speak right away. With a harsh clearing of his throat, he said, "I would be more than honored." After taking a deep, cleansing breath, he asked, "Who is the best man?"

"Dad's gonna stand in for my brother." He could hear the emotion in Osbourne's voice.

Drug cartels tied to Melissa's sister had murdered Osbourne's brother to send a message. "That's very cool," he said.

"Dad thought so." He took a deep breath. "I have a few more calls to make, but I'll shoot you the deets. My dad has already covered the cruise for the team and their plus ones. Norton confirmed block leave dates last week of May with me before I called you. You were next on my to do list."

"I guess we'll all be on block leave together, then," Jerry laughed. "Thanks, man. I'll let you get to that list. Shoot me your dad's number, too."

"He already has yours."

"Okay. Well, count on me. Whatever you need."

"Thanks, Jerry."

"Talk later."

After he hung up, he sent Olive a message.

> Jerry: Hope you're sleeping. Headed to chow.

She immediately called him. "Hey there," he said as he answered, "doesn't sound like sleeping to me, young lady."

"Yeah. The snowplow came by the hospital about five minutes ago. Someone said the interstate's clear. I'm trying to decide whether I want to try to make it home or just wait it out. I'm off until Wednesday, so if I could get home, I could just stay there."

"Still coming down hard here." He looked out the window at the snow pouring down. "I could come get you. The truck has four-wheel drive."

There was a long pause. "I'm so close to saying yes."

He checked the time. "Let me grab some chow and see what the weather does here."

"Thanks, Jerry."

After he hung up, he opened the weather app on his phone. The storm looked like it would pass through in the next hour. He took a screenshot and texted her.

> Jerry: Be there around two. I'll call when I get there.

Her response came five minutes later.

> Olive: You're the best. 💀

When he stepped out into the courtyard, the cold hit Jerry in the face like a sucker punch . He tried to walk in Fisher and Brock's footprints, placing his steps very carefully to avoid slipping on the ice. His foot broke through a top layer of snow, through a layer of ice, and through more snow. As he entered the chow hall, he slipped his cap off and put it in his coat pocket. He didn't see anyone working the grill, but the sandwich bar and salad bar looked open, so he headed that way.

He piled roast beef and cheese onto some rye bread. The tomato soup smelled good, so he added that to his tray and made his way to where his buddies sat.

"What's up with Doc Oz?" Fisher asked as he slathered peanut butter on an apple slice.

"Would you believe wedding bells are ringing?" Jerry replied. "Apparently, we're all invited. He already cleared block leave dates with Daddy."

A smile covered Fisher's face. "Kinda presumptuous, but still awesome. Be great to get down to Florida again."

Jerry shook his head. "They're getting married on a cruise ship."

"No joke?" Brock asked.

"I went on a cruise when I was a kid," Fisher said. "Pretty

cool. Lots of cartoon characters on board, so probably a slightly more grown-up venue this time around."

"It really is pretty cool."

Brock pulled his phone out of his pocket. "Do you have the dates? I need to get it on the calendar before Erin adds something to the honey-do list."

He looked at the text from Osbourne. "All expense paid cruise sailing 22 through 28 May. Miami to Bahamas to Haiti to Miami."

"Wow," Brock said. "Erin will be quite impressed with me. She's all about cruises. Goes on like three a year with her mother."

"You're going to be boyfriend of the year." Fisher licked the peanut butter off his thumb. "You'll be able to ride that wave for a few weeks at least."

They ate in silence for a while. They had spent so many hours a day together that none of them felt the need to fill the silence with useless banter. They ate and then stood in unison to take their trays to the belt that carried them off to the dishwashing section in the back.

Fisher said, "You're off to a good start. Ready to finish losing?"

Jerry looked at his watch. "Nah. I concede. Split up my stuff. I'm going to pick Olive up and take her home."

"Oh! Man down! Man down!" Brock teased.

"Her knight in shining pickup truck," Fisher grinned, slapping him on the back. "Be careful. Call if you need us to get you out of a ditch or something. We'll send a Chinook."

"Yeah. You know they did that back in the late 80s

once." Jerry put his cap on and checked his pockets to make sure he had gloves.

Fisher said, "Not completely sure you have the same amount of stars on your shoulder boards to merit that kind of treatment, Sergeant First Class."

"*Est quod est.*" Jerry quoted the Latin for it is what it is. "And it's 'promotable.' Sergeant First Class promotable. It's going to take an hour to de-ice the truck."

"I'd help, but..." They walked outside, and Brock looked up at the sky. The snow had slowed down considerably. "Well, you know, it's cold out here, bro."

Jerry laughed and waved them on, then carefully walked out of the courtyard and over to the parking lot. He used his key fob to remote-start the truck, then went up to his room. He'd give it about five or ten minutes to heat the windows from the heater inside the truck before he attempted to get the ice cleared.

Clarksville, Tennessee

Casablanca's black-and-white glow danced across her living room as Olive snuggled closer into Jerry's side. The empty soup bowls that had contained leftover chicken noodle she'd made Wednesday sat stacked on the coffee table, a faint thyme taste lingering in her mouth.

She tilted her head, studying him. She liked the shape of his face, the beard that covered his jaw, the way his eyes crinkled when he smiled. In the weeks since Christmas, she'd relished every moment spent with him and wanted more and more. She shouldn't have accepted his offer to come get her. She should have just stayed put. But the thought of another day not seeing him had not appealed.

"Still can't believe you drove through that," she murmured, her Alabama drawl soft against the film's dialogue.

Jerry's grin flashed, dry and quick. "Four-wheel drive's no joke. Couldn't leave you stranded. Plus, I missed this." His fingers brushed her arm, sparking warmth under her sweater.

She smiled, snuggling closer. "Well, you are certainly my hero."

The movie rolled on. Rick and Ilsa at the airport, tension in the scene thick. They would always have Paris. Olive enjoyed the layers of solid muscle and the heat of his body beneath his clothes as she snuggled into him. Yet despite his raw strength, each time he made contact with her to stroke her arm or tuck her hair back, his touch felt so gentle, as if petting a newborn kitten.

Jerry shifted, his voice low. "Speaking of not leaving people behind—Phil called this afternoon."

"Ozzy?" She perked up, remembering the time years before when she had met Phil Osbourne and all the stories Jerry had told her about his team's former medic.

"Yeah. He and Melissa set the date. They're getting married on a cruise in May."

"A cruise?" She shifted so she could face him fully. The movie droned on, but she wasn't paying attention anymore. "Seems like an odd venue for former SF. Kind of a closed-in environment.”

He chuckled. “I thought the same thing. And no weapons. The security on a cruise ship is *serio dicere*.”

“What?”

“Oh. That was from the philosopher Seneca. *Serio dicere.* Meaning to be taken very seriously. Cruise ship security is no joke.” He enjoyed her curiosity and her fearlessness in asking for clarification.

“Showing off again, soldier?”

He chuckled. “More like I feel comfortable being myself with you.”

She felt heat rush up her neck into her cheeks and squeezed him tighter. His body felt so hard and strong. And warm. “Never been on a cruise. Seems odd to have the ceremony on a ship, too, really.”

“Phil has his reasons.”

“What reasons?”

He shook his head. “Not my reasons to tell.” His hand began rubbing lazy circles on her back. “We’re all invited.”

Curiosity made her want to know more, but she didn’t push. “A cruise is expensive.”

“His dad’s covering our tickets and travel. From the chatter on the group chat Phil created, most of us who served with him are invited. Our team went through a lot. We’re close. I think his dad knows that and wants to bring his extended family there to represent.” He brushed a hair off her cheek in a gentle manner that made her heart skip. “So, anyway, how would you like to go with me? Be my plus one?”

The idea of being isolated with Jerry for a week, surrounded by the people he loved and respected, getting to know them in a unique way sounded very appealing. She studied his face, searching for any indication he didn't mean it. She found none. "I would love to. When are the dates?"

They discussed minor details, then settled back on the couch for the rest of the movie. When the credits rolled, she glanced at the clock—11:47 PM. No wonder she kept having to fight off yawns. She used the remote to turn the television off and disengaged herself from his arms. She stood and stretched her back. "It's late. The roads are probably still bad. You're welcome to sleep on the couch if you want."

Jerry stared at her, his expression thoughtful and introspective. "Well, that's a very tempting offer." He stood with her and pulled her to him. "I appreciate it, Captain, ma'am, but I think I will respectfully decline. For now."

As much as she wanted to dismiss his concerns, she understood them. Still, she felt a twinge of rejection. "Okay."

He cupped her cheek with his palm, his eyes darkening. Suddenly, her mouth went dry and her pulse started to pound. When he spoke, she somehow knew what he would say. "Olive, listen," His voice dropped, raw. "I'm in love with you."

That tiny little twinge of rejection vaporized. Quick tears burned her eyes. "I—" She took a deep breath, and spoke through the joy that burst from her heart. "I love you, too." It spilled out, deep and true. How could she feel this strongly after such a short amount of time? It didn't make sense.

His lips found hers, warm, the kiss holding a promise. She melted into it, fingers running through his beard then curling into his hair, breathing in his scent, until he eased back, forehead resting on hers. "Yeah. So, I won't be staying. I better leave right now."

She bit back the temptation to once more extend an invitation they might both regret. Instead, she smiled. "Drive safe. Let me know when you get there."

After one last, soft kiss, he grabbed his coat. She stood at the door, listening to his boots crunching their way out to his truck.

FOURTEEN

Fort Campbell, Kentucky

May

Bach's Orchestral Suite No. 3 played softly in the background as Jerry neatly folded a shirt and set it on top of the stack on his bed. While he folded laundry, his mind wandered back to thoughts of home. Mabel was so jealous that he was going on a cruise. He needed to remember that. Maybe he could take her over the holiday block leave at the end of the year. They could do one of those theme park-type cruises. She would have as much fun as a seven-year-old with the activities and the characters. He wished he'd thought of it sooner.

He wondered if he could find a cruise that would accommodate people with Down Syndrome. He should look into that.

He glanced over his suit jacket hanging on the outside of his closet. He couldn't believe that in just a few days, Phil Osbourne would get married. He'd worried about his friend ever since the harrowing trek through the Katangela jungle. Watching the decline in his personality and spirit had physically hurt.

As someone who made his living—a calling he answered, really—based on his physical strength and mental acuity, he couldn't imagine what life would look like with any of that ripped away. Yet, every mission he went on came with the risk that he might return no longer whole—if he returned at all. That risk came with the job. He often prayed that God would give him the mental and emotional strength to handle it if anything ever happened.

He'd added Osbourne to those prayers over the last couple of years. Thinking of him now, in love, hearing the contentment in his voice, filled Jerry with a peace for his friend he didn't know he could ever feel since Katangela.

His eyes glanced over the maroon velvet box on his bedside table. Nestled inside was a platinum ring with a traditional round-cut diamond. Just thinking about it made his heart race.

Was it too soon?

Probably. Regardless, it felt right. No one had ever made him feel like Olive Duncan made him feel. He could talk to her about anything and everything. She even understood the soldier aspect of his life, having served herself. In fact, she respected everything about him, and he thrived in the light of that respect.

The question was whether she would want the military lifestyle to be a part of her life again. Duty stations changed. In his twelve years in the Army, they'd assigned him to four different duty stations, and he knew they'd PCS him again soon. Uncle Sam didn't keep soldiers in the same place for very long. He knew his place on the team would count for something, but eventually they would all disperse.

She had also left the army as a Captain. The lifestyle of a Commissioned Officer was not the same as the lifestyle of a Non-Commissioned Officer. They had different processes, different politics, and much different pay.

In an early conversation, she'd talked about buying her house and how it felt good to claim Clarksville as her home now. Would she want to live that transient Army life again? Would she want to live with his constant deployments—oftentimes with very little notice? Could she continue to handle the secrets, the things he could never share even with her? Or would those stack up until they toppled like a mountain of resentment? Jerry had seen so many relationships collapse under the pressure of his type of work.

Did Olive want children? He had always wanted children. Lots of them. So many questions still to ask and answer. He wouldn't know the answers until he asked a very specific question.

Until then, conjecture and five dollars would buy him a cup of over-roasted coffee.

Someone rapped on his door, then pushed it open. He

glanced up as Calvin Brock lumbered in. "Yo."

He had thinning brown hair and a pink tint to his skin. His frame filled the entire doorway. He looked like a professional wrestler, though, in truth, he had once boxed. A judge had recommended he join the army at age eighteen because his trajectory had him landing in prison in a few years. Jerry didn't know a lot more about his past life, but this current Brock was someone whose life he'd place his hands in—and had done so more than once.

"'Sup?" Jerry asked, folding a pair of socks together, then rolling them into a neat cylinder. He picked up the empty laundry basket. "Burgers ready?"

"Just about." His Bronx roots came out when he spoke in complete sentences. He pointed at the speaker. "Doesn't that noise make you want to nap?"

Jerry chuckled. "I learned to appreciate it in sniper school. Helped me focus. Didn't distract me."

"That what you listen to when you're up in a tree in your Gillie?"

Jerry set the basket in his closet. "When I'm not having to listen to your inane chatter."

"I got you, bro." He held up his phone. "Erin wants to know if she can get Olive's number. Something about packing and being roommates."

"Sure." He swiped his phone and sent Brock a text with the requested number. "Erin ready for the full team experience?"

Brock's cheeks turned bright red. "Don't know, bro. I've cooked on it for a couple of weeks. I mean, what if it ain't her cup of tea?"

"What 'it'? Us?"

"Yeah, like, the whole brothers in arms thing. I mean, what if—"

Jerry put his hand on Brock's shoulder. "Listen, this is who you are. You told me how much you found your real home when you had your first formation in basic, remember? If she doesn't like this part of you, you might ought to consider that when thinking about making any future plans."

"Yeah." He paused for a moment, then went back to his lighthearted normal. "I'll get this to Erin, and I'll see you downstairs. Daddy said ten minutes."

After Brock left, Jerry looked at the packing list he'd made. He had everything accounted for except his shower kit. He'd need that in the morning.

They had to be at the Nashville Airport by 0600 hours. He planned to pick Olive up at 0430. Sunday morning traffic shouldn't cause a problem, but he didn't feel comfortable without that thirty-minute buffer.

With everything in order, he left his room and went down to the courtyard. On the stairwell, he could smell the grilling meat. Per tradition, Norton fed the team lunch before breaking for block leave. Several members of the unit would be at the wedding, but not most of them. Osbourne had been gone a long time in Army years.

Norton watched him approach from his station in front of the grill. "How's things, Jerry Maguire?"

"Smooth and steady, Daddy. Ready for tomorrow?"

"My entourage has it all planned out," Norton said,

smiling under his red beard. "All I have to do is show up." Norton had to let the Secret Service coordinate a lot of their travel, which was the price he paid for having married the only daughter of the Vice President of the United States.

"Are they going to be on the ship?"

"Apparently." He grinned. "Cynthia said she better not see them."

Jerry laughed. "I can actually hear her say that in my head."

Norton grinned a loving grin and looked up, staring at a memory. In a rare moment of vulnerability, he said, "We hadn't been married long, and we just got that place near the gate."

"The blue house," Jerry filled in.

"Yeah, with the pool. Anyway, it's late one night after a jump, and I can't sleep because—reasons—so I decide it would be a great idea to sneak out of bed and clean my pistols down in the garage. So I had just broken down the Springfield .45, and she storms in there barefoot in her nightgown and, man, I never heard Cynthia read anyone the riot act like that, all about guns and killing. I will never forget that."

Norton shook his head, still grinning.

"What did you do?"

"Well, I figured out that right then, Cynthia was much more interesting than my Springfield, so I took her back to bed. She's really something when she gets up a head of steam like that, let me tell you."

Jerry accepted a plate from Ibrahim and wandered over

to the table with the toppings and sides. Cynthia was a physician and the daughter of the VP, but women were women at the end of the day. He didn't think Olive would scold him for performing maintenance on his gear in their home. They had really never had a disagreement. He wondered what might get her goat.

Captain Peña arrived with his wife, Emma, who had often acted as their tactical debriefer under the callsign 24-10 in years past. They made their way to Norton's side, so Jerry made his way to elsewhere.

Some other wives and girlfriends had already arrived. Olive would have joined them today, except she had to pull her final shift before vacation. No getting out of it.

Tim and Leanne Waller arrived late. Jerry spotted the pair and cut across the courtyard, his grin pulling wide at the corners. Weeks back, Leanne barely looked pregnant. Now she rocked side to side with each step, palm splayed across the taut dome pushing out her shirtfront.

She smiled at him. "Hey, Jerry."

"You look rather radiant," Jerry said, accepting the hug from her. He shook Waller's hand. "Tim. Glad you made it."

"Yeah. We had a doctor's appointment."

Patting her baby bump, Leanne teased, "Uh, 'we' had a doctor's appointment. Tim was just a straphanger." US Army Airborne soldiers referred to paratroopers who added themselves to the jump manifest to fulfill their mandatory jumps as strap-hangers.

Tim said, "Glad I made the manifest."

Leanne pouted her lip. "Well, 'we,' as in me and little

Waller, are officially off the cruise manifest."

"That's too bad." He looked at Waller. "What about you? Am I going to have to double down on groomsman duties?"

"Nah. Leanne and her mother are insisting I go. Her parents are coming here tonight. We have exit strategies in place for wherever we are in case I need to rush home."

Major Norton stood beside Captain Peña and First Sergeant Wade "Commando" Chandler. He tapped a trill atop the grill with his spatula. "Hey, guys. Can we get your attention real quick?"

Everyone settled down and moved closer, Jerry included. Norton continued, "First of all, I want to thank all of our special guests for joining us today. Thank you all. It's great when we have beautiful women here instead of just a bunch of hairy gorillas."

Polite laughter.

"So, you all knew this was coming. I will now confirm the rumors. The President and the Joint Chiefs, in their infinite wisdom, have determined that I can better serve at a posting closer to the flagpole."

First Sergeant Chandler said, "So, in other words, you got too old to stay on a team?"

Everyone, including Norton, laughed.

"No, that would be you who's old, Top." More laughter. "Anyway, I have to tell you," His face turned stern. "It has been the honor of my life to serve alongside every single one of you. You are the very best at what you do. I will never forget you, no matter where the Army takes me." He laid a hand on Peña's shoulder.

Peña cleared his throat. "Come the first of June, we'll officially do the whole dog and pony change of command with much pomp and fanfare and ribbons and flags. Heck. We might even march in lines and whatnot. And I'm sure there will be cake. As you probably guessed, I've been selected to be your new team commander. Daddy would rather I take over his duties starting today."

"I'm sure he would!" Chandler yelled.

Everyone laughed.

Norton held up his hands, asking for room to speak again. "We also get to surprise your very fine First Sergeant with the news that he has been accepted into the Sergeant Major's Academy effective August first."

Chandler's eyes widened. "What?"

"Obviously, there's been a terrible mistake. But you should take advantage of it before they get to know you. Now who's too old?"

Jerry laughed with his teammates and clapped Chandler on the shoulder. "Congratulations! Well done, Top."

Norton continued. "We will announce the new First Sergeant when all of the paperwork gets finalized. I don't think that announcement is going to surprise anybody." He gave Jerry a meaningful look.

Jerry didn't realize how much he wanted that position until now. He knew his ultimate goal, of course, but now that it *might* be his, he could almost taste it.

Norton held his hands out to the crowd. "Today is

about food and family. We have good food and beautiful women here. Let's just get to that before we get ahead of ourselves. I'd like to pray."

The men wearing them took off their hats.

"God, thank you for watching over us. Thank you for memories we will cherish but can never share. Thank you for a promising future. We trust You have made plans for us and that Your plans for us are good. Be with us today. Bless these fine men and amazing women. Bless this food. Amen. Let's eat."

Jerry loaded his plate, missing Olive. He felt just a hint of envy when Cynthia arrived, and Major Norton laid a huge kiss on her until she laughed and pulled back.

Jerry overheard him say, "You missed my big speech."

Cynthia, straight-faced, replied, "Oh, thank goodness."

"It was a moment. I had a moment," Norton protested.

The warm May sun felt good on Jerry's skin, and increased his anticipation of the coming week. He imagined Olive by his side at events like this in the future, and it felt exactly right. He could not imagine anyone else he would rather have in his life.

He suddenly realized he had already started thinking of the two of them in the future tense. Married. Together. Committed. One, no longer two. Not "me and you" but "us."

He even imagined his dad and her parents doting over their future children. What would they look like, those little people he and Olive would bring into the world with her spirit and his sense of duty?

That settled it in his mind and heart. He needed to plan

to make that future he imagined into a present reality sooner rather than later.

Clarksville Memorial Hospital

Jerry gently revved the engine of his Indian Motorcycle before parking beside Olive's assigned parking space, the deep rumble vibrating through his chest as he sat in the hospital employee parking lot. The late afternoon sun cast a golden glow over the parking lot, warming the air with the promise of a perfect evening. He'd polished the bike that morning, its teal and gold paint gleaming under the clear sky. Strapped to the seat behind him was the spare helmet he'd brought just for her—ruby red with a subtle visor tint, the one he'd picked out thinking it would suit Olive perfectly.

He checked the time. Her shift should end any minute now. The anticipation built in him like a quiet hum, mingling with the engine's idle as he powered the bike down. When he spotted Olive walking toward him, still in her scrubs with her backpack slung over one shoulder and typing into her phone, a wave of genuine elation washed over him. Olive looked tired from the long day, but her smile lit up her face as she spotted him, and in that moment, everything else faded.

"Hey there," she called, quickening her pace to a light jog.

The world shrank down to Olive and nothing else, as if he watched her through his optics. In the space of a heartbeat, he saw her hurrying to greet him when he returned home from a deployment, her backpack transformed into a toddler that looked like her, and looked like him, with her smile and his eyes. The future no longer stretched out before him. Instead, it floated above him and surrounded him, and it no longer existed without her.

Jerry swung his leg over the bike to stand, pulling her into a quick, warm hug to delay her attempt at a quick kiss of greeting. "Hey yourself. Good shift?"

"Nothing I couldn't handle," she said, her eyes sparkling as she glanced at the motorcycle. "This is a surprise."

He grinned, handing her the spare helmet. "Thought you might like to ride. I promised months ago, and it seems like we never got around to it. It's such an amazing and perfect day—blue skies, no wind. Figured we could take the scenic route."

Olive's laugh sounded light and delighted, falling on his ear like subtle windchimes. "You know me too well. Lead the way, soldier."

Before she could don the helmet, he placed his hands on her shoulders and stared into her eyes.

"What?" she queried. "What is it? Is something on my face?"

Jerry let his eyes do the talking and saw the moment when Olive realized this was the perfect time to shut up. He pulled her slowly closer, leaning down, moving his lips closer to his future. When he captured her mouth with his, it was not a friendly kiss. This kiss communicated his need, his want, his desire for their future together. For forever.

She moaned slightly in the middle of it and carefully wrapped her arms around him, one hand still clutching the bulky helmet.

As they kissed, Jerry felt like he suddenly understood everything: the heart, the soul, the reasons that Olive and his life had become inextricably entangled since the second they met all those years back. The world turned beneath their feet, and they stood still, in the perfect stillness of this moment that was now, and shared their hopes and dreams to the exclusion of every other sense. This is what he wanted more than anything. This is what had been missing from his life all his life, and he was on the edge of making himself whole.

He broke the kiss and straightened, his eyes still staring into hers. Olive's eyes stared back, a look of confusion and wonder and hope and desire all blended into one. "Wow," she breathed.

He shrugged. "Missed you today."

They mounted the bike, Olive settling in behind him, her arms wrapping around his waist with a comfortable ease that made his pulse quicken just a little. Jerry started the bike and kicked off, guiding them smoothly out of the lot and onto the road before making his way to the backroads of Clarksville that skirted the edge of town. The wind rushed past, carrying the scent of well-maintained farm fields, and he felt the world open up around them.

As the miles slipped by, Jerry's mind drifted to the changes on the horizon. The team's transition weighed on him—not with dread, but with a growing sense of rightness.

For years, he'd served as the primary sniper, the one perched in silence, waiting for the perfect shot. His role demanded precision, patience, and a steel nerve he'd honed through countless missions.

Now, stepping into the 18Z slot as the new First Sergeant felt like the natural next chapter. A tremendous relief settled over him at the thought of handing off the sniper duties to someone else—maybe someone new to the unit or one of the up-and-coming X-rays after they got through training. He would mentor whoever took the mantle he passed. He was ready to lead from the front and serve and shape the team in broader ways.

He thought of Captain Peña, the man who'd be his commander come June. Peña's steady presence, his sharp tactical mind—Jerry respected him deeply, the kind of respect forged in shared trials. Looking forward to being his "top" sergeant filled Jerry with a quiet excitement. Together, they'd keep the unit strong, adaptable, unbreakable. Though his goal for years, he realized that serving in that role was also an honor—an honor he hadn't fully anticipated, but one that fit.

Olive's arms held him securely, her warmth pressing against his back in a way that made everything else seem secondary. It was amazing—simple and profound—how right it felt, how right she felt, her trust in him as they leaned into the curves together. She wasn't just along for the ride; she made herself part of it, part of him, in a way that brought contentment to his soul. She partnered with him. The rhythm of the road, the hum of the engine, her gentle hold—it all wove into a moment of pure peace.

Spotting a wide shoulder ahead, Jerry signaled and eased the bike to a stop, the gravel crunching softly beneath the tires. He killed the engine, the sudden quiet amplifying the birdsong in the nearby trees.

"Ready to take the reins?" he asked, turning to her with a smile.

Olive's eyes widened in surprise, then delight. "Really?"

"You know how, right?"

"I do. But do you trust me with your baby?"

"Absolutely," he said, dismounting and helping her slide forward. "You've got this."

As she took the handlebars, Jerry carefully settled in behind her, his arms encircling her waist now. The reversal felt playful, intimate in the sweetest way. After restarting the engine, she revved the engine tentatively, then with growing confidence, and they pulled back onto the road. Jerry rested his chin lightly on her shoulder as she walked through the gears and tested the brakes. Slowly at first, getting the feel of the bike with Jerry behind her. Soon, he watched the landscape blur by, his heart full. This was the kind of day, the kind of life, he wanted to build—with her, always with her.

FIFTEEN

Olive pulled in next to her car and turned the bike off. The thrill at driving the motorcycle, being the one in control, still coursed through her. She'd loved the wind in her hair, the feel of Jerry's arms around her, the way she felt one with the road as they leaned into turns and corners.

Jerry slipped off the bike and helped her with the kickstand. Sad to see the evening end, she pulled the helmet off and handed it to him. A grin covered her face. "That was just incredible," she said. "I understand how people get addicted to it."

He secured her helmet to the back of the bike and slipped his off. A contented smile covered his face. "Glad you enjoyed it."

She stepped forward and framed his face with her hands. "Gerald McBride, I love you. And I love this side of you."

His eyes flared, and he pulled her closer. She eagerly met his kiss and tried to pour the love and desire she felt into it. Her arms went around his neck, and she stood on her tiptoes. She couldn't get close enough to him.

She finally ripped her mouth away. He rested his forehead against hers, his breathing fast. He put his hands on her hips and set her away from him. "We need to go for a ride more often," he said, his voice hoarse.

With a chuckle, she stepped all the way back, breaking all contact. "I don't disagree."

After pulling her purse out of the saddle bag, he handed it over to her. "See you at oh-four-thirty," he said.

"Oh-dark-thirty. Can't wait." Her lips felt swollen, and she ran her tongue over them. "Be safe getting back to post."

With a wink, he strapped his helmet back on and turned on the bike. He sat there, idling. She knew he waited for her to drive away before he left.

Olive arrived home just before 8:30 that night, thanks to light traffic for once and hitting only a few stoplights along the route. She immediately began her final packing and checking off her departure list. Not a minute after forwarding her mother her itinerary, Olive's phone rang. She grinned as she answered the video call. "Well, hello. I just emailed you."

"I saw," her mom said as she walked through her house. "You all packed?"

"Yes, ma'am. We have to be at the Nashville airport at six."

"Yikes!" Her mother sat on her front porch. Olive imagined that the late Alabama spring provided a humid blanket. "What time does the ship sail?"

"Three-thirty." She settled into her chair. "Seven beautiful days away from the hospital and the chaos."

Her mom's eyes shone from behind her glasses. "Every girl's dream." After a pause, she asked, "And how are things going with Jerry McBride?"

The kisses they'd shared tonight mingled with mental images from the last several months. She couldn't help the silly smile that accompanied the memories. Since confessing their love, she had felt a freedom of expression she had never felt before. He made her feel safe. She could see spending the rest of her life with him by her side. She wanted to spend the rest of her life with him.

But did she want that life as a soldier's wife? That would be the deal breaker. The more she thought about it, the more she went round and round in her mind about it.

Oh, but the way he made her feel. The way he filled her heart with love and desire. And the way he—

They had not once talked about a future together. They had always existed in the moment. She was just projecting. But she could dream.

And hope.

"Pretty serious." She paused. "I can see a future there."

"Is he career Army?"

She chuckled. "He's third generation career Army, Mama. Grandfather, father. And before you say anything, I know. That's been on my mind lately, too." She paused. "Although we both know how much I enjoyed the culture when I was in."

"We do." Her mom took a drink of water.

"You know, when I got out and started making plans, I

felt pressed to stay here. I just didn't know why." A grin covered her face. "I think I know why God wanted me here, now. I believe it was to meet Jerry that morning at chapel."

"We've been praying for your future husband your whole life. I have a feeling we'll finally be able to add a name to that prayer."

Heat flooded her face, and she changed the subject. "How's Irene's new job?"

"Oh, you know, having to work her way through the ins and outs. I think she'll like it more by the time summer's over."

They chatted for a few more minutes. After they hung up, she read the text message that had come in from Erin Carpenter, Calvin Brock's girlfriend. They'd been assigned the same cabin on the cruise.

She had no idea about cruise culture, but apparently, Erin did. They coordinated decorations for their door, supplies, and accoutrements that they had each packed. She bypassed Erin's nervous energy about meeting Cynthia Norton. She'd met her a few weeks ago and enjoyed the time they spent together tremendously. No one would ever know her father was the Vice President of the United States from just talking to her over tea. She knew Cynthia would prefer it if people didn't define her by her pedigree.

Olive finished writing the note for her neighbor's teenager detailing which plants got watered, on what day and where to leave the mail, then put the requested sodas in the refrigerator. She looked around the kitchen before wandering into the living room.

With all of the pre-vacation nervous energy coursing through her, she didn't think she'd sleep. So, she changed into the dress she planned to wear tomorrow, then grabbed her latest Violet Pearl mystery and curled up in her big chair.

The doorbell surprised her. She must have dozed off. As she got up, she checked her phone. 4:10! She had slept for hours.

Jerry stood on her doorstep wearing a pair of knee-length khaki shorts and a white shirt covered in red palm fronds. "Morning, soldier. You look ready for the tropics," she said, sleep clinging to her voice.

He wiggled his eyebrows. "You look like you just woke up, bed head."

"Sure did. My alarm should be going off in about five minutes." She stepped back as he walked in and gladly accepted his kiss. Then said, "I'm going to go freshen up."

"I can take your bag to the truck."

"I still need to pack my makeup bag. Give me five minutes." On her way to the bedroom, she said, "Coffee maker's prepped if you want to get that brewing."

In the bathroom, she quickly brushed her teeth, then brushed her hair and pulled it into a braid. She ran her hands down the front of her green sundress. It had handled sleeping in the chair well. After repacking her makeup bag, she tossed it into the open suitcase on her bed and zipped it shut.

When she wheeled it into the living room, she found Jerry standing near the door, a travel mug of coffee in one hand and his phone in the other. As soon as he heard her, he slipped the phone in his pocket and smiled, holding out the coffee. "Mine's still brewing. All set?"

"Yep." She traded him her suitcase for the cup, then took a sip. He had added exactly the right amount of cream. She closed her eyes, savoring the creamy brew. While he took the bag outside, she ran through a mental checklist as she entered the kitchen and grabbed his coffee cup. She rinsed everything out and wiped it all down, then met him back in the front room.

"I am so excited!" she said, slipping her tote bag handles over her shoulder. "Let's get this party started!"

"There's something I need to tell you before we go," he said.

His serious tone gave her pause. A nervous flutter started somewhere in her chest. "Okay."

"This is between you and me. You can't talk to your roommate about it. Brock told me he hadn't said anything, and he really shouldn't."

"So, unofficially," she offered.

"Let's go so far as to say hypothetically and completely off the record."

Less alarmed and more curious, she perched on the arm of the chair. "Understood."

"Phil's fiancée, Melissa? Her sister's in witness protection."

Olive raised an eyebrow. Of all of the things she might have thought would come out of his mouth, that didn't even make the long list. "Really? Do you know why?"

"I do. Can you keep a secret?"

"You know I can," she nodded.

"So can I," he answered without any additional elaboration.

"Oh, so you're funny in the early morning hours, too, are you?"

Jerry winked and took a sip of coffee. "The reason they're getting married on a cruise ship is to provide a protected and enclosed space for her sister to attend the wedding."

She quickly worked through the logistics. "Wow. That's kind of big. How did they pull it off?"

He shrugged slightly. "I don't know the details. Phil's dad's a federal judge. And Cynthia Norton will be aboard with her Secret Service detail."

Despite her sleepiness, Olive noted the understandable little snarl on Jerry's lips whenever he mentioned DHS. He continued, "Anyway, I imagine things were arranged at a very high inter-service level." He slipped his hands into the pockets of his shorts. "Between Federal Marshals and Secret Service for Norton's wife, we'll likely have several security checkpoints, and all of our events are exclusive and private."

"That's fair." She paused. He didn't move. "What else?"

He rubbed the back of his neck. "I don't know how to explain this." He let out a breath. "If something bad happens—"

She stood and put a hand on his chest. "Hey, Jerry, it's good. I can follow orders, and I don't want you to worry about me if something goes sideways. I want you to focus on what you have to do."

"I will, but we should have a plan."

She felt her head cock to the side as she considered. "Do you have a plan if something happens?"

"I do, yes."

She nodded. "Then I'll trust your plan."

After a moment, a slow grin spread across his face. "I love you, do you know that?"

"So you say," she said, stepping closer. "I love you, too, by the way."

He cupped her cheek and gave her a small kiss. "Ready to roll? Getting late."

She scoffed. "We have time for one more kiss."

Miami, Florida

Jean Desalin leaned against a conex, the night air thick with salt and diesel from the nearby Miami docks. An enormous street light painted the shipyard with a silvery light in the pre-dawn morning. The low groan of mooring lines creaking against the tide hummed in the background, punctuated by the distant clang of a loose chain

Despite the darkness, Jean wore his sunglasses in case a camera captured his face.

"What's the ship's status?" he asked in Haitian Creole as three people emerged from the shadows.

"Definitely something buzzing," René said. "The crew shifted this week. We've lost four of ours. I've never seen it happen like that."

"A VIP is coming aboard with some tight security," Marie

said. "Hao doesn't even know the details. The manifest contains no names."

"No names? How?"

Marie shrugged. "Hao said even the captain didn't know."

His mind whirled. What did this mean? The last thing he needed was his crew getting removed. "Can we proceed?"

Claude shrugged. "That gives us four to add to the island plan. Most of the manpower is there upfront. We can add them to the ship after."

Jean looked at Marie. She said, "My cover name so far has held up under scrutiny. I don't think we need to worry about my position."

"We still have two on security, which will help. And we have Hao on the bridge," Claude added.

Jean nodded and asked, "Do you believe we can truly trust Hao?"

Marie didn't even blink. "Absolutely."

Impatience crawled up Jean's neck, but he pushed it back down. Emotions could ruin this kind of careful planning. "I don't have a way to recover the money we paid to Wei. Not like he gave me a receipt. We don't have a lot of choice but to continue with the plan."

René nodded. "Wei provided his people. We have about half of them still vetted for the ship because they already worked for the company. I just don't know if we can rely on them entirely when it all goes down."

"We may not have a choice," Marie said. "This is our last chance, and our ship numbers aren't enough."

"Wei is a professional, and our success means his success," Jean said. "I'll see you in three days. Contact ends after today. René, coordinate our Chinese team. Claude, you're still lead on the island. Marie takes lead on the ship." He turned to his sister. "Use caution. Our success hinges on complete surprise."

"We know the plan."

SIXTEEN

Valiant Voyager, Port of Miami, Florida

The cruise ship Valiant Voyager sailed with much ado and fanfare. They stood on the deck and waved at the Miami dock. All around them, those who chose to toasted the port with a splash of champagne they had brought for exactly that occasion. Jerry stood in a circle with friends, trying to recall the last time they were all together.

Then it came to him. Katangela. Brass had tasked them with the straightforward mission to interfere with the ongoing reign of terror a warlord had imposed on the tribal communities there. The mission took a turn when the then Vice President passed away, and Cynthia's father took over the office. Cynthia had been serving the locals as a missionary doctor when the warlords took her hostage. Suddenly, the clear path became a very crooked road through a dangerous jungle. They had succeeded in all their objectives, but Bill "Drumstick" Sanders and Phil "Ozzy" Osbourne had come home with bullet wounds and one less limb.

As the cruise ship's horn blared and pulled away from the dock, they all gathered near the railing, shoulders brushing, their laughter cutting through the sea breeze. In deference to the civilian crowd around them, no one mentioned past missions, but their glances—quick, knowing, crinkling at the edges, sometimes accompanied by shallow nods of respect—spoke of shared secrets only they understood.

In all, eight of the original team had come, not counting him and Osbourne. He knew that spoke volumes about Phil Osbourne's reputation and their admiration for him as a person.

Jerry caught sight of Waller standing alone at the railing. Osbourne had gone to school with Timothy Waller in Texas. Waller had medevacked Osbourne out of the Jungle, and Waller later moved into Osbourne's slot on the team, so Bourbon was here, too, even though they had never directly served together on the team. Leanne clearly occupied the man's thoughts.

Someone slapped Jerry on the back, and he turned to find the groom. "Jerry Maguire in the flesh. Know something? You complete me."

Osbourne looked good. He had joy in his eyes and sported a healthy tan. Jerry looked him up and down, from the toe of the shoe covering the end of his prosthetic leg to the cap he wore over his blond hair, announcing his status as the groom.

"Well, there he is," Jerry said, pulling Osbourne close for a hug. "I wondered if you'd missed the boat."

"Been on board for a minute. Was helping out with some of the details."

In a crowd like this, mentioning his fiancée's sister and her witness protection status would lack prudence. "Understood." He shifted and pulled Olive closer, leaving his hand resting on her hip. "I'd like you to meet Olive. Olive, Phil Osbourne, aka Ozzy."

The smile lit up her face as she took his hand with both of hers. "We've actually met. Back in Germany, when you brought Jerry in with that arm thing."

Osbourne studied her face and declared, "I remember you. He was flirting pretty hard with you back then, as I recall."

"Well, can you blame him?" Olive chuckled. "Anyway, I've heard a lot about you since then."

"Really? Probably lies. Mostly lies." He shot Jerry a sideways glance. "I'd love to sit down and hear what he had to say. In exchange, I promise to tell you some stories about a young Jerry Maguire that are guaranteed to curl your hair."

An announcement interrupted their conversation. "Good afternoon, everyone, this is your Cruise Director! Welcome aboard our 7-day adventure! Kick off the fun today at 5:00 PM with a dazzling magic show in the Grand Theater, or join our shuffleboard showdown on Deck 12 at

5:30 PM. Don't miss our live band performing at 8:00 PM in the Ocean Lounge! A quick note: on day 4, all passengers must disembark between 7:00 AM and 11:00 AM to spend the entire day enjoying our private island while the crew conducts mandatory training and safety drills. Check your newsletter for details. Let's make today amazing!"

As soon as the ship's crew cleared them to find their quarters, their group navigated to the passage with their cabins. Everyone in their party occupied the same passage, except Rick and Cynthia Norton, who had a VIP suite on the upper deck, and Osbourne's family, who settled into a spacious family suite. Jerry and Calvin "Hobbes" Brock claimed rooms across the hall from Erin and Olive. Most of the team in one area gave him a sense of security that helped belie the fact that they were unarmed and surrounded by a thousand people. He also liked that, with Olive's room just across the hall, he could hear her if something happened and she needed him.

"How much time do you need?" he asked as they paused at their doors.

Olive looked up at him, the excitement of embarking making her green eyes shine, and the ring in his pocket suddenly felt like it weighed a ton. He prayed this evening might give him the perfect moment. "Unpacking won't take long."

Bill Sanders pressed by them. "Can't stand boats. This is why I never joined the Navy. We're going to be huddled together like sardines in this tin can," he said.

He held his wife Lynda's hand. She chuckled. "At least

we won't smell like it," she said.

They stopped at the door next to Jerry's. Lynda turned toward them as Bill unlocked their door. "Are you two decorating?"

Erin's black curls bounced with her nod. "Yep. You?"

"Of course! Much to his dismay," she said with a grin.

"What does that mean?" Bill growled as he pushed the suitcase into the room. "I don't mind your frilly, girly ways, woman."

Jerry shook his head. "I'll be five minutes. I can help."

Olive brushed her lips against his. He tasted the salt air. "Looking forward to it."

Jerry tossed his bag on the bed and examined his surroundings. The room had two twin beds, a desk, and a shower that a grown man might fit into if he held his breath just right and left one foot outside.

"Beats Mogadishu," Brock said as he neatly lined a dresser drawer with perfectly folded shirts. "Remember those conexes? I don't know why they thought four of us would fit in one."

"Good times," Jerry said, remembering the extreme heat, the cramped quarters, and the bomb that detonated their fourth night there. He'd had a lot of opportunities to feel terror while performing his job over the years, but that night, as a burning beam pinned him and burned him, topped a lot of them. He pulled his shower kit out of his bag. "Anything's better than Mogadishu. Nobody shooting at us here, though I've heard there will be sand."

"Always with the sand."

They enjoyed the rapport as they unpacked. They left their cabin door open and listened to their friends coming and going down the corridor. He couldn't believe Osbourne's family had gone through such care and expense to bring his people to him.

About ten minutes later, he heard Olive's voice in the hall. He wandered to the door and watched Erin hang a banner spelling out "Bon Voyage" at the top of the door.

"What's the purpose?" he asked.

She grinned over her shoulder at him. "One, so you know which room is yours." She gestured down the hall. "Everything looks the same."

He raised an ironic eyebrow and tossed a thumb over his shoulder toward the number on his cabin door. She laughed. "Yeah, yeah."

Olive slipped by her and held out a cardboard anchor. "Want to put this on your door?"

He looked at the anchor, then looked into her eyes. "Is no an acceptable response?"

Bill stood across the hall from his door while his wife swooped a banner of colorful pom poms across the top of his door. "Does 'no' look like an acceptable response," he asked, "because this is what I get."

Olive chuckled and pulled it back. "'No' works." She fastened it to her own door. "You can be a boring old grumpy landlubber."

"Boring is my favorite when I'm on vacation." He looked at his watch. "Ready for a walk before dinner?"

"Sure." She stepped back and looked at the result. Blue

and white anchors, ropes, and ship's wheels covered the door in fun patterns. "Looks great," she said.

He suddenly thought of his mother and her long tradition of decorating doors for special occasions. Olive looked just as delighted as his mother or Mabel ever had.

Olive patted her dress pocket and said, "I have my key."

He stepped forward and held out his hand. "Let's get the lay of the ship, shall we?"

As the cruise ship's gentle sway rocked her cabin, Olive slipped a yellow dress from its hanger, the silk cool against her fingers. It fell to the tops of her white sandals, each peppered with cute little yellow leather daisies across the toes. After fastening the daisy earrings, she twirled before the mirror, heels clicking on the polished floor. Each night this week, she planned to slip on a beautiful dress, pairing earrings with flowing skirts or tailored jackets. She loved the idea of dressing for dinner.

"You look terrific," Erin said. She came out of the bathroom in a red dress that fell just above the knee. Her dark skin shimmered under the glittery lotion she'd applied. She wore a large necklace with a rhinestone hummingbird sipping from a red rhinestone flower.

"Not quite as shiny as you," Olive replied. "You look gorgeous."

"You know it, queen." She grabbed her purse from the bed and slipped her key card into it. "Let's go see if the men think so. Maybe we can elevate their heartrates."

Olive's time in the Army had broken down any intimidation presented by sharing close quarters with virtual strangers, but she had still felt a touch of apprehension, hoping her personality would mesh with theirs. With Erin, she already felt like they were old friends. It also helped to room with someone who had several cruises under her belt. It removed a lot of the fear of the unknown.

Jerry and Calvin waited for them in the passageway. Jerry wore a pair of khaki pants and a blue-and-white striped shirt that he'd left open at the collar. When he saw her, his eyes lit up, and a slow smile spread across his face. As he looked her up and down, her heart beat a bit faster, and a flush started somewhere deep inside her chest. He whistled under his breath and said, "Remind me to take you to more places that require dressing up," he said. "You look beautiful."

"Thank you," she said. She whirled around and then lifted her foot. "Do you like my shoes?"

He stared at them and dryly said, "They're, without a doubt, the most amazing shoes out of all the amazing shoes I've ever seen in my entire life."

She threw her head back and laughed. "You barely looked at them."

"The woman wearing those amazing shoes is much more interesting to look at."

She snorted. "Well, the cool thing about these shoes is that I bought them for two dollars at a thrift store. Then I found not one but two dresses that match them perfectly.

That makes me a winner." She winked and slipped her hand into his. "I'm also starving."

He brought their joined hands to his mouth and brushed a kiss over her knuckles. "Me, too."

They had wandered the ship's labyrinthine decks for a solid forty-five minutes, scribbling notes on a folded map—here a bustling buffet hall, there a sun-drenched pool deck, over there a neon lit gym pulsing with distant thuds. But the clock's relentless tick forced them back to the cabin for quick changes, vast swaths of corridors and decks and theaters still unexplored.

They held hands as they navigated through the ship, heading to the banquet room Phil's parents had reserved for their evening meal. At a juncture, Jerry paused and gestured to the door that would take them to the deck.

"Want to watch the sun set before we go in for dinner?"

"Oh, I do," she replied. They left Calvin and Erin in the passageway and went outside. The warm breeze brushed her bare shoulders. "I don't know why I expected a chill in the tropics," she said. "I'm glad it's so nice."

"Me, too." He drew her close, her back nestling against his chest, his arms a warm anchor around her. To the west, the sky unfurled like a painter's canvas, awash in violet and tangerine, the colors deepening, shimmering, as the sun kissed the horizon's edge. A salty breeze carried the ocean's sigh. The sun—a molten orb—slipped below the sea, its final rays making their entire world glow red and pink.

"Incredible," she said, turning to face him. She cupped

his cheek with her hand and pressed her lips to his, enjoying the feel of his beard beneath her palm.

He pulled her closer, and she wrapped her arms around his neck, pressing against him. As he gentled the kiss, he put his hands on her hips and took a step back. She looked up at him, seeing the same love and desire she felt mirrored back.

His eyes searched her face, then suddenly turned serious. "Would you ever want to leave Clarksville?"

Nervous butterflies began dancing in her stomach. Suddenly, all of the apprehension she'd felt at the possibility of shifting roles from serving soldier to soldier's wife disappeared. She knew now she very much wanted that. "Depends on whose asking," she said, "and where we're going."

He took another slight step back and brought her left hand up to his mouth, brushing his lips across the knuckles. "My mom had a sign she hung up in every home at every duty station. It read, 'Home is where the Army sends you.'"

In her time in the Army, she'd lived in North Carolina, Germany, and Kentucky. She imagined a thirty-year career would come with many more duty stations than that. "I would think home is wherever we are."

As the sun dipped lower, leaving behind the darkening purple and orange, Jerry whispered, "Close your eyes, Olive."

She happily complied, looking forward to whatever treat he had in mind this time. Shock ran through her entire body when he slipped a ring onto her left ring finger. She could feel the weight, but when her eyes flew open, she didn't even glance at it. Instead, she kept her eyes locked with his. She didn't need to look at anything except his beautiful eyes.

"I never thought I would ever find anyone who could understand my life and what I do for a living. The last few months have shown me that God has always known there was someone for me. He had a plan for us. I know it. I love you. Marry me, Olive Duncan. Let's make our home together, wherever the Army takes us."

Nothing in her heart or mind told her to say anything but yes. She barely had the word out before she stepped back into his arms with a kiss that felt so much more than before. As he broke the kiss, he wrapped her in his arms, and they stood like that for several minutes, watching the sky turn from indigo to black.

"I guess we should join the party," he said, his voice vibrating in his chest.

"That *is* why we're here." She looked up at him. Surely his arms around her kept her from floating away in sheer bliss. "I'm still starving anyway."

"Me too." He laughed and stepped back, then took her hand, and they strolled to the private event room. Back in the light, Olive raised her hand and admired the round-cut diamond winking back at her. It sparkled, dazzled, and danced, elevating and enhancing the jubilation she felt in her heart.

Two men in suits stood at the door with briefcases on

the deck beside them. One held a scanner. Jerry froze, tensed up a bit, and studied them, his eyelids lowering slightly and his jaw tightening. Then, he slowly held out his left wrist so he could scan the cruise bracelet. Olive followed his lead, and as soon as they scanned them, the Secret Service agents from DHS opened the door for them.

Inside, the expansive windows reflected the crystal chandelier back into the room. The intimate space shimmered with elegance. Ivory linens draped six round tables, each adorned with low bouquets of roses and eucalyptus, their delicate petals kissed by flickering candlelight. Gold-embossed place cards, tied with satin ribbons, sat in front of already plated salads. A welcome sign proclaimed "Love Sets Sail" in graceful script, framed by Phil Osbourne and Melissa's story in photographs. The air hummed with acoustic melodies, weaving through the laughter and clinking glasses, as the room embraced the gathering with warmth.

Jerry kept his hand on the small of Olive's back, lightly guiding her as they walked through the room. She had met most of the men in his unit at one point in time or another, and had spent time with some of them, so she didn't feel too out of place. She loved the way he relaxed, the way he laughed and smiled, and the way he shook hands and slapped shoulders. She could see the love and respect he had for the men in the room, and they for him.

About fifty people mingled, sipping sparkling lemonade and munching on the hors d'oeuvres the wait staff offered from silver platters. Soon Phil Osbourne tapped his fork against his glass and said, "Dinner is served. Please find your tables."

They worked their way to their assigned table. She recognized Lynda and Bill Sanders. Lynda wore a dark blue dress with a simple cross necklace. "Hello," Olive said as she sat down. "Love what you did with your door."

Lynda smiled and rubbed Bill's shoulders. "That makes one of you."

Jerry gestured to the other couple at their table. He wore a tan suit. She wore a deep emerald green silk abaya with gold embroidery along the cuffs and neckline. A matching hijab, pinned neatly with a pearl brooch, framed her face.

"You've met Abe, but I don't think you know his wife."

Jared "Honest Abe" Ibrahim nodded and said, "It's good to see you again. This is Rania."

Rania's warm smile lit up her eyes. She extended a graceful hand. "It's so nice to meet you at last," she said, her voice soft yet sincere.

Lynda patted Ibrahim on his shoulder. "We were married once, Abe and I."

Jared nodded. "Yes. It's true. Until my appendix got the better of me."

"Then you condescended to marry me," Bill said, wiggling his black eyebrows and pulling her closer.

Olive smiled at Rania. "It's nice to meet you as well."

Jerry leaned in and spoke softly. "Undercover op. I'll tell you about it later."

"But, aren't Bill and Lynda married?" She had seen that

they shared the same cabin, and they wore rings.

Jerry chuckled. "Yeah. Now they are. There was this undercover op where they faked it first, though."

Bill watched Olive take a drink from her water and raised an eyebrow. "Speaking of wives, got something to share, Jerry Maguire?"

Lynda saw her hand and smiled, bringing her hands together. "Oh, how exciting!"

Heat fused Olive's cheeks. "I think we'll let the couple of the hour take the spotlight for now," she said. "Our time will come."

Jerry picked her hand up and kissed the knuckle near the ring. "It certainly will."

SEVENTEEN

Jerry settled back against his chair in the promenade lounge, listening to Fisher grumble into his laptop. Sanders nudged his elbow. "What's he doing?"

Jerry pointed at the Cybertruck sitting in front of the casino, about fifty yards down the promenade. Apparently, it could be won by signing up for an unwanted membership in the casino. "Some guy he knows from a hacking course he went to a few months ago dared him. Said he couldn't hack into it."

Fisher paused and looked at him, narrowing his eyes. "Certified Ethical Hacker course. He was the class leader, and I was the senior NCO. He's never outdone me. He's not going to this time."

"Memaw never did say I was the smartest person in the room," Sanders said, opening the lid of his soda. "Certified, eh? Hysterical."

"You say that now," Fisher said, "but assume your

infrastructure goes down—because some bad actor got into the system—and those of us with training don't exist. You'd be the first to complain about your warm soda pop." With that, Fisher hit the ENTER key and raised an eyebrow as the lights on the truck turned on.

"Well, heck yeah, I would be." He shuddered. "Who'd want to drink a warm soda? Heaven forbid."

A ship-wide announcement interrupted their jovial conversation. "Hello, passengers, this is your Activities Coordinator! Ready for some fun? Join us at 1:00 PM for a comedy juggling act on the Lido Deck, or test your skills at our 4:00 PM trivia challenge in the Starlight Lounge. Shuffleboard fans, meet us on Deck 12 at 5:30 PM!"

"Shuffleboard, anyone?" Jerry chuckled and shook his head. He popped a peanut into his mouth, its salty, roasted crunch grounding him amid the sprawl of stories, chased by the faint, caramel fizz of his soda.

Swanson arrived and grabbed a chair from an empty table. "Pot Pie," Sanders said, "What's the good word, brother?"

"Daddy and Peña will be here momentarily. Ozzy too. He's meeting with the chaplain's assistant right now." The waitress appeared, and he ordered a sparkling water before directing his attention back to the group.

"Found a skeet shooting game in the arcade," Jerry said. "Sites are way off, though."

Yet another announcement interrupted them. "Hello again, passengers. Just a friendly reminder: on day 4, everyone must disembark between 7:00 AM and 11:00 AM for our private island visit while the crew completes essential drills and maintenance. See your newsletter for more. Have a fantastic day!"

Sanders said, "If they keep doing that every few minutes, I will find it mighty tedious."

"You know, there was a time," Brock said, "when you could shoot actual skeet with an actual firearm right from the deck."

"No kidding?" Jerry shook his head. "The way security screened us when we boarded, I can't imagine them allowing that these days."

Sanders said, "I think it was more on account of the broken skeet and buckshot littering the ocean could hurt the fish and such."

Jerry said, "So, not an issue that people would have live ammo and firearms then?"

"Whatever. But there's ways they could have done it. Just like ranges, you know? Laser shots instead of birdshot. Skeet made of fish food." Sanders rubbed his chin. "I mean, if it hasn't been invented yet..."

"Get on that in all your spare time, partner," Swanson said. "Don't you worry about a thing. I'll handle our caseload."

Daniel Swanson and Bill Sanders had formed a private security company, utilizing the many skills they'd acquired during their time in the Special Forces. Brock chuckled. "You guys busy?"

"Dude. The second y'all get out, you need to come see us. We have so much work, and there are just some things that we can't handle." He gestured at Fisher. "Like our boy here. I could use him nine ways to Sunday and still have work piled up."

Jerry shook his head. "Not getting out any time soon."

Swanson said, "Going for that third rocker, are you?"

"I want it. I need it," Jerry grinned. "The SFC rank is just so unbalanced with three up and two down. Now, the Master Sergeant rank... that three up three down? The only thing more perfect is to slap a diamond right in the bullseye."

Fisher glanced up from his screen only briefly. "Private sector is on my list in seven more years. Oh, you little..." he started typing furiously. "Ah-ha!" He ripped his hat off and pointed at someone across the wide promenade. "Got you, Heisman!"

A dark-haired and very tall, very blond, and very muscular man stood and strolled across the carpeted floor, laughing. He looked like a bodybuilder or a linebacker. When he got to their table, Jerry had to crane his neck to look up at him. How tall was he? Six-seven? "Well done, Trout."

Jerry looked at the Cybertruck. It had rolled forward about two feet. "Did you just—?"

"I did. Lights are too easy. Automated self-driving system? That takes *actual* skill." Two ship security guards approached the Cybertruck, clearly expecting to find someone inside. The tall man twitched his chin in their direction and observed, "They look so confused."

Fisher gestured at him. "Captain Chase Anderson, meet my team. Swanson, McBride, Sanders, and Brock."

Anderson shook hands with each one. "Nice to meet

you all. Heard some stories.”

Fisher gestured at him. “Chase’s with 11th Cyber at Schofield Barracks.”

“Nice,” Jerry said. “My dad was stationed there when I was a kid.” A memory surfaced of Sunday services at the beach, waves crashing against jagged rocks as the preacher’s voice carried over the breeze. Mabel giggling as she played in the sand with her Beach Barbie. A wave of warm nostalgia hit him, tinged with a sudden pang of missing his mother.

“We enjoy it. I’m ready to get back to the lower forty-eight, though.” He pointed across the promenade. “My wife is hoping for Meade next.”

“Busy area,” Swanson said. “Baltimore isn’t Northern Virginia, but it’s close. I think I’d choose somewhere else.”

“Well, some things have to be experienced to fully understand,” Anderson said. “And Vi likes the easy trip to Manhattan from there. She regularly goes.”

Brock pushed his hat back on his head and scratched his temple. “I’m from the Bronx. I’m happy to be stationed in Kentucky.”

“I bet,” Anderson said, a grin stretching across his face. “But I’m looking forward to not having to fly six hours just to get started on a trip.”

“Fair enough.” Jerry gestured at a chair. “Would you like to join us?”

He shook his head. “I’m with my wife. But we’d love to get together.”

“Violet’s with you?” Fisher asked. “How is the world’s

most famous novelist these days?"

Anderson grinned. "I don't know about all that, but this is her trip. She's here on a writing retreat with a bunch of other authors."

Fisher laughed. "So you're just strap-hanging?"

Anderson nodded, "I'm Mr. Violet Pearl, so yeah. Free cruise? I'm in. Maybe we can do lunch?"

Jerry glanced at Swanson, who knew the schedule for the wedding events. The way his friend could keep those kinds of details straight should be considered a superpower. Swanson nodded, so Jerry said, "Lunch is perfect."

After Anderson rejoined his wife, Fisher shut the lid of his laptop. "Solid man there. His wife is Violet Pearl. She writes those Mandalyn Clementine mysteries."

Jerry mentally pictured the book Olive read on the plane. "Olive reads those."

"I've read every one of them," Swanson said. "Chase Anderson. I recognize the name. Didn't he play for A&M?"

Jerry shook his head. "Everything I know about college football is nothing."

"Communist," Sanders teased.

Jerry raised an eyebrow. "Since everyone knows *baseball* is America's pastime, remind me, Drumstick. Who won the World Series last year?"

Sanders shrugged. "If it ain't the Braves, who cares?"

Jerry shrugged. "Braves are my favorite team whenever they play the Yankees. Actually, my favorite team is whoever plays the Yankees."

Brock said, "So you like all the losing teams, Maguire?"

Swanson persisted, "Anderson was a legacy player, right?"

"I think so," Sanders said. "I think he played the same years I did. We never played against each other, but he always made the news because his father played for the Eagles in the Super Bowl, so they made a big deal of him."

"He's brilliant behind a keyboard," Fisher said. "He's probably forgotten more than I've ever learned about hacking. Guy can subnet in his head. Probably dreams in code."

Swanson snorted. "Since you're just about the smartest guy I've ever met, that's saying a lot."

Fisher's cheeks turned red, but he was saved from replying by Peña and Norton's arrival. "Ozzy will be here in a minute," Peña said. "Then we can decide what we want to do next."

"I'm good with doing this," Sanders said, sticking his legs out and tossing a peanut into the air, which he caught in his open mouth. "There's worse ways to spend an afternoon."

"It's good to just sit and be able to talk guy talk," Brock agreed. "Seems like there's always business getting in the way."

The group spent the next hour catching up. Osbourne and his father joined them, and the conversation turned to the Category 5 hurricane that hit Miami during Thanksgiving a year ago. "It was pretty bad," Osbourne said. "I've been in some storms, but cat five is something special."

"Well, you were busy, too," Norton said.

Osbourne nodded and smiled sheepishly. "That I was."

Osbourne spent the night the hurricane hit Miami protecting the shelter Melissa ran for battered men and women from a drug cartel that took an interest in one of her tenants. In the middle of the hurricane, the cartel bore down on them, leaving Osbourne alone to defend it. He used his honed Special Forces skills to single-handedly protect Melissa and her sister from eight other men.

"With salt shot, no less," Jerry said. "I'm sure it would have been nice to have actual buckshot or, you know, anything better. Anything at all."

"Well," Sanders drawled, taking a pull of his soda, "it's not about the ammo, it's how you use it."

Jerry shook his head. "Sometimes it's just about the ammo, bro. *Carpe munitionem*. Seize the ammo."

Everyone laughed and listened as Osbourne told the story, answering questions and adding anecdotes. "Long night," Osbourne said casually. "It was good to see the sun come up. But the city's still recovering, and it's been eighteen months."

Olive curled in the corner of the couch and listened to Melissa and her sister chatter about life. In the suite's kitchen, Phil's mom, Candace, and Cynthia Norton filled platters with fruit and sandwiches. She looked around the room, at the woman who had joined their party.

Olive had to run the gauntlet of Secret Service agents and US Marshals before entering the suite. She had arrived last despite arriving fifteen minutes early.

Lynda Sanders handed her a water bottle and slipped into the chair next to her. "How are you?"

"Good," she said, twisting the lid off. "I've enjoyed getting to know everyone."

"I've met most of these women over the years," Lynda said, looking around the room. "Except Erin and Lola. They're new to me. I think Brock is going to have his hands full with Erin."

"Erin's been great," Olive said, nudging her friend. Erin paused in talking to Rania and looked over at her. "She's the cruising master."

"My mom loves cruising," Erin said as she fiddled with the wristband and looked at the spiral staircase that led up to the bedrooms. "Ever since my dad passed, I've been her go-to partner. I've never been in one of the suites, though. This is really nice."

"It is," Cynthia said. "We're in a balcony suite, but it's not as big as this. I do have two bedrooms, because of the detail, but it's certainly not so grand."

Olive looked around, noting all the closed doors. "Compared to our cabin, it's huge."

"There are only two of these on this particular ship," Candace said. "We were blessed to get it. I really didn't want to try to plan and produce a wedding from a stateroom."

"You guys have been so generous," Olive said, "Thank you again for this trip."

"It's our pleasure. Phil and Melissa are precious to us." For a moment, tears filled her eyes. Olive knew she must be thinking about her son who was killed. "Doing it on a cruise ship was a great idea. The Marshals suggested it."

Melissa joined the conversation. "We appreciate everyone coming. I told Phil I would be fine with eloping, but he knew his mom wanted a ceremony, and he surprised me with the work he put into figuring out how to get my sister here."

Olive remembered the briefing at the opening dinner. They couldn't ask her new name or where she lived. And they weren't to mention her children. "It's wonderful."

Candace set a tray of sandwiches on the table. "I think having the Secret Service here with Cynthia helps. The Marshals were acting a bit nervous, even though it was their idea."

Cynthia, who apparently overheard, snorted. "It nearly took an act of Congress to get approved to be here. I wish I was kidding."

"I'm sure it's fine," Rania said. "The security getting aboard seemed a little over the top."

"It's always like that," Erin confirmed. "Very thorough. Are you guys going ashore in the morning?"

Olive shook her head. "Jerry's cool staying aboard. I don't really want to go without him."

Cynthia came all the way into the room after setting the fruit on the table. "Rick said he had no interest in getting off the ship. I've been to the Bahamas before on a mission trip. I'm good with not."

Erin nodded. "I've been so many times. Right off the ship, it's mostly tourist things. And the vendors can be a little aggressive. Past that, it's not such a great neighborhood in any direction, if you know what I mean."

Lynda chuckled. "I'd love to see Bill deal with some aggressive vendors just one time. By the time he would get done talking to them, they wouldn't know if they should be selling or buying."

Cynthia gave a half-smile, staring back at some private memory. "That's because he'd read who they are deep in their souls within a second of speaking to them. He uses that against them."

Lynda nodded and grinned. "Oh my, yes. It's definitely a gift he has." She shook her head. "Then he speaks with that slow drawl, and they underestimate his intellect, and it's all over from there."

Olive chuckled. "I'll remember that when I'm talking to him."

"Oh, it's far too late," Lynda drawled. "He's already figured you out. You can ask him to sum up his analysis of you if you want."

Emma interjected, "I spent years conspiring with Bill. I do miss him in the field." Emma said. "He's brilliant at reading faces, knowing lies and truth."

Olive turned to Emma. "It fascinates me that you can do what you do."

"Yeah, if I thought about it too much, I probably would feel the same." She brushed her dark hair off her face. "But the more I do it, the better I get at it."

"Where are you from?" Lynda asked Olive. "I definitely can hear the Alabama."

"Mobile. Just north of Mobile."

"Thought so."

"But I love living in Clarksville."

"Oh, nice area," Lynda said. "We were there right before Bill got out."

"Yeah, I got out of the Army at Campbell and stayed. Definitely nice to have four distinct seasons."

The women chatted and celebrated the bride. At one point, they moved into the dining area and fixed plates of lunch. Olive piled her plate high with fruit and cheese. She sat down again as she popped a chunk of pineapple into her mouth. The ripe sweetness of pineapple burst on her tongue with the first bite, juicy and sun-kissed.

Melissa spoke up once everyone had a plate.

"I appreciate all you ladies being here. Our guys are so close and such a strong force together that I had hoped we would become friends, too. The more I speak to each of you, the more I'm discovering you all are my sisters as much as our men are brothers." She held up her lemonade. "This party is for you. Something to give you a quiet moment away from the crowds and a chance to get to know your sisters without our men."

They chatted and ate lunch, and the longer Olive spent in the company of the women, the more at home she felt. This group didn't even flinch at the idea of her being a veteran, of her time spent serving. They embraced that about her and shared their own stories and experiences.

She listened to Cynthia recount her story of a harrowing escape from the jungles of Katangela and Lynda's fake marriage to Bill on a mission in Istanbul. Emma talked about the time terrorists took her prisoner and how the entire time she knew Jorge would find her. Melissa and Lola shared the story about the hurricane in Miami and how Phil had protected them against the cartel members. She knew she was with women who could think like her, love like her, and pray like her.

Long after lunch, she looked at her watch. "I guess we should start getting ready for the evening," Olive said. "Jerry and I have plans to go see a show."

"Oh, we are, too," Emma said, setting her plate in the sink. "We can walk together so we'll sit next to each other."

She hugged her new friends and some old ones, then walked out of the suite with Emma. She and Jerry had made plans to meet outside of their rooms at three. She rubbed her thumb over the large round diamond on the new ring on her finger.

EIGHTEEN

After a full day on the water, they woke up in port at Nassau, Bahamas. Most of the group met for breakfast, securing a large section of the dining room. Olive and Jerry sat across from Phil Osbourne and Melissa. Jerry nodded at Swanson as he sat across from Ibrahim and his wife, then turned his attention to Osbourne.

"Are you two going to play tourists today?" he asked, spearing a melon cube with his fork.

Osbourne leaned back and slipped his arm over the back of Melissa's chair. "We live in Miami, brother. We can get a tropical tourist city vibe any time we want."

Olive chuckled. "I've always wondered what people who live in tourist towns do when they go on vacation."

Melissa took a sip of her coffee. "We know what not to do, mostly." She set her cup back in the saucer. "It was so good to spend yesterday morning with you."

"Same," Olive answered. "I suddenly wish Kentucky

wasn't so far from Miami." She spread cream cheese on a piece of toasted bagel and topped it with some smoked salmon. "What are your actual plans, if you're staying on board?"

"We're going to finalize everything for tomorrow. We have a little bit of coordinating to do today. And I'm going to spend as much time with Lola as possible."

Olive swallowed the bite and then wiped her lips with her napkin. "It must be hard to be so separated from her."

Melissa sat forward and grabbed Olive's hand, inspecting the ring. "How did I miss this yesterday?" she gasped. "Have you made any specific plans yet?"

Osbourne raised an eyebrow and looked at Jerry, who shrugged nonchalantly. "No."

Osbourne said, "You sneaky sniper, you."

"We decided to get through your wedding before we started talking about ours," Jerry said. "I'd be happy with an elopement next weekend."

Heat filled Olive's cheeks. "Oh yeah?" She leaned into him, and he hugged her against him. "I wouldn't say no to that. Maybe the ship's Captain can marry us."

Osbourne chuckled. "I approve of an elopement," he said, "especially after seeing the bill from the cruise line."

"Oh, please," Melissa said, "like that mattered to your parents."

Olive looked over at Jerry. The glow of happiness on her face filled his chest. He squeezed the back of her neck. "I didn't want to wait another second."

"Don't blame you," Osbourne said. He held up his orange

juice. "To love and forever."

Olive considered Jerry's suggestion to elope next week. She wondered what her family would say if she just announced that she'd gotten married. Her mom and her sister would have a fit. Maybe she and Jerry could just elope, and then they could throw a party in Mobile? But the more she thought about it, the more she thought about Mabel and how much she wanted Jerry's sister to be a part of a ceremony. She needed to talk to him about that.

After the toast, Olive said, "Seriously, though. I doubt Jerry wants to wander around an island. We're here for you."

"We appreciate the offer," Osbourne said. "My mother is the task master. We're supposed to go to her suite at eleven."

Rick set his tray on the next table over. "Morning, everyone."

"Daddy," Jerry said, knowing how much Rick hated that name outside of the times they wore the uniform. "Looks like you got some sun yesterday. Your freckles are redder."

Rick cut his eyes to Jerry. "Unlike some of the other folks here enjoying this venture, you still work for me."

Jerry bit the inside of his lip to keep from laughing. "Sir, yes, sir."

Cynthia placed her tray next to her husband and settled into her chair. "Good morning. Isn't the view stunning?" Jerry looked out at the shimmering turquoise waters of Nassau port.

"Quite striking."

Cynthia tilted her head as she looked at her husband.

"Looking at your burn with the full light, I'm thinking you should avoid the sun today."

"That right?" He drained his water glass. "You'd think with as much time as I spend outside, this wouldn't have happened."

"Closer to the equator. Sun's stronger. Plus you were hatless." Cynthia spread her napkin in her lap.

"You've clearly never had the sun reflect off the Sahara's sand right into your eyes."

"You've never seen how red you are when you come home from some undisclosed desert," Cynthia said. Then she winked at her husband and looked to Melissa. "How can I help?"

"You've done so much already with your dad's help with my sister," Melissa said. "Relax. Enjoy the downtime with your husband. I have a feeling you don't get a lot of that."

Cynthia rubbed her hand over Rick's shoulders. "True. We might find some shade and play some chess or something."

"Is that what you kids are calling it these days?" Sanders asked, slipping his tray onto the table and taking the seat across from Cynthia. "I mean, I'm down with that vernacular. What exactly is castling? Is that when the knight jumps the queen?"

Laughter rippled through the group. "Morning, Lynda," Cynthia said. "How was the movie last night?"

Lynda picked up her knife to butter her toast. "I enjoyed it. But it triggered something with Bill. I guess modern war movies play with some of his memories. He didn't sleep well."

Jerry remembered a nightmare he had after watching *Black Hawk Down*. "I feel that, bro."

Sanders cleared his throat, and his cheeks turned red. Jerry continued, opening the door for Sanders to regain some footing. "Want to talk about it? I hear Melissa's a pretty good counselor."

"Hush your mouth, Jerry Maguire, 'fore I stitch it shut like a hog's ear." He took a long drink of his cola. When he set it down, the flush had cleared his face, and he looked more relaxed. "We're not venturing out today. Thought we'd enjoy some of this here ship's amenities without the crowds."

They chatted about their plans as more of their friends arrived for breakfast. Soon, they filled their corner of the dining room. At one point, Jerry leaned toward Osbourne. "This was a good idea. Not only for the reasons you did it, but because of this. If we were all just in hotels in Miami, we wouldn't have this."

"Yeah." Osbourne looked around them. Jerry could see the raw emotion on his face. "You guys are my family. In a way, I wish we could freeze this in time."

Lynda leaned over her husband to talk to Cynthia. "Is tonight your Captain's dinner?"

Cynthia shifted her empty plate away and said, "Yes. Phil's parents will be there, too."

"The DVs among us," Sanders said. "I bet the Captain looked at the roster and had a panic attack about a federal judge and VPOTUS's daughter on board at the same time."

Norton shook his head. "None of our names are on any itinerary. We're all incognito."

Melissa nodded. "That was part of the negotiations with the cruise line."

"Then how did they know who to invite to the Captain's table?" Olive asked.

"State Department gave them our VIP statuses." Cynthia's cheeks turned red. "I long for the days when that is no longer my identity."

"It only is in official channels, my love," Rick said. "To us, you're either mom, wife, or free medical care."

Lynda nodded. "Bill appreciates your skills."

"My heart belongs to you," Sanders said. He tossed his napkin. "Literally."

Jerry could see the amusement on Olive's face, even though he felt his own muscles tighten with tension. "You know that story?"

"Yeah, Cynthia told us yesterday."

Sanders narrowed his eyes. "What else did y'all talk about?"

Lynda propped her chin in her hands and looked sideways at her husband. "Oh, you know, all of the things. Just girl talk."

Olive fit in. He'd hoped she would, of course, but as he watched her tease Sanders and chat with Lynda, certainty chased away his doubts bit by bit. These were his people, lifetime friends as close as family, and she could claim them as hers, too.

He put his arm over her shoulders and leaned close to her ear. The smell of her strawberry shampoo teased his nose. "Want to go somewhere just the two of us?"

She shot a glance in his direction. "Sure. Do I need to get my bag?"

"I don't necessarily want to leave the ship." He shook his head. Almost as an afterthought, he asked, "Do you?"

"Not particularly." She looked back at Melissa and Phil Osbourne. "Enjoy your prep time. Let us know if we can do anything for you."

Melissa shot her a bright smile. "We have all hands on deck. You enjoy today. Tomorrow we'll occupy all of your time."

After saying their goodbyes, they walked hand-in-hand out of the dining room. Olive leaned into his arm. "Where to?"

He did a quick mental survey of what he knew of the ship. "That lunch cafe should be empty."

"Sounds good. My room is, too. Erin and Calvin had plans this morning."

"Rather cramped quarters," he said. "Not really anywhere to sit."

She thought of the desk chair and the beds. No other surfaces. "True."

They strolled down the passageway and through glass doors that swished open for them. A faint, mingled trace of chlorine from the nearby pools and fried dough from the arcade wafted through.

Two more turns and they found themselves in an empty pizza and ice cream cafe. He knew it would fill up in a couple of hours with teenagers and kids.

They settled at a two-top table. Olive propped her chin in her hand and said, "Okay. Explain Cynthia Norton and all of that emotion in there."

Jerry thought back to the first day he saw Cynthia through the scope of his sniper rifle and the events that unfolded after he squeezed the trigger. The back of his neck tightened slightly at the memory. "It's a long story," he began. "What did she tell you?"

Olive leaned forward and smeared sunscreen on her calves. The sun warmed the lotion, filling the area with the smell of coconut sunscreen.

They sat in an isolated area of the nearly empty pool. Jerry lay on his stomach, a hat covering his head. She didn't know whether he dozed or relaxed, but she just enjoyed sitting next to him, not talking.

Despite the relative emptiness of the ship, an announcement came over the loudspeakers. "Good afternoon, folks, this is your Cruise Director! Tonight, catch our spectacular Broadway-style show at 7:30 PM in the Grand Theater, followed by a karaoke extravaganza at 9:00 PM in the Moonlit Bar. Tomorrow, day 4, all passengers must head to our private island between 7:00 AM and 11:00 AM for a day of fun while our crew conducts mandatory safety training and lifeboat drills. Bring your cruise card and check your newsletter for disembarkation details. Enjoy your afternoon!"

Olive's eyes scanned Jerry's bare back and legs. She

knew what caused the scar on his left upper arm, but she had never seen him shirtless or in shorts above his knees before. She loved looking at the muscles of his strong back, shoulders, and arms.

But the long scar on the left side of his back resembled a nasty burn. Then there was the obvious bullet wound in his mid-left thigh. Her curiosity nearly overwhelmed her, but she had no intention of disturbing him right now.

He'd spent the morning adding to Cynthia's story about the harrowing escape from the jungle with a very seriously wounded Bill and more seriously wounded Phil. He told her a little bit about Emma's capture in a small village outside of Djibouti and the team's rescue mission. He couldn't talk much about Lynda and Bill's story except to say that it had been a joint operation with the FBI and a few other agencies, and how that mission had unexpectedly reunited the two college sweethearts.

Jerry had never once mentioned anything that would correlate to a bullet in his leg and a nasty burn on his back. She started to wonder if he had even more scars beneath his swim trunks before she purposely turned her thoughts away from that area.

Clearly, the work Jerry and his teammates did involved a high degree of risk and danger, but she had never considered how those threats could spill out into ordinary life. She'd learned about Melissa and Phil's troubles with a drug cartel in Miami, and how it tied into Phil's brother's murder. The story of how Cynthia and Rick met, and the few details she had learned about Bill and Lynda had intrigued and thrilled her. Finding out about how Jorge had saved Emma from certain death left her speechless.

Thinking about how she and Jerry had met in a chapel in Kentucky made her think about how incredibly boring their story would be compared to the others. A small part of her barely recognized wished she and Jerry had some adventure tale to tell.

She smiled and shook her head at the silly thought. Life came with its own kind of adventures. She didn't need guns and danger piled onto it—even if she could honestly say she first met him in a trauma center with a life-threatening bullet wound to his arm.

"Mind if we join you?" Emma asked, gesturing at the empty chairs next to her.

Olive shifted her sunglasses to the top of her head and looked up at Emma. She wore a yellow bathing suit that glowed against her dark tan skin. "Of course not," she said. "You look so nice."

"I wasn't sure if you were seeking privacy. There's a lot of group time lately." Emma said.

"We spent the morning alone. It was lovely, but we're here for people."

Jorge set a pool bag on the ground next to Emma's chair. "Want anything from the bar?"

She nodded. "Some of that sparkling lemonade, if they have it."

He raised an eyebrow at Olive, who shook her head and held up her water bottle. As he walked away, Emma clipped her towel to her chair then settled on it. "What did y'all do with your time this morning?"

"Chatted," Olive said. She put her sunglasses back on and settled her head back. "Jerry was telling me how he met you and Cynthia and Lynda."

"Really?" She leaned over Olive and looked at Jerry. "Seems like a conversation like that would have a lot of holes in it."

Olive chuckled. "I'm sure it did. I was just sitting here looking at all the holes in his body he hasn't explained yet. And I was thinking about how exciting it all sounded and how comparatively boring my military service was."

Emma gifted her with a skeptical look. "Can't see how a surgical nurse in Landstuhl would find any day boring. I imagine you have all sorts of exciting stories."

Her mind wandered back to the years she spent there and the countless traumas that came her way. "Good point," she murmured. "I guess for the patients, though, it was the end of the excitement and the beginning of long days of nothing to do but recover and heal."

Jorge returned with two lemonades. "Did you guys venture out at all?" he asked.

"No. Neither of us really wanted to."

"We started to, but the police carrying SIG Sauer SIGM400 rifles quickly turned me off," Jorge said. "I'd rather not know why there were so many obviously untrained uniformed men so well armed."

Jerry lifted his head. "That would be a tad disconcerting," he said as he shifted his chair and sat up. "So Olive, why are you thinking about my holes?"

Olive grinned, "Deep subject, holes."

Jerry grinned. "I'll tell you someday."

"Why not now?"

"Okay," he agreed amiably. "See that?" He pointed to the scar on his thigh. "Got shot right there." He turned his body and tossed a thumb toward his back. "See that? Got burned."

"Very informative," Olive said.

"Very hot, actually. You already know about this one," he said while flexing his scarred left biceps.

"Some of my best work. But why all on your left side?"

"I'm right-handed?" Jerry shrugged. "*Etiam sanato vulnere cicatrix manet.*"

Emma piped up, "Even though the wound is healed, the scar remains. Publilius Syrus."

"*Non turpis est cicatrix quam virtus parit.* Ibid.," Jerry quoted.

Olive surprised them both by translating, "No scar is ugly which is born of valor." Jerry cocked an eyebrow. Olive said, "I've been brushing up."

Jerry said, "No need. You're perfect in every way." While Olive pondered that, he turned to Emma. "Erin said it was kinda like a souk but filled with tourist junk."

Olive frowned. "What's a souk?"

"A marketplace in the Middle East," Emma said. "Like a bazaar. Bunch of stalls. Everyone trying to get your attention, barter with you." She took a sip of her lemonade. "I liked going to them, but nothing really stood out to me. Then we turn a corner and there's like fifteen police or militia or whatever they are standing around with their fingers on the triggers of their automatic rifles, weapons off safe, and all the fun kind of evaporated."

"I don't blame you," Olive said. She imagined that would be a little scary, especially if you didn't know why and what. "Did you just turn back around?"

"Yeah. Nothing we'd want to get mixed up in." Jorge leaned back in his chair and closed his eyes. "We're on vacation. Not a mission."

"Preach," Jerry said with a grin. "You two both would have just gone ahead and strolled right on in if it had been the latter." He stood up and stretched his arms over his head. "I'm going to cool off in the pool."

Olive slipped her sunglasses off and stood up, shifting the straps of her swimsuit. "That's a great idea."

They strolled side by side around the pool, the deck warm beneath their bare feet, and reached the deep end. Only a single towel lay crumpled on a nearby chair. Most of the other passengers had gone ashore. Jerry launched into a smooth dive, slicing the water with barely a splash. Olive followed, the cool water enveloping her, sending a shiver of delight down her spine. She swam upward, tilting her head back as she broke the surface, her hair slicking away from her face. Wiping water from her eyes, she felt Jerry's arm slip around her waist. She opened her eyes, a grin spreading across her face, and looped her arms around his neck with ease.

"Having fun?" Jerry's voice carried over the gentle lapping of the pool water.

Olive grinned, her feet dangling in the cool water. "Definitely."

"You know what I keep thinking?" His gaze steadied, searching her face as the sun glinted off the deck.

"What?"

"That we get to spend the rest of our lives together, having little adventures like this one."

Her chest tightened, warmth spreading through her as she blinked back tears. "God is good to bring us together."

"I'm grateful." He leaned in, his lips brushing hers, a faint, mineral bite of pool water tinged his lips, cool and crisp like the thrill chasing her pulse. He pulled back, a playful glint in his eyes. "You any good at swimming?"

She let out a nervous laugh, shaking her head. "No."

"Good." He flashed a mischievous grin. "Race you to the other side."

She flicked her wrist, sending a playful splash of water his way as he launched forward, his strong arms slicing through the pool's shimmering surface. She took her time, her strokes slow and deliberate, enjoying watching him glide ahead. The water lapped gently against her skin, and a warmth bloomed in her chest, her mind drifting to quiet mornings and shared laughter in years to come.

NINETEEN

Near Northwest Providence Channel, Caribbean Sea

Jean Desalin sat alone at the bow of the private yacht, the Caribbean night air humid and heavy with salt. The vessel rocked gently, anchored just beyond the radar range of the cruise line's private island in the Bahamas—silent, waiting for Claude's signal from the night shift confirming they had taken out the island's radar. Its low creak groaned against the hull like a held breath, muffled by the lap of dark waves whispering threats below.

The yacht owners' blood stained the teak deck, a reminder of their violent takeover of the vessel. Jean's notebook lay open on his lap, pages dense with scrawled plans, timelines, and names—too many names, too many points of failure. He did not like how the plan had shifted.

Behind him, the yacht's deck split into two worlds. Six

of his countrymen, hardened by Port-au-Prince's streets, clustered near the stern. Any other night, they'd pass rum around a table covered with dominoes, but tonight demanded sobriety. Five Chinese operatives, Liang Wei's handpicked men, kept to the cabin's shadows, their Mandarin clipped and faces blank. No mingling, no need to form friendships—just a shared goal: twenty million dollars' worth of weapons and explosives loaded tomorrow, smuggled to Haiti via the cruise ship.

He would have the hardware to overthrow the current government, save his people, and maintain power against the pig Americans. Of course, China would have a toehold very close to the American empire. Not a bad price to pay.

They would sneak the weapons in through the cruise line's Haitian island, and by the time anyone even knew something had happened, Jean and his fellow patriots would have dispersed the weapons into the hands of his loyal men.

Jean's jaw tightened as he mentally went over the next twenty-four hours. They would secure the island at 0400. One radar ping, and the plan crumbled. They had to take control of the island before anyone suspected their motives. The entirety of their plan hinged on that little scrap of sand in the water. While Jean did not plan to engage in wholesale slaughter, he recognized that before dawn, some corpses would litter the sand. Such costs came with revolution.

They would then shuttle the remaining staff off that island to another one they had stocked with supplies of food and water. The next morning, Marie would call the Royal Bahamas Defense Force and give them the location of the hostages.

His mind flicked to another issue—the VIPs. Jean finally received some intelligence concerning the possible armed resistance they may encounter. While his assets aboard the ship had not gathered the identities of the principals, they had informed him that security personnel guarded them night and day. Jean assumed these men came from, at best, a personal security company or, at worst, were trained mercenaries. Given that the principals were all American—they had at least confirmed that—a personal protection firm seemed much more likely.

Regardless, the additional scrutiny the VIPs brought to this voyage had upended his crew setup, forcing out four plants and doubling the scrutiny of the staff. Bad timing, bad luck. The extra security could choke their window when the ship weighed anchor at the island tomorrow. Thankfully, they had reinforced the island team with the four extra bodies.

More problematic was the news that the entire VIP party did not plan to disembark and head to the private island along with every other passenger during the mandatory ship exercises. Apparently, they intended to remain aboard and perform a wedding ceremony during that time. That meant Jean would have to contend with them somehow.

While it aided his cause to know that the ship's Captain would be in the Sky View Chapel along with the

American VIPs, their mere presence during his planned takeover of the ship caused him some concern. Daphnée would want to simply kill them all. Wei would probably not object so as to avoid any entanglements between China and America. Jean preferred to have some hostages to use in case he needed leverage in the future.

He fisted his hands, impatience clawing his chest. Too many moving parts in too many different spots. Marie leading on the ship, Claude on the island, René and the others playing loyal crew. He hated not being everywhere, not gripping each thread himself. The cruise's passengers did not worry him. They were unarmed, and many would over-imbibe on the free rum offered on the island. They likely wouldn't realize anything had even changed until the weapons were already offloaded into Haiti and the entire "crew" of the ship disappeared into the jungle with them.

A trained security detail, though, their experience taught them to sniff out trouble. Even though they went into this with the goal to avoid killing any passengers, they might not have a choice. Their protocols, communication with the chain of command, and their very presence risked the mission. The wisest thing to do would be to strike swiftly and surely.

Henri and Julien came up onto the deck. They immediately found him in the dark. "Papa," Henri said, "Mama has food for you."

He nodded. "Any word from the cargo ship?"

"*Oui*," Julien said. "They are waiting on location."

He looked at Henri. "Did you stock the island with water and food?"

"I did. And Marie and I checked the dock yesterday. It should work."

Jean slapped his hands on his son's shoulders and stood, boots scuffing the deck.

He turned and headed down into the belly of the yacht. As he walked down the stairs, he smelled the spices of the chicken he knew Daphnée prepared and suddenly realized the depth of his hunger. They would have a long day tomorrow. Now he needed to fuel and rest.

TWENTY

"Why NCO? Why not officer?"

Jerry looked up from his perfectly prepared lamb chop. "Hmm?"

Olive set aside her napkin. "What made you decide to be an NCO? Isn't your father a retired colonel?"

He looked at the tables around them before speaking and kept his voice low. "Yes. He was an 18 Alpha, a team Daddy, then went on to USASOC and JSOC, then a bunch of other duty stations before heading back to USASOC and retiring as a full bird."

She pursed her lips. "But you enlisted. Didn't go the officer route."

Anger suddenly burned in his chest. It surprised him how fast it hit him. "Didn't especially want to. I wanted to stay on a team as long as possible."

Jerry studied her face. What was this? He couldn't help but overlay her words with the last conversation he ever had with his mother. He left that day feeling like he wasn't good enough, as if all his hard work, school after school, and all the accolades and awards didn't mean anything to her because he had an E instead of an O in front of his pay grade.

"Officers have better pay, more responsibility, higher housing reimbursements, and a larger retirement."

She said it as if these were unknown facts, something he didn't know. "I'm aware."

"Then why not get a commission? OCS or whatever. You're clearly qualified."

He narrowed his eyes at her. "Was my answer somehow insufficient?"

Her head went back as if dodging a blow, and her eyes widened. Perhaps she could hear the caution to not go any further in this conversation with him.

"I didn't mean to make you angry," Olive said, her eyes wide with caution.

"Oh? What was your intention?" He took a breath and puffed it out.

She sat up straighter. "If I were still in the Army, we couldn't even be here together. Because I was an officer."

"Ma'am, yes, ma'am." He realized his voice didn't sound particularly friendly. "As I recall, we covered that the first time we met. I told you I wouldn't hold it against you. You holding something against me?"

When Olive sat silently, instead of saying anything else, he set aside his utensils and napkin, crossed his thick arms over his broad chest, and met her gaze. The silence stretched until Olive opened her mouth to speak again, apparently thought better of it, and closed her lips.

"Say it," Jerry prompted. "You know you want to."

"Fine." Olive leaned forward. "I just don't understand why someone who is thirty years old isn't looking at his future more seriously."

"More seriously? You don't understand? Well, first of all, I don't recall asking you to understand. But let me put it this way. I can explain it to you, but I can't understand it for you."

"Then explain it," Olive's voice rose a bit.

"Fine. Apparently, you think this is all just some game for me?" he snapped. He tried to keep the anger out of his voice, and failed. He did, however, manage to lower his voice to a cold whisper. "Olive? I am one of the top five shooters on the actual planet Earth. Did you know that? So why not the best man for the hardest job? If I were an officer, they'd take me out of my tree or off the rooftop or out of my Ghillie and hand my rifle over to maybe the sixth-best shot, or the tenth-best. Why not use my God given talent and skill the way God intended and, oh by the way, preserve lives along the way?"

Jerry felt his jaw clenching and the muscles in his neck bunching like springs. He shut his mouth to stop the words and to keep from raising his voice. He did not want to say something in anger that he could never take back. He also did not want anyone at a neighboring table to hear him.

"You're really angry." Her eyes snapped wide, jaw slackening as color drained from her cheeks.

Angry? She didn't know the half of it.

"What 'I am' is done with this conversation." He tossed his napkin atop his nearly untouched plate, rose to his feet, and stalked away.

He did not look behind him. He had to get away from her right now, put some perspective into that conversation. Remove the hurt his mom caused him and try not to project that onto Olive.

He understood her point of view. She had just agreed to marry him, and suddenly their intertwined futures lay before her. Maybe doubts or fears had started nagging her, and she wanted to alleviate some of the worst of it.

That didn't make him feel any better about how angry he'd gotten and how quickly the hurt had returned.

He went straight to his cabin, thankful Brock had not come back from dinner yet. Energy thrummed up his spine, and his hands formed fists. He paced inside the tiny space, going from bed to door to desk and back again.

Finally, he threw himself down onto the bed, pushing the idiotic towel, folded and twisted into an elephant shape, out of his way. He covered his eyes with his arm and started breathing slowly. In through his nose, out through his mouth. As he breathed, he began mentally going over Psalm 91, making sure to form every word.

He who dwells in the secret place of the Most High Shall abide under the shadow of the Almighty.

The relaxation technique began to take hold, and the tense anger started to dissipate.

"You should look at the future. More stability, better

retirement." Olive might as well have quoted his mother directly. When Jerry told his mom that he had turned down the opportunity to go to Officer Candidate School, she couldn't believe it.

His mother had scolded, "You've had your fun. Now it's time to look to your future."

The last time he'd seen her alive, they'd had that conversation, and he had resented her words, because he knew he lived the life he'd always dreamed of. He needed her to respect him and feel proud of him. Every little boy on the playground says, "Look, Mom!"

Look how strong I am, look how fast I am, look how good I am, watch me. Watch me, Mom!

He murmured aloud, "Look what a good shot I am. Look how my teammates respect me. Look at all the lives I just saved. Look at how fast I got to Sergeant First Class. Look at my badges and medals. Look at this amazing woman who agreed to marry me."

He needed her approval, and he didn't have it. What he heard was, "You're not good enough." He'd left angry, her standing there with her silly gingerbread apron tied around her too-thin body with the snowman hat on her bald head.

Olive had no reason to know how much his mother had hurt him, and how she'd died before he could fix that relationship. Knowing her heart and how she cared so deeply for the people around her, he couldn't believe she would intentionally bait him. He also didn't think she thought less of him for enlisting instead of going the officer route. She had just wanted to have a conversation, and he'd lost his well-known cool.

Perhaps Osbourne's wedding and asking Olive to marry him at the same time had added some stressors to the back of his mind that he didn't anticipate. Something had certainly reared its ugly head.

He spent a while praying for God to ease the pain in his heart. Oh, how he wished he could call his mom. He needed to hear her voice one last time—without scolding or recrimination in it. *Look, mom!*

Jerry sat up, harshly clearing his throat. He needed to speak to Olive, to help her understand what happened.

He checked the time. Eleven-thirty. She might still be awake. Brock never came in before two. Erin always found some late-night show or activity on the ship and dragged Brock along. That meant Erin probably hadn't returned, either.

He opened the cabin door and peered down the passageway, sensing and seeing no movement. In one step, he'd crossed over to Olive's door and lightly tapped on it.

It only took a few seconds for her to open the door. She had changed out of the dinner clothes and into a pair of shorts and a tank top. Her hair fell out of a sloppy bun on the top of her head, and he could see the tearstains on her cheek. She'd scrubbed her face clean of makeup.

Her eyes widened when she saw him, then narrowed. "Hey," she greeted, her voice harsh.

Jerry slipped a hand into his pocket and rubbed his neck with the other one. "I, uh, need to explain something."

"Okay."

"Can I, uh, come in?"

She crossed her arms over her chest and leaned against the doorframe. "Better not."

After releasing a breath, he said, "I'd like to tell you about the last conversation I had with my mother. She died just hours later."

"Well," All of the righteous indignation radiating from Olive just went away. She straightened and pushed her door wide. "In that case, you'd best come on in."

Sunlight poured through the ship's dining room windows, casting golden streaks across the tables as Olive sipped her coffee. Jerry had spent two hours in her cabin the previous night, explaining the story of his mom in a way that clearly took a toll on him. She realized as he spoke that she'd used almost the exact same words as his mom had, and that caused his angry reaction.

The vulnerability he showed her last night, the tears on his face, and the pain in his voice only made her love him more. She knew she didn't have anything for which she ought to apologize, but she did anyway. She hugged him and told him that she would never hurt him on purpose.

In typical Jerry fashion, he had said, "*Amoris vulnus idem sanat qui facit,*" which apparently means "The wounds of love are healed by the same person who inflicts them."

They prayed together, talked some more, and then finally kissed goodnight.

She hadn't seen him today, and didn't expect to. Jerry had groomsman duties to perform, and so much time spent in social interactions had left her a little drained, too. She hadn't slept well and had a slight headache. She decided to dine alone—just her and her latest Mandalynn Clementine mystery, written by the brilliant Violet Pearl.

Early, a ship-wide announcement came over the loudspeakers. "Good morning, ladies and gentlemen, this is your Captain. Today is day 4, and we've arrived at our private island! All passengers must disembark by 11:00 AM to enjoy the island's beaches, activities, and complimentary dining options. The ship will be closed to guests today as our crew conducts mandatory safety drills, including lifeboat testing and ship-wide maintenance. Please follow the disembarkation instructions in your newsletter and proceed to the gangway with your cruise card. Crew members, report to your designated areas for today's training. We look forward to welcoming you all back on board this evening. Enjoy your day ashore!"

Passengers around her scarfed down eggs and toast, their forks clinking as they glanced at departure schedules, their chatter buzzing with plans for the day. The ship had weighed anchor about 250 yards from the cruise line's private island before dawn, its turquoise waters sparkling under a cloudless sky. Every thirty minutes, the intercom crackled in three languages: "All passengers, please proceed to the queues to board tenders to the beach." A staffer's voice followed, promising an island lunch at noon and a reggae band to serenade dinner, along with a host of activities. "Our staff have security drills to perform, so please remember that this is a mandatory fun day."

Olive's lips curved into a smile as she imagined the night sky erupting in fireworks before the tenders ferried everyone back to the ship. All morning, the announcements came every fifteen minutes until the last one at 10:45 AM, ferrying the final round of the island goers to the private beach.

The tenders could hold more than 200 people. She couldn't believe how efficiently the ship emptied.

Their party, however, had remained aboard. After all, they had a wedding to put on. With the security for Melissa's sister and Cynthia Norton and a skeleton crew left manning the ship, they pretty much had the ship to themselves.

She found a nice corner of shade near the empty pickleball courts and settled back in with her book. When she realized she had read the same page three times, she closed the cover and closed her eyes.

The faint, briny tang of sea air laced with sunscreen drifted from the decks below, the smell enhancing the edge of her headache.

"God," she breathed, "help us stay open with each other so that any unintentional hurt can be quickly set to right. Thank you for last night."

She wiped her eyes and took a drink of water, the cool liquid quenching her throat. Then she opened her worship music playlist. She adjusted the earbuds in her ears, then leaned back in the chair and put her arm over her eyes. "God," she whispered, "I trust Your plan. I love you and I know You brought Jerry into my life on purpose." She began praying for him, for his friends, and for their time together that day.

Every member of the crew had an assigned lifeboat. Today, they would conduct drills at each lifeboat and check the equipment. They should have done this before leaving Miami, but the first mate had a family emergency and could not return in time to conduct them. They decided to make leaving the ship for the passengers mandatory and to do it properly here on the island stop.

Hao, as First Mate, of course, helped provide the perfect cover to gather all of the crew in one place at one time—and to empty the ship.

They all gathered in the main dining hall. They would eat lunch before heading to their assigned spots. Daphnée Desalin, who had arrived from the island via tender twenty minutes ago, led the team of servers to the hall, eyes moving all around to make sure no surprises lurked in the corners.

The servers with the carts dispersed themselves around the room, then paused, waiting for their queue to serve the staff. Daphnée chuckled to herself about her choice of words, even though she said them internally. Then she clapped her hands.

"Welcome, crew. Change of plans. Everyone, please form a single-file line, and we will head to the tender that is waiting on you."

A maid in a tropical shirt and khaki skirt asked, "Who are you?"

Daphnée smiled, a bright smile inspired by the fact that, finally, finally, after over a year of careful planning, the day had arrived, and her husband could now move forward in the plans to take control of their country. "Let me explain." She gave the signal to her men.

The "servers" pulled the covers off their carts and pulled out AK-47 automatic rifles. Screams, gasps, and cries erupted from the crowd. Daphnée grabbed a suppressed pistol from her tray and stepped forward, waving it in the air. "You heard me, friends. Form a line. No one will be harmed if you stay quiet and obey our commands."

One of the chefs stepped forward, anger firing darts out of his eyes. "What are you doing? There are three hundred and fifty of us, and what, twenty of you?" He looked around at the crowd. "We can take them!"

Daphnée very calmly aimed and shot him between the eyes. He crumpled to the ground, and the woman next to him started screaming.

"Shut up!" Daphnée screamed, menacing her with the pistol. The woman stifled her screams and quietly sobbed in fear.

"Any other volunteers?" Daphnée asked. When only whimpers and tears responded, she ordered, "Take your cell phones out of your pockets and drop them on the floor at your feet, then form a single file line." The room filled with the sound of phones plopping onto the ground like hail. She aimed her gun at a bartender who tried to hide dialing her phone. "Must I waste another bullet on the likes of you?"

The woman shakily dropped the phone and held up her hands, turning to follow the line out of the dining hall.

TWENTY ONE

Olive sat up with a start. She must have dozed off. She didn't remember ending her prayer. When she looked at her phone, she gasped. 11:45!? The wedding would start in fifteen minutes!

She grabbed her book and phone, then rushed through the entirely empty ship. It felt so strange to encounter absolutely no one as she ran down empty corridors and down vacant stairwells. She burst into her cabin. It didn't surprise her to find Erin already gone.

Despite the time, she had to shower, but she could get away with not washing her hair. She also had to run an iron over her dress. Argh! Why hadn't she done that last night?

Because she'd thought starting a fight with the man she loved the day before his best friend's wedding would somehow be a good idea.

Stupid, she thought to herself as she waited for the iron

to heat. *God, please help me.*

The clock mocked her as she quickly put on the high-necked, sleeveless dress the color of the turquoise ocean covered in white and yellow flowers.

12:13.

At this point, should she even go? Of course she should go. It's why Jerry brought her.

She pulled her hair into a Chignon and quickly applied her makeup. Taking a deep, calming breath, she slipped her sandals on and stepped back, checking her appearance in the mirror.

She grabbed her phone and her beaded purse. Now, she had to get up to the fifteenth deck. She rushed to the end of her corridor and paused, trying to decide if she could run the stairs faster than the elevator could take her. With such an empty ship, though, she decided the elevator would win the race. While she waited, she slipped her shoes off. That would just make for more efficiency once she got to the top.

She left the elevator on the fifth deck and rushed down the promenade. Designed to accommodate thousands of people, the corridors and passageways loomed like vast liminal spaces, as if she'd swallowed a strange elixir and dwindled to a third of her size.

Just as she passed the casino, she heard, "There's one."

The voice surprised her. She turned and saw a man and a woman in crew member uniforms. They approached. The woman waved her arms in a sweeping gesture. "Where are you going, ma'am?" she asked.

Olive glanced at her nametag. *Marie, Haiti*

"I'm heading up to the wedding on the top deck," Olive said.

"*Mwen pa gen tan pou sa,*" Marie spat out. She looked at Ming. "Just take her."

The man with the nametag, *Ming, China* said, "You need to come with us."

Olive could sense a strong aggression radiating from them. That didn't make sense. Everyone with whom she'd ever interacted on this ship had so far treated her with patience and cordiality. Not aggression. Not anger. She slowly dropped her purse and one shoe, shifting the other one so that she held it with the heel out like a blade. "I am going to go on to the wedding now," she informed.

Ming shook his head. "No." He lunged at her. She pivoted, muscles coiled from the second she'd seen his weight shift forward. Shifting her stance, feet sliding wide, she swung out with the shoe. His eyes widened with surprise, and he howled, grabbing his cheek, blood seeping from his fingers.

Before Olive could swing again, Marie punched her in the jaw with a vicious uppercut. Olive's arms went weak, and spots danced in front of her eyes. Just like when Bryan struck her, her jaw went out of socket. She fell back, landing against the Cybertruck. Ming lunged at her, grabbing her by the back of her hair. Limbs still limp, she had no defense against his fist as it pounded into her temple. The metallic tang of blood flooded her mouth from a split lip, coppery and hot, as the world spun into black.

★ ★ ★

Daphnée stood with her back to the tender driver, facing the staff under her guard. The hot sun beat down on the little boat, baking the occupants on this lower deck. On the top deck, Julien guarded another group. They followed the tender carrying the remaining staff, guarded by Henri and another member of the Chinese group.

No one spoke. No one made eye contact with her. She had them exactly how she wanted them—terrified and compliant.

About a mile from the cruise ship, they stopped at a dock built on a sandbar very close to a tiny island. The dock would hold everyone on the tender. It would be an easy swim to the little island.

Daphnée could see the forty island staff members delivered that morning by Claude on the beach of the little island. They yelled and waved their hands. When they saw Julien unloading the crew above Daphnée, the excitement at a possible rescue slowly vanished, and anger took its place. They yelled and cried.

Daphnée ignored them.

"You will find water and American relief meal packets on the island. You will all survive," she explained, hearing her counterpart give the same information above. "We will send someone for you tomorrow morning."

A British engineer stood. "You can't mean to leave us here!"

She raised an eyebrow and trained her pistol on him. "You

can get off and live or refuse and die. Are you volunteering like Chef Juno?"

His eyes widened, and his face paled. He sat back down. She nodded in approval.

"You will leave this boat and go onto the dock. From the dock, you can easily get to the island. We don't want to hurt you. We just want to get you out of our way for the next twenty-four hours."

A security guard wailed, "Why are you doing this?"

Daphnée looked him up and down and said, "*Liberté ou la Mort!*" She saw the last of the top deck finish filing off the tender and waved toward the dock. "Out, now. Move."

Right at noon, a side door creaked open, and Phil Osbourne, his father, and Jerry stepped into the Skylight Chapel, taking their place beside the chaplain under the stained-glass window. Sunlight poured through the colorful glass, casting flecks of color across their navy suits, white shirts, and light blue patterned ties. His eyes scanned the rows of seats, but he did not immediately see Olive.

What?

He looked again, carefully checking each row. Still nothing.

Irritation scratched at the back of his mind. Did their midnight talk not straighten things out? Surely she wouldn't do this to him—to them.

Of course she wouldn't.

If not that, then what?

In six months, she had never made him wait. In fact, most of the time, she arrived early or waited on him to get there. He couldn't fathom that, here on a cruise ship with nowhere else to be and nothing else to do, she was just simply late. That made no sense to him.

The soft strains of music filled the Chapel. Sharon, Melissa's business partner, stepped down the aisle, her bright pink dress perfectly complementing a bouquet of pink and white lilies cradled in her arms. A few paces behind, Lola, Melissa's sister, followed, the hem of her pink dress swaying with each step. When she reached the front and turned to face the crowd, the music paused, then changed.

The chaplain lifted his arms, and everyone stood and faced the back.

Melissa came through the door on the arm of her uncle. The sequins in her ivory dress reflected the bright sunlight streaming through the windows. She stood tall, eyes forward, holding a simple bouquet of white lilies cradled in her arm. A veil covered her face, and her black hair danced in curls down her back.

Jerry tried to peer past Melissa to the open chapel door, but did not see Olive. The irritation started to transition to actual worry.

As Melissa reached the front, Osbourne stepped forward. Her uncle responded to the chaplain, then turned to sit in the chair in the front row next to his son. Everyone sat and bowed their heads as the chaplain began his prayer.

The faint, waxy bloom of fresh lilies mingled with the

polished wood's subtle varnish. When an "amen" chorused through the room, Jerry raised his head and scanned the room again.

It took every ounce of control he had to stand still and not bound down that aisle to initiate a quadrant-by-quadrant search for Olive.

Jerry barely paid attention to the vows exchanged by bride and groom. The chaplain spoke about love, marriage, and God's perfect plans. They slipped the rings on each other's fingers, then clasped hands and smiled at each other, anticipating the chaplain's command to kiss. "Phil," the chaplain started, "you may now kiss—"

Nearby automatic gunfire interrupted the chaplain.

TWENTY TWO

Before Jerry had time to react, the chapel door burst open. "Everyone get down!" the Secret Service Agent he knew as Agent Guthrie yelled. Then the agent raced up the aisle toward Cynthia, his Glock 47 pistol drawn just as rapid gunfire echoed from outside the chapel doors.

The 7.62×39mm caliber bullet is the preferred round used by non-NATO forces and fired by Kalashnikov rifles like the venerable AK and variants such as the SKS or the MAK-90. A tremendous amount of 7.62 automatic gunfire echoed around the chapel from the corridor outside, interwoven with short, controlled bursts of 9mm return fire from right outside the double doors.

Instinctively, Jerry turned toward the direction of the shots. He and Osbourne pushed Judge Osbourne toward the women and stepped in front of them. A federal Marshal named Stalling emerged from the back corner of the room, pistol drawn, and guided Melissa, Judge Osbourne, Lola, and Sharon toward the back of the room. When Agent Guthrie reached Cynthia, Rick Norton stepped out of the pew and ran for the door.

Jerry made sure the wedding party was well away from the door before rushing down the aisle. Before he got to the door, it burst open. The Federal Marshal named Black burst through, staggering to the deck.

Osbourne got to him before Jerry. Blood covered the front of his white shirt. While Osbourne ripped the shirt open, Jerry took the Glock 47 from his limp hand and quickly searched his belt and pockets for spare magazines. As he stood, he rapidly released the nearly spent magazine and replaced it with a full one, then checked the remaining rounds in the first magazine. Three rounds. He slipped that magazine into his pocket, then stood and looked at Peña.

The gunfire had ceased. The sharp smell of cordite and the metallic smell of blood began to waft into the chapel. Peña gestured toward the door. He joined Norton, Ibrahim, and Fisher at the door. Sanders, Waller, Brock, and Peña took up the other side. Out of long habit, they "stacked" at the doorway, prepared to breach. At Peña's signal, Jerry held the pistol ready, holding it directly in front of his face and chest, his arms forming a relaxed triangle prepared to move in any direction in his working space, and Fisher turned the handle.

He quickly assessed the situation outside. Secret Service Agent Butler, Secret Service Agent Young, and Federal Marshal Nguyen lay on the deck, motionless. Norton and Peña quickly scooped up their discarded weapons: a Glock

47 pistol from Marshal Nguyen, and a Heckler and Koch MP5K fully automatic carbine from Secret Service Agents Butler and Young. These had been disguised in their briefcases.

They then joined Jerry on point. Fisher retrieved another Glock 47 from the downed Secret Service Agent Young, and also retrieved his spare magazines.

They moved out, almost moving in unison, covering every corner and angle like a deadly synchronized dance. Jerry slowly approached the man on the deck of the corridor closest to him. The man lay on his back, his lifeless eyes staring up at the awning above. Chinese?

He glanced at the weapon. Not a Soviet AK. Was that a QBZ-191? He'd trained with one, had fired it even, but months had gone by since that class. If it wasn't QBZ-191, it was definitely Chinese. Not an SKS, perhaps an AK-103. He held out the pistol he carried, and Swanson immediately took it. Keeping an eye on the four other bodies, he retrieved the rifle, snatched up the muslin bandolier holding six fresh 30-round magazines from around the man's neck, and slung it around his own neck, then checked for a round in the chamber.

Assured, he held the rifle at the ready. The weight felt comfortable, and Jerry felt more secure with a long gun in his capable hands. He had always found a long gun more to his taste than a pistol, even in close-quarters combat.

"Blessed be the Lord my rock, who trains my hands for war, and my fingers for battle," Jerry murmured, quoting Psalms 144:1. It was as much of a prayer as he could spare at the moment.

They crouched as they walked. They maneuvered above the entire ship, and by crouching, they stayed out of the visual range of any snipers below. Waller, Swanson, and Fisher each retrieved weapons and ammunition. One by one, they replaced spent or partially spent magazines with fresh magazines.

They found three Chinese military QSW-06 pistols, all equipped with built-in suppressors. Why hadn't the OPFOR used these in their initial assault? They would have taken them completely by surprise. Jerry offered a quick prayer of thanks that they had not.

Chase Anderson, Fisher's friend, had joined them, and he and Sanders each retrieved the remaining available rifles. They quickly frisked the bodies, finding radios, phones, and yet more magazines. Four wore the uniform of the cruise line's crew. On their name tags, the home country listed below three of the men's names read "Haiti."

The fifth, a Chinese woman, wore black cotton fatigues with many pockets and no markings or patches. Once they confirmed no one remained alive, Norton opened the elevator door and dragged the Chinese woman's corpse into the opening to block the doors and keep the elevator from getting called down.

Anderson reached up and knocked the lenses out of the security camera. He and Brock, both taller than the rest, circled, disabling the cameras on the deck and in the elevator. Then they met at the elevator, blocked from view below by the elevator wall.

"No one left alive," Fisher said.

"All clear," Swanson added.

Sanders rolled his head on his shoulders. "What the actual?"

"Haitian?" Norton shook his head. "Pirates, maybe?"

"Does it matter?" Jerry asked. Impatience clawed at his gut. "Olive never made it to the wedding."

"You're right," Peña said. "Emma looked for her but didn't see her."

He wanted to rip open that door and sprint down those stairs and find her. But he resisted the urge. Right now, he considered three possibilities. One, Olive was dead somewhere on the ship. Two, Olive was hiding somewhere on the ship. Three, Olive was captured somewhere on or off the ship.

He could affect nothing if Olive was dead. If she were alive and hiding or held captive, he could not keep her alive by abandoning his team. What he needed to do instead was stay with them, figure out what all this meant, and affect a positive outcome.

He hated it, though. He wanted Olive alive. He needed Olive alive.

"I want to clear the stairs," Peña said. He motioned at the stair door.

Jerry nodded and, weapon ready, stacked on Peña. Peña held the handle with his finger and thumb, then raised the remaining three fingers. He dropped one finger at a time, and when he had made a fist on three, he opened the door. Jerry did a quick look, confirmed no one hid inside, then slipped into the stairwell and cleared the corners, Ibrahim and Swanson close behind. They silently maneuvered down the single flight to the deck below and looked through the porthole. Nothing and no one moved.

They made their way back up the stairs. Anderson disabled the cameras in the stairwell while they thoroughly cleared the bodies, grabbing phones, radios, knives, and anything that might prove useful. At Agent Lewis's body, Jerry pulled out the satellite phone and held it up to Fisher. He frowned at the bullet hole in it.

They returned slowly back into the chapel, crouching the entire way, leaving Waller and Brock guarding the open door.

Osbourne had the agent's shirt and vest off and examined the bullet wound under his arm. He looked over at the ship's Captain, a man named Ege, who hovered near the judge and the Marshal. "Is there a first aid kit here?"

Captain Ege ran his hand over his smooth head. He spoke with a shaky, weak voice. "Uh, yeah, yeah," he said, his Norwegian accent more pronounced than before.

The chaplain's assistant, Sergeant Blackwell, stepped forward. "Think I saw it in the back."

Osbourne pressed the agent's shirt to the wound. "Is there a table back there?"

"Yeah. A table and counters all around. A sink and a small fridge, too."

Osbourne looked at Melissa's uncle. "It's not good. Help us get him back there. I can work better on a table."

"Any other entrances to this room?" Norton asked

Captain Ege.

Ege shook his head. "No. Just those double doors. What is it? Pirates?"

"Maybe," Peña said.

Emma looked out the window and waved Peña forward. "Jorge, look."

They risked going to the wall of windows to look out. A large nondescript cargo vessel had navigated next to the cruise ship and appeared to have rafted up alongside on the cruise ship's port side out of view of the island. Peña turned to Ege. "Can you get us to the bridge?"

Captain Ege shook his head. "Protocol would have the bridge locked down. There's no way we can get in there until the threat is over." He gestured at the foreign ship. "Until that is no longer attached to my ship."

Jerry forced his mind to focus on the situation. "Chinese and Haitian. Could be a false flag, but doesn't feel like it. Their weapons are all PRC manufacture." He quickly inspected his procured rifle. On a hunch, he pulled a magazine from the bandolier and examined the case head of the topmost round. "No serial numbers or identifying marks on the weapons. No manufacturer engravings on the rounds. Ghost guns. Ideas?"

While they spoke, two men on the deck of the cargo ship took a crowbar to a wooden crate. They reached inside and each pulled out what looked like QBZ-191 rifles.

Norton whistled under his breath. "If all of those crates on that cargo ship are filled with weapons, that's a heck of a lot of firepower."

Lynda, an FBI analyst with a hyper-organized brain, got to work. She rubbed the back of her neck and kicked her heels off. She paced from the window to the pew and turned, then came back. "There's buzz about China funding Haitian militants. These weapons are new and as untraceable as they come. Without anything to go on, I'm going to guess some sort of collaboration with the two nations. But what's the point of this? Like, here, now?"

Cynthia came out of the back with her arms full of water bottles. "Hydrate. Everyone."

Rick snorted but took the water. Jerry absently drank while he studied the foreign vessel. "We're docking in Haiti tomorrow."

"Yes." Lynda snapped her fingers. "They're using the cruise ship as a Trojan horse to transport weapons onto the island, maybe?"

Peña shook his head. "Why go through all this?"

Lynda paced back and forth again, then answered her own question instead of Peña's. "That's probably it. If they load the ship here and unload it there, no one is the wiser until it's all done. Too much security at the cargo ports. There's been a weapons embargo on Haiti for years." She pivoted, paced, not even looking at them. "Before any word about today gets out, those weapons are already in Haiti."

"To feed an uprising?" Bill asked.

"Exactly." She turned and put her hands on her hips. "Then China has the gratitude of the new regime and is that much closer to American sovereign soil."

"Think this was just the first wave of a larger ongoing attack?" Jerry asked.

"No." She shook her head. "I think they're just putting pieces together so the first wave can happen." She paused. "In theory, of course."

Bill squeezed the back of her neck and then hugged her to him.

Marshal Stalling said, "Public ports closed down weeks ago. Government's in chaos. Rival gangs are warring on the streets. But the port where the ship docks is privately owned. Security to and from the resort is always tight. Maybe they've compromised it."

Lynda nodded. "Like they compromised this crew. So, they have this security drill, and all the passengers are on the island. Then they can load the weapons, and no one is the wiser. They must have people on the island."

Ege said, "But the island is staffed with cruise ship employees year-round. There is radar and security to protect the island. An alert would have gone out."

Bill crushed his water bottle. "Nope. They're too organized. They took the island last night at a minimum. Anyone there now besides the passengers should be considered bad actors."

"Five of the bodies out there had staff uniforms on." Fisher drained his water. "I'm going to guess this is a plan that has been a long game."

Peña nodded. "It's what we'd do. That's certainly what China would do."

Ege shook his head. "No. Impossible. That would mean

hundreds of crew and staff."

Anderson said, "If we're talking PRC, as in People's Liberation Army of China, they could take a resort island without a sound. Throw a thousand mercenaries at it. PLA SOF could take that little island with a company-sized element without getting their boots dirty. Thing is, though, they'd need to keep it quiet. As soon as word gets out, the Haitian civilian port would shut down and they'd never get their weapons unloaded."

"They would have had that Island crew infiltrated as well," Swanson said. "Get someone on the inside to disable security."

Peña caught Norton's eye. "What are your orders, Daddy?"

Norton slipped his tie over his head and unbuttoned his top button. "I think you're the Daddy here, Jorge. I'll follow your lead, sir." He slung the strap of his rifle over one shoulder and the bandolier strap over the other. At Swanson's questioning look, Norton said, "We announced it the day we took leave. They're sending me to D.C."

Anderson spoke up for the first time. "But why would China risk an international incident?"

Norton rubbed his beard. "Seems like they're using Haitian nationals to do most of the heavy lifting. Gives them plausible deniability."

Sanders took off his jacket and loosened his tie. "You're gonna fit right in up in D.C., like a hog in slop."

Panic danced along Jerry's neck. "As much as I appreciate all this speculation, we're burning daylight. They're going to wonder where their minions disappeared to if they don't report back soon. They'll definitely notice the lack of security cameras. I'm guessing they came to collect or eliminate us since they would figure our DHS friends were armed."

Marshall Stalling said, "Didn't count on Secret Service *and* US Marshals. I got one for sure. Maybe two."

Lynda shook her head. "We can't assume that. If they infiltrated the crew, they could have known there were armed agents here. They came to take out the Secret Service and the Marshals. Secret Service has constant communication as well as small arms. *If* the mission—and I stress *if* because obviously I don't actually know—but, if the mission is to transport weapons into Haiti in a clandestine operation, then the Secret Service raising the alarm would directly interfere with their plans."

Agent Guthrie stood in the doorway of the back room, guarding the entrance while Cynthia remained inside. "My partner Lewis had the satphone."

Fisher said, "It's fried. Took a bullet."

Guthrie lifted his eyebrow. "I just tried to use the courtesy phone in here to contact the bridge or comms room, but it's dead.

Fisher pulled out his cell phone. "Jammer. Russian R-330Zh Zhitel set, or more likely Chinese JN-1105A."

Chase Anderson added, "That means our OPFOR must be using TBR-121s for comms, unless they whitelisted their other devices." He picked up a handheld radio they had retrieved from one of the corpses. Blood dripped off it, and the top of it had vanished under the impact of a bullet. In an almost arrogant display of strength, he casually smashed the device against the deck to crack the case open, then inspected the electronic innards. After a momentary inspection, Anderson let out a low whistle.

Glancing over his shoulder, Fisher confirmed, "State of the art. They got us on comms."

Peña walked over to Captain Ege. "Are ship's comms separate from the bridge?"

Ege's eyes darted all around, as if suddenly realizing that well-armed men in tuxedos and dress suits surrounded him. His breathing increased, and his voice rose a little. "Who are you people? What are you planning to do?"

Calmly, Peña slung his rifle and rapidly snapped his fingers three times in front of Ege's nose. "Are ship's comms separate from the bridge, Captain?"

Ege looked at all the men as if he realized that every man in this room radiated a lethal intent. He took a deep breath and said, "Yes. They are. Same deck, different entry."

"Stay calm. Cooperate. You'll get through this alive. Understand?" Peña asked.

Ege nodded.

"Good. Draw me a map. Then draw me a map to the armory. Don't blow smoke. I know you have one." He turned his back on the captain, fully expecting the man to comply, and said to the group, "We need to reestablish comms. Trout and," he paused, looking at Anderson, "Heisman can hook us up."

A voice speaking Chinese came over one of the radios. Peña looked to Emma. She said, "He's asking what's taking so long."

Norton gestured at the radio. "There was a woman out there. Not in crew uniform. Black fatigues."

Emma tapped the radio's antenna against her lip. "Chinese or Haitian woman?"

"Chinese."

She raised an eyebrow. "Shall I answer?"

Peña's lips pursed, then he said, "Worth a shot. Say you encountered resistance, but you're headed back soon."

Emma covered the microphone of the sophisticated handheld with the hem of her dress, clearly trying to slightly muffle her voice. She quickly rehearsed some Mandarin. It sounded like a nursery rhyme to Jerry. Then she cleared her throat and transmitted. As soon as Emma finished her transmission, Jerry said, "We need to move before they send someone to find out why they haven't made it back yet."

The voice came again, and Emma translated. "Asking how many hostages."

Peña shook his head. "Stall him from now on. You're busy securing the hostages and whatnot." Emma nodded. Peña took the paper from Ege. "Okay, comms, then armory." He looked at Ege again. "Where is that cargo bay in relation to the deck that has the loading dock for the tenders?"

Captain Ege took the paper back and quickly sketched out the ship. He explained the decks. "Cargo elevator would go down to decks one and two."

"They shouldn't be expecting resistance," Jerry said. "They've removed all the passengers." His mind shifted to Olive, and he intentionally shut that down.

"Obviously, they picked the wrong boat," Peña said. He pointed to Emma. "I need you with us to translate the radio transmissions."

"Yes, you do," she said. "But I'll do it from here. We don't have gear, and I don't want to be in the way."

Jerry checked the time. They'd wasted five whole minutes. Tension tightened his neck. He said to Captain Ege, "Give us your badge. We don't want to break down doors or get stalled at sealed steel portholes."

Ege fumbled with his badge clipped to his crisp white uniform shirt. "Of course. My keypad code is 112233."

"Original," Jerry observed, pocketing the badge.

Peña said, "Listen up. Challenge is 'white dress.' Password is 'bowtie.' Straphangers, take rear guard. The rest of you stack up as usual. Stealth is the one ROE until we get loud. We'll use these suppressed pistols, blades, or hands and feet until we have to pivot. Clear?"

Everyone said, "Roger."

"Absolutely no one," Peña said, "And I mean no one is authorized to get himself killed. I do not need that kind of paperwork hassle. Jerry. You're my senior NCO. All set?"

Somehow, the fact that Jerry was the most senior non-commissioned officer present had eluded him in his concern for Olive. Jerry nodded, "*Semper Paratus*, Daddy." Always prepared.

Norton put his hand on Ege's arm and said, "Thank you, sir. We'll get your ship back. Listen to the agents." He released Ege's arm and turned to Chaplain's Assistant Tyler Blackwell. "You and the Chaplain better get some prayers going. I'd join you, but we're pressed for time."

"Yes, sir," Blackwell said.

Peña said, "Good. Let's roll."

Between the available rifles and pistols, they all left armed. Ibrahim took point going down the staircase. They moved as one unit, silently, communicating with hand signals and gestures—two fingers, forward; fist clenched, hold. Anderson impressed Jerry, staying with them, following their lead, even though he'd never trained with them. He also moved quietly for a man of his bulk, much like Brock.

They encountered no one. The ship's usual hum—voices, laughter, piped music, regular announcements — had vanished, replaced by a hollow silence that pressed against Jerry's ears like tinnitus. The bad guys must have swept through deck by deck and cleared each one before coming to the chapel.

At the stairwell door to Deck Eleven, Ibrahim froze, fist raised. The team sank into a crouch, weapons up, breaths shallow. Jerry knew if he were in charge of the invading force, he'd have guards at comms. But they needed to move silently and swiftly. Peña dispatched Brock and Sanders to conduct reconnaissance. Jerry slipped out of the doorway and crouched in the corner of the corridor, his weapon ready. What he wouldn't give for a nice high perch and his beloved Cassie.

Swanson, his old sniper spotter, crouched on the other side of the corner. They made eye contact, nodded once, then focused their attention down the corridor.

TWENTY THREE

Olive's eyelids fluttered open, but harsh and very bright white LED light stabbed into her eyes like shards of glass, forcing her to squeeze them shut once more. A vicious throb exploded behind her temples, sending waves of nausea churning through her stomach, as if the ship's gentle sway had turned into a violent storm.

What happened?

She let out a low, involuntary moan, her hand drifting instinctively to her head. Her fingers brushed the swollen, tender spot at her temple, and she flinched, the contact sending fresh sparks of pain radiating outward. Fragments of memory clawed their way back: she had been rushing down the promenade, late for the wedding.

Then...

Her eyes snapped wide, ignoring the searing stab that lanced through her skull. Bars. Thick, cold metal bars enclosing a stark holding cell.

She pushed herself upright on the floor, wincing as a deep ache pulsed along her left jawline. Gingerly, she traced her fingers over the bruised skin there, the touch confirming the dull swell and the obvious dislocation. That's right, she thought, the recollection sharpening like a razor. The woman—Marie, with her cold eyes—had swung a closed fist straight into her jaw. She realized her jaw had been dislocated exactly as it had been by Bryan her freshman year of college nearly a decade ago. And the man—Ming, broad-shouldered and silent as a shadow—had followed with a ruthless strike to her temple, the world dissolving into black.

"Hello?" Her voice came out ragged, muffled around the tender throb in her jaw, the word tasting like copper on her tongue. "Hello? Is anyone there?"

Silence echoed back. She rolled to her hands and knees, her stomach rolling with the movement, and stayed there for a moment, panting, praying she wouldn't get sick. Gingerly, she stood, wrapping her hands around the cold and unyielding bars of the cell to steady herself.

When the world quit tilting and her feet steadied under her, she shook the cell door with desperate force. It rattled faintly but held fast, mocking her with its immovability.

Nothing made sense. Tears pricked hot at the corners of her eyes. She couldn't tell if it was the relentless pain carving through her body or the clawing fear of the unknown that caused the tears. Slowly, she sank onto the bench, the chill of the metal seeping through her dress, and buried her face in her hands.

At this point, all she could do was pray. Silent words tumbled through her mind, fervent pleas for strength, for rescue.

And for Jerry.

She had no doubt he'd find her.

Marie and Ming had done a deck-by-deck sweep and encountered no one except that redhead, so when Marie opened the door to the office in the engine room, seeing Emanuel Ramirez typing away on a laptop almost gave her a start.

"Emanuel," she said.

He looked up, eyes absent before focusing on her. "What are you doing in here?"

"We had mandatory training. I was sent to find you."

He raised an eyebrow. "Bug off. I'm doing something important here."

With a sigh, she lifted her pistol. "No, Emanuel. I'm doing something important here."

He looked at her again, and a startled look replaced the irritation on his face. "What are you doing? What is this?"

"Come with me."

He started to shake his head, and Ming leaned forward and grabbed him by the collar.

The clanging noise startled Olive. She jumped up from the bench as the woman, Marie, and man, Ming, marched a man in an engineer's uniform toward the cell. He had long black hair pulled into a ponytail and light tan skin. Marie held a gun on him. Ming said to Olive, "Move to the back."

Unwilling to risk either of their lives, Olive swallowed her rising panic and stumbled to the back corner of the cell. Ming swiped a key card across the digital lock beside the door. A soft electronic beep cut through the tension, followed by the sharp click of the magnetic mechanism disengaging.

The door clicked open, and Marie shoved the engineer inside. Ming slammed the door behind him with a clang that vibrated through Olive's bones.

Olive stood still until the two captors left, then she stepped forward. "Are you okay?"

He spun around, eyes wide and shadowed with confusion and shock. "Who are you?"

"Olive Duncan. I'm a passenger."

"Are you okay? You're hurt. What's going on?" He whirled toward the cell door and grabbed the bars with both hands, shaking them hard. The door rattled but did not budge. He put his face against the bars and yelled, "Hey! Let us out!" He rattled the door again. "What is this?"

She sat back on the bench. "I don't know."

"Where is the rest of the crew?"

He asked the same questions she had thought over and over again. "I don't know." After a moment, she asked, "What's your name?"

He looked over his shoulder at her. "Emanuel. Emanuel Ramirez."

She rubbed her arms with her hands. "Well, Emanuel, we have no choice but to just wait." She gestured at the control panel on the wall next to the door. "Unless you know how to hack that thing."

He reached through the bars and ran his fingers over the keys. "I could," he admitted, frustration etching lines across his forehead, "with equipment. I don't have any way to. Not here."

She took a deep breath through her nose and slowly let it out. "Then we wait, I guess." She didn't mention Jerry and his friends. One, she didn't know if she could trust Engineer Emauel Ramriez. Two, she couldn't know for certain where Jerry and his team were right now.

TWENTY FOUR

They stacked up in the corridor around the corner from the comms room, backs tight against the bulkheads. Fisher had confirmed at least one guard at the door.

Ibrahim traded Fisher his Glock 47 for a suppressed QSW-06 pistol, and Brock accepted one from Anderson and handed him his Heckler & Koch. Ibrahim weighed the pistol in his hand as if trying to imagine how it would fire. From behind him, Jerry put a hand on his shoulder. Brock raised his pistol to the ready position and nodded. Peña put a hand on his shoulder.

At Fisher's mark, indicating that the guard turned away from them, the two men rushed around the corner. Jerry watched as Ibrahim reached the far man and incapacitated him while Brock slipped inside the room.

The pistols fired almost silently, the steel firing pins making more noise than the bullets exiting from the muzzles. Jerry heard a faint grunt, then Ibrahim gave the all-clear signal, a low whistle, before he dragged the body of the Chinese militant into the room.

They moved with stealth and precision, silently making their way further down the corridor to the comms room. Jerry had expected a small room with some communication equipment. However, when he walked in, Sanders looked around and said, "Well, turn off the smoker and call me done. Who knew we could run a country from here?"

Walls of screens and workstations lined one bulkhead. He identified a sonar detector, a ham radio, VHF radios, a UHF rig, a wall of telephones, and three fax machines. The other equipment was foreign to him, but Anderson whistled under his breath and slipped his suit jacket off. He walked over to the sonar and tapped the screen. "The ship rafted up alongside isn't the only one here. There's something else just out of sight."

Peña walked over to him. "Any idea what it could be?"

Anderson shook his head. "It's been a few years since I took the Navy course at Little Creek, but it's smaller than the cargo ship outside."

Brock gestured to the corner. "Three crew dead."

Peña nodded. "Plus the two we took out."

A dull gray device about the size of a bread machine sat like an uninvited guest in the middle of the aisle in front of the fax machines.

"JN-1105A," Fisher said. "Blocking cell signals. When we unplug it, it might alert the OPFOR." He looked at Anderson. "Heisman?"

"Never trained on it. Only ever seen pictures."

Fisher nodded. "Same. Why couldn't they be good commies and use a Russian Zhitel?"

"Very inconsiderate of them," Anderson agreed.

Peña said, "I'd rather not let them know we're onto them, much less coming for them."

Fisher nodded and pulled a chair out to sit at a work station. He used his handkerchief to wipe blood from the screens. "Let's see if we can get our voices back without alerting our new friends."

"When you do, let Ozzy and my wife know. Emma is Twenty-Four Ten moving forward. She'll get us all connected." Peña looked at Anderson. "Chase, do you have your phone?"

"I do."

"Fisher will hook you up with the app as soon as you have connectivity. We'll use a group chat app for comms." He gestured at the wall of phones. "Can we call the chapel from here?"

Anderson chimed in. "Depends on what they did to disable the equipment. Looks like an S-VOIP system, so it should be localized and unaffected by the jammer. They might have just powered down the router or the dish. We can find out."

"If they don't respond, try using the phone. But, Ozzy knows it's coming either way."

"Roger."

"Daddy," Ibrahim said from the back of the room. "You'll want to see this."

Jerry followed Peña through a door. Two walls of screens filled the room. Clearly, this was a security room.

The screens showed different decks, passageways, and dining rooms. "Heisman!" he called.

Immediately, Anderson stood in the doorway. "Jorge?" His eyes lit up, and he came further in. "I would have thought this was in security."

"Same." Peña gestured. "Get us some eyes?"

"Gladly," Anderson slid into a chair and pulled a keyboard closer. He examined the screen in front of him and flipped through a binder at the workstation. The system instruction set had helpfully been written in six languages. He nodded and started typing. Immediately, the screens changed, showing passageways, the cargo area, and the promenade.

Jerry examined the cargo area. A Chinese man used a small forklift to carry a crate from the open dock door to the freight elevator. "I'm counting seventeen baddies just on this screen."

Anderson flipped pages in the binder, then typed. Three screens filled with different angles of the loading dock.

Sanders whistled under his breath. "That's enough firepower to wake the devil on a Sunday morning."

Norton said, "I'd want all that under my Christmas tree if I were overthrowing a government."

Crates and crates lined the loading dock as forklifts carried more to the cargo elevator.

"Whatever this is," Peña said, "it was worth taking control of the island and this cruise ship." Peña looked at Norton. "Thoughts?"

The latest crate contained familiar markings. "That's definitely Semtex. And that crate is likely mines or grenades.

Been awhile since I went through the recognition cards." Norton sighed, then pursed his lips and crossed his arms. He stared at the activity in the loading dock. "We don't have enough ammo."

"No." Peña rubbed the back of his neck. "And the longer our attackers above go without reporting in or escorting us wherever we ought to be going, the less likely we can maintain the element of surprise."

Jerry stared at the cargo bay. "There's ammo in there." He pointed at the crates on the screen.

Peña turned fully in his direction. Jerry found it odd to talk like this out of their gear. They had no protection, no vests, no helmets, no gloves, no optics, no eyes in the sky, no backup, no solid intel keeping them informed in their ear—nothing. Not even boots. Peña wore a light pink collared shirt and navy pants. What made them think they could battle this small army?

"If we could secure you a weapon with a proper scope, what do you think about the island?"

Jerry looked at the screens again, knowing what his Captain asked him. Could he, as a sniper, find a perch on the ship and start taking out bad guys to help them secure the island? He noticed several uniformed crew members working in the cargo hold.

"I think the infiltration was deep," he muttered. "We have no idea which crew were involved and which crew on the island are ignorant."

Sanders raised an eyebrow. "What does that mean?"

He tilted his head. "To answer your direct question, I

could definitely provide overwatch tactical fire support from a high perch on the ship. The beach is less than half a klick away. Even with iron sights, I could do a passable job. The chapel sun deck is actually ideal.

"However, once I go hot, we don't know what will happen to the civilians on the island if we don't know which crew members are involved. They could have explosives, grenades, or other fun toys. There is a risk of significant collateral damage and considerable potential political fallout. Your call."

Peña stared at him for what felt like a long time, then said, "Understood. That's a problem for future me. Right now, we need to get control of this vessel. Preferably without anyone on the island knowing."

"What's the plan?" Ibrahim asked.

"We need more firepower to get more firepower because we need more firepower. Deck five. Armory."

Anderson typed, and a passageway appeared on the screen directly in front of him. Two armed Haitian men in crew uniforms stood on either side of the door, while a Chinese soldier, all in black, covered the entrance to the corridor nearest the elevator and stairwell door.

Peña looked at Anderson. "Work with Fisher. Get us comms. Coordinate with us from here. Get a message to DC any way you can. See if they can scare up some help ASAP. Then see what you can do to disable the bandit handheld radios. In that order. Clear?"

Anderson nodded his understanding. "On it."

"After we leave, seal this room. No one in or out without

the challenge and password."

Anderson said, "On it, Jorge. Whatever you need."

Back in the comms room, he said to Fisher, "Think you can at least get the ship's Wi-Fi reestablished so we can communicate?"

"Affirmative. Working on it, sir. Minutes or seconds away."

"Seal up behind us. Keep the Glocks and extra mags in case you have visitors. Give someone else those long guns." Peña paused and added, "And between you and Heisman, get me that truck." He pointed at the screen, which displayed the casino on the promenade deck.

"Yes, sir," Fisher said.

"Right. Let's move," Peña said.

Jerry smiled as he followed Peña out of the room. The Tesla Cybertruck was both silent and fairly bulletproof. It would get them most of the way down the wide-open promenade, which happened to be on the same deck as the armory.

In silence and with precision, the team moved through the decks, using the Captain's pass to unlock doors to hidden stairwells. When they emerged on deck five, they paused before entering the promenade. So many signs, banners, lights, distractions. So many hiding places. He looked up. This design resembled a small-town main street, featuring second floors on the building facades. Any one of those windows could hide a sniper.

Moving as one, they walked low and steady, maintaining a three-hundred-sixty-five-degree lookout, and made it to the entrance of the casino, crouching behind the Cybertruck.

Less than three minutes later, Fisher's voice came through Jerry's earbuds. "Wi-fi is up. Heisman says the truck's all yours."

"Roger," Peña said in a low voice.

Jerry moved to the side of the truck and froze, his tongue going dry as a coppery panic taste filled his mouth.

On the ground next to the Cybertruck lay a white high-heeled sandal.

With yellow leather daisies across the toe.

And blood covering the heel.

"Olive," he whispered, bending down to pick it up. He saw her in his mind, twirling in her dress, then showing him these shoes.

Peña bent down with him. "Doesn't look like her blood," he whispered, pointing at the black hair mixed in with flesh caught on the heel of the shoe. Jerry clenched his jaw and nodded. Peña put a hand on his shoulder. "You good? Need you with us, now, Top."

Was he good? He closed his eyes. He had no choice. As he opened them, he nodded.

Peña slapped his shoulder, then turned and made a motion with his finger. He directed Jerry and Sanders to the top of the truck. Norton quietly opened the door and slid behind the wheel. Ibrahim slid into the passenger's seat. Waller, Brock, Swanson, and Peña got into the back seat.

The truck silently moved down the promenade. Jerry kept watch for any bandits. He held Norton's suppressed pistol at the ready, not wanting to fire with the rifle just yet. The longer OPFOR didn't know about them, the better.

Norton drove it well through the wide-open space of the promenade deck, slowly and silently navigating around tables and chairs, velvet ropes, and fake palm trees. Finally, he came to a full stop before the final turn. Speaking quietly through the connected call, Peña ordered Jerry and Sanders off the top of the truck. Jerry slid down and took point. He pulled Cynthia's compact from his pocket and used it to look around the corner. Fisher said over the comms, "Spot. Visual. One bandit starboard. Five meters. Dressed as crew. Rifle. Comms. Over."

The bandit didn't move. He stood still, leaning against the wall. He had his eyes trained away from them, clearly bored and in his own head. "On your mark," Peña said through comms.

Jerry closed his eyes and took a deep, steady breath. He had one chance to make it a clean shot. Holding the suppressed pistol with both hands, he rested his finger on the side of the trigger, then crouched on one knee. Using the wall as a shield, he peeked around the corner and aimed, then pulled the trigger four times.

A look of surprise covered his opponent's face as he slid down the wall. Jerry's bullets had caught him twice in the chest and twice in the skull in shot groups smaller than half dollars.

He stepped away from the truck, pumping his fist. Norton drove the truck around the corner, then floored it, Jerry and Sanders running along behind. At the end of the corridor, he stopped the truck, and Ibrahim and Brock threw open their rear doors, firing with deadly precision in three-round bursts as they emerged. The enemy guards did not get a chance to return fire.

Emma relayed the code to open the armory's iron gate just inside the door. They did a very quick inventory. Sanders and Ibrahim slipped flares into their pockets. Jerry grabbed a stun gun and tossed the other one to Norton. Deeper into the room, they found a locked cabinet. While Waller picked the lock, Peña opened the map the captain had drawn.

"We need to get to deck one, but because of their numbers, we have to flank them to even have a chance."

Swanson looked over his shoulder. "Big area. Lots of room to maneuver."

"And hide," Sanders said. "Do we have a good count yet?"

Anderson replied over comms. "We've identified thirty-three on the loading dock and twelve in the first deck cargo bay."

"To our eight," Norton said. "Hardly a fair fight."

"It doesn't always have to be a challenge. We can take the easy win," Peña said in a dry tone.

"Done," Waller announced. He opened the cabinet. Inside, they found Benelli M4 shotguns and unopened boxes of double-aught 12-gauge buckshot.

"Well, that's rather underwhelming," Jerry observed.

"Were you hoping for a Barret?" Waller asked ironically.

"It will have to do," Peña said. "We need the ammo. Plus, shotguns are fierce, so there's a psychological effect."

He sighed and looked at Norton. "I want to call you Daddy."

"You're my Daddy now." He ran his hand through his red beard. "I'm Coppertop again."

Peña smirked but did not laugh.

Jerry joined the others in filling his pockets with shotgun shells. He strapped a Benelli to his back, the canvas strap digging into his shoulder through the thin shirt. He slipped the pistol into his belt against his lower back and gripped the rifle in front of him. He didn't think he ever appreciated the straps, holsters, fasteners, pockets, and compartments of his uniform and gear more than this very moment.

"Coppertop," Peña said, sounding a bit pained, "Jerry Maguire, Pot Pie, Hobbes, you four make your way to the main dining room—quietly—and rappel down to deck three. Then take the kitchen stairs to deck one. I'll take the others through the back stairs. When we get into the flanked position, we'll signal and go in full force. Put them on the X. No need for quiet, then, just surprise. Make a lot of noise when we hit."

Jerry nodded. "Roger that."

"Hoo-ah," Sanders uttered sarcastically, imitating the Marine Corps motivational saying.

"Guys," Peña said. "Make it hurt."

TWENTY FIVE

The corpse of Baptiste Dumas lay in the corridor outside the ship's armory. Marie knelt next to the still-warm body, examining the shots to the head and the chest. She checked his pockets. He still had a radio, but no weapon, no extra ammunition.

"Still warm." She looked up at Ming, indicating how close together the entrance wounds were and their precise locations. "Obviously professional."

He grunted and nodded but did not reply.

They turned the corner and stopped short. The Cybertruck from the casino raffle sat unmoving in front of the armory door, the doors open, lights still on.

They approached the open armory door with caution, guns out and ready. Marie hugged the wall next to Ming. He went in first, then came back out again, shaking his head. She could smell the gunpowder.

"What is going on?" she asked. She went into the armory

and saw the other three bodies, the open security area, and the empty gun cabinet.

A very uneasy feeling wormed its way through her core, spreading up into her chest, making her heart race, her vision tunnel, and her mouth go dry.

She cautiously made her way back into the corridor. "Something is very wrong. Get an update from Ying Yue."

Ming unclipped the radio from his belt and spoke in Mandarin to the MSS operative tasked with bringing the wedding guests to a waiting tender. After several seconds, she replied. Marie waited for Ming to translate. "She says there are more hostages than they thought, and it's taking longer than it should."

She stared at Ming with narrowed eyes. "That's what she said twenty minutes ago." He gave a single stiff nod. "Challenge her."

He spoke rapidly. Again, the reply took much longer than they'd expected. "I asked if she was Li Hua. She said yes."

A sharp headache appeared behind her eye. She rubbed her temple. What to do? "We need eyes."

Ming switched the channel on the radio and spoke into it. After about thirty seconds, he spoke again.

Marie shook her head. "We can't wait here. Let's go see."

"That could be dangerous."

"What other option do we have?" she snapped.

They took the staff elevator up to Deck Eleven, moving with more caution than before. They exited the elevator with weapons at the ready. They paused at every juncture, fingers on triggers, peeking around corners before going forward. Outside of the comms door, blood spatter covered the bulkheads, and the carpeted deck had two big blood stains. Marie reached over and tried to turn the door handle. It didn't budge.

She rubbed her temple. "We need to speak with Hao."

Ming shook his head. "That is against protocol."

She grabbed the front of his shirt. "What does it matter now?"

They slipped down the passageway and went around the corner, then paused at the reinforced bridge door. Marie used her fist to tap a code out on the door. Seconds later, Hao Jun stepped aside on the threshold, his lean frame clad in his crisp white uniform, epaulets glinting under the bridge's lights.

His sharp eyes swept the empty passageway behind them before he pulled the door shut with a decisive steel thunk.

"You two take great risk in coming here, Marie," he murmured, his voice low and edged.

She reached up without hesitation, her palm cupping the warm plane of his cheek, thumb brushing the faint stubble there as she drew him down for a kiss. "We have a problem," she whispered against his lips, pulling back just enough to search his eyes.

Hao arched a brow, a sardonic curl touching the corner of his mouth. "How could we have a problem when your brother so carefully arranged everything in his uniquely overbearing way?"

Marie let the barb slide past, her expression unchanging as

she straightened, the weight of the mission settling back into her shoulders. "What do we know about our VIPs?"

He shrugged, the motion fluid and dismissive, then clasped his hands loosely behind his back. "A couple attended the captain's table last night. One was a judge. He had no security. The other was a blonde American. She had two security agents."

"Armed?" Her tone sharpened, eyes narrowing as she leaned against the edge of a chart table, the cool metal grounding her.

Hao's gaze flicked away for a fraction of a second. "I didn't ask."

She followed his line of sight to the corner of the bridge, where the navigator's body slumped against the bulkhead—limp, lifeless, a dark stain on his chest. The sight twisted something low in her gut. "I could have taken him to the island," she breathed, the words barely audible.

"Reginald decided it was more expedient to remove him." Hao slipped his hands into the pockets of his white uniform pants. "What is the problem?"

Marie pushed away from the table and crossed to the wide forward window, her reflection ghosting across the reinforced glass as she gazed out into the endless blue. "The team sent to collect the wedding party with the VIP guests did not return," she said, her voice steady but threaded with steel. "Comms is not replying, and the weapons room has been breached."

Hao gasped, the sound raw and involuntary, his composure cracking as he stepped closer. "How is that possible?

She shook her head, dark hair swaying against her shoulders, frustration coiling tight in her chest. "We can't know. I was hoping you'd have inside information that you've not shared yet."

From the captain's chair at the heart of the bridge, Reginald Hall stirred—former MI-6 agent turned MSS sympathizer, his silvered hair cropped close. He leaned forward, elbows on the armrests, his British accent clipping the words with dry precision. "You've received all of the intel you need. We don't have any information on the VIPs despite our best efforts."

Marie whirled toward him, her lips curling into a sneer that bared her teeth, heat flushing her cheeks. "Perhaps you should have anticipated resistance."

"Based on what?" Reginald's tone remained even, unflappable, his pale eyes meeting hers without flinching. "We are dozens of armed, trained fighters. They are fifty unarmed wedding guests."

"Unarmed?" She closed the distance in three strides, until her face hovered inches from his—close enough to feel the warmth of his breath, to see the faint lines of calculation etched around his mouth. She put her nose near his, voice dropping to a venomous hiss. "And now?"

He calmly shrugged, the motion lifting one shoulder as if shedding an unwelcome coat, his gaze steady. "Now we need to get more intel, obviously. If our signals weren't jammed, I would try to search images from last night's dinner and see if I can identify anyone."

"Bah!" Marie spat the word like a curse, recoiling with

disgust, her hands balling into fists at her sides. "Useless!" She turned sharply to Hao. "We have one of the wedding guests in the brig."

His eyes widened, dark irises flaring with surprise. "Is that so?"

"Can you force her to give you information?" Her words came out urgent, laced with the desperation of a plan forming on the fly.

Hao thought about it, his brow furrowing as he rubbed a thumb along his jaw, the faint rasp of skin on skin the only sound for a beat. "Perhaps. If I were also a prisoner." He turned to Reginald. "Knock me out. Make it bleed."

Reginald rose smoothly from the chair, his movements economical, crossing to a nearby cupboard embedded in the bulkhead. He swung the door open, revealing a toolkit for the endless minutiae of shipboard life. His fingers closed around a heavy wrench. He hefted it in his palm, as if testing its balance. "You might want to have a seat."

Marie clutched Hao's hand, her grip fierce, nails digging crescents into his skin as their eyes locked one final time. "I love you, Hao," she whispered.

He nodded, a ghost of a smile touching his lips as he eased into the nearest console chair, the leather creaking under his weight. "Stay in earshot," he ordered Ming. "I'll let you know when I know something."

She turned her back then, steeling herself, shoulders squaring as she stared fixedly at the blue sky. The wrench whistled through the air, a dull, meaty thud echoing off the bulkheads as it struck his head. She winced.

Jerry twisted the curtain strip into a makeshift rope, then secured the end of it to the column on the third floor of the dining room by tying a bowline knot. He pulled and tugged hard, ensuring the anchor knot would stay in place and bear his weight. He made an overhand knot in the tail about every three feet until he reached the end. He glanced over at Brock, who nodded, then to Norton, who made an adjustment to his "rope" before nodding.

He didn't look forward to this. They didn't have gloves, and the friction burns on their hands were going to be real. They also didn't have boots on. No way these dress shoes would grip the "ropes" to provide friction and braking in any meaningful way, nor would they offer any cushioning or ankle support upon landing when they reached the steel deck below.

They quietly laid down their rifles and shotguns on the carpeted deck while ensuring their pistols remained secure and would not alert anyone below by falling to the deck. Then Norton and Brock half-slid, half-climbed down to the second floor while he kept watch. As soon as he got the hand signal from Norton down below, Jerry pulled both of their improvised ropes back up and secured the long guns to them. One by one, he lowered the weapons down.

Finally, Jerry slipped over the railing and climbed down himself. The faint, muffled creak of the curtain fibers straining under his weight whispered up the line, barely louder than his pulse thundering in his ears. While not perfect, the knots he'd placed at intervals mostly helped reduce friction, protected his hands, and gave his shoes something to grip.

Mostly.

This time, the clang of the outer door slamming shut barely registered with Olive. She rose alongside Emanuel, eyes fixed on Ming and another man as they hauled an unconscious figure between them—gripping his limp arms, his boots scraping lifeless trails across the floor. Blood fell from the side of his head, pattering softly in their wake.

"Get back," Ming said. He nodded to the other man, and they laid the body between them while Ming typed the code in the panel. The latch unlocked, and they dragged the man in, leaving him in a heap in the middle of the cell.

Olive charged toward the door. "Can you at least give me a first aid kit for him?"

The silver-haired man with Ming turned and looked at her. His expressionless eyes made a chill go up her back. Without a word, he went into the outer room. Ming followed him.

"This man is injured!" she yelled.

Seconds later, the man returned with a red bag, the white cross on the outside identifying it as a first aid kit. He unzipped the bag and removed the shears, checked the other contents, then tossed it in through the bars.

"Thank you," she said.

He didn't speak. Not long after he left, she heard the

sound of the outer door clanging shut.

"Can you help me?" she asked.

Emanuel stepped forward and helped her roll the man over. He gasped when he saw his face. "That's First Officer Jun," he said.

The nametag on his uniform read, *Hao Jun, Hong Kong*.

"Nasty blow to the head," Olive observed, pulling a pair of gloves out of the kit. She took his pulse first, then probed the wound. "Can you see if there is any superglue or butterflies or anything like that in the kit?"

While Emanuel searched, she took the bottle of saline and a stack of cotton pads and gently irrigated the wound, pushing the hair out of the way while checking for any kind of debris. Then she pressed a stack of pads against it and looked at the bottle that Emanuel held up. "This?"

She nodded. "Open it, please."

She released the pressure on the wound and lifted the pads. The bleeding had slowed considerably. "I'm going to press the skin together. I need you to squeeze the glue along the top of the seam I'll make."

Emanuel nodded, and she pressed the wound together, then cleaned up the blood that covered the seam. She nodded to Emanuel, and he squeezed the glue slowly along the gash, following Olive's directions. The sharp, chemical sting of superglue fumes bit her nostrils, mingling with the underlying coppery reek of fresh blood seeping through.

She maintained the pressure on the wound for about a minute, letting the glue dry. As she gently released it, she held her breath, praying that the glue would hold.

"Great job," she said.

"First time I've ever done that," Emanuel said, sitting back on his heels. "But this doesn't look like your first day."

She chuckled as she taped a cotton pad over the wound. "Correct. I'm a surgical nurse. This is not my first day."

After she pulled the gloves off, she started to stand, but First Officer Jun moaned and his eyelids fluttered. She put a hand on his forehead, wanting to comfort him. Instead, he moved quicker than she would have thought possible and grabbed her wrist.

"Ahh," she said, pain flooding her arm. She wrenched her hand free.

His eyes opened all the way, and he blinked, then looked at each of them. He muttered in Chinese. Olive shook her head. "I'm sorry," she said, "I speak English."

He moaned again and put his hand to his temple. "What happened?" he asked, his voice hoarse.

Emanuel put himself in his view. "We don't know, sir. Two men brought you here already unconscious."

"Two men?" He gasped and sat up quickly. "I was on the bridge. There was a ship, then I don't remember anything else."

"Where is the Captain, sir?" Emanuel asked.

"He..." he winced and touched the bandage. "He was at a wedding."

Olive started to speak, but reconsidered. She didn't know either of these men. If Jerry and his friends had managed to evade capture, she didn't want to say anything that might put them in danger.

TWENTY SIX

When they reached the first level of the dining room, Norton broadcast, "This is Coppertop. Deck one. Over."

Anderson replied, "Roger, Coppertop. Kitchen to your port side. Over."

Fisher guided Peña's team while Anderson guided theirs. They worked their way toward the kitchen. Hundreds of abandoned cellphones littered the hallways.

"Trout to Colada. Move to starboard and standby. Over."

Jerry mentally blocked the sound of Fisher's voice, focusing only on Anderson as he cleared rooms for them.

"Coppertop. Heisman. Bow clear. Port and starboard clear. Over."

"Heisman. Coppertop. Roger. Moving toward bow. Over."

"Coppertop. Heisman. Possible bandit to your twelve. Bandit is prone in the kitchen. Over."

They stacked and breached the kitchens. The smell of burning food mingled with the scent of recent death. In the kitchens, they found the corpse of a crewmen. The murdered chef had taken a round to the forehead. Nothing they could do for him. As Jerry went by the smoking oven, he turned the burners off.

Brock whistled and held up a baggie of heavy-duty zip-ties. Norton nodded once and threw up a thumb.

Through the kitchens, into a large corridor, and on to the end. They moved in a tight group, their upper bodies barely moving, their legs moving almost synchronously beneath them, carrying them smoothly down the corridor.

"Colada. Trout. All clear to stern. Lift clear. Over."

"Trout. Colada. Moving to lift. Over."

Norton waved the team to the entrance of the freight elevator. They stacked until it arrived, cleared it, and breached as soon as the doors opened. It smelled of produce and seafood. Jerry kept his foot in the threshold, keeping the elevator on their deck and the doors open.

"This is Coppertop. Set. Over."

"Colada set. On your mark. Over."

Norton replied, "Roger, Colada. On my mark. Over."

Norton broadcast to Peña as he pushed the "1" button. "Mark, mark, mark."

With the group in a defensive posture and Anderson speaking into the comms, they silently emerged from the elevator, weapons ready.

They could hear the high-pitched whine of a light-duty electric forklift rolling through the space, stacking cargo to port and starboard. The intruders had packed their end of the cargo bay with row upon row of large crates stacked up to eight high. The crates would certainly affect Jerry's ability to maneuver and fire within the target space. Conversely, they would provide adequate cover and concealment, preventing their opponents from freely maneuvering as well.

Anderson signaled, "Coppertop. Heisman. Four armed Bandits to your eleven, twelve, and one. Be advised. Colada to your twelve. Over."

Instantly, Fisher signaled, "Colada. Trout. Three armed bandits to your twelve and one. Be advised. Coppertop to your twelve. Over."

Norton whispered, "Alright, ladies. Check your targets on every shot. Just like we've done a thousand times—except no gear whatsoever."

They nodded.

Peña broadcast, "Colada to Trout. On your mark. Over."

Fisher, keeping his voice needlessly low, broadcast, "Roger. Standby."

Norton whispered, "Tighten up."

Jerry already felt relatively tight.

A few very long seconds later, Fisher, hypothetically waiting for the opportune moment to strike based on what he and Anderson could observe through the cameras, finally broadcast, "Mark, mark, mark!"

Both teams instantly opened fire with their noisy borrowed Benelli shotguns. In confined spaces, the shotgun's semi-automatic design allowed for rapid target acquisition and follow-up shots. The tight spread of the eight double-aught buckshot pellets in each shell allowed for a wider impact area at close range, without traveling far beyond the target. As available weapons went, the shotgun worked for close-quarters combat by limiting the risk of friendly fire. Also, they epitomized overwhelming violence, often making opponents freeze or hesitate after the opening salvo.

"Contact right!"

Jerry, crouching behind a crate, peered around it, firing two shots in rapid succession, then moving to the next crate.

"Strike one!"

"Contact left!"

"Strike two!"

They spoke into their comms, filtering out the explosions of shotgun blasts and men yelling, moving with precision and purpose.

Jerry emerged from behind the row of crates and suddenly pain sliced through his left cheek. He reacted, spinning to find the target, firing two shots at a woman with black and gray dreadlocks just as she brought her pistol to bear again. She gasped and fell backward without firing another shot.

Back behind cover, Jerry swiped his left hand to his cheek. He could feel the blood and the burn. Thankfully, it felt like the bullet had just grazed him, although the pain seemed disproportionate to a flesh wound. Annoyed, he superfluously used his sleeve to swipe at his face. He heard one of their opponents open fire with an automatic weapon. He moved back out from behind cover, his shotgun at the ready.

When the smoke cleared and the dust settled, none of the armed enemy surrendered. They had to take out all the armed opponents. Finally, the six remaining unarmed enemies threw up their hands.

Menacing them into compliance with their shotguns, Peña's team shouted orders, "On your knees! On your knees! Hands on your heads!"

Brock set all his weapons on a crate and retrieved the zip-ties he had acquired in the kitchens. He towered over the prisoners, each of whom individually he outweighed by a hundred pounds or more. They did not resist as, one by one, Brock zipped their hands and ankles together. He then zipped them together in pairs. Peña kept them covered the entire time, his eyes hard.

When the second-to-last captive started to speak, Brock shoved him to the deck. Staring into the man's eyes, Brock raised a finger to his lips in the universal symbol of silence. The man never said another word.

"Guys," Swanson broadcast. "I have a bit of a personal problem."

Meanwhile, Jerry and Norton verified that the casualties the team had shot were all beyond saving. They were. Special Forces soldiers never trained to wound. They trained for lethality, and their real-world execution of that training followed suit.

As they confirmed the elimination or capture of all potential threats, Waller's voice came over the comms. "Bourbon here. We need Ozzy, over."

Jerry rushed from behind the crates and dashed to

where the team medic knelt over Swanson.

"Talk to me," Osbourne said over the comms.

"Pot Pie caught one. Lower right abdomen. We need more than compression." Jerry could hear the tension in Waller's voice.

Ozzy responded, "Roger. Meet me in sickbay. Trout. Walk me in."

Waller looked up at Jerry as he pressed on Swanson's wound. "Nice face, Maguire. You need anything?"

Jerry realized that the wound on his face must look terrible. He felt blood sliding down his neck and into his dress shirt. He shrugged. "I'll be fine. Just a graze."

Marie sprinted across the loading dock of the cruise ship, her boots pounding the smooth deck. The clamor of forklifts beeping and the ocean slapping against the hull of the ship drowned out the sound. She lunged forward, fingers clamping around Henri's arm like a vice, yanking him mid-stride from his inventory checks. "You need to go right now," she hissed.

Her nephew's eyes—wide, dark mirrors of her own—flared with instant alarm, the tremor in her grip translating straight to his bones. Without a word, he slapped the tablet in his hands to the top of a nearby crate.

"Where?" he demanded, already pivoting toward her, his lanky frame taut as a bowstring.

"Tell these men to get serious," she gestured toward the six guards idling nearby. "Then, go to the cargo ship."

She jabbed a finger toward the hulking silhouette of their cargo vessel rafted up alongside the cruise liner, its ramp connecting the two vessels.

Marie spun away, eyes raking towering stacks of containers. There—Julien, hunched over the controls of a forklift, its yellow arms laden with a crate of ammunition. She bolted toward him, waving her arms like signal flags. He slammed the brake.

"Auntie Marie," he called, twisting in the seat. His face creased with confusion, sweat beading along his brow in the humid press of the afternoon. "What's the matter?"

"We have to go right now." The words tumbled out sharp and unyielding.

He frowned. "But—"

"Now, nephew." She vaulted onto the step beside him in one fluid surge, her face inches from his, nose brushing close enough to catch the faint soap scent clinging to his skin. "We are all about to die. This is a fail. Come with me now."

"I don't understand." His voice cracked, gaze darting past her to the oblivious bustle of the workers unloading the cargo ship, searching for the threat. "Where's Henri?"

"Already safe. Come on."

He powered down the forklift and hopped down. "Where are we going?"

"Follow me." She seized his wrist and led him to the cargo ship.

Jean stood near the ramp that spanned the gap between the two vessels. Henri stood before him, one arm jabbing back toward the dock in urgent arcs, his words spilling fast and heated, swallowed by the noise of loading dock.

"We need to get you out of here," Marie cut in, her voice slicing through like a knife's edge, halting Jean mid-sentence as she closed the distance.

Jean shook his head. "What is going on?"

"We don't know." She gripped his elbow. "Security force of some sort. They're about to take the loading dock. We already lost the armory, communications, and the cargo bay."

Jean pressed his hands to the sides of his head, fingers threading through his hair as if to hold his skull intact against the fracturing of his world. "Daphnée is in the cargo bay."

She stepped closer. "Jean. We have to go."

"I can't leave her!" The yell tore from him, raw and guttural, propelling him toward the ramp in a blind surge.

Julien lunged, arms wrapping around Jean's waist in a vise, hauling him back with a grunt, their boots scuffling in a tangle of desperation. Marie's voice lashed out. "Daphnée can take care of herself. She knows as well as I that you are the face of this movement. We need to get you to safety. If we lose you, the movement dies."

She didn't release her hold on his arm, steering them away from the cruise ship toward the lifeboat davits slung along the cargo ship's rail—a bulky orange shell swaying gently on its falls. "We will regroup and save Daphnée," she said as she wrestled the release pins free.

"What about Hao?" Henri asked, his voice suddenly small. "Shouldn't he come with us?"

Marie's stomach clenched as she pictured the blood pouring out of his head and Ming and Reginald Hall dragging him between the two of them. "Hao is deeply undercover," she forced out. "We can't risk that right now. As long as he is not compromised, he'll be fine."

She bundled them into the boat, Jean's resistance crumbling into numb compliance as Julien and Henri clambered over the gunwales. Marie shoved off as Henri lowered the small engine into the water. The air filled with the smell of the small engine fuel as he started the engine. It made her stomach churn.

Just as the gap widened to safety's illusion, an explosion erupted behind them, followed by the sound of yells, confusion, two more explosions, then the sound of gunfire.

Jerry and the team searched the crates, locating a crate of grenades and another crate of ammunition. They armed themselves and reloaded.

As Jerry pried up the heavy lid of a long crate, he felt a sudden sense of elation. The crate held what looked like about thirty QBU-202 sniper rifles.

He only needed one.

He unceremoniously set the shotgun down on the deck and retrieved one from the crate. As he examined it, he whispered, "Hello, gorgeous. You may not know it, but I think this is the beginning of a beautiful friendship."

Jerry would have preferred to find a CS/LR4, the modern Chinese army's long-range rifle, but this gorgeous piece of firearms history would suffice. It had a range of up to 1,800 meters, and the generous Chinese had even graciously equipped it with appropriate optics. The true beauty was that Jerry had fired about 600 rounds through one of these less than two years ago.

He held the rifle up and announced, "Listen up! I need to find the 8.6×70mm Lapua Magnum rounds. They have to be in here somewhere."

Sanders, from across the aisle, immediately said, "I think I got 'em. Look at that. One line. No waiting."

As they stocked up and supplied, they discussed the plan. From here on the first deck, they needed to get up to the loading bay on the third deck.

"We could use the elevator again," Sanders said.

Peña jerked his head in the direction of the elevator. "It's full. They sent another load down. We have it locked so they can't recall it."

"Won't be long until they realize it's been too long," Norton said. "We need to move."

"Better to get into position there and wait." Peña tapped the map. "We need to flank them again."

Jerry said, "Sir. We have grenades, now. Team can stay intact. Frontal assault is much faster."

"Fair point, Top," Peña acknowledged. Jerry let the verbal promotion go without remark. "But a pincer is more effective. I don't like this playing out under the watchful eye of that cargo ship, either. So, we breach here and here, simultaneously. Three-man teams." They quickly went over the specific details of the plan.

"Once we start making noise up there, there's going to be a problem for the prisoners on the island." Ibrahim rolled his head on his neck. "That loading dock door is open."

Peña nodded. "I don't disagree. But we're down to six. We can only do one thing at a time. Right now, that's securing the ship."

"Roger dodger," Sanders said. "Let's do this."

They parted ways at a juncture in the corridor. Jerry stayed with Brock and Norton. Peña, Ibrahim, and Sanders went the other way.

They moved as a single unit, with no need to direct or explain who needed to do what. They communicated with clicks and low voices in their comms, while listening for Anderson and Fisher to give them direction. Soon, they took their positions on the third deck, with each team on either side of the loading dock.

Jerry's pulse thudded in his ears as he dropped to a pushup position, the cold deck pressing against his palms. He glided forward slowly, every muscle taut, aware that one wrong shift could expose him. His breath came shallow as he peered around the opening from less than a foot above the deck. The loading dock sprawled out below—crates stacked like jagged teeth, the rafted-up cargo vessel bobbing ominously against the ship. Armed figures clustered near the doorway, their postures rigid, rifles slung low but ready. One wrong glance their way, and it was over.

He reversed just as carefully, heart slamming against his ribs, and rose to his feet, bringing his newly acquired sniper rifle to the ready. Sweat trickled down his back, and blood trickled down his chest. He raised his hands, fingers flashing silent signals: control room up on the catwalk—

clear line of sight over everything. Hostiles grouped, facing the door, alert and ready.

Norton clicked twice into the comms. Fisher came over, voice a low rasp. He relayed the room's layout and pinpointed enemy positions like dots on a map. Jerry knew maps didn't account for the human factor.

Finally, Peña quietly broadcast, "On my mark."

The wait stretched like a wire about to snap. In the loading dock, a Chinese woman argued with a man at the cargo elevator, her voice sharp and rising. The man spun away, barking French into his radio, the words echoing faintly. Jerry's grip tightened on the rifle; any second now, that radio could summon reinforcements or initiate executions of the passengers on the island.

At Peña's whispered command of "Mark. Fire in the hole," they tossed the Chinese stick grenades into the mix, then crouched and shielded themselves around the corner of the corridor until the grenades detonated. The blasts roared through the deck, a concussive wave that rattled Jerry's teeth and sent debris skittering.

With no more need for quiet, they yelled directions to each other, staying in constant communication, voices cutting through the ringing in his ears.

The dock erupted in chaos as each three-man team surged forward, their feet clad in dress shoes sliding treacherously on the salt-slicked deck while pounding against the clamor of automatic fire.

Adrenaline surged as Jerry broke for the metal staircase leading up to the office overlooking the loading dock.

Norton covered him. Shouts erupted from the dock—confused, angry. Gunshots broke out. Jerry half-expected a bullet to whine past his head. He took the stairs two at a time, thighs burning, rifle bouncing against his back. The door loomed at the top, slightly ajar. What if it wasn't empty? What if someone hid inside in ambush?

He kicked it open hard, hitting his dress shoes like a hammer hits a nail, and swept the muzzle across the dim room—desks, shadows, nothing moving. Empty. For now.

He exhaled sharply, positioning himself at the window, scope scanning the smoke-filled dock below as the fight erupted in full.

He used the buttstock of his QBU to break the glass out of the window overlooking the operations below, scattering glass to the deck. He lined up on a target. "How are your optics, QB?" He squeezed the trigger, and his target went down from a dead-center shot. "Already knew my zero? You shouldn't have."

Jerry methodically started eliminating threats, one by one. He would observe the action below, identify the enemy combatant who posed the greatest threat to his team members, and remove that bandit from the board as if checking off tasks on a prioritized list.

"Hao Jun," the first mate said, extending his hand, his voice steady despite the blood matting his dark hair along the crown of his skull, the drying rivulet down his temple that stained the collar of his white uniform.

"Olive Duncan," she replied, rising from her corner to clasp his offered hand. It surprised her how much it hurt to move her jaw, so she tried not to move it as she spoke. Her voice came out slightly slurred as a result.

"Where are you from, Olive?"

"Tennessee. Little town near the Kentucky state line." She studied his face in turn—the subtle wince as he shifted, the way his jaw tightened against the pain. "How are you feeling now that you're up?"

He inclined his head in a small, formal bow, the motion careful, as if testing the waters of his own balance. "I would feel better if my head didn't hurt so much," he admitted, a wry twist touching his lips, though it didn't reach his eyes.

"I could say the same." She eased back into the corner, turning her back to the unyielding wall of the cell—close enough to the bars to feel their chill radiate against her shoulder blades. "You took a pretty hard blow."

"You, too," Emanuel interjected from his perch on the bench. He lifted a finger to point at her face, tracing a slow, circular motion in the air over his own temple and jaw. "Bruising on your temple, your jaw."

She shouldn't have felt a flush of embarrassment creep up her neck—not after the raw violence that had dumped her here, bruised and caged like an unwanted pet dumped at the puppy pound—but the heat bloomed anyway, warming her cheeks. She ducked her chin slightly, fingers brushing self-consciously at the tender swell. "I fought back," she said, the words tumbling out a touch sheepishly. "But that guy, Ming, can throw a punch."

"Where is everyone else?" Hao asked, his tone shifting to something keener, more insistent.

Emanuel shook his head. "We don't know, sir. She was in here when I got here."

Hao's brow furrowed. "Who brought you here?"

"One of the Director's assistants, Marie Allard," Emanuel replied. "The man had a cook's uniform on, but I didn't know him."

"Ming," Olive added, the syllable clipped. "The nametag on his uniform said his name is Ming."

"I know Cook Ming." Hao lowered himself onto the bench beside Emanuel. "He makes a chicken and mushroom soup that reminds me of what my Nǎinai would make." His voice softened on the word, a faint smile ghosting his lips. "My grandmother."

They sat silent for a while, the only noise Emanuel's fingers drumming a silent rhythm on his thigh.

Then, a distant explosion ripped through the air—a muffled thunderclap that swelled to fill the brig, vibrating the bars and rattling the control panel's keys like chattering teeth. Hao surged to his feet. "What?" He craned his neck, eyes flicking upward to the ceiling as if he could pierce the decks above, then pressed close to the bars, straining to peer into the front room.

Another boom followed, then another nearly overlapped it—deeper, closer, shaking dust from the vents and sending a shiver through the floor. Gunfire cracked in its wake, sharp and erratic, a hail echoing from somewhere amidships, punctuated by muffled shouts that clawed through the bulkheads.

Olive pressed the heels of her hands to her eyes. To be trapped here, listening to the sounds of the battle, alone and defenseless, with two men she did not know nor could she trust.

And her head hurt. A lot. And her jaw hurt. A lot more.

She did not want to show weakness in front of these men. Instead, she forced a calm expression and raised her head. But, inside, she began a litany of prayer. *God*, she thought, *if that's them, guard them. Keep them. Shield them. Help them find me.*

Help Jerry find me.

Thirty-three enemies, each armed with rifles chattering wildly, should have cut them down in seconds. But their response revealed their lack of discipline and training. Panicked shouts in a foreign tongue, bullets spraying high and wide, sinking into wooden crates or ricocheting off metal decks with sharp pings that echoed like angry hornets.

With the smoke still curling from the grenade blasts burning his nose, Jerry steadied his breath and peered through the QBU's optics, the crosshairs sweeping the chaotic loading dock below. The enemies—now down from thirty-three—numbered only twenty-seven strong. Fractured by panic, they scrambled for cover behind crates and machinery, their automatic fire wild and unfocused.

One combatant popped up from behind a forklift, rifle aimed at Peña's position. Jerry's finger caressed the trigger. The shot cracked sharp and true, dropping the man before he could fire.

"Strike one. Bow," Jerry murmured into comms, his voice calm despite the adrenaline surging through him. Below, the team advanced in tight formation, Norton and Brock laid down suppressive bursts that pinned clusters of enemies, while Peña, Ibrahim, and Sanders flanked right, their movements a symphony of practiced precision.

Peña signaled forward, dodging a haphazard spray of bullets that chewed into the deck plating nearby. Jerry's heart tightened—too close—but he refocused, spotting another enemy reloading clumsily on the rafted-up cargo ship's gangway. Another squeeze, another enemy slumped. The rifle felt like an extension of his arm, familiar and reliable, even if it wasn't his usual gear.

The dock thrummed with noise—people shouting, the roar of gunfire, metal pinging from ricochets. Sweat beaded on Jerry's forehead, the office air thick with the scent of gunpowder and sea salt wafting up from below. A near-miss shattered more glass from the window frame, shards tinkling to the floor as a stray round whizzed past his left shoulder. He ducked instinctively, pulse racing, then rose again. What he wouldn't give for a plated vest and a Kevlar helmet.

His team pushed hard, exploiting the enemy's disarray—some combatants fumbled magazines, others argued amid the haze, shouting conflicting instructions, their coordination crumbling under pressure.

"Clearing central crates—cover the ramp!" Norton's voice crackled. Jerry shifted his aim, eliminating threats emerging from the cargo ship's shadow, their rifles barking futilely into the smoke. The team surged ahead, dress shoes slipping but steady on the debris-strewn deck. Brock vaulted a low barrier, firing on the move, while Ibrahim dragged a wounded teammate.

Who?

No, just a shadow. He missed Waller in his ear. Jerry blinked sweat from his eyes, scanning for the next priority.

As the last pockets of resistance faltered, Peña waved toward the dock. "Boarding now—Jerry, overwatch the deck!"

The five-man team below funneled toward the gangway as if they had practiced it a thousand times, weapons up, crossing the narrow gap to the rafted cargo ship. Jerry's shots kept the pressure on, making the bandits keep their heads down. The vessel loomed like a steel behemoth, its hull groaning against the cruise ship's side with each swell of the water.

An enemy leaned out. Jerry hastily fired and missed, the impact echoing faintly. But the man retreated. Brock saw the bandit and moved in.

Heart steadying with each breath, Jerry watched his team secure the boarding point. The fight wasn't over—not with Olive still out there somewhere and an entire island of hostages—but they had gained ground.

"Moving," he broadcast. He slung the QBU and moved

to rejoin them below. Jerry, Brock, Ibraham, and Sanders cleared every corner of the loading dock while Peña and Norton kept the gangway covered.

Upon signaling the all clear, the six men moved inexorably up the gangway. Peña, Norton, and Sanders took the lead with Jerry, Ibraham, and Brock bringing up the rear and covering rear security. One by one, they boarded the ship.

Jerry's senses sharpened in the dim, echoing corridors. The vessel's hull groaned softly with the ocean's rhythm. The ship appeared lightly manned by an all-Chinese crew, but the faint hum of machinery below decks could mask potential footsteps.

They moved swiftly yet tactically, stacking up in tight formation: Peña at point, weapon sweeping low; Norton covering high angles; Brock and Ibrahim alternating flanks while Sanders brought up the rear. Jerry, QBU ready, scanned for elevated threats.

His mind raced through contingencies. What if the crew had rigged traps? What if reinforcements hid in the engine room?

They cleared compartments methodically—breaching doors with controlled force, cutting into corners to expose threats slice by slice. In one narrow passageway, a crewman in black fatigues emerged suddenly from a side hatch, hands empty but eyes wide with alarm.

"Down! On the ground!" Peña barked in English-tinged Mandarin. Brock zip-tied him swiftly as the man complied without resistance.

"Mandarin, Jorge?" Norton observed.

"Married to Emma? I picked up some things. Important words, anyway."

No shots fired—yet—but the encounter ratcheted Jerry's tension. They pressed on, the air growing thicker with the scent of oil and salt and sweat despite the ventilation fans whirring overhead. A muffled shout echoed from deeper inside the ship—Chinese voices, urgent but indistinct.

The team communicated in hushed clicks and hand signals. Finally, the bridge loomed ahead, its reinforced door a final barrier.

Jerry shot through the door's lock with a precise round, the report echoing sharply down the hall. He kicked it in, the impact reverberating up his leg through the thin soles of his dress shoes. He raised his weapon instantly, sighting in on the man obviously in charge.

An older Chinese man in full black battle fatigues stared at them with cold contempt, silently raising his hands. Peña approached with pistol drawn, grabbing the man and pressing him against the wall to zip-tie his wrists.

Norton broadcast, "Trout. Coppertop. Smothered mate. I say again. Smothered mate. Over."

Fisher's voice, responding to the chess reference, crackled over comms. "Roger, Coppertop. No movement on the ship's deck. No movement in the loading bay."

They lacked the manpower for a full sweep, so vigilance remained high—eyes on every shadow, every unlocked door.

Anderson chimed in. "Be advised. Just confirmed DC is sending reinforcements. DHS and a detachment from Fourteenth Group inbound." Reinforcements dispatched by the Secret Service and a detachment from the 14th Special Forces Group (Airborne), previously conducting training in Puerto Rico, were en route.

"ETA?" Peña demanded.

After a few seconds, Anderson replied, "Twenty-two mikes."

They moved back to the loading dock with their prisoners in tow. Upon arrival, Jerry handed off his Chinese prisoner to Ibrahim, who herded him toward a makeshift corral of stacked crates they had moved into place to confine their few captives.

"We're gonna need medical support for some of their wounded. Trout. Prioritize that," Peña broadcast.

"Roger," Fisher replied. "I'll put them on the list right behind Pot Pie."

Peña scoffed, then whistled sharply. "Jerry Maguire, Hobbes, Honest Abe…" he hesitated, "Coppertop. Do another sweep of that ship. Drumstick and me will keep these fine folks company. Make it quick, boys. Most ricky-tick. Spike the punch bowl on the way out."

An eternity passed in the next twelve minutes. Once the all-clear echoed—tentative but necessary—they tossed grenades into the ship's engine room. After getting back on the cruise ship, they severed the mooring ropes and sealed the cruise ship's cargo doors, isolating the threats. They returned to find that Peña had made no meaningful progress in getting any information out of their guests.

Norton keyed his comms. "We need Twenty-Four Ten. Anyone available to escort her?"

"I'll go get her," Peña replied.

Emma chimed in over the channel. "Send pictures. I need to start research."

Jerry quickly snapped a few photos of the Chinese leader's face and texted them to Peña's wife.

"Glad I didn't join the Navy, for whatever good that did me today," Sanders quipped in his droll voice.

Abruptly, Anderson cut in, "Jerry Maguire, we located Olive."

His heart leaped in his chest. Already halfway to the door, he demanded, "Where?"

"Brig. I'll guide you," Anderson said.

TWENTY EIGHT

Hao stared at Olive with narrowed eyes, his probing gaze prickling the fine hairs at the nape of her neck. She shifted on the bench, finding the intensity of his stare more disconcerting than the sporadic bursts of gunfire that had sounded for the last five minutes.

"You don't seem scared," he said, his voice low and edged with suspicion. "What do you know?"

Olive shook her head, the motion sending a fresh twinge through her bruised jaw. "I'm terrified," she confessed. "Just used to tense situations. Helps me internalize my emotions."

"What does that mean?" His brow furrowed.

Olive licked her lips, tasting salty tears she'd hidden from them. The hostility rolling off him in waves coiled tightly around her chest, making her breath come shallower. "I'm a surgical nurse and served in the US Army," she explained, keeping her tone even. "I can be afraid but still function."

He glared at her for a long beat, his dark eyes unyielding, before the hard lines of his face eased. "I see." He lifted a hand to the back of his head, fingers tracing the edges of the bandage with deliberate care. "You patched me up."

"I did."

Emanuel interjected from his spot on the bench, leaning forward with his elbows on his knees. "I was in the Navy."

She turned to him, summoning a smile. "What did you do?"

He shrugged. "Same thing. Engineer. Pay's better on this ship, and it docks a lot more often than the aircraft carrier I was on."

"Right." The casual rhythm of their exchange grounded her. "Wish I knew what was happening," she murmured, frustration threading her voice as she rubbed her palms along her arms, chasing away a chill that had nothing to do with the air. "None of this makes sense!"

"Pirates," Hao said, his mouth turning downward at the corners, pulling the skin tight across his cheekbones. "They are getting worse."

"The Valiant Voyager seems like a big ship to try to pirate," Emanuel countered, glancing toward the barred door as if it might yield answers.

Hao shrugged. "Everyone is on the island. It's the perfect opportunity." He sighed then, deep and rolling from his chest, tilting his head side to side as if to loosen the knots in his neck, vertebrae popping faintly in the quiet. "We need better security."

"We hear scuttlebutt of course," Emanuel added, his fingers drumming a soft tattoo on his thigh. "But I've never seen anything."

"It's a big ocean." Hao tilted his head, ear cocking toward the door, the silence stretching taut around them. "The shooting stopped."

Emanuel pushed to his feet, crossing the narrow cell in two strides to press his face against the bars, cheek squishing against the cold metal as he craned to peer into the outer room. "Maybe we'll get rescued after all."

Under Anderson's clipped directions coming through their earpieces, Jerry led the way down the narrow passageway, Sanders a silent shadow at his right flank, Ibrahim mirroring on the left. They held their weapons ready. They made the stairwell without incident, ascending to the fourth deck in taut silence, breaths measured, eyes scanning every bulkhead and corner. No other soul stirred the corridor—no footsteps, no voices, no litany of announcements.

They emerged at an intersection. Anderson's voice cut through the comms, low and precise. "Someone is just inside the door. I don't have eyes there, but I keep seeing a shadow."

"Roger," Ibrahim murmured, his voice a rumble in the quiet, his broad frame easing forward. He leaned out, weapon sweeping the angle, then snapped back. "Just closed doors."

Jerry's jaw tightened, the itch to charge thrumming in

his veins like a live wire. "Heisman, which door?"

"Fourth on the left," came the steady reply.

He glanced at his friends. Sanders gave a short nod, and Ibrahim's eyes already locked ahead. "Let's do this."

They advanced with predatory caution, hugging the bulkheads. Jerry's pulse hammered a restrained rhythm. Every instinct screamed to run and burst through the door. At the fourth door on the left—a plain slab of reinforced steel with a porthole, they halted, backs pressed flat. Jerry fished Cynthia's compact from his pocket, the sterling silver warm from his body heat, and flipped it open, angling the mirror up to the glass in a practiced arc. One man, Chinese features, clad in a cook's uniform. He leaned against a desk, arms crossed tight over his chest, his posture deceptively lax, a holstered sidearm bulging at his hip.

Jerry held up one finger, then jabbed it toward the target's center mass. Sanders positioned at the handle while Jerry stepped back from the door, feet planting wide, the suppressed Chinese pistol rising in a two-handed grip. He nodded once.

Ibrahim swiped Captain Ege's badge to unlock the door as Sanders twisted the latch and shoved it wide in a fluid surge. Jerry swung through the gap, body low and coiled, the world narrowing to the target's arc. The man in the cook's uniform snapped upright, eyes flaring wide in shock, mouth parting on a half-formed shout. A heartbeat later, his hand clawed for his gun, leveling it in a blur toward Jerry's chest.

Jerry fired twice, the suppressed rounds whispering

through the air, punching center mass with dull thuds that dropped the man back against the desk, his gun clattering unfired to the deck. Two more precise shots as the man slumped, arms unfolding limp, a bloom of red staining the white fabric as he slid to the floor.

Jerry pivoted, clearing behind the desk in a swift sweep while Ibrahim mirrored on the other side of the room. One glance revealed the man no longer lived. His nametag read, "Ming, Hong Kong." Jerry retrieved the unfired pistol from the deck and jammed it into his belt.

Clear.

They converged on the inner door, a heavier barrier etched with the brig's utilitarian warning in six languages. Jerry rose on his toes, peering through the porthole's wire-mesh glass. He could see the holding cage on the right. It held three figures—Olive, face swollen and shadowed with bruises, flanked by two men, one in an officer's whites crusted with blood, the other wearing an engineer's jumpsuit.

Ibrahim gripped the handle, and on Jerry's count, he wrenched it open. They flowed through, weapons sweeping the space in overlapping arcs.

"Jerry!" Olive's sob shattered the hush, raw and breaking as she rushed to the cage door. Tears carved tracks down her bruised cheeks. "I knew you'd come."

He crossed the room in three strides, eyes raking the men with her. The bloodied officer stood rigid with guarded tension. The other edged back, hands half-raised, uncertainty etching his features as he stared at their weapons. Sanders and Ibrahim fanned deeper as they cleared the far corners of the large room, muzzles trained on blind spots.

Clear.

Jerry reached the bars, his free hand threading through to cup her face. Brushing gently against the swollen curve of her temple and cheek, thumb tracing the purple bloom with a tenderness that knifed his gut. "I've been distracted, worrying over you," he murmured, voice rough.

Tears streamed unchecked down her face, glistening on her lashes. "I'm sorry. I fell asleep—"

He shook his head, the motion firm, silencing her with a press of his thumb to her lips. No time for that. Plus, it looked like it hurt every time she spoke. "Trout, can you do anything about this door?"

"Standby," Fisher's voice came back, fingers no doubt flying over keys.

A second ticked, then the latch clicked and buzzed, and Jerry stepped aside as Olive launched herself through the gap, colliding into his chest. He wrapped his arms around her, pulling her against him. Nothing in his life had ever felt as good as her at this very moment. He closed his eyes, blocking the world for one stolen beat, savoring the thunder of her heartbeat syncing with his, the simple, shattering truth that she was whole, here, breathing, alive.

They separated too soon, the press of duty clawing him back. He wanted to bundle her close, sweep her off to somewhere safe and sunlit, but they still had to contend with the island. "Who are your friends?"

Olive gestured first to the man in the officer's crew uniform. He spoke up. "First Mate, Hao Jun."

Jerry dipped his chin in acknowledgment. "Sir. Captain Ege has been worried for you."

"I would like to know what has been going on with my ship," Hao replied, his voice biting.

Jerry nodded once, his eyes locked on Hao's. Something about the man's tone raised his hackles. "Expect so."

Olive nodded to the other man. He likewise spoke up. "Emanuel Ramirez. An engineer on the ship."

The two men did not shake hands. Olive tilted her head then, her gaze snagging on the ugly groove scoring Jerry's cheek where a bullet had nicked him. "Can I patch you up?"

Jerry did not like the way it clearly hurt her to speak. He wondered if she had lost teeth. Before he could tell her it was a minor wound, Sanders said. "Getting antsy in my pantsy, Jerry Maguire. We should move out soon."

Jerry nodded and drew the guard's pistol from his belt. He handed it to Olive. "Loaded," he said. She nodded, performed a quick function check on the weapon, and held it ready.

Ibrahim approached from the corridor off the room they were in. "Rest of the area is secure, Top."

"Daddy," Jerry said into his comm, "we have Olive as well as two civilians."

After a loaded pause, Peña's voice came back. It almost surprised Jerry when Peña replied instead of Norton. He would have to get used to that moving forward. "Roger,

Maguire. I read three civilians. Stand by."

It struck Jerry as odd to think of Olive as a civilian. He didn't think of her as a civilian, though in this context it fit. The line hummed with muted discussion—Peña and Norton's low tones working logistics. Peña returned. "Bring them to the loading dock and regroup. We'll consolidate everyone after we contend with the island."

"Roger." Jerry's gaze found Olive's, and he said another silent prayer of thanksgiving. "Let's go," he said.

TWENTY NINE

Olive desperately wanted to ask Jerry a thousand questions, but she could feel an intensity radiating off of him that told her not to distract him right now. So, barefoot, packing a loaded QSZ-193 pistol, and feeling rather underdressed in a turquoise sleeveless dress with yellow and white flowers all over it, she followed him down the staff stairwell and into the bowels of the ship.

As they filed out of the brig, she pointed and said, "That's Ming. He brought us here."

It surprised her how much it hurt to speak, now. Her head throbbed as they moved, and her jaw hurt like nothing she had ever felt.

Jerry nodded and said, "We've met."

While all the spaces occupied by the passengers had carpet, wallpaper, decoration, and elegance, this area of the ship had metal painted floors, white walls marred with scrapes and nicks, and harsh white LED lighting. Such a dichotomy between the two.

Bill Sanders led their group, Jerry stayed beside Olive, and they stayed behind the two men, while Jared Ibrahim covered their rear. At every intersection and stairwell, they paused while Jerry and his teammates took directions from someone named Heisman.

On the third deck, the corridor became very wide, double the width of the promenade. After a turn that took them toward the outer part of the ship, they went through a wide door and entered the loading dock.

The astringent smell of the ocean and gunpowder mixed with the citrus smell of explosives burned her nose. Some of Jerry's team stood near Jorge Peña. She spotted Calvin Brock guarding some people contained by a pen made from crates, some wearing black fatigues and some in crew uniforms, all bound hand and foot.

She could not help but notice the long line of bodies covered by tablecloths.

Emma rushed toward her, wearing a golden gown, her hair pinned up in a French Twist, and also barefoot. High heels clearly were not the preferred tactical footwear. How odd they must look in their gowns among the ruins of battle.

"Olive!"

The women hugged. "We were so worried," Emma said.

Olive chuckled. It hurt, but she managed, "Me, too."

Hao cleared his throat. "I would like to get back to the bridge. Is there someone who can escort me?"

Jorge approached. "One moment, sir. We're in touch

with the Captain. Let me see what we can do."

He pulled Jerry and Olive out of earshot. Before he could speak, Jerry said, "Colada, I strongly advise not taking that man to the bridge."

"Oh? "Jorge raised an eyebrow. "Why's that, Maguire?"

Jerry released a big sigh before he spoke. "Call it a hunch." He paused and said, "Sir."

After glancing back at Hao, Jorge said, "Got it."

"Wait," Olive said. She stepped closer. "He was dragged in unconscious. I had to stop his head wound from bleeding. He's not faking."

After this speech, her hand instinctively clutched the side of her jaw, and she felt herself wince.

"Maybe," Jerry said. "Maybe not."

Rick Norton approached. "If I get a vote, I agree with Maguire."

"Your vote counts, Coppertop." Jorge nodded. "Okay. He stays here."

He looked at Olive. "Ozzy is in sick bay. Pot Pie caught a bullet to the lower abdomen. He needs surgery. They could use an extra hand. The Secret Service boys have Cynthia locked in tight. No help there. Feel up to helping out?"

Jerry leaned in. "She got beat up pretty bad."

Olive put a hand on his chest and smiled up at him. "Should have seen the other guy."

Jerry stared blankly into her eyes. With absolutely no inflection, he said, "I met him briefly."

Olive tried to read any kind of emotion in Jerry's expression. She realized he was compartmentalizing at that moment. Remorse and second-guessing would likely wait for some vulnerable night of bad dreams weeks or months from now.

To Jorge, she said, "I can't do what you all do. But, I know how to assist a surgeon." Jorge's eyes narrowed, clearly inspecting her injured face, evaluating her slurred and painful speech. "I can do it," she insisted.

With a deep sigh, Jerry said, "I'll take you. It's on this deck. Not far."

"Drop Olive, then get back to work," Jorge said. "Fourteenth Group is 'Talon Strike.' They are about twelve mikes out. Fast movers inbound, too. Hate to do this to you, Maguire, but you're who we got."

"Roger, Colada."

Confused at the code speak, Olive looked at Jerry, who nodded. But she could see his jaw clenching. "What? What is it?"

Jerry turned her to face him. "Long conversation. Promise we'll have it soon."

Jorge put a hand on Emma's waist. "Twenty-four Ten, go with them. I don't think we'll need you for a while."

"You got it, Colada," Emma said. She patted him on the cheek and looked at them. "Ready, Maguire?"

Olive realized they didn't trust who could hear what, and their work depended on secrecy. They used their call signs even in casual conversation, even here, to remain clandestine.

"Gonna need Bourbon," Jerry said.

Olive frowned. Bourbon? Since when?

"That you will." Jorge turned back briefly. "Pick Bourbon up when you drop Olive off. Then make your way up top with Twenty-Four Ten."

"Sixty seconds. Need to grab some gear," Jerry said. "Drumstick. Give me a hand."

He and Sanders lifted one of the sheets and pulled a black backpack off the person under it. Jerry dumped its contents on the deck. He and Bill Sanders shifted the lid of a crate and loaded the backpack with ammunition. Then they quickly moved to a different crate. Jerry retrieved a long rifle that looked identical to the one strapped to his back, including the same elaborate-looking scope. He detached the scope from the second rifle and casually stowed it into the backpack.

As he slipped the pack onto his back, he said to Jorge. "Set."

Jorge spoke into the air. "Heisman or Trout, guide Maguire to sick bay, then to the chapel, if you would be so kind."

Jerry led the way down the corridor and around two corners to the sickbay. The doors automatically slid open. Inside, Phil pressed a thick pad to Daniel Swanson's abdomen while Tim Waller ransacked cabinets for supplies. Blood covered Daniel Swanson's white dress shirt and his forearms up to his elbows.

Olive assumed Tim had started the saline IV and placed the pulse oximeter and blood pressure cuff while Phil managed the wound. She rushed forward and went straight to the sink. "What do you need?"

Phil lifted the towel on Daniel's abdomen and probed the wound. "A surgical theater would be nice."

Tim turned with a look of relief and announced, "Swanson, Daniel. Older than dirt male. Single GSW to the lower right abdomen about 20 mikes back. I carried him here, maybe 10 mikes back. It was not a fun trip. Ozzy just showed up. Entry with no obvious exit, likely lodged internally. No other injuries noted."

Jerry spoke from behind her. "Bourbon. You're with me when you can break it off."

"Roger that," Waller nodded, then spoke to Olive again. "Patient is conscious but in a lot of pain—rating it 8 out of 10, oriented times three. BP's low at 92/58, pulse 112 and thready, respirations 24 and shallow, O2 sat 94% on room air. Skin's pale, cool, and clammy—signs of early shock. Likely internal bleeding. No allergies reported, no meds on board yet. Just found morphine and fent. I've got a 16-gauge IV in his left AC with normal saline wide open, about 500 mL in so far. BP cuff and pulse ox are on. No active external bleed now, but abdomen's rigid and tender. Haven't done a FAST yet."

"Anything else?" Olive asked.

"No time to look around. Got what I needed when I saw it. There's probably a surgery or clean room further in."

Jerry asked from the doorway, "You good?"

Olive gave Phil a thumbs-up, and Phil said, "We're all good. Go."

Tim and Jerry hurried away.

Phil lifted his chin toward the door that led further into the sickbay. "I haven't been able to leave him yet, either. See what we have back there. A theater would be nice, but if not, see if you can find a surgical kit of any kind. I need—everything—but scalpel, forceps, clamps, sutures, gauze at a minimum."

"Yes, doctor," she said automatically, her speech somewhat slurred as if she had a lisp.

The cold of the tiled deck seeped into her bare feet as she went through the door into the inner part of the sick bay. Her head throbbed with every step. She passed a nurse's station, grabbed a stethoscope from the back of a chair, and then went through a treatment room into a back corridor that showed signs for X-ray and a procedure room. When she peeked in there, she looked around and rushed back to the front room. "Found one. Small surgical room."

Phil taped the IV against Daniel's arm and looked at the wheels on the bed, kicking the lock loose. "Let's get him back there."

"I found scrubs."

"Good. We'll get dressed for success before we really get going."

Olive made note of Daniel's blood pressure while Phil expertly applied Betadine all around the wound. He lifted his chin toward her. "Take out the earbud, will you? It's distracting me. You can just set it down somewhere. I can compartmentalize it if it's not right in my ear."

Olive stripped her glove off and took the earbud out of his ear, then put his phone on speaker. He held his hand out. "Scalpel."

While she assisted Phil, she prayed. The pain in her head and jaw distracted her. Her jaw throbbed with each heartbeat. Soon, the full metal jacketed steel core bullet he pulled out of Daniel plinked into a metal dish.

"Vicious round. Surprised it didn't go right through or bounce around a little inside you, Pot Pie. Let's see what you did," he murmured, then said, "Shine the light this way, please."

Phil thoroughly searched the path of the bullet, making sure he didn't have to stop any more bleeding. When he felt sure he hadn't missed anything, he began closing. Watching Phil's beefy fingers perform this delicate work fascinated Olive.

She anticipated his needs, having the instruments and implements in hand before he even asked for them. She secured the needle with the suture thread in a pair of needle forceps and held them out as he opened his mouth to ask for them.

His eyes crinkled around his mask. "Anyone ever tell you that you should be a nurse?"

She chuckled and said, "More than once."

THIRTY

Jerry, Tim Waller, and Emma Peña silently moved through the ship, taking precautions and letting Anderson guide them while watching out for anyone out of place. They did not encounter anyone.

The chapel door did not open automatically. He tapped on the door and waited. Marshal Stalling called from the other side of the door. "White dress!"

Jerry said, "Bowtie!"

Marshal Stalling opened the door with his Glock 47 ready. The group slipped inside. A body lay against the back wall, covered by a tablecloth. He assumed the tablecloth had been pilfered from the back room, and he assumed the corpse was once Marshal Black.

Jerry asked, "Everything okay?"

Marshal Stalling nodded. "Lost Black. Nothing anyone could do. We've been keeping up with everything on comms. Mrs. Peña connected us."

Cynthia Norton came toward him with a first aid kit in her hand. "Let me see your face."

Secret Service Agent Guthrie stepped forward, a note of warning in his tone. "Ma'am?"

"Thank you, Doc." He smiled and shook his head. "Later. Still on the clock."

"I can see bone," she protested, while gifting Guthrie a withering stare.

"Later," he explained.

Cynthia turned her scornful look upon Jerry. "You're just as bad as the rest of them."

He half-grinned a tight-lipped grin. "Then I'm in very good company, ma'am."

He looked at Captain Ege, intending to ask him about the first mate. The man did not look well. His skin had a grayish tint, and deep circles had formed under his eyes. Jerry looked over at Waller and made a gesture with his head. Tim immediately walked over to the Captain and knelt in front of him. "Hi, sir, can I take your pulse?"

"Dr. Norton? I'm gonna need Bourbon with me. Right away. Can you do anything for the Captain?"

Secret Service Agent Guthrie interrupted. "Ma'am, we can't allow that right now."

Jerry took a deep breath to keep himself from audibly expressing his personal opinion concerning DHS. "Look Guthrie. I need my guy. I have neither the time nor the crayons to explain the situation to you. So here's the juice. He's stepping back, and the Captain is now your problem. Okay? Good talk."

While walking toward Captain Ege, Cynthia directed her words toward her protection detail. "I'm treating him. Figure it out."

Jerry tapped Waller on the shoulder. "Need your eyes, Bourbon."

Jerry thoughtfully unslung "QB" and leaned the long rifle against the chapel bulkhead, then slipped carefully out of the backpack rig he had improvised, squatting to let the carbine make gentle contact with the deck.

He handed Stalling the carbine and the ammunition for it, then said, "We have support inbound. Just about to take back that island. This will all be over soon."

Jerry handed Waller the pilfered set of optics, followed by the backpack containing his sniper rounds, and they moved to the windows. At the windows, Jerry raised his rifle and used "QB's" optics to survey the entire visible island while Waller used the dismounted scope like an ancient telescope. In his suit, he looked comically akin to a sixteenth-century sea captain while doing so.

The cruise ship had dropped anchor about a quarter of a kilometer from the small private island, making the morning taxi runs for the tenders a breeze. QB had an accurate range of up to 1,800 meters or nearly two full kilometers. Through the powerful scope, Jerry could see each person, make out their facial expressions, and even read the nametags on some of their uniforms.

"Fish in a barrel," Waller murmured.

Jerry found his suit jacket slung over a chair where he had left it and picked it up. He caught Waller's eye and said, "Let's go. Burning daylight."

Waller threw him a thumbs-up, and together they left the chapel and walked around the area near the stairs. Jerry once again slung QB and found a foothold that allowed him to climb onto the chapel's roof. Here, he had the highest vantage point of the ship.

Waller passed up the backpack, followed by his dismounted scope and carbine. Then Jerry gave him a hand up to the roof.

"You good?"

"I'm good," Waller answered.

Jerry laid his jacket on the burning hot deck. Waller tossed the backpack in front of it like a sandbag, and Jerry settled on his stomach, then set up the long gun for accuracy and harmonics. Once he had everything in place, he took his time looking through the scope, keeping his finger alongside the trigger but not on it. He spied the obvious baddies. Now he just needed to figure out who else had joined the gang.

"Bravo Four set," he reported.

Anderson came back. "Roger, Bravo Four. Talon Strike now 2 mikes out."

A long twenty seconds or so went by, and Anderson broadcast, "I have comms. Talon Strike, this is Neptune's Dagger. Welcome to the party. Over."

A new voice came over their comms, linked in by Anderson. "Roger, Neptune's Dagger. We brought some party favors. Save us some snacks. Talon Strike inbound in...ONE MINUTE!"

"Tighten up," Jerry whispered. "One minute."

Without hesitation, Waller began feeding Jerry much-needed intel on the objectives in a low voice. "I confirm eleven bandits. I spot six on our declination. From your right. Bandit one is three six zero meters. Male, tactical vest, comms, AK slung, pacing near the east dock. Bearing zero-nine-zero from your position. Wind from nine o'clock, four knots full value. Dial elevation minus one point five MOA. Hold center mass, favor left edge for wind. On target?"

Jerry felt himself relaxing and completely focusing on the task. Waller knew the work. "Confirmed. Set next."

Waller called wind, distance, declination, and bearing on four more targets before Talon Strike hit the beach on the far side of the Island.

In their ears, they heard, "Go, go, go!"

Through his scope, Jerry watched the facial expression of one of the baddies keeping watch. He could tell the moment he realized something unstoppable was coming for them. Jerry zeroed in and fired before he could sound the alarm. Then, he moved quickly and found the next obvious target, then the next.

"Turkey!"

Waller said, "Friendlies on the field. Check left."

Through his scope, Jerry identified a Fourteenth Special Forces Group team member emerging from behind a building on the island. At the very same time, three heavily armed F-16's flew low and fast over the island, hitting afterburners and causing multiple sonic booms from perhaps 30 feet off the ground. This caused a panic among the thousands of passengers, but also badly demoralized the enemy.

Jerry didn't realize the heaviness in his chest until the sight of support made everything feel lighter. He whispered a prayer of thanksgiving and continued to support the Team from his position—though he never had to fire another shot—until Peña called him down.

Olive wheeled Daniel out of the operating room and into the main triage room. She had no doubt Phil could have done it alone, missing leg or not.

Phil broke open the pharmaceuticals cabinet and said, "Monitor vitals every ten minutes. Keep fluids running, saline, 100 cc per hour, no overhydration. He's got a liter of blood loss, maybe more, but I won't be able to do anything about that until the team gets to a stopping point."

He fished through the medicine cabinet, checking labels and doses. "Push 500 mg ceftriaxone IV now if you can find it. That should hold the infection off. Give him morphine, 4 mg IV push. In four hours, we'll do it again if we have to, though my prayer is he'll be outbound to a genuine no-kidding hospital by then. Watch for fever or tachycardia."

Olive made notes on an index card she'd found in a drawer, nodding as he spoke. He hadn't said anything she didn't already expect.

From outside the ship, they heard tremendous explosions

and the ship vibrated. Phil nodded. "Fast movers. Prolly 18s or 16s."

After she finished writing, Phil held out his hand. She hesitated, then handed him the pencil and card. He set them on the counter and slipped on a fresh pair of gloves. "Let's have a look at that jaw."

She shook her head. "It's not so bad." Her voice sounded even more slurred, as if she had just had a teeth cleaning and the Novocain hadn't yet worn off.

Phil raised an eyebrow. "Nurse Duncan, sit down and let me examine your jaw. Now."

Chagrined, she settled onto the triage chair and folded her hands in her lap. Phil prodded the left side of her face, from the temple down to her jawline. When he pressed a specific way, she gasped and winced back.

He centered himself in front of her and said, "Open your mouth just a little." When she complied, he put his thumbs in her mouth and gripped her jawbone with his hands. He made eye contact and said, "This is going to hurt."

Before he finished the word, "hurt," he pulled and adjusted her jaw. Pain exploded behind her eyes and her field of vision became a field of solid red. She nearly missed hearing the popping sound. As the pain subsided, so did the residual pain she'd suffered since regaining consciousness in the brig.

"Wow," she whispered, gingerly touching her jaw. "Wow. So much better."

His frown darkened his face. "He hit you hard enough

to knock your jaw out of socket."

She shook her head. "She."

With a raised eyebrow, Phil said, "She?"

"Yeah. A woman punched me in the jaw. A man punched me in the head." She carefully felt around her temple. "Knocked me out." She prodded her jaw again. "I had this happen once before. A boyfriend…" At the dark cloud that crossed Phil's face, she stopped talking. "Anyway, that was a long time ago."

Phil pulled out his cellphone and turned on the flashlight feature. "Look right at me," he said, then moved the light toward her eyes, then away. He nodded. "Slight concussion. You might do well to go to the hospital with Pie when we're done here."

She screwed her nose up at him. "I'd rather not."

He patted her shoulder. "My hospital would be best. I'll make arrangements as soon as I have comms."

He unmuted his phone, still on speaker, and said, "Pot Pie is recovering nicely. Needs medevac soon for volume. What's the news, boys?"

She recognized Travis Fisher's voice. "Medivac is seven mikes out. Heisman will guide you to the helipad."

As he finished speaking, Jerry appeared in the doorway. She went straight to him, putting her arms around his neck. He hugged her tight and spoke over her shoulder to Phil. "I'm here to take you to the helipad." He pulled back and looked down at Olive. "You, too." He gave her a small kiss on her left cheek. "It's over. Cavalry's here."

The US Navy frigates and destroyers had towed the cargo ship away and now floated on the horizon. They had reloaded all the illicit cargo back aboard before tugging it clear. Jerry and his friends sat in deck chairs and watched the new cruise ship, the Opulent Odyssey, pull up alongside. The ship was the cruise line's most exclusive vessel. Under the supervision of the Secret Service and other DHS agents, the new crew would relocate all the passengers' belongings onto the new cruise ship and then bring the passengers aboard by tenders. None of them would step foot on this ship again.

Because the Valiant Voyager sailed under the Bahamas flag, the Royal Bahamas Defense Force would conduct a very thorough search and inspection of the ship before any future passengers could come aboard.

Captain Ege walked off the bridge and welcomed the other captain onto his vessel.

Three SH-60 Seahawk helicopters circled the island. He knew they would land on the far side of the island and take the Nortons and Ozzy's parents back to the mainland. A Medivac helicopter had already departed with Daniel Swanson and Olive Duncan. Ozzy rode along, taking them to his hospital in Miami.

The Marshals and Secret Service had worked it out with the cruise line to give their people the opportunity to finish their trip aboard the Opulent Odyssey or leave. They all decided to go ahead and leave, and another transport would arrive to take them all back to Miami soon. Melissa's sister, Lola, and Marshall Stalling had simply disappeared. Jerry hadn't even realized they'd gone until long after everything ended.

Peña and Emma walked up to Jerry where he lounged. She had changed into a pair of loose pants and a jersey top. "Well, that happened!"

Peña slapped Jerry on the shoulder. "Nice work, Top." Without changing his stoic expression, Jerry simply lifted his chin in acknowledgement. "We have a tender on the other side of this deck. It's going to take us to a fast boat that will take us to Miami in style." He looked at Sanders. "You, too, Drumstick, according to your wife. She'll join you when she's done here."

"Oh, goodie. Another boat. More ocean. Can't wait. Hey! Maybe we'll be attacked by pirates." Sanders drained his soda and said, "Well, let's skedaddle." He looked around. "They get our luggage already?"

"That's my understanding," Peña said. "We have everyone accounted for."

Three hours later, Jerry followed Phil Osbourne through the emergency department and on into the doctor's lounge. The bandage on his left cheek covering the sutures interfered with his field of vision and generally annoyed him. Inside the quiet room, he found Olive sitting on a couch, her bare feet up on the coffee table in front of her. She had her head back and eyes closed.

In the hours since he'd seen her, the bruising on her face had darkened. The bruise from her temple had spread to around her eye, and her eye had started to swell shut slightly. Her jaw had purpled all the way to her ear.

Anger boiled in his chest at the sight of her. He had to stop briefly and take a breath. Osbourne put a hand on his shoulder and squeezed, as if he understood what made him pause.

"Excuse me, ma'am?" Jerry greeted softly. She slowly opened her eyes, then blinked and smiled. "You call for a cab?"

She laughed and stood, steady on her feet. He noticed she still didn't have on shoes. "I am so ready to be gone from here."

"Hey," Osbourne said, "why do you want to be mean like that?"

She hugged him. "Thank you, Phil. Thanks for everything."

"You're welcome. Next time you get beat up by pirates, I'll be happy to patch you back up again."

"Next time," she said, then turned to Jerry. "You. I've missed you so much today. Does that hurt?"

"Not even a little bit." He pulled her into his arms. "Tried to call you to tell you I was coming, but it went to voicemail."

"Yeah. My phone was in my purse. That didn't make it into the brig with me. That's the kind of thing we can worry about tomorrow." She framed his face with her hands.

He flinched. "Okay. Maybe it hurts a little bit."

She pulled her hands back. "Sorry."

"It's okay. I've had worse, as you know."

"Did you decide to get shot again to meet more hot chicks?"

He shook his head, "You're the only hot chick I ever wanted to meet, Olive." He hugged her and, out of her line of sight, raised an eyebrow and gave Osbourne a questioning look.

Osbourne waved a hand in her direction. "She's good. Jaw imaging is good. Headache's getting better instead of worse."

Jerry gently brushed the hair off her forehead and gave her a light kiss. "I'm so sorry you got hurt."

The tears that filled her eyes surprised him. "I'm sorry *you* got hurt. I'm sorry I was late. I'm never late."

He brushed her lips one more time. "I know. That helped my worry."

Osbourne held out a set of keys. "Remember my address?"

"Yeah. It's in my phone, too. Hey. You sure about this?" Jerry asked. "Where are you two going to stay?"

"Cabin in Tennessee. I called and arranged to come a few days early. Melissa's meeting me at the airport in," he looked at his watch, "thirty-five minutes."

"Safe travels, brother," Jerry said, holding out his hand. They clasped hands, then hugged. "Enjoy the honeymoon. Hopefully less eventful than the ceremony. Despite all that, congratulations. Melissa's amazing, and you deserve amazing."

"Yeah, you know, good times were had by all. But the best is yet to come."

Epilogue

Jerry pulled Olive into his arms as the music began. She fit easily, one hand on his shoulder, one hand clutched in his.

He wore his dress uniform, what the Army community called the pinks and greens. The earthy brown-green coat and beige dress shirt made his hazel eyes shine bright. He had his trousers tucked into the tops of his brown leather jump boots and sported a chest full of ribbons and badges.

Her dress, a cascade of intricate floral embroidery in purest ivory, hugged her shoulders with delicate spaghetti straps before flowering into tiers of soft ruffles that skimmed her waist and hips, then flaring into a graceful skirt that brushed against the wooden floor.

Friends and family, brothers in arms, watched as they waltzed to the music, staring into each other's eyes. Olive couldn't help but remember Jerry the first time she saw him, so close to losing life or limb. Had she truly started to fall in love with him way back then? Or maybe when he uninhibitedly flirted with her outside the hospital while dosed with painkillers? Or that day they met again years later at chapel?

Whenever it started, she couldn't imagine a future without him now. The shadows from the events of the spring had started to fade. But the remnants of those shadows didn't stop the love she had for Gerald Adam McBride, for the desire to live as his wife, his one, as he served his country with love and honor.

He twirled her, laughter in his eyes, then pulled her close and dipped her, his lips covering hers. Their friends and family cheered, and her head spun with the love and desire she had for him.

As the cheers and clapping swelled around them like a warm tide, Jerry lifted her upright, his forehead resting against hers, their breaths mingling in the quiet space between heartbeats. The orchestra's final notes lingered, a soft echo of violins fading away, but the world narrowed to just the two of them—his callused fingers tracing the lace at her back, her palm pressed over the steady thrum of his heart beneath the crisp wool of his jacket.

In that instant, Olive saw it all: the sweet grin he'd flashed her in the recovery room, the fierce protector who'd shielded her from those who would harm her, the man who'd vowed his life to her in front of their friends and families. The events on the cruise ship faded to faint etchings on the canvas of their story, overwritten by the bold strokes of this new beginning.

"I love you, Mrs. McBride," he murmured, his voice

rough with emotion, eyes gleaming in the candlelight.

"And I love you, Master Sergeant McBride," she whispered back, rising on her toes to seal the promise with another kiss, deeper this time, tasting of forever and the adventures yet to come.

As the DJ's voice invited the guests to join them on the dance floor, Olive let herself be swept into the joy, her hand never leaving his. A new battle to fight would certainly call him away. The world might test them again. But here, in the circle of their chosen family, they had come together, as one, loving each other in an unbreakable way. No matter what the world threw against them, love would make a way.

The End

LOVED THIS BOOK?

Dear Reader;

I created the Love and Honor series in order to get to this story. I just had a vague idea of what it looked like: a Special Forces A-Team on board a cruise ship for a wedding when pirates take over the ship. It becomes a very bad day for the pirates.

I said to my husband, "I need to take a 7-day cruise."

He said, "As long as I don't have to go."

(heh)

I went alone, watched passengers, took tours, explored the ship, and tried to figure it all out. On day five, I got it.

Then I plotted and drafted the other books in the series and couldn't wait to get them written so I could write this one!

I would love to know your thoughts.

I really would.

Writing is often a solitary profession, but it doesn't have

to be. I personally read every single book review, positive or otherwise. I'm not exaggerating. It would mean the world to me if you shared your thoughts. Hearing from my readers helps me prayerfully craft the next story. An honest review also helps other readers make informed decisions when they seek an exciting, romantic Christian book for themselves.

Please use the link or your smartphone to scan the QR code on this page, and leave an honest review telling me what you liked or didn't like about the story. I would so love to hear from you.

halleebridgeman.com/products/love-makes-way

Yours in Christ;

Discussion Questions

"For I know the thoughts that I think toward you, says the LORD, thoughts of peace and not of evil, to give you a future and a hope." (Jeremiah 29:11, NKJV)

1. In what ways do Jerry's scars from his career and Olive's nursing career illustrate how God's "thoughts of peace" might weave through seasons of healing and service, only to converge in a romance thousands of miles away from their initial meeting? How does this challenge our tendency to view past wounds as roadblocks rather than God's plan?

2. How can we steward God's hope not just for ourselves, but to foster peace in the lives with which we intersect?

3. Olive believes God wanted her to get out of the Army so that when she encountered Jerry again, she would be available to be with him. Do you think God works in such

a way? Do you believe that His plans mentioned in this verse apply to your life today?

He who dwells in the secret place of the Most High Shall abide under the shadow of the Almighty. I will say of the LORD, 'He is my refuge and my fortress; My God, in Him I will trust.' Psalm 91:1-2, NKJV

4. Jerry uses this verse to steady himself when he's afraid, to center himself when he feels overwhelmed. Do you have a verse that provides peace to you?

5. What does it look like in your life as you ponder the words, *"He is my refuge and my fortress; My God, in Him I will trust"*?

"Have I not commanded you? Be strong and of good courage; do not be afraid, nor be dismayed, for the LORD your God is with you wherever you go." (Joshua 1:9, NKJV)

6. Olive is terrified when she's locked in a cell with two men she doesn't know, beaten and hurt. In that situation, do you think it would be easy to pull courage from within, knowing that whatever happens, God is on your side?

7. The men in the unit did not hesitate when everything happened, even as unexpected and out of place as it was. How much do you think the courage of God was infused in those soldiers at that time? Or do you think their strength was derived from training?

"Blessed be the LORD my Rock, Who trains my hands for war, And my fingers for battle." Psalm 144:1, NKJV)

8. Jerry's role as a Special Forces sniper demands lethal accuracy that Psalm 144:1 attributes to God's training; how does this verse tie into his job, where each trigger pull spares innocents at the cost of enemies—challenging us to discern if such "hands for war" glorify God or merely justify our capacity for violence?

9. Years ago, Jerry had reconciled the lethal facts and results of his occupation with his Christian faith. Do you think that contradicts his Christian faith?

10. Olive has to reconcile herself to Jerry's profession and specialty. Do you think this was wrong on her part, or should she have trusted his faith and his belief in God's plan?

Recipes

Beef Sliders with Caramelized Onions on Homemade Rye Buns

Ingredients

For the Seeded Rye Buns

- 2 cups (300g) bread flour
- 1 cup (120g) dark rye flour
- ¼ cup (30g) whole wheat flour
- 1 packet (2¼ tsp) active dry yeast
- 1 tablespoon brown sugar
- 2 teaspoons salt
- 1 teaspoon caraway seeds, ground
- ½ teaspoon fennel seeds, ground
- 1 cup (125 ml) warm water (110°F/43°C)
- 3 tablespoons melted unsalted butter
- 1 tablespoon apple cider vinegar

Nordic Seed Topping:
- 2 tablespoons caraway seeds
- 1 tablespoon fennel seeds
- 1 tablespoon sesame seeds
- 1 tablespoon poppy seeds
- 1 tablespoon sunflower seeds
- 1 teaspoon coarse sea salt or flaky salt
  For Brushing:
- 2 tablespoons milk mixed with 1 teaspoon maple syrup
  For the Caramelized Onions and Beef Sliders
- 4 tablespoons (½ stick) unsalted butter, divided
- 1 large sweet onion, thinly sliced
- 2 pounds ground beef (80/20 for juiciness)
- 1 TBS Worcestershire sauce
- 1 tsp salt (Kosher or sea salt is best)
- ½ tsp black pepper
- 1 tablespoon fresh thyme leaves (or 1 teaspoon dried)
- ½ teaspoon onion powder
- ½ teaspoon garlic powder
- 8-12 slices Swiss or Gruyere cheese (enough to top each slider)
- Optional: Sesame seeds for topping (1 tablespoon)

Instructions

Step 1: Make the Rye Buns

1. In a small bowl, combine the warm water and brown sugar. Sprinkle the yeast over the surface and let sit for 5-10 minutes until foamy and active.

2. In a large mixing bowl, whisk together the bread flour, rye flour, whole wheat flour, salt, ground caraway, and ground fennel.

3. Make a well in the center and add the activated yeast mixture, oil (or melted butter), and apple cider vinegar.

4. Mix until a shaggy dough forms, then knead on a lightly floured surface for 8-10 minutes until smooth and slightly elastic. The dough will be denser than regular white bread dough due to the rye flour.

5. Place the dough in a lightly oiled bowl, cover with a damp towel, and let rise in a warm place for 1-1.5 hours until doubled in size. (Rye dough rises more slowly.)

6. Punch down the dough and divide into 8 equal portions (for standard sliders; divide into 12 for smaller ones).

7. Shape each portion into a tight ball by pulling the dough down and under to create surface tension. Place on a parchment-lined baking sheet, leaving space between each bun.

8. Gently flatten each ball slightly with your palm—they should be about 3-4 inches wide and 1 inch thick for sliders.

9. Cover the shaped buns with a damp towel and let rise for 45-60 minutes until puffy but not doubled.

10. Meanwhile, preheat the oven to 400°F (200°C). Combine all seeds and coarse salt in a small bowl for the topping.

11. Brush the tops of the risen buns gently with the milk-maple mixture, then generously sprinkle with the seed mixture, pressing lightly so the seeds adhere.

12. For an extra crusty exterior, place a small oven-safe dish with hot water on the bottom rack. Bake the buns for 18-20 minutes until golden brown and they sound hollow when tapped on the bottom.

13. Cool on a wire rack for at least 30 minutes before slicing in half. (These buns stay fresh for up to 3 days in an airtight container or freeze for 3 months.)

Step 2: Caramelize the Onions

1. Melt 2 tablespoons of the butter in a large skillet over medium heat. Add the sliced onions and reduce the heat to medium-low.

2. Cook, stirring occasionally, for 25-30 minutes until lightly caramelized and golden brown. If the onions start to look dry or stick, add a tablespoon of water to the pan. Season lightly with a pinch of salt. Set aside.

Step 3: Cook the Beef and Assemble the Sliders

1. In a large bowl, mix the ground beef, Worcestershire sauce, salt, and pepper.

2. Form into 12 patties. Heat the onion skillet to medium-high heat. In batches of 4, cook the patties to a medium-well doneness (4-5 minutes each side).

3. Preheat the oven to 350°F. Lightly grease a baking sheet. Slice the cooled rye buns in half and fit the bottom halves tightly on the baking sheet (cut more buns if needed for smaller sliders).

4. Place a beef patty on each bun. Evenly distribute the onion mixture over the bottom buns. Top each with a slice of Swiss or Gruyere cheese.

5. Place the top bun halves on the cheese.

6. In a microwave-safe bowl, melt the remaining 2 tablespoons butter with the thyme, onion powder, and garlic powder. Brush this mixture generously over the top buns (rye absorbs flavors well, so don't skimp). Sprinkle with sesame seeds if using.

7. Bake uncovered for 15-20 minutes until the cheese is fully melted and the bun tops are lightly browned and toasted. If the tops brown too quickly, cover loosely with foil midway.

Tip: For medium-rare beef, assemble and bake immediately after browning to avoid overcooking. These sliders reheat well, but the rye buns hold moisture better than sweeter rolls.

Peppered Fries

Ingredients

- 2 pounds russet potatoes (about 4 large), scrubbed and cut into ½-inch thick wedges (skin on for rustic texture)
- 3 tablespoons olive oil or avocado oil
- 2 teaspoons salt, divided (Kosher or sea salt is best)
- 1½ tablespoons coarsely cracked black pepper
- 1 teaspoon smoked paprika
- ½ teaspoon garlic powder
- Chopped fresh parsley or chives for garnish

Instructions

1. Preheat your oven to 425°F (220°C). Line a large baking sheet with parchment paper or a silicone mat for easy cleanup.

2. In a large bowl, toss the potato wedges with the oil, 1 teaspoon salt, cracked pepper, smoked paprika, and garlic powder until evenly coated. The pepper should cling to the potatoes.

3. Arrange the wedges in a single layer on the baking sheet, cut-side down, without overcrowding (use two sheets if needed for even crisping).

4. Bake for 25-30 minutes, flipping halfway through with tongs, until golden brown and crispy on the edges. For extra crunch, broil on high for the last 2 minutes, watching closely to avoid burning.

5. Immediately sprinkle with the remaining 1 teaspoon salt and any optional garnishes while hot.

Festive Red Cabbage and Apple Slaw

Ingredients

For the Slaw

1. ½ medium head red cabbage (about 1 pound), thinly shredded

2. 2 crisp apples (like Honeycrisp or Granny Smith), cored and julienned or thinly sliced

3. ½ cup walnuts, roughly chopped

4. ½ cup raisins

5. ¼ cup thinly sliced red onion

For the Warm Cider Vinaigrette

- ¼ cup apple cider vinegar
- 2 tablespoons olive oil
- 1 tablespoon maple syrup
- 1 teaspoon Dijon mustard
- ½ teaspoon ground cinnamon
- ¼ teaspoon ground cloves
- Salt and black pepper, to taste

Instructions

Step 1: Make the Vinaigrette

1. In a small saucepan, whisk together the apple cider vinegar, olive oil, honey, Dijon mustard, cinnamon, and cloves over low heat for 2-3 minutes until warmed and emulsified (do not boil).

2. Season with salt and pepper. Let cool slightly—the warmth helps the dressing penetrate the cabbage.

Step 2: Assemble the Slaw

In a dry skillet, toast the walnuts over medium heat for 3-4 minutes. Roughly chop.

1. In a large bowl, toss the shredded cabbage, apple slices, walnuts, cranberries, and red onion until combined.

2. Pour the warm vinaigrette over the slaw and toss thoroughly to coat. The cabbage will soften slightly but stay crisp.
3. For best flavor, cover and refrigerate for 30 minutes to let the flavors meld, or serve immediately for more crunch.

Warm Spiced Cider

Ingredients

- 6 cups (1.5 quarts) fresh apple cider (unfiltered for best flavor; avoid from concentrate)
- ¼ cup maple syrup
- 2 cinnamon sticks (2-3 inches each)
- 6 whole cloves
- 6 whole allspice berries
- 1 orange, peeled in wide strips (or 1-2 orange slices for subtle bitterness)
- 1-inch piece fresh ginger (sliced)
- 1 star anise

Instructions

1. In a medium saucepan (at least 2-quart size), combine the apple cider, maple syrup, cinnamon sticks, cloves, allspice, ginger, star anise, and orange peel.

2. Place the saucepan over medium heat and bring to a gentle simmer (do not boil, as it can make the cider cloudy). This takes about 5-7 minutes.

3. Once simmering, reduce heat to low and let it infuse for 15-20 minutes, stirring occasionally. Taste and add more maple syrup if you'd like it sweeter—the spices will mellow the tartness of the cider.

4. Transfer to a slow cooker on low for 2-3 hours after the initial simmer.

5. Remove from heat and strain through a fine-mesh sieve into a heatproof pitcher or directly into cups.

6. Garnish each cup with a cinnamon stick or orange slice for a festive touch. Serve immediately while steaming hot.

Excerpt

If you enjoyed this story in the Love and Honor series, let the story continue. *Chasing Pearl* from Hallee Bridgeman's Jewel Series tells the story of the incredible chain of events that led to Chase Anderson and Violet Pearl falling in love. Meanwhile, enjoy this exciting excerpt from *The Seven Year Glitch*, which tells the story of Timothy "Bourbon" Waller and Leanne Corwin, from Hallee Bridgeman's Red Blood & Bluegrass series.

The helicopter circled the house that looked more like an island at this moment. The rotor wash from the straining helicopter blades kicked up little muddy ripples on the surface of the water by the thousands and fanned the roof of a nearly submerged small green car that bobbed in the water like a giant sea turtle shell. Floodwater rose up to nearly the second-floor windows of the house, and billions of gallons of water waited to pour into the improvised cove with nowhere to go but up.

Searching the floodplain below—which always made her experience at least a tiny bit of motion sickness and vertigo—Leanne Corwin counted a family of three who had sought refuge on the rooftop. A tree had fallen onto the power line next to the house, tipping the pole, and the water rose dangerously close to the heavy transformer fastened to the pole. Leanne prayed the local co-op had already cut the power to this area.

She wove two each three-quarter inch ropes into the stainless-steel figure-eight—which she preferred to a traditional snap link—in the center of her harness. She carefully but quickly stepped out onto the skid of the helicopter, letting the ropes take her weight. The helicopter skids each supported supplemental five-inch-wide scuff platforms precisely for this purpose. As quickly as she could safely manage, she leaned her body out and back into an L-position and kept her eyes on Martin, her team leader. Despite the gear, the helmet, and the warm waterproof clothing, the constant downwash of the blades overhead always managed to blow cold, wet wind directly down her neck and the front of her shirt. Had she not worn thick heavy-duty leather gloves, the wash of the rotors would have frozen her fingertips just as it numbed the tip of her nose.

Martin shot a thumbs up. Without so much as a nod

for an answer, Leanne bent her knees and kicked off, simultaneously releasing the tight grip on the paired ropes tucked into the small of her back with her gloved brake hand. She fell twelve feet before she braked the first time, and then performed a nearly flawless free-rappel with her eyes facing the ground all the way down to the rooftop.

Just seconds later, after she freed herself from the ropes with a flip and a twist—the kind of quick-release a figure-eight made easy, and the primary reason she preferred it—Martin retrieved the ropes back into the helicopter. Remaining "hooked-up" could result in Leanne having a terrible day at the office, not just if the helicopter suddenly shifted in a crosswind, but if it lost ground, the static discharge could give her a nasty shock. Even in wet weather, helicopters generated a tremendous amount of static electricity while in flight.

Leanne threw off her heavy gloves energetically, like a hockey player preparing to have a kinetic debate with an opposing player. The gloves were far too bulky for her to perform any work requiring fine motor skills. She used them only to slide a few stories down a pair of nylon ropes or controlling a trail line. She stowed them in the roomy inside pocket of her day-glow vest. She would put them back on when she had to control the trail line. Once Martin had stowed her ropes safely in the aircraft, thus eliminating the risk of twists or fouling, he hoisted down the Stokes Litter and rescue yoke on the braided steel wire rope cable.

Eyes on the helicopter, Leanne rapidly assessed the

situation on the rooftop with her peripheral vision. Leanne saw no evidence of injuries. The trio—a man, woman, and small child—all looked soaked to the bone, and cold and exhausted, but uninjured. The man stood back a few yards away from them as if guarding some unseen perimeter. She knew he instinctively prioritized the rescue and safety of the woman who held the small child ahead of his own, just as men had instinctively done from the beginning of time.

Good men, anyway.

Straightforward rescue, then. No one was panicky or belligerent. Yelling over the sound of the helicopter, Leanne pointed to the small boy and said to the woman, "We need to put him in the basket first! I may need you to help me reassure him because he's going up alone."

She didn't call it a litter. She had found that word litter carried negative connotations in this context. The word basket brought to mind images of Easter or clean laundry. Leanne took the young boy from her arms. He couldn't have been older than four, and the whites of his wide eyes testified to his fear. "Hey there! What's your name, little man?"

The boy looked at her, then looked up at the hovering helicopter, then back at her with big brown eyes. The woman yelled, "His name is Frankie."

"Okay, Frankie. I'm going to zip you up in this big red sleeping bag, then my friend Martin up there is going to pull you up inside the basket, and your mom will be next. Then you guys get to fly in a helicopter. Won't that be fun?"

As Leanne helped the little boy into the litter, Frankie started crying and thrashing against her, reaching for his mom. Leanne made sure her boots gripped the shingles of the roof securely and that the trail line remained far away from anyone's feet. Slipping or tripping into the rushing floodwater would create a secondary emergency that no one had time to deal with right now. "It's okay, Frankie," the mom said, reaching around Leanne to touch his tiny face. "Mommy will be right behind you."

Leanne quickly fastened the straps around him and secured the aluminum latches on the litter. "Hey, Frankie? I'm going to zip you all the way up just so the wind doesn't blow in your face so much." *And so you won't be utterly terrified while Martin hoists you up to the helicopter*, she didn't say aloud. "I want you to close your eyes and count as high as you can count. Can you count to a hundred?"

He nodded.

"Okay. My friend Martin up there is wearing that spaceman helmet. He's going to unzip you when you're on the helicopter. I bet you a ride in a firetruck you won't even get to a hundred before Martin unzips you. Deal?"

He nodded again, his eyes on his mother.

"Okay. You're *so* brave, Frankie. You are like a superhero. Close your eyes and count, now, buddy." Leanne zipped him in, covering him entirely, then cinched the straps tight, slipped her heavy gloves back on, and retrieved the trail line.

She looked up and shot a quick thumbs up to Martin before taking control of the trail line with both hands. He hoisted the litter up in pretty good time, then recovered the precious cargo. From the ground, Leanne saw Martin lift his face shield so the little boy could make out his smile and his bushy mustache.

In no time, Martin had lowered the yoke, and Leanne held the trail line loosely in one gloved hand. She bit the glove on her right hand and pulled her hand out of it, then stowed it before she turned to the mother and held out the yoke, which resembled a canvas seat and explained, "I'm going to help you get into this, safe and secure. Then Martin and I will get you up to Frankie."

The mom nodded. Leanne could see the tension around her mouth and the fear in her eyes. As Leanne bent over her to hook her into the yoke, she asked, "What's your name?"

"Francis" Just like her son, Francis looked up at the helicopter then looked at Leanne. Unlike her son, she looked at the deep, murky, rushing water surrounding them on every side, as if contemplating making her getaway by some other means.

"Okay, Francis, you can do this. We got you. Trust me. It's really loud, and a little scary, and the wind from the rotors is going to feel really cold when you get close, but I promise we've done this a hundred times. It's completely safe. Frankie needs you up there with him. Now, put your arms through right here."

Putting her focus on her son gave Francis the courage she needed to nod. The entire time Martin hoisted her up into the aircraft, Francis gripped the steel cable with both hands as if she might never let go. She kept her eyes trained upward at the helicopter hoist and never looked down even once. After Leanne confirmed that Martin had her securely aboard the helicopter, she bit her right glove and pulled it off with her teeth while the descending trail line slid through her gloved left hand. Finally, she turned her attention to the man on the roof.

For a frightening moment, Leanne felt as if she might have been electrocuted. She stared at his face in utter shock. She couldn't even think over the sound of her roaring pulse. Her heart beat so loud, it drowned out the hovering helicopter noise.

It couldn't be. How?

He obviously hadn't recognized her yet. Her helmet covered her red hair, and she wore yellow safety glasses to shield her eyes from FOD and rotor wash. "Timothy!" She exclaimed around the thick leather glove still in her mouth. She spit the glove out and stowed it quickly in her vest. Taking a deep breath, she blurted out exactly what she didn't want to say. "What are you doing here?"

Timothy Waller had filled out in the seven years since she last saw him. The lanky teenager had turned into a well-muscled man with broad shoulders and stout thighs. He wore his blond hair cut military short, and crow's feet crinkled at the corners of his blue eyes as if he laughed a lot. The sight of him standing there in front of her stripped all thought from her mind until she nearly forgot how to function while standing on this rooftop in all of her gear with the helicopter hovering above her and dangerous water rising all around.

In the emptiness of her mind, an unparalleled elation at seeing him again flooded her soul only seconds before the memory of acute pain and embarrassment reminded her of what he'd done. Instead of a roof, she found herself transported to that June day seven years ago and into the Charula, Kentucky, town square, running past the "Brothers Against Brothers" statue.

A look of surprise crossed Timothy's face, and his jaw dropped. "Leanne?" She witnessed his expression as recognition caught up with him. He closed his gaping mouth, and his lips formed a smile just as slow and sweet as sorghum sliding over hot buttermilk biscuits. The drumming of her pulse transformed into roaring machine-gun fire at the sight of that grin.

He gestured toward the boat secured to the house's rain gutter. "I was part of the volunteer rescue. Just about had 'em in the boat when the downed power line trapped us."

His voice hadn't changed. That was her first rational thought. She used to love talking to him and listening to the faint southern twang in his deep voice. He used to sing to her. His singing voice always made her chest vibrate on the low notes.

How was he here? How was he back here—volunteering to rescue flood victims in Hooper County, Kentucky—when he was supposed to be at some army base thousands of miles away in Germany?

The yoke brushed against the back of her shoulder, jostling the trail line. It startled her, dragging her back from the day after high school graduation and the unforgettable humiliation of waiting for Timothy on the courthouse steps while he made his way to Basic Training without so much as a goodbye wave. She held out the yoke so he could secure himself, and he took it from her. "I got this. Just like STABO operations, but looks like more fun."

Just like STABO operations, whatever that meant. Leanne watched as he expertly strapped himself in, and after he checked all of the straps, he gave her a sharp nod. He hadn't missed a thing, so, gloves back on, she looked up and gave Martin a thumbs up before holding the trail line with both hands.

Leanne would come up last. Unlike the civilians, no one would anchor her ascent by holding a trail line. Martin and the pilot were professionals with years of experience, but Leanne would still spin or oscillate—or both—all the way up.

Before long, Martin had everyone in the helicopter and all the gear stowed. They flew away from the rooftop and toward the Hooper County high school. Leanne decided to focus her attention on Frankie, who clung to his mother so tightly his little arm muscles trembled.

Francis looked at her and yelled over the engine. "It came so fast. My husband was at work. He called and told me about the flash flood warning just as my phone emergency alarm went off. I was packing a bag, and I went to go downstairs, and the water was already up the staircase. I didn't know what to do. The car started floating around the yard! It even hit the house once! I can't swim, and I have Frankie."

Leanne put a reassuring hand on her knee. "It's okay." She spoke as softly as the noise of the helicopter would allow. "The important thing is you're safe now. So is Frankie.

Francis pointed at Timothy and said, "We would have been fine if that tree hadn't fallen. He was worried the line might electrocute us."

"Probably wise. That transformer could have been dangerous if you had been on the water." Unlike in Hollywood thrillers, pure water was actually a terrible electrical conductor. However, muddy floodwater suspends and insulates all kinds of solid matter that usually makes for highly unpredictable and very efficient electrical pathways. She glanced at Timothy, catching him staring at her with such an intense look in his eyes that she felt her breath catch. She quickly averted her eyes and looked back at Francis. "Glad we were able to get to you before the water reached the roof."

"You reckon it's gonna cover the roof?" Francis asked. "We had that flood three years back, and the water barely made it to the driveway."

Martin interjected. "It's not looking good for anything downstream. Saint Louis to New Orleans is getting covered up. Over in the east, the Gorge is backed up, too, clear to Corbin and down to Knoxville."

No one else spoke for the rest of the ten-minute flight. The pilot set the helicopter down by first touching the earth lightly with one skid to discharge static electricity, then executed a soft landing on both skids. He landed in the middle of the high school football field that the county had designated as a staging area for emergency flood relief. Once the pilot had the engine powered down, Leanne helped Francis and Frankie out of the bird and walked them to the Red Cross tent so they could get some hot chocolate and a dry blanket. When she turned around to leave the tent, she barreled right into Timothy's solid chest.

Somehow, she knew what he would say. "I think we should probably talk."

"I see. Well, I think there was a time for talking, but that was a long time ago." She brushed by him and headed toward the emergency management services trailer.

"Leanne! Hang on!" He kept up with her. "Hey! Just stop for a minute."

She stopped so suddenly he very nearly ran into her. "What?"

He looked all around them, at the tents and the trailers and the people. He finally looked back at her. "This obviously isn't the time or place, but I would like to sit down and have a conversation with you while I'm here."

Searching his face, she saw nothing that would indicate any kind of remorse or shame at what he had put her through back then. Nothing. She saw frustration, an uncomfortable shyness that he had always exhibited, and even a touch of anger that she couldn't decipher. "What good would it do to have a conversation? I think you were pretty clear seven years ago."

"You think I was clear?" His eyebrows furrowed, and

the tiny little spark of anger burst into actual flame behind his suddenly cold blue eyes.

"You were. And sorting that out might take hours. Honestly, I don't have the time right now." She gestured toward the trailer. "I have to work. Every second I stand here talking to you—when I don't even want to talk to you—is another second someone's life could be at risk. Leave me alone, Timothy."

This time when she walked away, he did not follow.

Look for *The Seven Year Glitch* at your favorite retailer today.

MORE BOOKS BY HALLEE BRIDGEMAN

Find the latest information and connect with Hallee at her website: www.halleebridgeman.com

The Love and Honor series:
Love in Any Language
Honor Bound
Word of Honor
Honor's Refuge
Love Makes Way

The Red Blood and Bluegrass Series:
Black Belt, White Dress
Blizzard in the Bluegrass
The Seven Year Glitch
A Change of a Dress

The Dixon Brothers Series
Ian, a prequel to the Dixon Brothers
Book 1, Brad
Book 2, Jon
Book 3, Ken

Virtues and Valor Series:
Book 1, Temperance's Trial
Book 2, Homeland's Hope
Book 3, Charity's Code
Book 4, A Parcel for Prudence
Book 5, Grace's Ground War
Book 6, Mission of Mercy
Book 7, Flight of Faith
Book 8, Valor's Vigil

The Jewel Series:
Book 1, Sapphire Ice
Book 2, Greater Than Rubies
Book 3, Emerald Fire
Book 4, Topaz Heat
Book 5, Christmas Diamond
Book 6, Christmas Star Sapphire
Book 7, Jade's Match
Book 8, Chasing Pearl

Standalone Romantic Suspense:
On the Ropes

Parody Cookbook Series:

Vol 1: Fifty Shades of Gravy, a Christian gets Saucy

Vol 2: The Walking Bread, the Bread Will Rise

Vol 3: Iron Skillet Man, the Stark Truth about Pepper & Pots

Vol 4: Hallee Crockpotter, and the Chamber of Sacred Ingredients

About the Author

www.halleebridgeman.com

With nearly a million book sales, USA TODAY bestselling and Carol award-winning author Hallee Bridgeman writes action-packed romantic suspense filled with realistic characters facing real-world problems. Her work has been described as everything from bold and refreshing to heart-stopping exciting and edgy.

Hallee and her husband live in central Kentucky, enjoying the beautiful changing of the seasons. When she's not penning novels, you will find her in the kitchen, which she considers the 'heart of the home'. Her passion for cooking spurred her to launch a whole food, real food "Parody" cookbook series. In addition to nutritious, biblically grounded recipes, readers will find that each cookbook also confronts some controversial aspect of secular pop culture.

Hallee has served as the Director of the Kentucky Christian Writers Conference, President of the Faith-Hope-Love chapter of the Romance Writers of America, Secretary and Assistant Programming Chair of Novelists, Inc. (NINC), is a member of the American Christian Fiction Writers (ACFW), and the American Christian Writers (ACW). An accomplished speaker, Hallee has taught and inspired writers around the globe, from Sydney, Australia, to Dallas, Texas, to Portland, Oregon, to Washington, D.C., and all places in between.

Hallee loves living in Kentucky, drinking really good coffee, watching campy action movies, going on regular date nights with her husband, and spending time with her children. Above all else, she loves God with all of her heart, soul, mind, and strength; has been redeemed by the blood of Christ; and relies on the presence of the Holy Spirit to guide her.

She prays her work here on earth is a blessing to you and would love to hear from you. You can reach Hallee at hallee@halleebridgeman.com

Newsletter

Sign up for Hallee's monthly newsletter (and get a free book)! Every newsletter recipient is automatically entered into a monthly giveaway! The real prize is that you will never miss updates about upcoming releases, book signings, appearances, or other events.

Hallee's Happenings News Letter

halleebridgeman.com/NewsLetter